Maybe

Also by Claire Allan

It's Got to be Perfect
Jumping in Puddles
Rainy Days & Tuesdays

Published by Poolbeg

Feels Like Maybe

Claire Allan

POOLBEG

Published 2008
by Poolbeg Press Ltd
123 Grange Hill, Baldoyle
Dublin 13, Ireland
E-mail: poolbeg@poolbeg.com
www.poolbeg.com

2

A catalogue record for this book is available from the British Library.

ISBN 978-1-84223-320-7

F828,035
£12

Typeset by Type Design in Caslon 11/15.5
Printed and bound by CPI Group (UK) Ltd, Croydon, CR0 4YY

www.poolbeg.com

About the author

Claire Allan was born and raised in Derry, where she still lives with her husband Neil and their four-year-old son Joseph. She is a self confessed homebird and spends more time with her parents than is normal for a grown woman.

She has worked as a reporter with the *Derry Journal* since 1999.

In her (very limited) spare time she loves reading, watching films with happy endings and drinking cold wine with friends.

Claire remains addicted to buying inexpensive handbags and shoes from Tesco and Next. She is actively seeking a 12 step programme to deal with her chocolate addiction.

Feels Like Maybe is her second novel. You can visit her website at www.claireallan.com.

Acknowledgements

There are so many people who need thanking, first and foremost my family. My lovely husband for hand-holding and encouragement, and our gorgeous son Joseph who makes me laugh every day.

My family, Mum and Dad – this one is for you – and also Lisa, Peter, Emma, my gorgeous Abby and our newest addition due around the same time as this book!

And also the Davidson, McGuinness and Allan clans – all support much appreciated.

Many thanks to all those wonderful ladies (and their partners) who spoke so openly to me about their experiences of infertility and allowed me to use their personal experiences to make Beth's as realistic as possible. Thanks go to Kathryn and her angel Aimee, Jann and Malcolm and their miracles Tallulah and Tabitha, Adele and her girls Eliza and Serena, and Nicola for allowing me to research a very personal subject in a very public way.

Thanks, as always, to my fabulous agent Ger Nichol for wine, craic and chat and for encouraging me to give Beth her own voice. I would be lost without you and our wee emails.

I cannot begin to thank Poolbeg enough for making the last year and a half feel like an amazing dream. Niamh, Connor, Kieran, Sarah and especially Paula Campbell, I thank you from the bottom of my heart for believing. I realise each day how very lucky I am to be a part of the team.

A special thanks to Gaye Shortland who helped make this book the best it could be and for her endless patience.

To everyone who helped make *Rainy Days and Tuesdays* a success story.

Many thanks to Lynda Laffan, formerly of Poolbeg, for being so kind to a first-timer. In particular I have to say thanks to the entire team of Eason, Foyleside. Your warm welcome meant the world. Huge thanks to all the booksellers across the country who welcomed me into their shops and said nice things about my book.

Thanks must also go to those members of the media who supported me over the last year, with a special mention to Keris and all at *Trashionista*, Radio Foyle, Lynsey Dolan at Country Mix FM, Catherine and all at *Verbal* magazine and Sue Leonard.

Once again thanks to the staff and management of The *Derry Journal*, especially my colleagues in editorial, for being so supportive. In particular Bernie and Mary – and Mary's daughter Maeve who asked so nicely if this book could have a Maeve in it!

Getting published has introduced me to some wonderful writing friends and I want to publicly thank my fellow authors for being there on the end of the phone or the email. In particular I want to thank Sharon Owens for daily (sometimes hourly) support and friendship, Melissa Hill for being my sage of good advice, and the amazingly wonderful 'Almost Famous Five' Fionnuala Kearney, Fionnuala McGoldrick, Clodagh Murphy, Emma Heatherington and Trina Rea for too many laughs to mention and a fair deal of hand-holding too.

I would like to take the credit for the name of this book, and indeed *Rainy Days and Tuesdays*, but both names were the invention of the lovely Emily Gale who deserves my thanks. I'm thinking of putting you on a retainer.

Without my "real life" friends though, this book would never have made it to print. So love and chocolate to Erin, Amanda, Lisa, Nora and Catherine. And not to forget, my wonderful VBF Vicki who championed this book from day one. I love you to pieces, missus.

Finally, to everyone who read and enjoyed *RD&T*, I hope you enjoy this one too.

This book is dedicated to

Mammy and Daddy.

Thank you for believing.

x

I

Aoife

When I die someone will write "*Aoife McLaughlin was very good at going it alone*" on my headstone. Then again, I will probably have to come back from the dead and write it myself.

That thought crossed my mind as I took yet another shallow breath and felt yet another contraction rip across my rounded, swollen belly. It shouldn't have been like this.

I should have had a loving husband mopping my brow and encouraging me through every wave of increasing pain. We should have jointly decided on a name and painted a nursery together – pausing only to leaf through the Yellow Pages and order pizzas with tuna and banana on them – and yet, here I was alone in a room where everyone spoke in a different accent to my own and struggled to pronounce my name.

There was no husband. There wasn't even a significant other. There was just me and my cervix which, much to my annoyance, was dilating at a painfully slow rate.

The pain came again and I breathed deeply on the gas and air that was my only salvation. The anaesthetist was busy, or so they had told me, so here I was with not so much as an epidural to make the whole experience more bearable.

All I had was a radio that was blasting out what seemed like the same four songs on a loop. I swore that if I heard the Outhere Brothers sing "Boom, boom, boom, let me hear ya say weyoh" one more time I was going to boom-fecking-boom the radio out the window.

A very cheerful midwife by the name of Peggy walked into the room just as the contraction reached its excruciating crescendo. "How are you doing, my lovely?" she asked, looking at the jumble of peaks and troughs on the monitor beside my bed. I wondered did she want the honest answer or the polite answer? Was this similar to when you go to the hairdresser's and don't like the disaster they've made of your barnet but you feel compelled to give a thumbs-up anyway?

But I have never been one for bullshit, it was one of the things my clients admired so much about me, so I decided to opt for the honest approach.

"You mean apart from this baby trying to squeeze its way out of my fandango while I lie here twenty hours into labour with no epidural? Just fucking peachy, thanks!"

"Oooh, if you're starting to swear, it must mean Baby is nearly here!" Peggy chirped, disappearing between my splayed legs for a quick look.

I was tempted to point out I had been swearing for most of the last twenty hours – being Irish it was as in-built in me as breathing. I wasn't about to stop now when my genitals were being shredded by a supposedly natural force.

"How far?" I asked, panting as the pain subsided.

Peggy held up a gloved hand, slightly stained with blood, and I felt a wave of nausea wash over me. Throwing up what was left of my breakfast I swore I would never, *ever*, believe anything that I saw in the movies again. You didn't get bloodstained hands in Hollywood.

"Seven centimetres, my lovely. Shouldn't be too long now. You should have this little one by morning."

I looked at the clock, it was 11.15 p.m. Damn fecking right I would have this baby by morning – even if I had to do the Caesarean myself. Another contraction hit and I sucked hard on the gas and air, sinking my teeth into the plastic mouthpiece, imagining it to be Jake's undersized penis.

"Sweet" – *gasp* – "Jesus" – *gasp* – "make" – *gasp* – "this" – *gasp* – "fucking" – *gasp* – "stop!"

Peggy, still smiling despite my clatter of swear-words tapped my knee, as if her gentle tapping held some magic anaesthetic quality.

"There, there, lovely! It will all be worth it when Baby is here." She smiled and walked out of the room, leaving me alone to my growing sense of panic.

Would it be okay when "Baby" – this nameless wriggling creature fighting to get out – was here? Somehow I doubted it. I had made some pretty major mistakes in my life before but this was a fuck-up of immense proportions and as my tummy tightened I knew it was too late to change my mind. What goes up must come down, I thought with a wry smile. I promised myself nothing was ever going up again.

I started to wonder if the gas and air was working any more. It made me feel woozy, that was for sure, but the pain didn't seem relieved in any way. What I really needed – really, really needed – was a king-size Nurofen and a bottle of vodka. That had always killed any pain I had before.

I mean, how much harm could a wee drink of vodka do to the baby now? Surely by the time the alcohol made its way down into my uterus, through the placenta and into the umbilical cord, the baby would be separated from me anyway?

3

A cigarette would be good too, or a nice big juicy joint. I closed my eyes, inhaling deeply on the Entenox and imagined I could feel the warmth of sweet smoke fill my lungs. Momentarily there was relief from the pain and then, *bam*, back at point zero. Tummy tightening. Back aching. Fandango fanning. Baby burrowing its way towards the light. There has got to be a more humane way to bring new life into this world. Beam me up, Scotty, I'm in trouble . . .

Much as I'm adverse to crying, I started to wail, crying big gulping, snottery tears born of fear, tiredness and pain the like of which I had never known. I'd heard giving birth was at best like having a big poo and at worst like a bad period. What utter shite! I would have cried out for my mother, if she wasn't the most annoying fecker on the planet – so instead I just cried. Peggy stuck her head back round the corner. "Now what's the matter, lovely? No need for tears."

I tried to tell her what was wrong. How it had all gone horribly pear-shaped and that I had never asked for this – never wanted it. It wasn't in the game plan. I was doing pretty damn okay before this, thank-you-very-much.

But all that came out was a muffled scream.

"I need to push!" I gasped, as soon as the power of speech returned to me.

It's hard to explain, but the feeling was beyond my control. I suddenly understood what bearing down meant. Every inch of my body, from the tips of my toes to the split ends of my auburn mop wanted to bear down and to push.

"No, dearie, you don't. You're only seven centimetres," Peggy replied.

"Yes, I do. I need to fucking push!"

"Now, now, lovely. Baby will come when Baby is ready to come."

"My name is not fucking 'Lovely' it's Aoife – Eee-fa!" I said, emphasising the pronunciation in the hope she would at last get it right. "And I'm telling you this baby is ready to fucking come now!"

I grimaced as my body contorted with pain and pressure. This was beyond my control and yet I felt strangely okay about it. This was my body and, by Christ, this was really happening and I was powerless to stop it.

"I'll go and get someone to check," Peggy said, making for the door.

"No! I need to push now!" I gasped, my body taking over and forcing me to push with every muscle available. "*Aaaaarrghhh!*" I could feel something move down to my pelvis, could see Peggy's eyes widen as she rushed to the end of the bed.

"I can see Baby's head!" Peggy said.

I took this as encouragement to keep going, and going, and going.

It wasn't so much that I longed to cradle the baby, I just longed for this pain to be over. My tummy tightened and I instinctively pushed again – my exhaustion gone as this primeval force took over.

"Pant now for me," Peggy said and I forced myself to stop pushing, to take small gasping breaths, as I felt this new life emerge from me.

Suddenly, although it had taken twenty-one hours, I felt a surge of relief. The pressure was gone and this little mewling creature was staring at me. The most perfect little girl in the world. I cried again, but this time it was because I knew that no matter how I had planned not to let this happen, I had already fallen madly in love with my daughter. My baby.

Ten perfect little fingers, with nails that needed trimming already. Those fragile little hands, curled up close to that button nose. I wondered had I ever felt skin so soft? Rubbing my nose against Maggie's cheek, I whispered my apologies to her.

"I'm sorry I didn't want you before but now that I know you, now that I've seen you, I want you more than anything." No one else could hear our conversation but then it wasn't for anyone else's ears. It was our moment alone and I could hardly believe how fulfilled I felt when just an hour ago I had felt more alone than ever before. I knew, I guessed, that I would never be alone again.

Peggy came back into the room, smiling now, the look of shock at Maggie's speedy arrival replaced by her usual calm demeanour.

"Do you want me to bring the phone in? You can let people know this little poppet is here."

I shook my head. There wasn't really anyone to tell. Beth would find the note in the morning when she returned from her break to Brighton. No one else really mattered, not now anyway.

"I'm okay, thanks," I said, never for one second lifting my gaze from my daughter.

"Well," said Peggy, "I'll be outside if you need me."

"Yes, thank you. Thank you for everything."

"All in a day's work, lovely, all in a day's work."

Peggy was clearly baffled by my reluctance to announce my new arrival. She had seen enough of me for one day. Letting her see my fandango was one thing, explaining my complicated set of circumstances was another. Some things were private. Exhausted, I placed Maggie in her little plastic crib by the bed and lay down, desperate for sleep but reluctant to let this little one out of my sight. All I could see now was a patch of pink skin, swaddled in blankets with a white hat on her tiny head. I put my hand to my stomach, now a gelatinous mass – like a balloon that has been partially deflated – and wondered had this little creature really been inside me just a few hours ago?

The name Maggie seemed perfect. I had no idea where it had

come from. I hadn't allowed myself to think of names before, but as soon as I saw all 6lbs and 9oz of my child, a tuft of dark hair and her face set in a determined little stare, I knew that no other name would suit the same.

No doubt Jake would have wanted something a bit more "out there". He would laugh and tell me that Maggie was "so suburban", "so bland", so "predictable". He could go and scratch himself. I was going to have a big enough problem selling this one to the folks back home without announcing the arrival of baby "Aisha" or "Bluebell". Nope, Maggie was just fine. Absolutely perfect.

2

Beth

My father once told me that the more things change, the more they stay the same. I used to believe him. Now I wasn't so sure.

I don't know why I couldn't sleep. In theory I should have been exhausted. The Brighton sea air should have been enough to knock me out, especially when combined with the huge dinner Dan and I had shared and the several glasses of wine that had washed it down.

He was snoring beside me. Gorgeous, naked, looking like he didn't have a care in the world, and yet here I was sitting up in bed, staring at the illuminated digits on the hotel clock and counting the hours till morning.

This bed was huge. Dan had joked that we would have had room to invite a couple of friends in for an orgy and still had room to sleep well all night if we had been so inclined. I had laughed, pulling him close to me, and had told him I wanted him all to myself. He had kissed me then, and for the first time in months I felt like he really and truly meant it.

I knew he loved me. I didn't doubt that for one second. It was just that lately acts of physical intimacy had become about much more than just being in the mood for a snog or a romp between the sheets.

I shook the thoughts from my head and got out of bed, padding to the bathroom. I could not allow those thoughts in my head now. This was not going to help. I had to stay positive, remain calm and relaxed and not, under any circumstances, get myself into a whole state about how my world was about to change and how everyone was about to learn just what a complete bitch I really was.

Aoife hadn't planned to get pregnant. I knew that. The rational side of my brain – which I do have despite being an airy-fairy-head-in-the-clouds type most of the time – knew that this was not in her plan. Her relationship with Jake had never been secure. I'd given up trying to warn her off, learning that sometimes it is better to stay quiet about a relationship than risk destroying a good friendship over it. I had been supportive. I'd even held her hair back when she threw up in the shop toilet as waves of morning-sickness swept over her. I had chosen the most gorgeous pram I could find for the baby and had helped design and decorate a nursery for it. I had even offered to hold her hand when she gave birth, something I knew could happen at any time.

Dan thinks I went a little overboard, but perhaps he doesn't realise just how much I was trying to convince him, and myself, that I was absolutely 100% okay with the fact that Aoife got pregnant with the drop of her knickers while I . . . well, I didn't.

Apparently twenty-three months is not that long, really, to be trying for a baby without success. I'm pretty sure a man came up with those statistics. After a year we had gone to the finest consultant money could buy and had a series of invasive and painful tests. (Well, mine were invasive and painful, Dan's simply involved a porn magazine, a plastic cup and his hand – he had been mortified but at least he didn't have to expose his undercarriage to complete strangers.)

They couldn't find a reason. Our infertility (how that word hung over my head like a badge of shame) was unexplained. I got really, stupidly excited that month. If there wasn't a reason then surely it was going to happen for us any time now. I imagined Aoife and me shopping for prams together, rubbing our expanding bellies and secretly I planned hiring a nanny to work for us both to share the childcare costs. And of course the nanny would bring our babies to Instant Karma every day so we could coo over them. Two proud mums together.

I cried for two days when my period arrived that month. Aoife never knew. I phoned in sick with a stomach bug and spent two days in bed, berating the unfairness of it all.

I'd come over all melodramatic and told Dan to leave me for a woman less barren and he had smiled and pulled me close.

"There is no reason why we can't have a baby," he soothed, "so you are stuck with me, Betsy."

He then fed me chocolate and Nurofen until the worst of my hormonal surges had passed and promised to shag me senseless for the coming month. This was not going to defeat us.

I sat in the bathroom of our hotel in Brighton and took deep breaths. Maybe this month it would happen. After all there was nothing wrong with us. Nothing at all.

3

Aoife

My waters had broken in the early hours of the morning. I had woken at three to some niggling pains in my back. Crawling out of bed I'd paced between the bedroom, the bathroom and the kitchen, trying my hardest to convince myself this was yet another false alarm. When a particularly harsh pain winded me I walked downstairs to the shop I shared with Beth to retrieve my antenatal notes from behind the counter and, if I'm honest, to escape the feeling that the four walls were closing in on me.

I needed the space of our shop, the comfort of its Aladdin's cave of pretty things. Instead of climbing back up the stairs I sat on the wrought-iron daybed which had been the focal point of Instant Karma since it opened four years ago. The rest of the shop had changed but this daybed would be there forever, Beth and I had vowed. We had spent many an hour sitting on its silken throws and cushions eating Jaffa Cakes, planning the transformation of clients' homes and putting the world to rights.

I pulled a throw – a dazzling and comforting silken creation in the brightest greens, pinks and golds I had ever seen – round me and leafed through my notes. They made little sense. I had never looked at them before. Looking at them would have made this all too real.

The pain was still coming in waves, some bad, some bearable. I still had two weeks to go, surely it couldn't be time? Matilda, our guardian angel – a crystal statuette which stood on a shelf behind the counter – looked at me with a sense of pity as I winced with pain.

"Don't give me your pitying looks," I chided her. "It's probably just those damned Branston Pickles things or whatever the feck you call them."

She didn't answer, of course – just carried on looking at me until I could take no more of her stares and decided to make my way back upstairs for a bath. As I walked past her towards the mahogany door that separated my working life from my home life, I felt a pop, followed by a trickle and then a gush.

"Ah fuck it!" I gasped to Matilda. "Either this is it, or I've just peed myself."

Beth was supposed to be my birthing partner but there was no way I could phone her now. Not only was it stupid o'clock in the morning but she'd had the audacity to bugger off to Brighton with her husband Dan for a weekend of mad sex and debauchery. Beth had been reluctant, worried she might miss getting a quick look at my fandango in the delivery ward, but I had encouraged her to go. I had noticed she looked tired lately, and stressed. She was even arguing with Dan, which never happened. As with so much over the last year, this was another decision which had seemed good at the time but that was coming back to bite me in the arse right now.

I was going to have to do this alone I realised as I looked at the ever-increasing puddle at my feet. It was clear from looking at Matilda that she was going to be no fecking help at all.

★ ★ ★

Staring at my watch now, I realised that Beth should be home. It had gone eleven. I lifted Maggie to me, latching her eager mouth onto my breast and marvelling at just how exceptionally clever she was. Here she was, just a matter of hours old and she already had this feeding malarky down pat. I'll admit I was a bit proud of myself too. I hadn't planned on breast-feeding. I hadn't really thought about feeding at all – it was part of my "total denial of pregnancy" strategy. Her burps came easily and I swear she knew my voice over the clatter of nurses and midwives who walked in to check on her and on my poor tattered perineum.

That day, Maggie's birthday, had been a day of extreme highs and lows. I still could not believe Maggie was mine. Beth would be most put out that this tiny creature had managed to do in five minutes what she had been trying and failing to do for nine months. Beth couldn't understand why I wasn't doing cartwheels over my pregnancy.

She was puzzled that I had resisted maternity clothes for as long as possible and had taken to leaving Formes catalogues on the counter for me from a week after I peed on that blasted stick. She didn't understand – couldn't understand – because her life was so different to mine. She had the loving husband, I had the love child – so many times over the last nine months I had wanted so desperately to swap. Now I knew that I would never trade my child – not for every designer daybed in the greater London area.

When the lows came they floored me. I had woken at 6 a.m., my bladder stretched to capacity. Buzzing a nurse I muttered that I needed to go to the toilet and she had helped me to the door. Sitting there I waited for the relief of a good pee. It was only when the stinging started that I remembered I had been stitched from hither to thither. This wasn't going to be easy, was it? And peeing was the least of my worries. Vowing that I was never, ever going to poo again I stumbled back to my bed and wondered just what the hell I had let myself in for.

I lifted Maggie to my shoulder. She had that delicious newborn smell, a mixture of Johnson's baby bath and milk. I stroked her white babygro, feeling her skinny legs curled up to her tummy and feeling the silken touch of her tiny hands. Leaning back on my pillow I closed my eyes and breathed every inch of her in – my contemplation only interrupted by a gasp of disbelief in the doorway.

I looked up and saw Beth, her mouth a perfect "O". Tears glistened in her eyes and it was all I could do not to giggle. Beth, gorgeous, lovely Beth – she was such an emotional person. I should have known the sight of me, in all my post-birth glory with this bundle of perfection on my shoulder, would have reduced her to tears.

"You've had the baby then?" she eventually stuttered.

"Nope, they just asked me to mind this one between contractions," I joked, but then again, looking at my stomach still swollen and round, I realised that was not beyond the realm of possibilities.

"What did you have?" Beth asked, walking towards my bed, her hands outstretched to my daughter.

"A Maggie," I answered, a smile of pride dancing across my face. "I did it, Beth, all on my own. I didn't even have one of those epidoodahs or anything." I decided it would be best not to tell her I wanted one, begged for one and even offered to pay for one.

"You should have called," she said, touching her fingers against the smoothness of Maggie's pristine babygro. "I would have come back."

"I didn't want to ruin the shagfest," I said. "Dan would never have spoken to me again."

"He would have been fine. You know he would have been."

I lifted Maggie down from my shoulder so that Beth could marvel at her button nose and unimaginably long eyelashes.

"Sorry about the mess at the shop," I muttered. I hadn't found the time or energy to clear up the puddle as I waited for a taxi to ferry me to the hospital.

"Don't worry about it. Dan was able to grab the counter before his arse hit the floor. He promises he won't sue." She reached her arms out again, taking Maggie from me and cuddling her tightly to her chest. She started to cry. "Oh Aoife," she said, "Maggie is just perfect. You are so lucky."

"I wonder if I'll feel the same at the two in the morning when she's screaming for a feed?" I said, knowing full well that I would. I already knew I would forgive anything of this child. Beth held her for a while, rocking her back and forth, whispering inaudible and soothing sounds into her ear. I looked on, contentedly – until, that is, Beth asked the question I had been dreading all day.

"Don't you think it's about time you told your mother you're pregnant?" Beth's eyes didn't meet mine.

"No, I don't think that would be a good idea."

"But you can't hide her, Aoife. She is here now, a real, live baby."

"Not today," I muttered. "I can't be dealing with Sheila and her crises today."

"But –" Beth started.

"But nothing, not today," I replied firmly and reached to take my baby back into my arms, suddenly feeling very protective of her.

Beth sighed. She looked hurt, but I had no time to think about her sensibilities at the moment. I was the one with aching breasts and stitches in my nethers. If anyone was getting sympathy right now it was me.

Beth had left after an hour. She had wanted to stay, she told me, as she stared longingly at Maggie, but there was business to be sorted out and I was hardly in a fit state to attend to it. With timing not being one of my strong points I had given birth three days before I was due to finish Elena Kennedy's yoga room. Elena is one of our most valued clients and while she obviously was aware that I was pregnant and that babies appear when they are good and ready, both Beth and I knew she would take a degree of soothing when she found out Beth would be doing the rest of this project alone.

It shocked me to find that after Beth left I felt slightly bereft. I had no one now. I should have told my family back home of course, swallowed down my pride and phoned them, but I could not bear the inevitable recriminations and disappointment. Maggie was not a disappointment. It wasn't that I had purposely kept this from them – there just never was a right time to tell them that I was knocked up by a feckwit of a man who didn't want to know. Fighting tears, I walked to the window and stared out at the grey evening. The wind was blustering through the trees and the light was already fading. I wanted to open the window as far as I could, and shout to the world that I was a mother. I had a beautiful daughter. I hadn't meant to make a mess of things, honest I hadn't, and what I needed now was a hug, someone to show me they really cared.

Tears tripping me, I wandered into the corridor, my heart thumping. I just needed someone, anyone, to listen. As it happens I found Peggy – feet up on the nurses' station, head buried in the latest edition of *Take a Break*.

"I've made a mess," I muttered and Peggy simply smiled.

"Never mind, sweetie pie. You wouldn't believe the kind of things we see here in the wards. Nothing about a woman's body after childbirth scares us any more."

18

"Not that kind of mess," I muttered before erupting into hysterical sobs. "I've messed up my life, every last part of it! My parents don't know about Maggie. Her father doesn't want to know her. No one cares. We're all alone!" My voice had risen to a roar, all the hurt and fear pouring out.

"You're tired, lovely," Peggy soothed. "How about I take Maggie for an hour or so to let you sleep?"

"That won't help," I said petulantly and I meant it. I mean, Peggy was hardly going to take Maggie for an hour or two every day of her life to help me, was she?

"Do you want me to call your parents?"

"My mother would have a stroke."

"What about your dad?"

"He would have stroke worrying about telling my mother."

"And the baby's father?"

"Even if I knew where he was he wouldn't want to know. He made that clear."

I could see Peggy start to run out of ideas, losing steam and patience.

"I'm sure it's not that bleak. A baby can be a great healer. Please don't underestimate the power of that little girl in there to make things better. I'm sure they will all fall in love with her as soon as they see her."

I wanted to believe Peggy. Maybe they would love her – Mum, Daddy, Joe, all of them – so I asked her to bring me the phone. I felt terrified but, if I'm honest, I was excited too. It was as if I had been given permission to phone Jake again after all this time. Peggy could be right, a baby could heal things.

I looked at Maggie again. She had her daddy's nose, his soft dark hair. I bet myself that if he could meet her, even if for five minutes, he would love her.

I wasn't naïve. I knew he wouldn't fall at my feet. My days of fantasising about him banging at the door of the shop at three in the morning begging forgiveness had long gone. I had binned them right about the same time that I had stopped allowing myself the fantasy of imagining myself giving birth back home, my family surrounding me and celebrating this joyous new arrival. Jake would have been there, flirting with my mother and keeping her onside. When our child arrived they would have congratulated me on my reproductive skills before Jake would have proposed, in front of them all, telling them I had made him the happiest man in the world. No, that fantasy had gone a long time ago.

But then again, I allowed myself a little hope. I thought that if he grew to love Maggie, he could grow to love me again too. The only problem was, I didn't know where he was. This was going to be far from easy.

"No way, Aoifs ," he'd said, jumping out of the bed as if it were on fire.

I used to love that, the way he called me Aoifs. It felt special at the time. Now I realised it was simply because he was too damned lazy to learn how to pronounce my name properly. It would have required effort and Jake was never about effort. He liked the world handed to him on a plate.

"I didn't plan this," I said. "I'm as surprised as you. I thought you might be happy."

"Happy? I'm thirty-two. I don't want a fucking child messing up my life, not when it's starting to go somewhere."

"It's not just 'a' child, Jake," I answered, my voice rising. "It's *our* child and at the end of the day I'm pregnant and you were the impregnator." I pointed my finger at him, as if the power of my gesture would awaken his senses and he would realise this could actually be a good thing.

"Well, you can get rid of it. How much do you want?" He was fumbling for his wallet.

Can you believe it? He never had money to pay for the cab ride home from gigs to my place, but here he was fumbling for his fecking wallet.

"I'm keeping it," I said, shocking myself.

Don't get me wrong, I didn't want this baby. I can only think she was a result of a split condom, or a dodgy pill. I had never taken a contraceptive risk in my life. My mother would have killed me if I'd got in trouble, no matter what my age.

My life had been going somewhere too, but when I thought about getting rid of "it" – my baby – my heart stopped, a mixture of overwhelming sadness and crushing Catholic guilt sweeping over me.

"Well, don't expect me to help out," he said, one foot in his trousers. "You're on your own with this one." Two feet in his trousers. "I can't believe you, Aoifs." T-shirt on. Inside out. "You're just like the rest of them – out to fucking trap a man. You are sad." Shoes on and jacket lifted. "Call me if you see sense, this could have been good." Door slammed.

And that was the last time I spoke to Jake Gibson.

4

Beth

I had coped better than I thought I would. I'd only cried a little and I was able to disguise that as happiness for Aoife. I was happy for her, of course I was. She seemed happy to have her baby and I had wondered over the last few months if she would come round to the notion of motherhood at all. In my weirder, hormonally mental moments I had allowed myself to hope or think that perhaps she wouldn't bond with her baby and she would give her to me to look after. I never told anyone that I felt that way. I knew those were not the thoughts of a rational woman – but since when did rational thought come into being broody?

It was strange really – the day I first felt the urge to have a baby. Dan and I had been together for ages, and married for a few months when the notion first hit me. Up until then the thought of parenthood terrified me. I liked our freedom, I liked that we could jaunt off to Brighton for the weekend without worrying about anyone else. Dan was working crazy hours in the law firm and I was busy with Instant Karma. When we weren't working we were out with Aoife and Jake.

I had even bought cream carpets for our flat. Babies and children were not even on our radar. So it shocked me to suddenly come over all maternal. Dan and I had gone to Morelli's for coffee. We were sitting there when a woman – a yummy mummy – walked in with the most gorgeous baby boy I had ever set eyes on cradled close to her in a sling. He had downy soft blond hair and his eyes were closed. He was perfect and I could barely take my eyes off him.

So I turned to Dan, who was talking about his latest case, and said in a very matter-of-fact manner that I wanted one of those.

He stopped talking, stared at the baby, then back at me and smiled. "If this means we get to have loads of sex you can count me in," he grinned and I reached across to him.

"Do you mean that?" I asked, searching his face for any sign of doubt.

"I never joke about sex," he said solemnly, and I sat back frustrated at his jokey manner. He took my hand again, rubbing it gently and simply said: "I can think of nothing I would like to do more than have a baby with you."

And that was our decision made.

I felt nervous as I threw my pills away – replacing those small white tablets with small white folic acid pills instead. I bought a book called *Taking Charge of Your Fertility* and within a few weeks I knew when the optimum time for our lovemaking was and what position offered the best chance of success.

I even discovered the "joys" of egg-white cervical mucus. Who would have thought I would ever have been interested in what leaked from my undercarriage? But soon I wasn't just interested, I was obsessed.

By some weird twist of fate we seemed to get a shocking number of commissions for nurseries and children's bedrooms at that time. I started a file – my best ideas – which I kept in the shop, just ready for the time when I would get to design my own nursery.

God, I wiled away so many hours, lying on the daybed, pencil behind my ears, looking to all intents and purposes as if I was working really hard on the Forbes' nursery or the Johnstons' playroom – instead I was choosing the ginghams and voiles that would adorn *our* nursery – the room where little Lulah or Lucas would sleep.

I hadn't looked at that file in three months – not since I finished Maggie's nursery.

5

Aoife

I had two pounds in twenty-pence pieces stuffed into a little film canister. Beth had given it to me when she helped me pack my hospital bag. "You can't use your mobile in the hospital," she had lectured, "so take this and that way you will have change for the phone."

I had nodded, stuffing the film canister in my case along with two packets of gigantic maternity towels, some breast pads and ten pairs of disposable pants.

Beth had given me a list of everything I would need. She got it from an internet forum where she spent time while planning her Big Day with Dan and she just couldn't bring herself to leave after the wedding.

"I can't believe I need so much stuff," I had muttered while folding yet another tiny vest into the case, alongside the babygros, nappies, cotton wool and baggy T-shirts for labour.

"Trust me," Beth had soothed. "The girls on my site said you need this stuff."

I smiled and continued packing, grateful that someone, even if it was only Beth's imaginary friends on the internet, was taking an interest in this pregnancy. If it had been left to me Maggie would have spent her first twenty-four hours wrapped in a hospital-issue towel.

I rattled my film canister as Peggy wheeled in the phone, praying that my two pounds would be enough to get some answers.

"Here you go, lovely," Peggy soothed. "I'll take this little one to the nursery to give you some peace and quiet."

I nodded, kissing my fingers and pressing them against my daughter's cheek. Then I started to make some calls.

The phone rang twice. He always answered on the second ring. Dan was nothing if not predictable.

"Hey, Dan," I started.

"Hey, Irish, congrats on the baby. Beth says she's lovely."

"Thanks. Listen, I need a favour." I heard his intake of breath and knew that he had been expecting this phone call ever since he had slipped on my broken waters in Instant Karma.

"I wish I knew where he was," Dan started, "but you know I haven't seen him in three months. He's keeping a low profile."

"But surely someone knows? You guys were so close."

"He is not the man we thought he was. He doesn't keep in touch with any of us any more. Too busy trying to make it big. What a dickhead!" Dan's voice was full of scorn.

I bit my lip, biting back tears. I knew Jake was a dickhead, but he was also my baby's father. Dickhead or not, I couldn't escape that fact. Dickhead or not, I still had feelings for him.

I nodded meekly at the phone.

"You okay, Irish?" Dan asked.

I nodded again, a soft sob escaping from my mouth.

He took a deep breath. "Look," he sighed, "I'll ask around, but I can't promise anything. Beth and I will come in later, okay?"

I nodded again before muttering a quiet "Okay".

I had used a whole pound of my allowance and still had no answers. Sitting back on the bed, I dropped another coin in and dialled another number.

The phone rang three times before a harassed-sounding woman answered: "Hello, McLaughlin residence."

Mum. There she was with her airs and graces – Derry's answer to Hyacinth Bucket. I wondered in that second how she had felt when she'd first held me in her arms. Had she considered me perfect? Had I completed her? She had the husband, the nice house, the perfect son and now she had her daughter. I wondered had she felt happy in those early days, because it seemed to me that ever since I had been a disappointment. Tears sprang to my eyes.

"Hello?" she repeated, still harassed. "Look, if you are one of those call centres, we aren't interested."

"Mum," I muttered, my voice cracking with emotion.

She didn't notice. "Ach, Aoife, how are you? I was just talking about you today to Úna O'Neill. She's getting her living-room done and I told her all about you and your fancy shop. You should have seen her face. There she was lugging her paint from Tesco – can you believe it, Tesco? Since when did they do paint? – and I was telling her how you were doing up a pilot's room."

"It's pilates, Mum." I didn't bother to tell her it was a yoga room. There was little point.

"Well, whatever it is, it is better than the room yer wan will have when she's done!" Mum sniffed.

She clearly felt superior. That's all I was to her – a tool to make her feel superior over lovely Mrs O'Neill who always baked fresh buns for the kids on the street.

"I'm sure her room will be lovely," I said. By now I was getting worried. How would I segue from this talk of Tesco paint to the rather life-changing announcement that I had given birth in the early hours of the morning.

"You'll never guess the news," she started.

"Funnily enough I was about to say the same thing," I replied, figuring that humour was my best approach now. Like "Ha, ha, Mum, you'll never guess, but I've just had a baby" – that kind of thing.

"Well, let me tell you first," she said.

I could hear her sit down, the cushions on the leather sofa squeak under her. This must be Grade A gossip.

"Are you sitting down?" she asked.

"Yes."

"Well, you'll never guess who's pregnant?"

And there she was, stealing another of my lines. I glanced around the room, wondering for a moment if it was bugged. I dropped another twenty pence in the slot of the payphone and waited for the bombshell.

"Who?"

"Jacqueline! She's early on, but we're so excited. Joe is over the moon. Can you believe it? I'm going to be a granny again. Odhran will be a big brother. It's just wonderful. We couldn't be happier."

Fuck. Perfect Jacqueline was pregnant again. My perfect sister-in-law, hugely successful Jacqueline who could do no wrong, was pregnant.

"She's hoping for a girl," my mother continued. "Well, to be honest, she says she doesn't mind but a girl would be nice. I'd love a wee granddaughter to fuss over."

I wanted to scream. I wanted to tell her she had a granddaughter to fuss over, but the words didn't come.

"Look, Mum, someone has just come into the shop," I lied. "That's great news. I'm delighted for them. Talk later, bye."

I hung up. I now had only twenty pence left. I got up and walked to the nursery and hugged my daughter so close to me that I feared I might break her.

"I'll take her back to our room now," I told Peggy and walked back to the ward, where I lay down with Maggie on my chest and slipped into my fantasy world again – one where my mother preferred me over Jacqueline.

A sea of blue and pink balloons bobbed past my door. I could hear the occasional yelp of excitement from a toddler meeting his baby brother or sister for the first time and high-pitched declarations from overexcited grannies that the baby they were laying their eyes on for the first time was the most beautiful in the world. I was sitting on my chair, Maggie latched on to my swollen breasts, feeling my body ache, tighten and heal, when Dan popped his head around the corner, turned a shade of crimson and disappeared again. I had the good grace to laugh, as did Beth who could barely control her mirth as she walked into the room.

"Dan will come in when you've put your baps away," she laughed. "Although between me and you I think he was secretly delighted to get a peek."

Beth handed me a huge pink teddy bear, a box of chocolates and a half bottle of champagne. "I thought you might need some sustenance," she said, stroking Maggie's back – despite its close proximity to my naked nipple.

I lifted Maggie to my shoulder and began to rub her back in soft, soothing circular movements, calling out the door to Dan that he no longer needed to avert his eyes.

He walked towards me, a bunch of flowers in one hand and kissed me on the cheek. "Well done, Irish," he smiled. "She is a princess."

I smiled back, wondering if it was too soon to ask him if he had found out anything about Jake's location. Telling myself to play it cool, I decided to bide my time with some small-talk.

I was able to ascertain that the shagfest had been most lovely, and that Brighton had been freezing. I found out that Dan was set to start a new case in the Crown Court that might just make the tea-time news and that Elena Kennedy sent her very best wishes and was only mildly put out that I wouldn't be completing her yoga room.

"When do they think you might get out of here?" Dan asked.

I hadn't really thought about that before. It was quite cosy here. There was always a nurse on hand to answer my concerns or take Maggie for five minutes if I needed to pee. Going home scared me.

My flat, or apartment as my mother insisted on calling it, was perfect for me. I had known as soon as we'd viewed the shop downstairs that I would feel at home in this building, so we struck a deal with the landlord to allow us to let both at a reasonable rate. (Well, this is London – when I say reasonable, I do of course mean extortionate.) I had used my flat as a place where I could test my ideas for clients' transformations. The upside is that I sometimes got to keep pieces that didn't quite fit with our clients' vision, the downside was that nothing really matched. The flat was an eclectic mix of multicoloured fabrics, rich silks, gruff Hessian, coloured glass baubles and inventive lighting. I loved it. I felt at home lounging on my sofa, the soft coloured glass of the Tiffany-inspired lamps glowing around me as I looked out of the sash windows, framed in voile and chiffon.

It was the perfect flat for a woman-about-town. It wasn't so good for a single mother and her newly acquired love child. Thankfully Beth had made sure it wasn't totally child un-friendly these days.

Relishing a challenge she had blagged enough goodies from our suppliers to transform my miniscule box room into a nursery of sorts. Cream walls, a white cot and rocking chair and a chest of drawers filled it completely. She told me she would wait until the baby was born before she bought either the blue or pink gingham to finish the job. I had shrugged her off. I didn't care about the nursery. I didn't want to think of someone else invading my space.

I'd kept the door to that room closed for the past month, hoping that if I'd ignored what was happening it would go away. It didn't, thank God. Weirdly now I wanted to buy the pink, or maybe red, gingham myself and get my sewing-machine out and make the finishing touches. I wanted to fill the white wicker baskets with nappies and lotions, bibs and vests. I wanted to sit on the rocking chair and coo at my child, singing lullabies. (Admittedly I was going to have to learn some first, Mum was more into singing hymns at us – or the songs of Tammy Wynette.)

"We've bought you a travel system," Beth announced, pulling me from my thoughts.

"A what? I have a car, you know," I retorted.

"Not a car – a travel system – you know, a pushchair, car seat and all."

"A pram?"

"Well, it's more than a pram. It's a Bugaboo. All the top celebs have it," Beth said proudly.

"Thanks, though I'm not sure Maggie will be mixing with the Richmond yummy mummy and designer-baby set – any old pram would have done."

"Not for this little one," Dan grinned. "She deserves the best, just like her Auntie Beth."

Dan was holding Maggie now, cradling her gently in his arms. I realised this was the first time my daughter had been held by a man and when I saw the look of love and admiration Dan had in his eyes for her, I started to cry.

"Fecking hormones," I muttered, drying my eyes with the sleeve of my dressing-gown.

"Hey, don't worry about it," Beth sighed, tears glistening in her own eyes. "I would be crying too if I had such a gorgeous baby."

It would have been churlish to tell her I wasn't crying out of love, but fear and self-pity.

Dan reached towards his wife and rubbed her hand and I felt jealous of them and their connection. I wanted to feel it too – to feel cherished.

"So, did you hear anything about Jake?" I asked.

"Not yet, I made a few calls. Sarah thinks he might be in Germany. She wasn't sure."

"Is she going to find out?"

"She'll see what she can do."

I sighed. This was frustrating. Why did he not have answers for me? Maggie was almost twenty-four hours old and her daddy knew nothing about her.

"Do you want me to come and pick you up tomorrow then? You know, if you are getting out?" Beth asked.

I nodded.

"You can come and stay with us for a few days if you want," Dan offered, but no, no matter how much I was dreading it I knew I would have to get into some form of routine on my own sooner or later.

"I'll think about it," I said, knowing that I had already dismissed the notion outright. Much as I loved and adored my friends – these two people who had become more of a family to me than my own flesh and blood – I just could not imagine fitting into their perfect home and their perfect existence.

Beth and I were great as a working team. We were the best of friends, but we could never be housemates. We tried it once shortly after I'd moved to London – it didn't work then and it sure as hell wasn't going to work now.

Our pram, or travel system, could never look right in their minimalist lounge. It would clutter the place. The Chi and the

Feng Shui would be fucked and there would be all hell to pay for it. Maggie's baby blanket could never look right draped over the Italian leather sofa and my mess of auburn hair and colourful clothes would make me stand out like a sore thumb against their chic designer labels and sleek hairstyles.

I knew they genuinely wanted to help, but I didn't want them to start resenting me. I had already gate-crashed so much of their lives over the last nine months – from the moment I called to tell Beth my period was late and she ordered me over to do a test – and I had to start proving to them and to myself that I could go it alone – well, with the help of Matilda, of course.

6

Beth

Dan was quiet the whole way home. I wasn't sure what to say to him. I didn't know if he was quiet because he just didn't know what to say to me, his hormonal madwoman of a wife, or because he had just promised Aoife he would help track down Jake.

Although they had grown up together and had been more like brothers than cousins, there was little chance of a Rolf Harris "Two Little Boys" type tearful reunion when they met again.

I once thought we were inseparable as a foursome. We were young, we weren't ugly and we were doing pretty well for ourselves career-wise. We were like the brat pack in *St Elmo's Fire* or the friends from *Friends*. We had it all and I'm not ashamed to say I was pretty smug about it. There was me, dating this up-and-coming lawyer, and my best friend and partner in business dating Jake Gibson, the next big thing in the music scene.

Of course, after a couple of years, things started to go wrong for our fantastic foursome. While Dan was doing well – really well –

and Aoife and I were becoming more and more in demand, Jake was still the "next big thing" but now it was only in his own mind.

He kept gigging, kept trying for that break but it didn't come. The more knock-backs he got the shittier he became to Aoife. Of course, she couldn't see it. She adored him. He treated her like rubbish and she let him.

Dan tried to talk to him, many times. He tried to get him to get his act together. He even offered him an internship at the law firm, but Jake didn't take it well. He accused Dan of being unsupportive and smug. And I tried to talk to Aoife, to show her she was worth more than that but she wouldn't listen and when we started having screaming rows about it I learned it was better if I just stayed quiet and helped picked up the pieces each and every time he hurt her.

But neither Dan nor I could see what was going to happen next. We knew Jake wasn't exactly reliable but we didn't think he would leave Aoife in the lurch like that.

I remember the day she took the pregnancy test at our flat. I had a secret stash of tests in the bathroom cabinet, but I couldn't tell Aoife that so I drove her to Tesco and she picked up a couple for herself. The thing is, I knew she was pregnant before she peed on the stick. I knew it because I knew fate had a very sick sense of humour. So as I sat and cried with her as the test turned positive, my tears were real – but for completely different reasons to hers.

Dan sighed as he pulled the car into our parking space and switched off the engine. He rested his hand on my knee – looking straight ahead – and said: "One day, Beth, we will buy one of those prams for our own baby, I promise."

I blinked back tears, knowing that he was blinking back his own and we walked to the flat in silence. I'm not sure if it was because there was nothing to say, or simply too much.

7

Aoife

I had been given the all-clear to go home just before noon. It had felt bizarre to get dressed. For some reason I hadn't noticed how flabby my still-distended tummy was while it was hidden inside my pyjamas, but dressing in my old maternity clothes I felt like a busted cushion. I had neither shape nor style about me. The heat of the ward made me sweat, bucket-loads of perspiration coursing between my swollen breasts even though it was February and the rain was beating down outside.

When I tried to slip my feet into my shoes they were swollen and I had to shoe-horn them in. I may have been bruised, I may have been stitched and bloated, but I was not walking out of hospital in my slippers.

As we travelled down to the ground floor in the lift, eager eyes staring into the car seat at Maggie, cooing and congratulating, I felt myself wobble, both physically and emotionally.

I wanted to go back inside, to have the nurses come and help me if I needed them. I was not ready for this parenting malarky and once again I told myself it was not meant to be like this.

After Jake had left me, swaggering out of my flat with his T-shirt inside out, I had tried to win him back.

I became, I can admit with the fullness of time, a little psychotic over the whole thing. I bombarded him with phone calls and when he changed his number I started with letters and emails.

I wanted him to know that I was as shocked by the whole thing as he was and that I had reacted myself with the same anger and disbelief but that it would and could be okay and sure we hadn't planned it, but that didn't mean a baby would have to be a bad thing.

He didn't reply. I would have handled the whole thing better if he had repeatedly told me to feck off, but he didn't. He just ignored me and that allowed me to tell my pregnancy-addled, hormone-riddled brain that perhaps he never got the thirty-six letters or forty-nine emails and that his phone must have a fault. Eventually, after I sobbed like a madwoman all over Janice Grayson's new nursery, Beth sat me down on the luxury rocker and told me that I needed to let go. I needed to realise he didn't want me or our baby. I nodded, agreed – I mean I hadn't really wanted our baby myself. So I decided that I had to change my tactics. He might not want us then, but surely that would change when his child was born?

Dan had carried Maggie in her new Bugaboo car seat over the threshold into Instant Karma. As I followed I wanted to close the door to the shop behind me, lie down on the daybed and stay there until my heart and body were healed.

Matilda stood on guard, that Mona Lisa smile on her lips,

staring down at me and my child as we walked past. "It will be all right," she seemed to whisper as I climbed the stairs and I wanted to believe her.

Having settled myself onto my sofa I held Maggie in my arms while Dan made us all tea.

"I've put the crib by your bed," Beth soothed and I wondered when I had got a crib. Pointing to a box on the floor she added that it contained nappies, creams, burp clothes, wipes and dummies. "We got you a baby bath too, on our Parent World account – I felt it was time we treated ourselves for a change. They said just to ring with whatever else you might need."

Do Parent World sell fathers? I wondered.

Dan appeared with tea and chocolate biscuits and we sat down staring at each other, a glorious whiff of "What now?" in the air. I nibbled my biscuit, cautious of spilling crumbs onto Maggie's head and wondered would it be too crazy to ask if Sarah had come up with the goods about Jake yet?

"Right," Beth said, taking a gulp of her tea. "This is what is going to happen. Heather is going to help out with the shop until you are ready to come back. If you don't mind, I'll pop in and consult with you but you can spend all the time you need with Maggie."

I nodded. I didn't know why Beth was telling me this. We had arranged this long before I'd gone into labour, but I liked her reassurance that some things were going to remain the same – Heather part-time in the shop, Beth and I sitting together dreaming up colour schemes and grand designs.

"You look tired," she said.

Again I nodded. I seemed, through exhaustion or whatever, to have lost the power of speech.

"Go to bed, sweetie. I'll look after this little one. Dan has to get back to work and I've no intention of opening up at this time of the day."

Gratefully I stood up and made my way into my bedroom. It had always been my sanctuary. I lay down on my bed, fully dressed, not even finding the energy to move the ten cushions I insisted had to live on top of my bedspread and fell into a deep sleep.

When I woke I could hear Beth singing softly to Maggie and the sound of her footsteps as she walked back and forth across the living-room floor. It was dark and cool as I went out and interrupted their moment – reaching my arms out for my child.

There were tears in Beth's eyes. "She's perfect, Aoife, I hope you realise that."

"I do."

Babies don't do an awful lot. Beth had left at around eight and I had started to realise just how strange this motherhood thing was. Yes, Maggie needed feeding, and changing and burping but she didn't actually "do" anything all that entertaining.

Our life was a constant routine of feed, sleep, feed, burp, poop (her not me), feed, sleep, and cry (me not her).

I dialled Jake's number – the old number, the one he hadn't answered in six months – but of course there was no answer. Then I called Heather and left a message on her answerphone to remind her to bring some milk when she arrived for work in the morning and then I crawled back to bed, leaving the light on and being scared to sleep properly in case I wouldn't hear Maggie when she cried even though she was in the same room as me.

We lay there, dozing and waking until dawn when I could at least make a decent effort to get my life back together.

It was still dark when I gave up the ghost and got up. Delicate fairy lights hung around the two sash windows in my bedroom and I switched them on and allowed them to twinkle softly. I was physically exhausted but my mind didn't want to switch off. Maggie was still asleep, her tiny chest rising and falling. Her arms were above her head, her hands two perfect fists. I knew I was supposed to sleep when she slept – even with my limited knowledge of parenthood I knew they advised that – but I couldn't and that added to the pressure. The not knowing when she would wake, or what she would want, seemed to switch on my "awake" button. Someone really should have made an instruction manual for early motherhood.

I made myself a cup of milky tea and poured the remainder of the chocolate biscuits from yesterday onto a plate before diving back under my duvet. Who cared that it was 6 a.m.? I had just created life – I was entitled to a chocolate biscuit or two. I switched the TV on, listening to the quiet hum of the morning news programme and I lifted my laptop onto my knee. It was time to take some action – of course in hindsight I know that less than forty-eight hours after giving birth with about ten hours' sleep was not the best time for taking any kind of action.

Clicking into my email I saw a message from Jacqueline – of course I already knew what it was going to say.

To: Aoife.McLaughlin@instantkarma.co.uk
From: jacqueline.McLaughlin@yahoo.com
Subject: Guess What?

Hi Aoife,
I'm hoping to get you before your mum does. I've been trying your phone but it's always off or just rings out. The life of a single girl, eh? Not that I would swap what I have for the world.

Anyway, thought you should know you are going to be an auntie again. I thought maybe you could think about a few new ideas for the nursery as a present for the baby.

There is a nice nursery in Homes and Gardens this month (March edition). Have a little look and let me know what you think?
Jacqueline

It wasn't so much that Jacqueline was annoying. It was that she was exceptionally annoying. She assumed that her nursery would be created for her – gratis. And she would expect all the fittings at cost too. Her first child, a chubby little thing called Odhran was a lovely child but spoiled rotten. I was pretty sure this second baby was heading for the same fate.

I didn't know whether to laugh or cry. Jacqueline would have a ball with my news. She would become my mother's confidante in her hour of need and yet I knew that the time was coming when I would have to break the news and allow them their little happy dance at my failure.

I did what I always do in times of extreme crises – emailed Auntie Anna. She would know what to do. She always had before. When I'd stormed out of the house in a teenage rage she had been my refuge. Surely she would be there for me now?

I should have told her before now. I realised that. Anna would have been fine with this. She was one of those cool aunties who bought you the odd drink and allowed you to swear. Having a baby out of wedlock would have been wee buns to her.

To: Annab60@yahoo.com
From: Aoife.McLaughlin@instantkarma.co.uk
Subject: Help!

Hi Anna,
Hope all is well with you. Sorry to do an Aoife and land a bombshell on you but I have some news. I hope you will okay be with this because the thing is, I have no one else to turn to.
I have kind of found myself in the family way – except, and I could die for telling you this – she is already here.
I gave birth two days ago to Maggie McLaughlin, the most perfect little baby you could ever hope to lay your eyes on.
I know your jaw has probably hit the floor by now, but I didn't mean

44

to keep her a secret. It just kind of happened. I'm not sure how to handle it.

Please, please, please don't tell Joe or Mum. I know that is asking a lot but you know they will only go off their heads.

Hugs to you,

Sorry for telling you by email,

Aoife

x

I sat and stared at the words before me for what seemed like forever. Would I be wise to send this email? It would mean Maggie wouldn't be my dirty little secret any more and yet I just wasn't sure I was ready for the inevitable shockwaves this little gem of information would send through my life.

My fingers hovered between the delete button and the return key and then, as my daughter woke – her mewling cry calling for my attention – I did what I had to do.

In precisely two hours and six minutes my auntie would switch on her computer over her morning cup of tea and find out all about Maggie.

The walls crowded in around me and as much as I loved my flat I knew I had to keep myself busy or drive myself to distraction. When Maggie was fed and changed and sleeping again I showered, each drop of water pounding against my skin in time with the thudding of my heart, making me wonder what I had let myself in for.

I dressed, my body hardly recognisable from the size 10 figure it had once been, and sore from the physical exertion not only of childbirth but of pregnancy. Nonetheless I found a pair of baggy trousers and a cream woollen jumper to slip on before ramming my still fat feet into a pair of loafers.

It was eight seventeen. I needed to get out.

I dressed my daughter in her snowsuit and we made our way downstairs to where the Bugaboo thingummy was waiting. It was raining outside, grey and cold on this February morning and Matilda gave me a look which let me know she was unhappy with my plans to take my child out into this rotten day.

"I won't be long," I muttered and pushed the pram (sorry, travel system) out of the little side door and through the lane into the main street. It seemed like London was waking up and cars were starting to crawl along the road, sleepy drivers with blurry eyes at the wheel.

Walking slowly I breathed in the damp morning air and made my way to Morelli's Home Bakery for a coffee and cream cake.

"Ooooh, you've had the bambino!" Mrs Morelli squealed, squeezing her ample frame out from behind the counter for a peek. Her doughy hands reached into the pram and she traced a small sign of the cross on Maggie's forehead. "*Bella, bella bambina!*" she said, pulling me into a vice-like grip of a hug.

"Her name is Maggie," I offered when I freed myself, lifting my daughter from where she was sleeping soundly and offering her to the jolly woman who smothered her in kisses.

"Eeva," she mispronounced my name, "she is an angel sent from God. You must be so very proud."

I nodded.

"And your parents? Are they coming to see her? I bet they are booking flights right now!"

"Maybe," I muttered, taking Maggie back in my arms and sitting down, grimacing slightly as my bruised bits hit the hard wooden chair.

A look of confusion flashed across her face. "I'm sure they will love her," she said sagely before offering me a latte on the house with whatever cake took my fancy.

"Better make it a decaf," I said as she bustled back behind the counter. I looked at the clock, it was eight fifty-five. In fifteen minutes Anna would open her email. My stomach tied itself in knots. Kissing Maggie's head I put her back in her carrycot and took the cup of warm coffee from Mrs Morelli.

She sat down opposite me. "Eeva, you know that if you need anything for you or your *bambina* then you can come to me, okay?" I nodded, a grateful tear sliding down my cheek and slap bang onto my vanilla square.

"Darling, don't cry," Mrs Morelli said, rubbing my hand. Her own hands – so soft, so warm and motherly made me cry harder. I may not have liked my mum all that much but I so wanted her here now, with her soft hands that smelled of Palmolive soap. "If your daughter had a baby and didn't tell you, would you forgive her?" I asked.

Her eyes widened – only a minute amount – and then she composed herself again. "I would forgive my daughter the world," she answered. "Wouldn't you forgive Maggie if she did the same?" I looked at my innocent child, asleep, her perfect cupid's bow of a mouth pursed in a quiet dream and, yes, I realised I would forgive her.

I would bust her arse first, but ultimately I would forgive her. It was eight fifty-eight.

I sat until I finished my coffee, then we bundled ourselves back out the door and back down towards the flat. Beth and Heather were outside, ready to open for the day.

"Where on earth have you been?" Beth gasped as Heather made a beeline straight for the pram and her first glimpse of Maggie.

"Just a little walk," I muttered, ashamed. Matilda may have been the queen of the holier-than-thou looks but Beth was generally the person who had the tone of voice to match.

"I went to Morelli's for a coffee. I felt claustrophobic."

"But it's too early to be out of the house with a baby!" Beth protested.

"Nonsense – she's fine!" I snapped. "I'm tired but fine, thank you, and the coffee was lovely." Bustling past, I left Beth and Heather standing open-mouthed in my wake.

As I walked into the shop I cast a stone glare in Matilda's direction. "Don't you start," I muttered.

I could hear the phone ringing as I climbed the stairs. My heart pounded, a sense of relief and a sense of dread vying with each other for attention. "It will all be fine, it will be fine, it will all be fine," I repeated over and over with every step.

"Aoife!" Beth called as I put my key in the lock and went to cross the threshold. "Wait there a moment."

"Come on up," I answered, making my way into the living-room and laying Maggie in her baby bouncer.

Beth stuck her head around the door, waving a white hanky as she entered. "Sorry if I was a little nutty there. It's just quite cold and damp out there and she is quite young." She nodded in the direction of the bouncer.

"I know, I just needed to clear my head a bit."

The phone burst into life again, ringing loudly and causing Maggie to wake – her startled cry immediately grabbing my attention.

"Do you want me to get that?" Beth asked.

"No, it's fine. It'll only be Auntie Anna. I told her about Maggie this morning in an email. I expect she wants to talk to me."

"I imagine she does," Beth replied coolly. "Shouldn't you talk to her then?"

"I will when madam is settled. I'm a little nervous." I lifted Maggie to my shoulder and shushed her as I bounced her gently in my arms.

"Do you want me to take her and let you get it over with?"

Beth asked, her arms already outstretched.

I paused, then kissed Maggie and handed her over. "I suppose that would be a good idea."

The phone rang again and I lifted it. "Hello?"

8

Aoife

"Aoife, I can't believe it. I just can't bloody believe it."

My heart skipped about a million beats all at once. I wondered momentarily if many thirty-one-year-olds in relatively good health suffered coronaries.

"A girl. I could have sworn you were carrying a boy," the voice continued.

It was Elena Kennedy, by far our most valued client. I like her, honestly I do, but I didn't want to talk to her then. I had been waiting for Anna to phone. The word was out and I needed to talk to my aunt and have her tell me I wasn't the blackest sheep ever known in the McLaughlin family.

"Yes, I'm home. Maggie is lovely."

"What a beautiful name," Elena drawled. "You really must pop over when you are feeling more yourself so that we can see her."

"Yes, I will do. That would be lovely."

"Or I could drop by?" she offered. "I've a lovely little gift for the pair of you."

"Yes, Elena. That would be nice too. Maybe next week when I'm feeling brighter. I'm still very tired."

"Oh yes, you must be. If there's anything I can do. I can recommend a night nurse if you need a little sleep."

I choked back a snort. It was far from night nurses I was reared and while Instant Karma paid the bills, it did not cover nanny expenses – not by a long shot.

"I'll let you know," I muttered, willing her to take the hint from my brisk answers that I didn't have time for idle chit-chat. If she had been anyone else I would have told her to feck off and that I needed to keep the phone line clear – but I couldn't risk it with Elena – not when I knew for a fact she wanted her bedroom transformed in the next few months.

Thankfully she picked up the hint and signed off, promising to call by and see us both and share a coffee and a chat. I looked around my flat. It was a far cry from her Richmond pad and I made a mental note to arrange the meeting for Stanford's Deli – a swish little bistro at the other end of the street.

I waited for Anna's call, staring at Beth with a growing sense of desperation.

"Do you think she's so angry that she can't bring herself to talk to me?" I asked.

Beth sighed. "Sweetheart, she might be shocked but I don't think your aunt has it in her to be angry with anyone for any length of time. She might just be busy.

"S'ppose," I muttered, walking to the kitchen to make a cup of tea – my fourth of the morning.

"Do you think I should phone her?" I shouted through to Beth who was still bouncing up and down gently, shushing Maggie even though she had been asleep for five minutes.

"If you feel you must," she answered.

I looked at the phone, staring at me from its cradle, and I realised I could stand there and drive myself to distraction for the next however long or I could dial a simple number and start to mend what I had broken.

The phone rang three times before Anna's voice answered – just to tell me she wasn't in and I was free to leave a message. Fighting every urge in my body to throw the phone through the window I sat down, a little too quickly, and felt the shockwaves dash through my battered body.

"You could just phone your mum?" Beth offered.

"And give her a stroke for breakfast? Are you mad?" I snapped.

Beth looked wounded but I didn't care. I was in this mess, not her – and she more than anyone should know that you don't just phone my mother and make grand announcements down the line.

"It was only a suggestion."

"Well, it wasn't a very good one. You know Mum. That would be entirely the wrong way to tell her."

Why I thought telling Anna via email was the right way to start spreading the news, I don't know – but it seemed the best choice out of a pretty shitty bunch of choices at the time.

Beth sat in silence and I immediately started to feel guilty. She was once again the victim of my hormonal mood swings and it wasn't fair. None of this was fair. I started to cry. "I'm sorry, Beth," I muttered and she came and sat beside me, nestling into me, careful not to drop Maggie.

"It will be okay. You've been through tougher than this."

"I guess," I answered, and at that the phone rang again. Taking a deep breath I lifted it. "Hello?"

"Are you trying to give me a fecking heart attack? Jesus, some things aren't funny, Aoife."

It was Anna.

"Sorry, I didn't know how else to tell you," I mumbled.

"Tell me? Isn't this a wind-up?" She sounded genuinely confused.

"No," I muttered. "It's very real. I have the stitches to prove it."

"Jesus," she said and went silent – totally silent – for at least a minute.

Then I heard her inhale. Anna always inhaled deeply when she was getting me out of a fix. It gave her time to think.

"This will be okay. We just have to come up with a plan."

I felt reassured. Anna was always able to work things out. She would find the answer.

"Feck knows what the plan will be, but we will come up with one," she added.

"I'm sorry for landing this on you."

"Don't worry about that. How are you, Aoife? How is the baby – Maggie? How are you coping? How did you manage to keep this quiet all this time?"

"I'm fine. Maggie is wonderful. I've Beth here to help me and there just didn't seem like a good time to tell you all."

"And the father? Are we allowed to talk about him?"

That was a very good question indeed. Were we allowed to talk about the father? God knows I'd thought about him a lot.

Jake was 5'10" but he looked taller. Maybe that was because the first time I laid eyes on him I had been staring upwards at a stage and he was standing there, eyes closed, guitar strumming, lost in Paul Weller's "You Do Something To Me".

I remember I laughed, turned to Beth and told her that "Yer man could do something to me any time he wanted."

"Oh him? Jake? He's the one I was telling you about – Dan's cousin."

I couldn't see a family resemblance. Dan was all clean-cut, sharp-suited and solid-jawed. Jake was balding, stubbly and dressed like your average scarecrow, but he had sex appeal by the bucket-load. His voice was deep, passionate, entrancing and I found myself utterly captivated.

When he sat with us after the gig for drinks I did my best to act like an interesting and intelligent grown-up – hiding the fact that I felt to all intents and purposes like a silly love-struck schoolgirl. We got talking – or more he got talking and I got listening and by the end of the night my heart had overruled my head and we ended up back at mine having rampant sex. I would like to say we made love, but I knew it was sex to him, pure and simple. I hoped it would change over time, but obviously it was always going to be just sex, to him. He never told me he loved me – well, only in a whiney voice when he wanted something – like a blow job. He once said I was his muse – as we drunkenly rolled into bed after a killer gig – but the "L" word was just not in his vocabulary.

I was, however, able to convince myself he did, in fact, have feelings for me because he spent so much time with me it would have been impossible for him to be "loving" anyone else. I became complacent, I can admit, because I thought it was only a matter of time before he came round to my way of thinking and realised he was mad about me too. He never did.

So were we allowed to talk about the father?

"Not really," I told Anna and she thankfully didn't ask any more about him. She knew enough of me to know that when I was ready she would get the information she wanted.

"I'm not sure where to go with this," she said. "If I can't tell your mum, can I tell Joe? He might be able to help."

"Oh God, he would go mad."

"Your brother is not the ogre you think he is," she sighed.

"No, but he is over-protective and he will be disappointed in me and if Jacqueline finds out it'll only be a matter of seconds before she is on the phone to Mum."

"You had a baby, pet. You didn't kill anyone."

I knew she was making sense but I wasn't ready to let them know. Not then anyway, not until I'd come to terms with it a little more myself.

"I know," I muttered. "Just give me a few days."

"The longer you leave it, the harder it will be. If you want me to do the telling I will. Your mum will love Maggie. I know it. Send me a pic, will you? I'll phone tonight to see how you're getting on."

"Okay, Auntie Anna. Thanks."

And she was gone. I wasn't sure if I was any further forward at all. Anna may have been convinced my mother would be okay with this, but I wondered if Anna really knew her sister at all. Mum hadn't been okay with anything I'd done for a very, very long time.

Beth stood up, placing Maggie in her cot and heading to the kitchen to put the kettle on yet again. Despite her presence, I felt utterly alone and put my head in my hands and wept like a baby.

"Sweetheart," Beth soothed, rubbing my back and kissing the top of my head, "this will all work out. C'mon, where is your 'This Too Will Pass' spirit?"

"It passed," I sighed, rubbing my eyes dry on the sleeve of my jumper. "These are just the baby blues," I continued. "My boobs are like watermelons, my tummy is like a bowl of jelly. My nethers are shredded, I can't get up and go out anywhere. I can't even relax in my own house or have a good sleep and," I spluttered, "and no one loves me."

"I love you," Beth answered.

"No offence, but that is not the kind of loving I'm talking about. I'm talking about you and Dan and your perfect relationship and your house. If you had a baby you know Dan would be a brilliant dad. He wouldn't be missing in action. He wouldn't offer to pay for a termination!" I was ranting, my sentences coming out between gulping sobs. My fingers pointed accusingly at Beth from time to time and yet I couldn't stop myself from letting the pain out. What did she have that I didn't? How come she got Mr Perfect and I got Mr Feckwit? "He would be one of those men who buys you a fifty-million carat ring just to say thanks for bearing the fruit of his loins and here I am, alone in my shitty flat with a child whose father doesn't even want to know she exists!"

Beth stared at me, dumbstruck for a while, obviously unsure of how to respond and then she muttered something about day three always being a killer and perhaps I would feel brighter tomorrow. She kissed Maggie, patted me on the shoulder and left – just as I started to cry again.

By evening I felt exhausted. Between the crying and the trying to latch her on to my boobs which had at least doubled in size in the last twenty-four hours, things were not as easy as I had hoped.

So I decided to switch off the outside world, unplugging the phone and curling up on the sofa, Maggie in my arms. We spent the afternoon watching Doris Day films and eating chocolate biscuits. (In fairness to Maggie she didn't do much of the film-watching or the chocolate-biscuit-eating – but she had the good grace to look content when the crumbs frequently fell on her downy soft hair.) I lost myself in Calam and Kate singing all about "A Woman's Touch". I felt myself calm down. Beth was right. This too would pass and I made a mental note to phone her later to apologise for my outburst.

9

Beth

She is addled with hormones, I reminded myself over and over again as I drove home, the cold February rain battering against the windscreen while tears poured down my face.

I felt my stomach start to cramp. This probably meant my period had arrived but then again it could be a sign of early pregnancy according to the website I had joined to get support while I tried to conceive. I tried not to let a little bubble of excitement swirl up inside me. A quick mental calculation reminded me my period was due two days from now, so it was much too early to get proper period cramps. It had to be implantation. I dried my eyes and allowed myself a little fantasy – one where I presented two little woollen booties to Dan and told him he was going to be a daddy. Parking the car, I took a few deep breaths. I should know not to allow myself these little indulgences. I should always wait until the positive result popped up on the test.

But maybe Maggie would be our lucky charm? She had settled so nicely in my arms today – her little body just seemed to fit in the crook of my arm. And my, did she smell delicious, so new, soft and fresh. My heart lurched that little bit at the very thought.

Walking into the flat I noticed that the light was flashing on the answerphone. I kicked off my shoes, poured a glass of water and pressed play.

"Beth darling, it's Mum. Just wondering how things are? Daddy and I were wondering if you and Dan might like to come down this weekend. I know you're terribly busy, but we'd love to see you."

I grimaced at the answerphone. There is no way Dan would be up for a visit back home and I doubt very much I'd be up for it either. If anyone was more obsessed with our procreation than us, it was my parents. They were so keen – too keen – to be grandparents. Each visit they dropped heavy hints that it was about time we added to the family line. Dan wanted me to tell them we were trying, and failing, each month, that we were "infertile" in an unexplainable way, but I couldn't do it. My parents weren't used to me failing at anything let alone basic biology.

I sat down and rubbed my temples. I could feel a headache come on. God, I was tired, so I curled up on the sofa and drifted off into a dreamless sleep.

I woke to a kiss, so soft and so gentle that it took my breath away. Opening my eyes to the now dark room, I reached my hand up to Dan's familiar face and felt a smile spread across my face.

"Hey, babe," I whispered, pulling him close to me.

"Hey, yourself," he said back, kissing me – at first gently and then deeply. I allowed myself to melt towards him and as his hand brushed against my breast, I felt myself wince with pain. Tender breasts: another sign. And then I was aware of the cramping again.

"Just let me nip to the loo," I whispered. Imagine how much

more amazing this could be if I knew I was pregnant for definite?

Of course, I didn't need to use the testing kit after all. The answer was clear as day in my underwear. No baby this month. No reason, just no baby. I didn't even cry, just wrapped myself in my dressing-gown, wandered through the living-room again and told Dan I was going to bed with a hot-water bottle.

He knew me well enough by now to know what that meant, so he kissed me on the top of the head.

"Maybe next month," he said and I nodded, just like I did every month.

"Maybe. Can you bring me a glass of wine and a king-size Galaxy, please?"

He nodded.

The same routine we played out every month. Even I was getting a little tired of it now. Twenty-five wasted opportunities. Twenty-four babies I wouldn't hold or coo over.

IO

Aoife

Beth and Dan have been together forever. Of course when I say forever I mean since 1994, but in my books that pretty much feels like forever.

When Beth and I started college on the same day and met at registration she was already one year into her relationship with Dan. They had met at sixth-form college and everyone was convinced it was never going to work. I was a hopeless romantic back then, however, and I knew from the first time I saw them together that it *was* going to work. They seemed together, so very madly in love, and as I welcomed Beth into my life as my new best gal pal I soon realised that Dan came as part of the package. He became like the brother I never had. (I do of course have a brother, but the ability of my parents to see the rays of sunshine pour from his arsehole has left our relationship tense to say the least.) I wasn't competitive with Dan. We just laughed, drank and partied our way through college.

After graduation, when we all moved en masse to London, that partying continued except that while I wanted to hit the clubs six nights a week (Sunday I devoted to *Where the Heart Is* and being hungover) I started to realise ever so slowly that Beth and Dan only wanted to party five nights . . . then four . . . then three . . . you get the picture.

It was around that time that they bought the "Ivory Tower" as we have dubbed it – a gorgeous two-bedroomed penthouse flat which has been the subject of some serious coveting on my behalf. I could never afford such a place – renting the flat above Instant Karma stretched me to my limits but, with Dan's career going into orbit at the law firm and Beth's tidy inheritance from her grandfather, it was well within their means.

I realised, as any good friend should, that if I owned a flat such as their flat I would want to forsake my partying to spend time lying on the shagpile rugs on the real oak floors drinking expensive wine from John Rocha Waterford Crystal and discussing the newest addition to the Bar. And shagging of course – they did lots of shagging.

I was jealous because love just didn't seem to come my way – until of course I met Jake four years ago and even then I could never have classed what we had as love.

It was hard to believe that Jake and Dan shared any of the same gene pool. They were so diametrically different and yet when the four of us went out together I felt like a Queen Bee. Here we were, me and Beth, businesswomen with a hip and happening boutique, Dan the hotshot lawyer and Jake the sexy singer in a band.

I knew people looked at us and envied us. There was a lot to envy and every night I would come home and Jake would follow and we would spend glorious hours entwined in each other. Oh yes. There was shagging. There was lots of shagging.

The highlight of our little ménage à quatre (even though we

never "ménaged" anything) was Beth and Dan's wedding day. She looked radiant in a shot-silk gown, her hair delicately dressed with a pale pink orchid. Dan looked handsome almost beyond words in his suit and there was me, all *Sex and the City* with my pale green tea-length gown, my tanned shoulders, my auburn curls cascading around my shoulders.

Jake could barely keep his eyes, or his hands for that matter, off me that day. He was entranced with me, bewitched with me, and I was with him. As he took to the stage to sing "Lean on Me" for Beth and Dan's first dance I thought my heart might burst with pride. I wanted to run on the stage, shouting "He's mine, he's mine!" and I imagined the day when we would dance together under the stars – me in the shot-silk gown, him in the handsome suit – and I couldn't wait. Mum would be so proud.

I'm not sure where it went wrong for any of us.

I picked up the phone and dialled Beth's number. Dan answered the phone and I knew something was wrong. I could barely explain it. Dan has a certain way of answering the phone, always emphasising the "o" of hello, showing off his bright and cheery disposition. I didn't get that from him this time, however. I got a subdued, monotone hello that unnerved me.

Immediately I asked if everything was okay.

"Hey, Irish," he responded, a deep sigh following, "Yes, things are fine."

"Is Beth about?"

"Erm, she's busy at the moment."

I felt my hormones surge a little just at the same time I felt my heart sink. This isn't what I expected. I expected Beth to answer, in her usual cheerful tone, all bad feeling forgotten, because unlike me Beth was never one to stay mad at anyone for long.

"Do you know when she will be free?" I asked, a little wobble creeping into my voice. I figured I'd better just come clean with Dan. "You see, we had a little spat today, I was a bit of cow – hormones, you know – and I just wanted to apologise."

"Don't worry about it," Dan answered. "She'll be fine. You know Beth, takes everything on the chin."

I should have been reassured by his words, but I felt there was something he wasn't telling me. The bounciness was still missing from his voice.

"Dan, you would tell me if something was wrong, wouldn't you?"

"Of course I would," he answered, and if there hadn't been a three-second pause between my question and his response I would have believed him.

The darned thing was I couldn't just jump up and rush over there as I would have done a month or two ago. It would require an operation of military precision now to get me and the baby out the door on a cold, wet evening and I wasn't sure if I was fit enough to drive anyway.

I looked at Maggie and realised once again just how much my life was changing minute by minute and I felt utterly useless. "Can you let Beth know I called and I'm sorry and if she needs me I'm here," I muttered, tears pricking at my eyes as I said my goodbyes.

An hour later I was still unable to settle so I wandered downstairs, baby monitor in hand, to the shop. In times gone by whenever I felt edgy – on those nights I sat in waiting for Jake to call for his requisite post-gig bonk – I would go downstairs, flick through the fabric books and work on my designs.

Of course now I was officially on maternity leave, I didn't have any designs of my own to work on so I would have to make do with casting an eye over the books and looking at the latest swatches sent in from our suppliers. I looked at our diary. Things were going to be hectic for Beth for the next few months, I realised. We had two living-rooms, a dining-room, a bathroom and a studio flat to complete before Easter. I gazed at her mood boards – sketches which showed off her talent, swatches which were very much 'now' – and I could see the warmth of her personality jump off the page. No one had the ability to transform a client's vision to reality just exactly the way Beth had.

I rubbed my fingers along some plush velvets and wondered just what was wrong with my friend and if this wee baby, my daughter, was already driving a wedge between us. Could Instant Karma survive such a change?

As I sipped from my coffee cup the phone rang and I jumped a little. I had been lost in a gorgeous design for a bathroom which Beth had half finished. It was my sad little attempt at a peace offering – a way of lightening her load.

It was Anna.

"Hey, you," she said. "How are you? How is the baby?"

"Ach grand, and you?"

"Just fine, sweetheart. Look, I've been thinking, and I think you need to come home. This will be much easier if they can see the little one in real life – then they will fall in love with her. And besides, I'm dying to give her a big cuddle. I'm willing to bet you could do with a hug yourself," she added perceptively. I knew she was right. Telling the folks would be easier face to face but I wasn't sure I felt that brave.

I mean, I would need a brass neck to walk down Shipquay Street, where everyone knew Mum, with my baby in her fancy pram. They'd think I was getting ideas above my station. Mum would be mortified. It could all go horribly wrong.

"I'll think about it," I answered.

"Please do," said Anna. "You can stay with me if you want. The spare room is yours whenever you need it, you know that."

"I'll call you in the morning. I think I can hear Maggie stirring," I lied.

We said our goodbyes and I closed my sketchpad and turned to head upstairs. There she was again, looking down on me. "Matilda, you know it was only a wee white lie that time. No harm done."

As some form of divine retribution, or instant karma if you prefer, Maggie did decide to be amazingly unsettled through the night. I'm sure something in her clicked that night to let her know she was outside the womb and there was a whole big world she could explore. Only wimps wait for daylight.

I spent that night pacing up and down in my battered dressing-gown, my eyelids drooping and my spirit, and boobs, sagging. I still hadn't heard from Beth, which worried me, but more than that I was mulling over Anna's suggestion that I go home and face the music.

Looking at Maggie, even though she had turned into a mewling terror with no mercy for her mother or anyone else, I knew that my mother would love her, eventually. I don't think I ever really doubted that if I was honest, it was her reaction to me that worried me.

I slept fitfully between four and six, waking to the sound of the rain battering off the window pane. Maggie was asleep now, curled into the smallest of balls in her crib, her tiny hands clenched in determined little fists. I knew she would tell me, if she could, to wise up and stop being such a coward. Beth, should she ever speak to me again, would agree and I know Matilda was certainly on the side of me coming clean – so I suppose all I had to do was bite the bullet and book some flights.

Only, if I went so soon, and Jake did find out about his daughter, it would look awful, wouldn't it, if he came to find us and we had left the country? My head was a mess, so at seven thirty I slipped on some tracksuit bottoms and a baggy T-shirt and sweater, wrapped Maggie up again and headed to Morelli's.

The cakes were still warm from the oven and the coffee was just percolating as I pushed open the door and walked in.

"Eeva, you look so tired," Mrs Morelli called, walking towards me with her arms outstretched at the pram. "Did the *bambina* give you a hard night?"

I nodded, sitting down wearily at the table while Maggie dozed comfortably.

"I'll bring you a nice breakfast, on the house," Mrs Morelli said, ignoring my protestations and calling to her husband in the kitchen to put on a Full English. "You need to keep your strength up with a little one."

"Thank you," I mouthed and dropped my head in my hands.

What was it about the kindness of this woman which reduced me to tears time and time again? I was almost embarrassed now.

"Now, now, Eeva. Let those tears out. Crying is good and no one is here anyway to see you but me."

I leant into Mrs Morelli, feeling the softness of her shoulder against my cheek and she patted my back comfortably, as if she were trying to get my wind up. I only stopped when the bell over the door tinkled and a man walked in looking for his morning coffee.

He glanced in my direction, taking in the sorry sight of the woman in battered tracksuit bottoms with the tearstained face, and quickly looked away. I was too tired and bereft to care and I simply let out the biggest snottiest blubber so far.

"Now, now, Eeva, everyone gets like this after they have a baby. You just have to take it easy and be kind to yourself." Kind to myself? How did I do that? All I seemed to do to myself these days was tie myself up in knots, lying to people, withholding information and making enemies of my best friends. I wasn't sure I could be kind to myself any more.

Mr Morelli set a plate down in front of me – sausage, egg, mushrooms and bacon staring back at me – and although I didn't feel even a touch hungry I started eating. Spearing a mushroom on my fork I looked and saw the man who had come in for his coffee give me a half smile. I figured he was afraid I was some care-in-the-community case and decided that being nice to me was the safest option. I smiled back – feeling the urge to run to him and tell him I wasn't actually mental. Instead, I decided just to keep quiet and keep eating.

As I ate I felt myself relax and as I relaxed I realised I would have to take action.

It was a quarter to nine by the time I got back to the shop. The shutters were already up and as I pushed my way in the door I saw Beth at her desk, a pencil pushed through a neat chignon on the top of her head. She looked up at us as we walked in and smiled a hello.

I should have known she would be okay. Beth can never hold a grudge for long – it is one of the many things I love about her – her ability to see the silver lining in every cloud and to leave the past in the past.

"Sorry," I muttered, and she waved her hand at me as if to tell me my words were unnecessary.

"If you can't let off steam at me, who can you?" she said,

stepping out from behind her desk and coming towards me and Maggie. "How've you been?"

"Okay, I s'ppose. Is everything okay with you and Dan? I called last night and he seemed a little out of sorts."

"Ach, tough day at the office," she muttered, reaching into the pram for a cuddle. "I swear she gets more gorgeous every day!"

"Hey," I answered. "I'm supposed to be the hormonal one."

She shrugged, kissing Maggie's downy head. "Were you down in Morelli's again?"

I nodded. "She helped me make a pretty big decision."

"What's that, then?" Beth asked, sitting on the daybed.

"I'm going to go home."

She looked at me, her jaw dropping ever so slightly in disbelief before she recovered herself enough to talk. "Really?"

"I think I have to," I said, sitting beside her. "She isn't going to go away." I nodded towards my daughter. "I need to let them see her and if they don't fall in love with her then they don't have hearts."

"You have always wondered about your mother," Beth said with a wry smile.

"I know, but who could not love this wee one?" I touched Maggie's head as if she were made of the most delicate china.

"I don't know. She had me from 'Wah'," Beth said, smiling as she quoted our favourite film.

We sat in silence for a moment, contemplating what I was about to do. Eventually Beth reached her hand to mine and squeezed it. "You'll be fine, Aoife. It will all work out. Just you wait and see."

With those words ringing in my ears I made my way upstairs, switched on my laptop and booked two return flights to Derry, leaving Stansted five days from then. When that was done I jotted off a quick email to Anna letting her know that we would very much love to take up her offer of a place to rest our weary heads. At that I lay down and allowed myself to drift off to a dreamless sleep until the mewling cries of a hungry Maggie woke me again. Fighting every urge in my body to go back to sleep for at least another three hours, I sat up, my gelatinous post-baby belly wobbling. Five days. I wondered if it was possible to lose a stone in five days.

II

Beth

"I refuse to define myself by my infertility," I told my reflection that morning as I got up and ready for work.

This was another month – another chance to start again and boy, it was going to be damned busy. Maybe the distraction would be a good thing.

Of course Aoife was entitled to maternity leave, but it didn't make my life any easier. We had hired an assistant Heather to help but she wasn't exactly what you would call talented, or organised, or particularly punctual, but she did at least make me laugh – mostly by continuing to refer to Laura Ashley as Laura Astley. The likes of Elena Kennedy and the rest of her Richmond set didn't appreciate her little faux pas, but Aoife and I found it strangely endearing.

If we weren't careful, really careful, we would find ourselves saying it too. It would become one of those private joke things that slip into everyday conversation. I made a note to correct Heather the next time she said it.

In some ways I was delighted that Aoife had told me she was going back to Derry – even if it did mean I would only have Heather to rely on for support. I wondered if her being away would make everything easier. As it stood I had to physically stop myself from reaching for Maggie every time I saw her and taking her home with me. I knew Dan was worried that I would find myself on the nine o'clock news as some mad baby-snatcher, so while it would hurt and while I would miss Maggie madly it might actually be a blessing in disguise.

I could at least pretend to focus on the jobs at hand which included a makeover of Dan's boss Karl Rodgers' house. Talk about pressure!

I sighed, scraps of fabric and wallpapers scattered on the desk in front of me. I was leafing through a lighting supplier's catalogue when the doorbell pinged and I looked up to see a tall dark stranger before me.

He wandered around, not really looking at anything in particular – with the distinct look of a man sent out by his wife to "get something for the house" but who clearly didn't know where to start.

"Hello there," I started. "Can I help you?"

He looked up, slightly startled by my voice. "Sorry, I didn't see you there," he said.

"No problem. Are you looking for anything in particular?"

"Just browsing," he answered awkwardly.

"Well, if you need anything . . ." I trailed off, turning my attention back to the selection of crystal chandeliers which would look fabulous hanging in the dining-room of Karl Rodgers' Chelsea pad. I loved lighting, it was my sad little obsession. No room looked complete without the correct ambience.

Mr Handsome Stranger wandered about for another bit, lifting trinkets from the dresser and putting them down without really looking at them. He gazed absent-mindedly at a drape fabric sample book before turning his attention to the daybed. I was, I admit, starting to wonder if he was going to shoplift. He didn't look the type but then again, they say you never can tell.

I watched him for another five minutes before his pottering started to irk me. "Are you sure I can't help you with anything? I'm the proprietor."

"Oh," he replied. "I thought the girl with the baby was the owner."

"Oh Aoife, no, well yes, but you see I'm the owner too and so is she. We're business partners, but she is on maternity leave at the moment so if I can help you . . .?"

"But I was sure I saw her coming in here earlier?" he replied, a look of bemusement on his face.

"Well, you did. She lives upstairs," I said, the words out of my mouth before I realised I knew nothing at all about this man and for all intents and purposes he could be some mad stalker and I had not only just A) told him Aoife's name but B) also told him she lived up the stairs.

I might as well have handed him a pair of her knickers from the washing line and given him written permission to terrorise her.

"It's just I saw her earlier in the coffee shop up the street and she seemed pretty upset. I don't know," he said, shrugging his shoulders, "I just wanted to make sure she's okay."

"She's fine," I answered. "You know, just a new mum. Actually she's going back home to Ireland for a bit. She should get a good rest then." There, that should put him off his mad stalking ways, I thought, congratulating myself on my cunning. "I could tell her you called by?" I offered.

"No. It was silly really," he said, looking rather embarrassed by the whole affair. "Just take care of her, okay?" And he left.

It was only as I started leafing through the catalogue again that I realised he might not be a stalker at all, but a burglar casing the joint and I had just told him the flat upstairs was going to be empty for a while.

How could I persuade Aoife to change the locks without revealing what an utter prick I was? I sighed, sipping water and popping two more Nurofen to fend off my cramps, and tried to cheer myself up by ordering an impressive chandelier adorned with Swarovski crystal.

12

Aoife

It turned out that, no, you can't lose a stone in five days. Most of that was down to the fact that Mrs Morelli was still giving me cooked breakfasts on the house each morning and I was still letting her. It was my escape, to leave the flat after sleep-free nights feeding an increasingly demanding baby and walk the short distance down the street to the welcoming cafe. The hours between Beth going home and arriving again for work had started to fill me with dread. It wasn't right, couldn't be right, that I had to do this on my own. It wasn't right and it sure as feck wasn't fair.

Between Beth, Mrs Morelli and Anna I had become sure that I was doing the right thing to go home and make my peace with my family. Of course, Anna had wanted me to at least confide in Joe before my arrival, but I just couldn't face it. I knew he was going to find out eventually and I knew that I would need him onside before I told Mum and Daddy, but the thought of speaking to him filled me with dread and shame.

I'd like to say we had a close relationship but with five years of an age gap he always seemed distanced from me. I'd looked up to him, yes, and he had looked down on me, or at least it had always felt that way.

"Please, Anna. I'll tell him before I come over," I finally conceded. "Just let me do it in my own time."

I said that every day for four days but then as I got ready to leave for the airport I knew I was running out of time. So the morning of our departure for Derry, I sat there, phone in hand and dialled my brother's number, praying Jacqueline would be at work. The phone rang and Joe answered, his voice heavy with sleep. He'd obviously been working the night before.

"Joe, it's me," I said.

"Aoife, how the feck are you? We can't wait to see you. Mum is talking about killing a fatted calf."

"Very funny," I deadpanned. "She only gets the fatted calves out for you. It will be Dohertys' sausages and beans for me."

Our conversation was light and easy and I wished it could remain like that – but as I looked at Maggie I knew I had to be honest with him.

"Look Joe, I have something to tell you and I don't want you to go off your head. I really need you to be supportive about this."

"You're not up the duff, are you?" he laughed.

"Not exactly," I answered, after a pause that probably wasn't long enough.

"Jesus, Aoife, what have you done now?"

I don't know why, but my defences always go up when I'm talking with Joe. I know he loves me and for the most part he has been a great big brother but sometimes I swear I hear my mother channelling through him.

"What do you mean, what have I done now?" I barked.

"Calm down, Aoife – there's obviously something up."

"But it's not for you to judge me!"

"I'm not judging you. For Christ sake, I don't even know what you're talking about!"

He sighed and I felt my heart sink. This was going to be tougher than I thought, but nonetheless I needed to do it. I thought back to the delivery ward, how I had to keep pushing even though it hurt like feck and I realised I had to keep on talking even though this too hurt like feck.

"I've had a baby," I said.

The world went silent. I wondered momentarily if the shock had killed him.

"Joe?"

"Christ," he muttered.

"No, it's Aoife," I answered, my weak attempt at a joke failing to raise a laugh from him.

Another pause.

"Is that why you're coming home then?"

"Yes, I think Mum and Dad have a right to meet their granddaughter."

"Why now?"

"What do you mean?"

"Why now, Aoife? I'm assuming you knew about this baby and it, he, she, whatever, was not a surprise. Why are you telling us now? Why not before?"

"No, she was not a surprise," I said. I felt embarrassed, ashamed even. Of course I should have told them before, but how could I explain it all now? How could I say "Well, I would have told you before but I was waiting for her daddy to realise he loved me after all and make us a family, but as it turns out he doesn't give a flying fuck and doesn't even know she has been born"? My cheeks burned and tears sprang to my eyes.

Joe sighed again – the same exasperated sigh my mother used so many times on me.

"I'll see you later, Aoife," he muttered. "I'll figure out some way to sort this mess out."

He hung up and I blinked hot tears at the phone.

"Maggie," I said to the dead line. "Her name is Maggie. And she's not a mess."

I never felt at home at home, if that makes sense, so as the plane pulled up on the runway of the airport the strains of "The Derry Air" were not playing in my ears. I wasn't one of the many on the plane who sniffed and wiped away a sly tear to be back on the banks of the Foyle. No, this was not my glorious homecoming. This was not the town I loved so well.

A gust of cold air filled the cabin as the harassed stewardess opened the door and welcomed us to the City of Derry.

Maggie looked up at me, her eyes wide as if to let me know she felt as nervous as I did about this whole episode.

"We'll be fine, darling," I soothed, knowing full well the words were to reassure me more than my daughter.

Walking across the tarmac to the small terminal building, the breeze whipped around us and I struggled to pull my scarf tighter while carrying Maggie in her car seat.

Long gone were the days when I skipped off a plane with a copy of *Cosmo* and a half-finished bottle of water. This was extreme travelling – balancing a car seat, changing bag, baby and trying to keep warm in the biting cold.

I was almost grateful for the warmth of the terminal building. If it were not for the fact that I was about to shame my family eternally, it would have been a nice moment.

Lugging my suitcase from the belt and onto a trolley, I balanced my precious cargo precariously on top and pushed my way through customs.

This is one time I wouldn't have minded being stopped and

searched. It would have killed another five minutes. Sod's Law of course meant I was waved on through and, as the door opened to crowds of excited family members waiting to greet their loved ones, I felt my heart thud in my chest.

It was then I saw Anna and tears sprang to my eyes. At that moment she spotted me and waved enthusiastically. Her face was a mixture of affection and concern and just seeing her there, empathy etched in her smile, I felt my resolve weaken. My eyes filled with tears and I thrust myself at her and sobbed in her arms as she smoothed my hair and ssshed in my ear. "I'm – so – sorry," I stuttered. "I – shouldn't – have – put – you – in – this – position!"

"Ssh now," Anna answered. "It's okay. It's going to be okay."

I wondered how everyone else could be so sure of that because I wasn't. Not one bit. Composing myself, I dragged one arm of my coat sleeve across my face to dry my tears.

"It's nice to see you," I muttered.

"You too," She answered, gazing past me to the pink bundle in the car seat. "And this must be Maggie."

I nodded, for the first time feeling a smile creep across my face. "She's perfect, isn't she?" I asked, not taking my eyes off my daughter for one moment.

"She looks just like you did when you little," Anna answered, rubbing Maggie's soft cheek.

"Really? I think she has a look of her father about her." I said the words before I thought about them.

There I was, mentioning the unmentionable – Maggie's father. I guessed that was one more demon I would have to face in the near future. Not, that is, that coming face to face with Jake was likely. He was still very much on the missing persons list.

Sensing my unease in that way only aunties ever can, Anna looked at me and assured me we could talk about that later. "Let's get you in the car. Parking costs a bleeding fortune here these days," she said.

Soon we were strapped in and heading homewards, the short journey to the city giving me insufficient time to gather my thoughts.

"I told Joe," I muttered as we turned onto the 'New Bridge' towards Anna's house.

"And how was it?" she asked.

"Not the best. He thinks I've made a mess. Which, I suppose I have. I'm not sure we can count on him to be our ally at the council of war with Mum and Dad."

"I'll have a word with him. If you ask me, me laddo's getting far too uppity for my liking these days."

"Easy to get uppity when you can do no wrong in your mother's eyes," I replied, a hint of bitterness in my voice.

"Your mum loves you, Aoife. She just has a funny way of showing it."

That was for sure, and it was definitely funny peculiar and not funny ha ha.

We pulled up at Anna's home, an ex-council house which made up in warmth for what it lacked in character. Carrying Maggie into the living-room, I breathed in the smell of home, the smouldering embers of the open fire, the faint smell of coffee from the kitchen. This was more of a home to me than my parents' house ever was.

"Sit down," Anna said. "Make yourself comfortable. I'll put the kettle on and then we'll work this thing out."

"I'm tired," I answered. "Can't I just have a little sleep first?" Suddenly, I felt as if I could barely keep my eyes open.

"Sure," Anna replied. "You know where your room is. I'll keep this little one here with me. Probably a good idea if you get a rest before we face your parents."

It seemed real then, the thought that I was going to face my parents. There had been obstacles in the way up till now, bridges to cross and things to do. Now, there was nothing between me and Mum and Dad but three miles and a sense of panic. I tried to block those thoughts out as I closed the door to Anna's spare room and sat down on the bed. I was a big girl now. I could handle this. As Anna has said, I hadn't killed anyone. I'd only had a baby. Millions of unmarried women have babies. And it's not as though I was a teenager when I got pregnant. I was thirty-one for God's sake. That's proper grown up. And I was in a relationship, albeit a highly dysfunctional one which meant that despite our three and a half years together I never actually referred to Jake as my boyfriend to my parents. No, I had nothing to be ashamed of. Nothing at all.

I lay down and pulled the soft pink duvet up under my chin. The rain was battering against the window and I was soothed by it. Closing my eyes tightly I curled up into a ball and wondered if I could make all these feelings of dread go away

I'm not a saint. After Jake had left, cursing and slamming the door I had sat in shock in my bed and wondered what the hell I would do. A wave of nausea had hit me and I ran to the bathroom and threw up until my throat was raw. I'm not sure to this day whether I was throwing up through shock at Jake leaving or if it was the start of morning-sickness. If it was the latter then you've got to respect its sense of timing.

Once I had stopped throwing up (and crying, and wailing generally) I sat with my legs pulled up to me and rocked back and forth trying to think out my options. I guess I knew there was a chance Jake wasn't coming back but I wasn't sure that I was ready to accept that. I had to start "Mission Make This All Better" – I just wasn't sure where to start.

Yes, I contemplated an abortion. As I sat there, my mouth tasting bitter from the vomit and my stomach still churning despite now being empty, I knew that Jake would come back if I did what he wanted and got rid of this baby.

But there was a part of me that knew I would never forgive myself. I would be as guilty of rejecting this baby as my own mother was of rejecting me – more so even. So as I cried bitter tears I realised "Mission Make It All Better" was not going to be easy. I couldn't get rid of this baby, and yet if I didn't I faced losing Jake. Both options were too painful to contemplate – even though having a baby was the last thing I needed or wanted.

I stayed on that bathroom floor until it started to get dark and then I dusted myself off and phoned Beth, who came around, hugged me while I cried some more and promised to support me whatever I decided. Dan, she said, would support me too and it was then I started to wonder if perhaps he could talk to Jake on my behalf and this could be salvageable after all.

Looking back now I realise I was grasping at straws. It's tragic really, tragic and funny. I was so utterly blind.

After I'd slept a fitful hour away I padded down the stairs to see Anna cuddling Maggie and singing softly to her. It was the same song she had sung to me when I was a child and I felt my heart swell with pride. How I wished in that moment Maggie would get to call Anna "Granny" instead of my insufferable mother.

That thought, of course, brought me back to reality with a bang. Now there was not even the excuse of being tired and needing a sleep to allow me to escape my mother's evil glares.

Seeing me standing at the door, Anna stopped singing and said, "Do you want to talk about it now then?"

I knew the question was a formality. This was her way of telling me we were going to talk about it now and there was to be no argument about it. I sat down, made myself comfortable (or at least as comfortable as you can be with a hungry baby latching on to your boob) and took a deep breath.

Okay, I was ready to start talking.

"It just kind of happened. I didn't plan it. The only thing I can think of is that I had this mild stomach bug. I threw up, but only once. I didn't think that would affect things. I didn't think I would get pregnant."

Anna nodded.

"Jake, that's the father by the way, and me, well, we had been together for about three and a half years."

"And you never thought to mention him to any of us?"

"It was complicated. And anyways, I did mention him. Remember I told you about the sexy singer I was seeing?"

"Dan's cousin?"

"Yep, well, that was him."

"But you never told me it was serious."

Anna looked a little hurt and I can't say that I blame her. I have confided everything in her since I was knee-high to a grasshopper. I could barely believe myself that I never told her every little detail of my relationship with Jake.

I sighed. "It was complicated. I would have told you but there wasn't really much to tell."

"Three years and not much to tell?"

"Well, he never really felt much for me. Not really." My face started to blaze a little. My aunt was pretty darned open-minded but could I tell her that I'd in all honesty spent the last forty months of my life as nothing more than a fuck-buddy to an aspiring musician? Every part of me cringed at the thought.

"Look, Anna. The fact is I was mad about him. A part of me is still mad about him, but we were never serious or, at least he was never serious. It took me telling him I was up the stick to realise just how unserious he was."

"You should have called," Anna said.

"Shoulda, woulda, coulda." I moved Maggie from one boob to the other. "I was embarrassed, Anna. And if I'm honest, I wanted him to come back. I hoped that after living without me on call 24/7 for a few weeks he would realise just how much he loved me and come back and make us a family. I planned to come over here and tell you all then. I had it all planned out in my head. Only it didn't happen. He never called again. He doesn't even know she has been born." My voice had started to crack just slightly. "And I just stuck my head in the sand and tried to pretend none of this was happening."

"Your poor, poor thing!" Anna paused, then added, "The birth? Was Beth there? Did you at least have someone to hold your hand?"

"I had a very nice midwife," I replied and Anna started to cry.

Then I started to cry.

Then Maggie started to cry.

"Do you think Mum will ever speak to me again once she finds out?" I said eventually.

"Let's hope so, eh?" Anna said with a half smile. "Now, let's figure this out. How are we going to tell them? I wouldn't think it would be the best idea in the world just to show up with Maggie."

Anna was right. The shock would kill them. But Maggie was my Ace of Hearts – the one trick I had to pull out of the bag to make them be okay with this. After all, she was their grandchild. They couldn't reject their own grandchild.

Anna and I talked more. We decided that she would head over there first and try and break the ice. She was going to phone Joe too, and invite (well, order, to be honest) him over to her house to meet the pair of us.

The thought of Joe and the way he had spoken to me on the phone earlier that day made my blood run a little cold. I had no doubt he would have already been on the phone to Perfect Jacqueline by then and that the pair of them would have tutted and felt all self-satisfied at my predicament. Joe may have fancied himself as all man but there were times when he was a right old woman. He revelled in gossip like no other man I knew. They say Derry men always remain tied to their mammy's apron strings – well, in Joe's case I was pretty sure he was still attached by the umbilical cord and every day a little bit more of my mother seeped into him. If he wasn't careful he would be getting a perm and playing the bingo by the time he was thirty-six.

Anna went to make the necessary phone calls while I burped Maggie. My mobile phoned beeped into life and I'm not sure why but I got the strangest notion it might have been Jake trying to get through to me. I thought just how wonderful it would be if he had somehow sensed I had been talking about him and felt this insurmountable urge to send me a message.

Of course, it only took the twenty seconds between the phone sounding and me fishing it out of my bag to find out that it wasn't Jake and was in fact Beth – just checking how I was doing.

I already missed her. "I'm surviving," I texted back. "Call u later. X"

Oh for our daybed and a bottle of gin! That would put the world to rights.

Joe arrived at four thirty. It was precisely the time he said he would arrive. It was one of the qualities my mother so admired about him – his ability to be on time for absolutely everything. In our childhood she often regaled the story of how he even managed to arrive on his due date. Unlike me. I was ten days overdue and Mum needed an induction. I don't think she has forgiven me since.

I heard the clunk of his car door and as I looked out the window I saw him walk up the garden path. He looked tired. His suit was a little dishevelled and he could have done with a shave. I would have felt sorry for him if I wasn't so sure the scruffy look was all part of his grand plan to have Mum fuss and coo over him when he went to her house. Fecking attention-stealer!

Running his fingers through his neatly trimmed dark hair he reached out to press the doorbell. I took a deep breath and opened the door. It was hard to know what to say. His disappointment in me was etched across his face and I felt that old defiance rise up again. I wanted to push him back out the door and tell him to take his smug, tired face and feck off. Instead I muttered "Hello" and walked back into the living-room, leaving him to follow me.

"So," he said, sitting down on the sofa, not even casting a cursory glance in the direction of the Moses basket.

"So what?" I replied. Yes, I was being childish but I couldn't help myself.

"What are we going to do about this?"

"*This*," I snapped "is my child. She is your niece. Her name is Maggie. The only thing I plan to 'do about this' is raise her the best way I can."

Joe sighed. "Don't be like that, Aoife. You know that's not what I meant." He rolled his eyes, and sat forward, his head in his hands. "You know I was talking about Mum and Dad and how you're going to tell them."

"I'm not telling them. Anna is." The childish tone remained in my voice, all that was missing was a triumphant "so there!" at the end of the sentence. I wanted to sit down and discuss this with Joe like the adults we were but I felt flustered, like a little sister again.

"But you have to face them," Joe replied, cutting through my thoughts.

"I know." It was my turn to sit down and put my head in my hands. "They're going to go mental, aren't they?"

"That you didn't tell them? Well, wouldn't you? If in twenty-odd years Maggie there" (for the first time he actually looked in her direction) "announced she had given birth and not told you about it, wouldn't you go off your head?"

"S'ppose, but you don't understand, Joe. You're their perfect child with the *perfect* wife and the *perfect* child in your *perfect* house." My voice had become high-pitched and whiney. I could barely hide my bitterness.

"For fuck sake, Aoife, grow up! This isn't a competition. This is about acting like an adult and you have been acting like a spoiled child. You've deprived Mum and Dad of so much and you can't even see how bloody selfish you've been!" His words hurt. Me? Selfish? I'd just done the most selfless thing of my whole life. I'd kept my baby. I'd had her even though I knew my support network was virtually non-existent. Aside from Beth, Dan and Anna (and Matilda too, I suppose) I was in this alone.

"Deprived them of what? Of feeling ashamed of me? You know they're still living in the 1950s! If they had their way I'd have been sent off to the Magdalen Laundries for this indiscretion and you know that. Who are you to judge me, Joe? You don't even know me!" I was shouting by that stage, unable to control my anger, and my raised voice caused Maggie to wake and start to wail. "See what you did!" I shouted and hurried to where she lay. Tears coursing down my face, I picked her up and held her close to me. "Sssh, baby, sssh! Mummy's here. Your own mummy is here." Her cries subsided.

I turned to face Joe, who was standing now with a strange look on his face. I couldn't place it. If I wasn't mistaken it could actually have been the teeniest, tiniest ounce of respect. "She's your niece, Joe," I said. "Don't you want to say hello?"

He stepped forward and reached his hand out to her. Her dark blue eyes stared out at him, her tiny fingers curling around his. "Can I hold her?" he asked, his voice soft now, and I nodded. Cradling her gently he bent his head forward and gently kissed her forehead. "You should have told us, Aoife."

For the first time I wondered if my brother was right.

13

Beth

"Your mother called again," Dan said as he poured me a cup of coffee.

I was standing by the kitchen counter, a thermometer under my tongue while I flicked through the morning papers.

"Wha didth she wan?" I asked.

Dan smiled, took the thermometer from my mouth and handed it to me. "Can I have that again, in English this time?"

I stared down at the figure in front of me, charting down the number in my notebook. Temps all normal for this time in the month. "What did she want?" I asked again.

"Same thing she always wants," he said. "She wants us to come down to visit."

I rolled my eyes.

"It has been a while, babe," he said, pouring just the right amount of milk into my coffee cup.

"Yeah, well, with Aoife away I don't see how we can manage it.

You know how busy I am at the moment. Karl's house isn't going to get finished if I'm swanning off all the time."

"You wouldn't be making excuses, now would you?" He raised an eyebrow.

"Of course not. I'm busy. You're busy. We are very busy."

"Well, you can't put it off forever."

"I know," I sighed. But I would put it off for as long as humanly possible. If I could put it off even for another three weeks – who knows, we could have an announcement of our own to make.

"She would understand if we told her, you know," Dan said.

"No. She doesn't need to know. Nothing is wrong, remember. The doctors couldn't find anything so there is nothing to tell."

Dan stood back, rubbing his temples. "I suppose."

I kissed him. I didn't like it when he looked unhappy. I didn't like that look of worry – that vague little look of disappointment he sometimes got when we talked about "things". I stroked his cheek, kissing him again.

"Next month," I said. "I promise. Next month we'll go home and see Mum. You never know, we might get lucky this month. My temps are doing exactly what they should."

He sighed again, kissing me lightly. "I'd better be off," and he left, his coffee cup still full and his croissant uneaten.

It made me feel uneasy, but I knew it was going to be a busy day and so I pushed those thoughts to the back of my head. Heather and I had a pitch to prepare. I needed to be on my game today – not worrying about whether or not Dan was annoyed with me.

We never rowed. It was something I was exceptionally proud of. We had the odd "discussion" but we never screamed at each other. Aoife used to say that no screaming out of the bedroom meant there was no screaming in it. She liked to think that her volatile relationship with Jake made them some mad passionate star-crossed lovers. Their passion proved their love, she said. I was happy to settle for security, contentment and, if I'm being honest, it didn't take away from the passion in the bedroom one bit.

Dan and I loved each other. We couldn't get enough of each other and yes, while admittedly at the minute our sex life was dictated by temperatures, discharges and optimum windows of opportunity, it was still pretty damn good when it got going.

No, Dan was probably just tired. I should not read too much into his still full coffee cup. We were just fine. He loved me and I loved him. Nothing was wrong. That was my mantra and it would stay my mantra – for this and for everything else in my life.

Arriving at the shop, I switched on the lights and lamps which gave the showroom its warm glow. We rarely had customers before eleven, so these two hours first thing were perfect for catching up on paperwork or putting the finishing touches to pitches.

I'd sent Heather out to pick up some more swatches of material from a supplier and was just settling down to work when the bell above the door tinkled into life.

"Beth, gorgeous. How are you?"

I looked up, seeing this familiar but unwelcome face in front of me and I felt my heart start to thud. I wasn't sure what to say. The power of speech was gone. I just sat there, staring, my mouth opening but no noise coming out.

"Aren't you going to give me a hug?" he asked.

I shook my head slowly. No, I did not want to give this man a hug. I most definitely did not want to hug the man who had impregnated my best friend and then run off, not bothering himself to contact her, or his cousin, or any of us at any stage over the last eight months.

No, I most certainly did not want to hug Jake Gibson.

"I think you should leave," I muttered eventually – standing up because I'd read once that you should always be at the same level as someone when having a confrontation.

"I don't really think that's up to you, babe," he said and I cringed at the use of the word babe. Why had I never realised before just what a slimy little creep he was?

"Aoife's not here," I said.

I didn't think he deserved to know Maggie wasn't here either. He didn't deserve to hear Maggie's name, never mind know her whereabouts. What kind of a creep has a daughter and turns his back on her? I could feel my face redden and my fingers start to clench. How dare he? How dare he stand here, and call me a babe, and have walked out on the most precious thing he could ever have been given?

"So I really think you should go," I added using every ounce of my strength to stop myself from telling him just what a complete bastarding fucking arse I thought he was.

"When will she be back?"

"Jesus, Jake, I didn't think you cared so much about people coming back. I thought you were a free and easy kind of a guy?" I didn't even try to hide the hatred in my voice.

"Look," he said, "I know she had the baby and she wants to see me so I'm trying to do the right thing and come to see her."

"You wouldn't know the right thing if it came up and kicked you in the balls," I snarled. "Just leave, Jake. Aoife will be back when she is back. It might be in ten minutes, it might be in eight months – we'll just wait and see, shall we? I'm pretty sure you don't mind, do you?"

"Whatever," he said, rolling his eyes. "Just tell her I called by." And then he left.

I felt sick. I sat down, my head in my hands and felt physically sick. I could not believe Jake was back. I could not believe he was going to waltz back into Aoife's life now – into Maggie's life and start messing them around again.

He didn't deserve to be a father. Why should I help him fulfil the role he had pushed away all those months ago? No, he could fuck off and if he wanted to get in touch with Aoife it would have to be without my help.

I clutched my hands to my stomach, rocking back and forth, and tried to block out all the horrible, evil thoughts I was having about him and then I picked up the phone and called the one other person who would understand.

Before Dan even had the chance to say hello I blurted: "He's back."

"Who? The mad stalker man?" Dan asked, a hint of a smile in his voice.

Yes, he knew I was a little scatty and he had taken great joy in ribbing me about the stalker man ever since that day I'd revealed almost every detail of Aoife's life to a complete stranger.

"No. Jake. Jake is back."

There was a pause – an almost inaudible sigh – one only I could recognise as the woman who loved him and knew just how much anger he now held in his heart for the man he had once considered his best friend.

"Does Aoife know?"

"No, and I don't think I should tell her."

"You have to tell her, Betsy, you know that," Dan said gently.

"No," I said, tears pricking in my eyes. "I don't have to tell her anything. I don't have to let that bastard into Maggie's life. He doesn't deserve her. He doesn't deserve to be a daddy."

Dan sighed again. It seemed to be a new habit of his. "If I know Jake like I think I know Jake, there is no danger of him acting the daddy for anyone."

"But he said he wanted to do right by her," I said.

There was a sniff on the other end of the line. "Jake Gibson has never done right by anyone his entire life."

"So I'm right then, aren't I? Don't give him the chance to hurt them again?"

"No, babe. It's not your decision to make. Aoife is a big girl. She can deal with this in her own way. You have to give her that chance."

"But Maggie's not a big girl."

"And she's not your responsibility."

My heart broke a little. I started to cry.

"Beth, are you okay?"

"Well, that's a stupid bloody question, isn't it?" I snapped.

Another sigh. "We'll talk about this later. I can't deal with this just now," he said and put down the phone, which of course just made me cry all the harder.

I walked to the front of the shop and turned the sign over to closed. Lifting my bag, I walked out and closed the door, locking it behind me. I couldn't deal with this either right then.

Calling into Morelli's, I was immediately soothed by the strong smell of fresh coffee and fresh baked breads wafting from the kitchen. This always worked. It always made me feel better, so I took a seat in the darkest corner and composed myself before stepping up to order a coffee.

I was grateful that Mrs Morelli didn't seem to be working that morning. I don't think I could have faced one of her inquisitions – well-meaning as they would have been. Aoife loved them, of course she did, she loved to natter to anyone who would listen and wasn't afraid to pour out her deep dark secrets to anyone who would listen (apart from her own family, of course). I preferred to sit alone, drink my coffee and quieten the chatter in my head.

Mr Morelli poured the coffee. If he noticed the red rims around my eyes, he didn't say anything. He just smiled as he took my money and handed me my change. I sighed with relief – just before turning around and narrowly avoiding spilling my hot, black coffee all over Stalker Man.

"God, I'm so sorry," I said, looking at him and seeing that same bemused look on his face that he had in the shop that day.

"No harm done," he said. "You missed."

I gabbled an apology again before moving to my seat, my face burning with embarrassment.

His voice followed me. "Are you okay?"

I looked up from my seat. "I'm fine. Honest. It missed me too."

"You look upset?"

"What are you – Dr Phil?" I snapped. I didn't need this. I just wanted to be alone.

"Sorry. Just asking. God, Instant Karma? More like Instant Depression!" he quipped and walked away – leaving my face burning once again.

It was still only 10 a.m., but Lord I wanted this day to be over.

14

Aoife

I swear I could hear my mother saying the Rosary as I opened the garden gate and started to walk towards the door. Joe carried Maggie in her car seat and I shuffled awkwardly up the garden path like a woman on her way to the gallows, or the guillotine. That said, at that precise moment I quite liked the idea of the guillotine. A quick drop of a blade and I wouldn't have to face my mother. Somehow it didn't seem so scary put that way.

Anna must have seen us coming because she opened the door, her face pale as if she had just come face to face with the Devil himself. I felt sick. I actually thought I would throw up in the rose bushes – but that would only make my mother more annoyed. She didn't like vomit in her garden. I'd learned that lesson when I was eighteen after a night on the tiles.

"It's been a shock," Anna whispered.

Joe snorted behind me and suddenly and inexplicably I found the whole thing hilariously funny. I mean, you couldn't write it, could you? I started to laugh – silent shockwaves of laughter tearing through my body and I was bent double with the power of it.

"Aoife, are you okay?" Joe sat the car seat down and ran to me.

I think he thought I was having some sort of fit. Tears, this time of laughter, coursed down my face and my sides started to ache. The look on Anna's face changed from concern to confusion and then I saw the beginnings of a smile creep on her face too.

"It's not funny," Joe said.

"It's really not, is it?" I answered but I was powerless to stop. It was like when you start giggling in church or at a funeral – your body convulsing with nervous energy. The more you try to stop, the harder you laugh until it is so sore you actually don't want to laugh any more.

"I mean it, this really isn't funny." Joe's eyebrows were furrowed together, his face tense with disapproval.

I was pretty sure that if I didn't stop laughing soon I would risk my weakened pelvic floor.

Unfortunately the thought of peeing all over Mum's *Welcome Home* rug made me laugh even harder and I leant against the door frame for support. As I stood there I could get a glimpse into the living-room and I saw my mother for the first time in two years. I imagine most good-living daughters would run to their mammy's arms and cry on their shoulders.

I didn't. I was still laughing anyway.

Mum hadn't changed. Perhaps there were a few more grey hairs but her hair was still styled the same way it always was – a sleek bob – cut just below the chin. She was wearing a burgundy twin-set and a tweed skirt. Her pink house-slippers showed the wrinkles in her tights at her ankles. The sight of her, sitting there dressed like an old woman, made me angry. She was fifty-five. She shouldn't be wearing house slippers at four in the afternoon and clutching Rosary beads at the thought of being a granny.

My laughter stopped.

"Oh fuck," I said. "I've really gone and done it now." My words had a sobering impact on Anna, who stopped grinning and moved her arm around my shoulder.

"C'mon, toots. Might as well get this over and done with."

I wiped the tears of laughter from my eyes and stood up straight, brushing myself off. Glancing back at Joe for support, and finding only a look of utter sympathy, I walked into the living-room.

"Mum, Dad," I said and waited for the onslaught. It didn't come. Nothing did. Dad shook his head. He took his glasses off, rubbed them clean on his shirt and put them back on. Then turning on his heel he walked out of the room to the kitchen. I felt my heart shatter.

"Where is this baby then?" Mum said to the floor. She couldn't bring herself to look at me.

"Joe has her," I offered, stepping out of the way just slightly to allow Joe into the room.

Mum looked at him. "So it's Maggie, is it? That's a very English-sounding name, isn't it?"

"Yes, Maggie," Joe replied awkwardly.

Mum looked at the car seat – at her grandchild.

"I suppose it's not her fault," she said, putting a bony finger to Maggie's delicate cheek.

I had to fight the urge to bat it away – to tell her to fuck off. "I don't know that it's anyone's 'fault'," Anna offered, taking a hold of my hand.

"Well, you would say that, wouldn't you, Anna?" Mum barked.

I felt a big fat tear well up and fall. I guess it's true when they say that a big cry always follows a big laugh.

I wondered what my father was doing. I wanted him to come and tell me this was okay.

"You should hold her," Joe said, bending down and taking

101

Maggie from her chair. Her small body looked even smaller in his arms. He looked like he could and would protect her but instead he handed her to my mother who bore the expression of someone just handed a worm-infested puppy.

"She's a good baby," I said. It was as if I wanted to prove I could do something, anything, right in my life.

Mum nodded. "They're all good when they're wee, Aoife. It's when they get older they break your heart."

Anna rolled her eyes. "For the love of God, Sheila! Stop being so bloody dramatic."

"When your child comes home with a baby born out of wedlock you can tell me to stop being so bloody dramatic!" Mum barked. "But for now you can stay the hell out of this!"

"If and when that day does come I'll be happy to welcome the baby into my family," Anna answered. "Jesus, Sheila. She's your bloody grandchild. Get over yourself."

Anna spoke to my mother the way I'd love to speak to my mother. I don't know where she got the courage, but I liked it. It gave me an inner strength.

"Give her to me," I said, my voice strong, unwavering and just that little touch too loud. "I wouldn't want you to catch anything from my bastard baby, now would I?"

Mum at least had the decency to look shocked.

"I didn't say she was *that word*." She whispered "that word" for effect – just to remind me my language was unacceptable.

"You didn't have to. You've made it patently obvious what you think of her, of me. I don't even know why I bothered to come here and tell you." I held my child to me. "I'm going to talk to Daddy."

And I stalked out, leaving my mother sitting there, her mouth gaping open, stunned into silence.

When I was growing up, if I was ever asked who my childhood hero was, my answer was fairly predictable. Depending on the time of year and how many times I had sat through *Star Wars*, I would answer either Princess Leia or my daddy. Yes, my father had the ability to supersede Leia and her buns of steel in my estimation. That was no mean feat.

We did a lot together when I was wee. Although he had Joe – his perfect son and heir – Daddy always took time out to be with me. He treated me like his princess and I put him so high up on a pedestal that there was no chance he could realistically get off it without injuring him or me as I stood gazing up at him.

We would walk together, sing together, read stories together. I was his shadow and he was this big, cuddly bear of a man who made me feel completely and utterly loved.

He didn't look like so much of a cuddly bear that day in the kitchen. Although I had only grown to a fairly unimpressive 5'6", Daddy looked small to me. And thinner.

He was standing, staring out the window at his garden, watching the branches of the crab-apple tree sway in the wind. I remembered when he planted that tree and how I had cried myself to sleep when I wasn't allowed to eat the fruit that fell from it.

"Daddy," I said. Funny how I still called him Daddy. Mum had long since lost her Mammy or Mummy titles, but Daddy could never be called by anything else.

He moved, just a little, on hearing his name.

"Daddy, don't you want to meet Maggie?"

He sighed and slowly started to turn towards me. "Your mother's heart is broken," he said.

"I know. I didn't mean to."

"I know, Aoife, but how could you do this to us?"

"I thought you would be angry. I thought I could make it better. That it would sort itself out."

He looked straight at me, his eyes misty with tears. "We could have been there for you, Aoife. We could have helped."

I nodded, ashamed to the core of my being. Daddy wasn't angry. He was hurt and confused – but he wasn't angry with me.

"I'm sorry," I muttered, head cast downwards.

"She's a wee gem, Aoife. Reminds me of you when you were a newborn." He reached out and I instinctively handed her over. She would be safe with him. He would never hurt her. He would never think badly of her. She would be his princess too.

"I don't want to know whatever you don't want to tell me," Daddy said. "Who the father is, all that nonsense. It's your business. Tell me if and when you want, but don't ever keep this little one from us again."

I nodded. "I'm sorry, Daddy." It was all I could say and it didn't seem enough.

He moved towards me, kissing my forehead gently. "I know you are, darling."

Maggie had enjoyed her first taste of Cow & Gate Formula, which was just as well because the wine I had enjoyed with Anna had gone straight to my head. God, before I got pregnant I could have had buckets of the stuff (and frequently did). Now one glass and I found myself lying in bed, the room swimming ever so slightly around me.

"It'll be all the excitement of the day," Anna said, pouring a second glass of Pinot Grigio for herself.

"Excitement?" I rolled my eyes, then winked.

"Ach, you know what I mean. The nerves, the travelling, the build-up. You fecking lightweight!" She laughed, throwing her hair back. She looked so much younger, so much more alive than Mum. How was that possible? There were only five years between them. It might as well have been twenty-five.

"It's been a mad week," I conceded as I yawned over the Pringles.

"Look, get yourself on to bed. I'll look after madam tonight. If she is on the bottle anyway you can get a great sleep. Your boobs will be like footballs in the morning, but the sleep will be worth it."

The thought of ten hours uninterrupted sleep seemed like heaven. After months of waking every hour on the hour to pee followed by the feeding demands of my daughter I figured it had been at least four months since I'd slept soundly. For ten hours I could pretend my life hadn't been turned upside down entirely. Someone was finally taking some of the responsibility off my shoulders and it felt good.

"Okay. You've twisted my arm," I said, rising to my feet and kissing Anna on the cheek. I then leant over the Moses basket. "Be a good girl, Princess. I love you," I whispered before climbing the stairs and curling up in bed.

I was just starting to fade out of this reality into another and more favourable domain where I had no stretch marks, an intact perineum and a mother who loved me when my mobile phone rang.

"Hello?"

"How did it go honey?" Beth asked.

Damn, I knew I should have phoned her. She would have been worried sick.

"Well, they stopped just short of treating me to a chorus of 'Love Child'," I said.

"So it went well?"

"Yes and no. Joe was okay – well, okay for Joe which is a start. Mum is disgusted. Daddy is upset, but he loves me and he adores Maggie."

"A good start then?"

I stifled a yawn. "Not the worst."

"You sound tired, will I let you go?" Beth asked.

"Sorry. I'm a bloody lightweight. I'm telling you, B, make the most of your wine and song now because once children come along you'll lose all street cred. Would you believe I'm already in bed? How sad is that?"

"Not sad at all. You've only given birth."

"Still, I'm thirty-one not fifty-one. Beth, you are so right waiting to start your family. Don't get me wrong, I love Maggie. You know I love her, but I don't see me ever getting a life back."

"Maybe not your old life," Beth replied. "But a different kind of life. It doesn't have to be worse."

"S'ppose," I answered. "Night night, honey. Tell Dan I said hi."

"Will do. And give Maggie a kiss from us."

"Will do."

She seemed to hesitate before hanging up. The silence was there but I couldn't resist breaking it. "Beth, hang on. I hate to ask but has Dan heard anything from Jake?"

She paused. "Sorry, honey."

We both sighed and then we hung up. I rolled over and closed my eyes, trying to block out everything that had happened that day. I imagine Beth went out to a swish wine bar and drank her bodyweight in Chardonnay. The lucky cow wouldn't even have had a hangover the next day.

15

Aoife

Apparently we mothers have some built-in genetic chip which programmes us to wake and start lactating at the very sound of our child crying. Mine must have been on the blink because I slept soundly through to seven thirty, only waking when rolling over in bed onto my swollen chest made me wince in pain.

I sat up, still feeling a little dizzy and called downstairs to Anna that I was going to jump in a shower. Expressing off milk contaminated with a good glass of Pinot Grigio was never going to be pleasant, and I knew I had to get it done sooner rather than later or risk my breasts exploding at the breakfast table.

In the shower I thought it odd just how my body had changed. My breasts were huge and firm with nipples the size and colour of Jaffa Cakes. My stomach, once my pride and joy, was flabby and saggy, marked with reddish-silvery lines like a modern art painting. Momentarily I wondered about *down there*. Every time I thought about what my poor fandango went through, I could feel it cringe. It gave me a little hope, if I'm honest. If it could cringe, then the pelvic muscles couldn't be totally fecked.

God, how had my life come to this? Standing in a shower in Auntie Anna's, hungover on one glass of wine and wondering if the stitches in my undercarriage had dissolved yet?

I swear Maggie put on three pounds overnight. She looked so much more filled out, more doll-like as I lifted her into my arms. I inhaled her baby smell, letting the weight of her settle in my arms.

"Was she okay?"

"A wee angel," Anna answered, getting up to put the kettle on. "Did you sleep okay?"

"Like a log. I don't think I stirred at all."

"Good, you must have needed it."

She set about frying some bacon and eggs and warming the pot for the tea. *Ireland AM* was on the small portable on the worktop and it all just seemed so homely.

"Have you plans for today?" Anna asked.

"Well, Joe said Jacqueline might call over later."

"That'll be nice," Anna replied sarcastically. There was little love lost between my aunt and my sister-in-law.

"And I'm going to take this wee one for a walk later."

"Grand," Anna said, pouring the tea. "Maeve said she might call over after work. She can't wait to see you again."

Maeve was my cousin, Anna's only child. Stunningly gorgeous but fiercely independent, she moved out of the house when she was twenty-one and Anna was lucky if she saw her once a month. I was indeed privileged to be getting an audience with her.

"It's going to be a busy one," I said to Maggie, wondering how on earth I was going to stay awake long enough to deal with it all.

Sitting down, Anna sipped from her mug. "Don't take this the wrong way, sweetheart. You know you are welcome here as long as you want. But how long were you thinking of staying?"

"I'm not sure. I want to get things sorted at home, but I can't be away from the business too long. Beth is run off her feet."

Of course what I didn't answer, and what I should have said, was that I didn't want to be away from London too long in case Dan was able to track Jake down and I could persuade him to meet his daughter.

"But aren't you on maternity leave?"

"Well, of course, but I like to be there so Beth can consult with me. Some of the clients can be very precious about their homes."

"I understand," Anna laughed, staring around her MDF kitchen, the dated tiles begging for a makeover. "It took me ages to get the place looking as good as this."

"One day, Anna, I'll transform this whole house for you. You'll have the coolest pad in Creggan!"

"Oooh, could you get that Laurence Llewelynn Whatsit to call round? I quite fancy the look of him."

We laughed and I pushed all thoughts of London, Jake and work behind me.

★ ★ ★

What I was going to do wasn't going to be easy, but I had to do it. I bundled Maggie up in her snowsuit and strapped her into her pram. It wasn't a long walk and it was a glorious February morning. The air was crisp, a hint of frost glimmered on the grass. I could see my breath escape from my mouth and I breathed in the familiar Derry air as much as I could. Home could be suffocating, I realised, but there were certain ties I could never escape.

The cemetery was quiet. A few cars were parked here and there. A couple of people milled around but it was as peaceful as it could be. I had promised myself that when I came home I would do this. I would come here to my grandparents' grave and introduce Maggie to them.

God knows what they would make of this or indeed what they

would make of me. Granny had died when I was sixteen and Granda a year later. It was hard to think my mother had come from their home because where she was as cold as ice to me at times, they were as warm and welcoming as Anna. I'd loved visiting them when I was young and I would sit with Granny, looking through her Littlewoods catalogue and planning all the things I would buy when I was a grown-up to put in my house.

She would let me tear the pages out and we would stick them down together, my first mood boards, my first attempts at design.

When I was eight, they had bought me a dolls' house and had let me choose the furniture myself. The dolls' house lived in their spare room and Granny and I would spend hours arranging and rearranging the furniture, sticking catalogue pictures of sofas and bedspreads to the walls with Blu Tack and make believing it was all true.

I knew Granny would be proud of me now – of my business – and I knew she would love Maggie if for no other reason than she was my child.

We walked to the top of the hill, Maggie and me. I still felt a little awkward talking to her as she lay in her pram. I explained where we were, who we were going to see and it all felt so strange. It had been so long since I'd been here. I hated this part of each homecoming and yet loved it at the same time. The memory of the loss was almost unbearable but the memory of the love that preceded my grief was more comforting than anything I had ever known.

I reached their grave, a green, frosted plot of lawn with a shiny black marble headstone declaring their names, the dates of their births and the dates of their deaths. I knelt forward and outlined the letters with my fingers. It made me feel closer to them in some weird way. I kissed the cold marble and stepped back, lifting Maggie out of her pram.

"Granny, Granda. This is Maggie. You'd have loved her to pieces. I wish she knew you," I whispered, holding her close to the ground.

The moment was among the most poignant of my life – until, that is, Maggie let off a rumble and an explosion in the nappy department. I learned a tough lesson that day. Formula milk has certain side-effects. Welcome to motherhood, I thought, where shit knows no boundaries.

I put Maggie back in her pram and walked back to Anna's. My leisurely stroll through the streets of Creggan humming Madonna's "This Used to be My Playground" would have to wait for another day.

The fire was burning when we arrived home and the kettle was on the boil. That's the thing about Derry – the kettle is always on the boil. A cup of tea is never far away.

"Did you have a nice walk?" Anna asked as I changed Maggie on the living-room floor, ploughing through a box of baby-wipes while wondering if a power-washer would be more effective.

"It's a nice morning. I walked up to Granny and Granda's grave. I know it's a bit silly but I wanted them to meet Maggie."

"They'd have loved her to bits," Anna replied, sitting down across from me.

"Do you really think so? I'm worried they would be ashamed – you know, because of me not being married and all."

"Your granny used to say every child was a blessing, Aoife. And any child of yours would have been a double blessing to her. You know that."

"Thanks, Anna," I said, standing up to take the poo-filled nappy sack to the bin in the kitchen. "I love you."

"I love you too, honey."

I love you too, honey. Five words. Six syllables. I couldn't remember the last time someone told me they loved me and meant it.

Jake did say it sometimes. But, like I said, it would always be in a whiney voice when he wanted something, like a blow job. "But, baby, I love you," he would say, puppy-dog eyes, pouting lips, big fat erection. They say men don't love girls that 'put out' but I figured if I did enough of what he wanted he would say the words some day without that whiney voice.

I heard him talking one night after a gig. God, it had been an amazing night. He was on fire. The place was electric. He'd sung all my favourite songs and even dedicated my all-time favourite "Signed, Sealed, Delivered" to me.

I was drunk on life, on Bacardi Breezers and love, and Beth and I had long since kicked off our shoes to throw some funky moves on the dance floor. By Christ, we thought we were hilarious. At the end of every dance we did our "jazz hands" and fell into each other's arms laughing so hard I worried I would pee my pants. How I wish now for the bladder control I had then. I don't think I ever enjoyed a night as much.

When the gig ended Jake had bounded over to me, his over-inflated ego adding a certain spring to his step. We had snogged – a full-on tongues-and-everything drunken fumble right there in front of everyone as if we didn't give a damn who was watching or who might shout "Get a room!".

We sat together drinking, Beth, Dan, Jake and me. The rest of the band were there too of course and the usual smattering of groupies but I had nothing to fear from them. We were draped over each other – wearing each other and our passion like a badge of honour and it felt amazing.

A short time later, stumbling back from the toilets, I saw him locked in a conversation with a tall blonde supermodel type. Creeping up behind him, longing to wrap my arms around his waist and pull him close to me in another full-on embrace I heard what he was saying.

"Aoifs is just a mate, seriously. Yeah, we mess about but she's a mate. Just like you're a mate, and Beth's a mate. Seriously."

I didn't want to make a scene. Jake didn't like it when I acted mean and moody, so I took his hand, kissed his cheek and pretended I hadn't heard. After all, love grew from friendships. And he did say he loved me, sometimes. In fact he said it later that night – when he wanted that blow job.

★ ★ ★

Perfect Jacqueline had perfect hair. I always hated that about her. While my mane was a mass of auburn frizz and curls, Perfect Jacqueline had a sleek blonde bob which was poker-straight. She didn't even need to bleach it, the sun did that for her – which was quite a feat given that the sun shone directly out of her arse. Yep, Jacqueline and Joe – the Sunny-arse Twins.

Jacqueline's hair was never out of place. It always had that 'just stepped out of a salon' look about it. Even when she was heavily pregnant with Odhran and when he was little and mad with colic, she still looked, well, perfect. It was almost too much to bear.

I'm not a bad-looking woman, even if I say so myself, but next to Jacqueline I always looked scruffy. We just were in different leagues and that was never more obvious than the first time I met her after my shameful return to Derry. My hair was scraped back off my face and I had just deposited the shittiest nappy in history in the bin when the doorbell rang and Anna made her way to the door.

Jacqueline never walks into a room, she glides ethereally. I was red-faced, the smell of my daughter's explosion hanging in the air when herself walked in, hair perfect, Doris Day glow about her face and wearing the latest Designers at Debenhams special offers. Her tummy was just ever so slightly rounded – I certainly looked more pregnant than she did. I swore under my breath. This was not how it was supposed to be. I was supposed to visit her, in her house, at a time that suited me, when I at least had a touch of make-up on, and perhaps some clean jeans and a top that didn't smell vaguely of sour milk.

It was not supposed to be while I knelt on the floor, jelly belly wobbling over my squirming daughter, as sweat coursed through my body in a most unattractive way.

While she did her very best to hide her mixture of smug superiority and disdain over my husbandless parenting status, there was a slight glimmer of glee in her eyes. She knew the battle was won. She had now officially replaced me as Number One Daughter in my mother's eyes and she couldn't have been happier.

"Aoife, how wonderful to see you and baby Margaret!"

"Maggie," I answered and stood up. It was hard to know what to do now. I hadn't seen Jacqueline in two years, but somehow a hug didn't seem appropriate. I was sure it wouldn't be appreciated anyway, not with the smell of poo clinging to me. Then again a handshake seemed much too formal. I settled for a nod of the head – the kind you would normally give to someone who let you out at a busy junction or for the old school friend you passed in the street but couldn't remember the name of.

"Sorry – Maggie. It's darling. Is it short for Margaret then?"

"Nope, just Maggie."

"Strange, to give a child a shortened name like that." She smiled at the end of her sentence as if the smile would neutralise the barb. It didn't. She looked at the sofa behind her, no doubt checking that it was suitable enough to cushion her royal arse and sat down.

"Maggie is a name in its own right, and a lovely one at that. Are you thinking of names yourself yet?" I answered, biting my tongue to prevent me from adding my own suggestions of Satan, Lucifer and Beelzebub.

"Oh, not yet, but we've loads of time. We want to focus on Odhran for now and think about the new baby when we're a little further along."

The use of the word "we" was not lost on me. I knew it was because Jacqueline was emphasising her married status. Her partner hadn't run off and left her at the first sign of a positive pregnancy test. No, he was still there and he would be there through it all. He would probably cut the cord and pan-fry the placenta and serve it with fecking chips.

She sat in a manner usually adopted by Hollywood starlets or C-list celebs. Her knees together, she balanced elegantly on the edge of the sofa.

"I think you're very brave, Aoife. Doing this alone. Parenting isn't easy. Well done for giving it a go."

She talked to me like this was an experiment – as if I was one of those teenage schoolgirls who brings home a baby doll which cries if you don't pick it up enough. Giving it a go? I was in this up to my swollen boobs and receding post-pregnancy hairline. I was hardly just giving it a go. I felt myself start to get flustered. I could not rise to the bait.

"It's not that tough," I answered. "Honestly, I don't know what all you couples complain about. I guess it's all about organisation, determination and patience. Isn't it?"

It didn't take a fizzle out of her. Without even an intake of breath she replied: "Yes, but alone, Aoife, without any company. You must get very lonely some of the time."

"Not so much. I have some great friends."

And I knew she'd won because friends were not the same as significant others and yes, I did get lonely – heartbreakingly lonely. Damn Jake and his disappearance. For three fecking years he was on my doorstep morning, noon and night and now not even the hardest core of the London Interior Design set could find him.

"Yes, I'm sure you do," she said with a curl of her lip – a slight smirk. No, friends were no replacements for a partner or family for that matter.

Once again I found myself thinking it should not be like this. I

115

should be here, with my baby on my lap, a doting partner and a proud granny. This little one's arrival should be a source of celebration and yet it seemed she was just something that made people look down on me – feel sorry for me.

I looked for Anna, hoping she would jump to my rescue, but she had gone to the kitchen and I could hear the kettle starting to whistle.

I lifted Maggie to me, and knelt back before standing up, my body still aching. I let out an involuntary groan as my pelvis stretched and pulled together.

A decent person would have offered to help, but not Jacqueline. She looked at me and put her hand to her own stomach while I sat back on the chair. I couldn't resist glaring at her and she glared right back.

"Oh, did you want some help?" she smiled with her usual annoying habit of being a complete bitch simply by the intonation in her voice.

No one would ever believe she was that nasty if I retold the story of how she offered to help.

"I'm fine, thank you," I said.

"I suppose you have to be. Still, I don't imagine all this unpleasantness will damage little Maggie too much."

At that I excused myself, still glaring, telling Jacqueline it was time for my daughter's nap. My resolve wavering, I walked up the stairs, sat on the bed and took out my mobile phone.

"Jake, please txt. We need to talk."

I pressed send and I knew it would do no good. He hadn't answered any of the other texts I'd sent since Maggie was born. This wouldn't be any different. Damn Jacqueline for making me feel so needy – so filled with guilt. Damn Maggie for making me feel so vulnerable. I'd never let Jacqueline get to me like this before – vowed that I never would – but sitting across the room from her and her perfect pregnancy, I felt as exposed as I had done when I lay – legs akimbo – on the delivery table.

I was doing okay till you came along, I thought as I put Maggie in the Moses basket. "I was an independent woman and you've taken all that away from me so that I'm some pathetic needy creature who sends text messages to fuckwits and lets fecking Jacqueline get the better of me." She slept on, blissfully unaware. "Damn you!" I snarled under my breath, kicking the bed and hurting my toe so much that tears sprang to my eyes. "Damn you," I said again, this time a whisper and then I cried – a mixture of the pain from my now probably broken toe, guilt at shouting at Maggie and biting loneliness.

I sat there for a while wondering exactly why I'd come back to Derry. I didn't need this. I wanted to feel good about myself again, but this trip was making me feel worse than I ever had. This trip was making me think the days since Maggie's birth had been a weird fluke and all those feelings of not wanting her – not wanting this – were all just waiting to come rushing back in.

At least in London, surrounded by Matilda and my daybed I could see that I had made something of my life. Here I was just Aoife – another unmarried mother who let her family down. Even my daddy, who loved me, was disappointed.

I lifted the phone again and called the shop. Heather answered in her usual sing-song voice. "Instant Karma, how can I help you?"

I had to hide the urge to bawl down the phone. Heather was young and scared easily. The last thing she needed was her boss wailing like a banshee down the line.

"Is Beth there, Heather? It's Aoife."

"She's with a client. Can I take a message?"

"Just tell her to call me," I managed before my voice broke.

"Is everything okay?"

"Yes," I squeaked in a voice so high I'm sure only dogs could hear it.

"Because I can get her now if you need her?" Heather was

starting to sound scared. That was not good.

"No – it's – fine." I stuttered through my tears.

"Seriously, Aoife, you don't sound the best. I'll get her now."

Like a sad little schoolgirl waiting for someone to confirm that I had a genuine reason to be upset, I muttered "Okay then" and launched into another almighty sob.

"Oh God, Aoife, is Maggie okay?" Beth's voice was filled with concern.

I wanted to shout back 'Stop asking about Maggie! Who cares if she is okay? Ask if *I'm* okay. What about *me*? Have I stopped existing now that I'm a fecking mother?', but of course I didn't. I just said: "I want to come home, Beth. Can Dan come and lift me from the airport tomorrow?"

"Already? You've only just arrived."

"I know but, Beth, it's horrible. I want to come home. This was a mistake. It's all been a bloody big mistake."

I was still sobbing on the bed ten minutes later when I heard a knock at the bedroom door. I ignored it, hoping it would go away. It seemed that was becoming quite a pattern for me.

"Aoife, darling. The Wicked Witch has gone. You can come out now. Are you okay?"

Anna's voice was filled with concern. I felt hateful to be letting her down again by leaving but I knew I had to get back to London.

"Come in," I muttered and she pushed the door open and walked in, taking a seat beside me on the bed.

"It's not that bad, Aoife," she soothed.

"I'm going home, Anna. I'm going to book flights and Dan is going to pick me up from the airport."

"I thought you were going to stay till this was sorted."

"Why should I?" I said petulantly. "If they want to think badly of me then they bloody well can. I can live quite happily in London without worrying about them and their snide remarks."

"They'll come round, Aoife. You have to give them time."

"Come round? But I've not done anything wrong."

"You could have told them – us – about Maggie. You have to expect them to be hurt and a little pissed off."

"So *you* are hurt and a little pissed off then?" I said, eyes blazing.

"If I'm honest, yes, Aoife. I am. I thought we were closer than that. I thought you trusted me." The hurt she felt was obvious in every word she spoke and for once I was speechless.

"I'm going out," I said, grabbing my coat and walking down the stairs.

"What about Maggie?"

"I don't give two shits about Maggie!" I blurted out, anger and shame pouring through me as I slammed the door and walked into the pouring rain.

16

Aoife

By the time I'd walked into town I was soaked through. The fleece jacket I'd pulled on wasn't all that great at keeping out the bitter Derry rain. I know I'd looked a disaster when I walked into Jackson's, pulled up a seat at the bar and ordered a double vodka and Coke.

I didn't care. I don't think I'd ever felt as wretched in my life as I did at that moment. This was worse – much worse – than giving birth alone, than being dumped the day I found out I was pregnant, than having my mother look at Maggie as if she were nothing.

Anna was annoyed with me. My one ally here at home had turned against me and to make it all worse I'd even turned against my own daughter. What kind of mother did that make me?

I loved Maggie. I knew I loved her with every fibre of my heart but life was easier without her. Yes, my family had been highly dysfunctional but at least we were all equally responsible for that.

Now it seemed like it was more or less all down to me and I didn't like that burden. I hadn't asked for any of this. I wanted children some day – not now, not like this. No amount of love for my child could change that. Right person, wrong time.

I lifted the glass to my lips and took a deep gulp, the sharp taste of the vodka making me take a deep breath. I felt it work its way down my throat to my stomach, leaving me feeling warm and cosy inside. I drank some more. Feck them all! I was going to drink for as long as it took for me to forget about this sorry mess.

My mobile rang and I lifted it out. It was Anna, but I wasn't in the mood for answering. She thought little enough of me as it was, so I didn't see the harm of going the full distance and making her hate me. I could live up to the name of the family fuck-up if they wanted.

I drank some more, sitting my phone on the bar.

My phone rang again. It was Joe. Again I ignored it. I knew Anna would have been on to him for help as soon as I slammed the door. Instead I ordered a second double vodka and Coke (not even Diet Coke – I was *that* much of a rebel) and pinned it as quickly as I did the first. I started to feel floaty, chilled out and more like the real me – the one who hadn't just had her life snatched from her. I could pretend none of it mattered.

I was on my fourth double vodka and Coke when my phone rang again. "Shut up!" I shouted at it, staring as the screen lit up. Why couldn't Anna just realise that I wanted to be alone for a bit. Why were they always, always on my back?

Except it wasn't Anna on the phone. The name displayed in big, bold letters was JAKE.

My heart thumped in my chest as I looked again at it. I wasn't sure that my mind, helped by the vast quantity of alcohol I'd just downed in record time, wasn't playing tricks on me.

No. It definitely said Jake. I opened the phone and held it to my ear, almost too afraid to speak in case it would break the moment and none of this would be real.

"Hello? Aoifs, is that you? Are you there?"

"Jake?" It was a statement as much as a question. It had been eight months since I'd heard his voice and yet I knew it as well as I knew my own.

"Look, Aoife. I hear you've been looking for me."

"You – we – have a baby," I slurred, the room spinning from a mixture of shock and alcohol consumption.

There was silence at the other end.

"I know. Are you looking for money or something?" he said eventually.

"I thought you might want to meet her. Your daughter. Maggie."

"Do you think that's a good idea?"

"You should. You have to," I said, sensing the slightest hesitation in his voice, knowing that if I tried, really tried, I could talk him round.

"Can I call round then?"

Fuck, fuck and treble fuck. He wanted to call round and I wasn't there. No, I was stuck in fecking Derry in a fecking pub and he was there, ready to call round and give me a chance to make him fall in love with me utterly and properly.

"I'm in Ireland," I said, trying and failing to hide my abject disappointment. Tears sprang to my eyes.

"Well, look, I've a bit of work to do. Call me when you're back. I'll set something up."

He hung up. No goodbye, just an offer to "set something up" sometime in the future. I hung my head in my hands and finished my drink. I was just about to order another when I noticed my top was soaking wet – and it wasn't from the rain. Two damp, round patches shouted out from my chest that I was a breast-feeding mother and here I was pissed as a fart in a pub having just lost out on the chance to make things right with the man I loved.

When they write the story of my life, this will be the bit they put in the chapter called "Not her Finest Moment".

I stumbled to the toilet, threw up and decided it was time to go home. As I walked out of the pub into the pouring rain, I'm pretty sure I heard someone say "Moo!" behind me. I walked on, head held as high as possible and threw up again in the street.

I was feeling pretty damned miserable. I had decided to walk home, hoping the fresh air and pouring rain would sober me up. Besides which, I doubt very much any self-respecting taxi driver would allow me into the back of a cab. I looked very much like the Creature from the Black Lagoon – a hardened street drinker with leaking nipples and weepy eyes and hair stuck to my face with rain. I'm sure I smelled of sick.

I cried the whole way home, gulping snottery sobs. I'm pretty sure I talked to myself the whole way too, cursing at myself for being so far away from London now when Jake wanted to get in touch. Cursing myself for being drunk when I was supposed to be a responsible grown-up adult. Cursing myself for showing my family they were right and that I was a fecking useless lump of a thing.

By the time I reached Anna's, I was incoherent. I braced myself for her anger. I knocked on the door and Joe answered – taking in my sorry state from head to foot. He shook his head. "Where the fuck have you been, Aoife? We've been worried sick. Maggie needs feeding. Have you been drinking? Jesus, you are a mess."

He continued in the same vein for quite some time and I just stood there, listening, nodding, crying. The fight that had kept me from falling to pieces for the last nine months had gone. They could say what they wanted now. It was all true.

As he ranted, his lips moving, my heart thumping and head swirling, I saw Anna walk into the hall, her face lined with worry.

"Let her be, Joe. She's been through enough," she said, but she didn't pull me into her arms and didn't offer me any comfort. Her eyes were dulled, her face white with worry. "Let's get you cleaned up." She turned to Joe and told him to be on his way. She would take care of things, she said, and there would be no need to be telling our mother or father about this sorry episode. He nodded, giving me one final look of disappointment before leaving.

As we climbed the stairs, Anna leading me by the hand, I asked how Maggie was.

"Sleeping like a lamb," Anna answered. "She's been as good as gold."

I nodded, my mind racing with a mixture of pride, guilt and shame. Anna filled me a bath and, as I soaked away the grime and the rain, she set my pyjamas out on my bed for me. She left her towelling robe there too. I was to put it on, she said, to get the chill from my bones. She brought me pint after pint of water and Milk Thistle to abate the churning stomach.

"Get dressed and come downstairs when you're ready," she said. "I'll put the kettle on and we can have a cup of tea."

I nodded again. A cup of tea sounded perfect. When I finished, the effort of bathing having wiped me out, I walked downstairs. Maggie's Moses basket was in the corner of the room. I walked to it and stared in at her delicate, trusting face. I kissed the tip of my fingers and pressed them to her rosebud lips, feeling the warmth of her breath on my hand. I stroked her soft cheek and prayed with every ounce of me that she would never, ever feel just how I felt at that moment.

I curled up in the armchair, letting the embers of the fire warm me. Anna walked in, teacups and hot buttery toast with her, and sat down.

"I don't want you to tell me you are sorry, Aoife. I know you are sorry. But I do want you to tell me what is going on with you. If you're going to stay here, be it for one night, one week, one month or however long, then you have to be honest with me."

"Jake phoned."

Anna looked at me blankly. The name Jake meant little to her and why shouldn't it? "Maggie's dad," I reminded her and Anna nodded. "While I was out. He wanted to call round to the flat to meet her."

"And you are here."

"I'm here," I said. "He's been ignoring me for nine months and now he wants to meet me and I'm in another country. You've got to admire the sense of cosmic timing there, don't you?"

"So he never once showed an interest in his baby?"

"Never. He walked out about twenty-three seconds after I announced the big news and went missing in action."

"Sounds like a rotten fucker to me," she said, biting into a slice of thick, buttery toast.

"Funnily enough, you aren't the first person to say that," I answered. "But there is something about him, Anna, that draws me in. I want to hate him. I really do want to hate his guts but I can't. He is Maggie's father and when we were good together we were very, very good."

"Not good enough that you ever told us about him," Anna said, one eyebrow slightly raised.

The woman had a point.

"Our relationship wasn't exactly the kind you phoned home about, Anna," I said, the vodka having loosened my tongue a little.

"Obviously," Anna said.

"I always hoped it would turn into something more. There were times when I really thought it could work out."

"But you don't still feel it can work out, do you?"

I know she wanted me to tell her that I never wanted to see him again, let alone get close to his todger, but I couldn't help it. I was addicted to Jake Gibson and if he had walked into Auntie Anna's living-room right there and then I would have done whatever he asked me to.

"I don't know," I muttered.

"Are you going to go back to London then?"

"I don't know the answer to that either. Present company excepted, I don't see much of a reason to stay."

"You have to give your family time, Aoife. It's been a shock. I don't like to be harsh with you when it's clear you're being harsh enough with yourself, but you are a grown woman and you need to start acting like one. Running away solves nothing."

"Nothing I do, or have ever done, has been good enough for them," I protested. "I should just let them get on with thinking badly of me and be done with it."

"Your mother is exceptionally proud of you, sweetheart. She might not show it but she is always boasting away about your fancy job and the fact you run your own business."

I sighed, because I know my mother loves my job. But that is just it: she loves the job – the success – not the individual behind it.

"I know," I replied. "It's the one thing I've managed not to feck up in my life."

"You do love it? Don't you?"

"Yes," I smiled. "It allows me to be me. And you know what, Anna, people like what I do! We have a waiting list of people waiting for a consultation. People have us on retainers to do their whole houses. We did it all ourselves, Beth and me."

I knew my face had lit up. I was in my conversational comfort zone. I had successfully steered the conversation away from Jake and my family and I could talk about something I felt utterly comfortable and confident about.

I could ignore what I had just done. I could push it to the back of my mind for a little while because the front of my mind was busy enough just now. I didn't need the voice telling me over and over again that I was a bad mother – who didn't deserve the gorgeous creature in the Moses basket across the room. I could ignore the voice telling me that what I had done – how I had

127

walked out – had been utterly, utterly selfish and wrong. I would beat myself up over that tomorrow, I decided drunkenly. And probably for a long time to come. That night, though, I wanted to pretend that everything was fine and that there was every excuse for how I had behaved, even if the nagging feeling in the pit of my stomach told me otherwise.

I went to bed shortly after that – still pushing those thoughts to the back of my mind. Positive thinking was the way forward, I tried to convince myself. So I decided, in fine drunken fettle, to phone Beth and tell her just how proud I was of us both. I wouldn't mention how I was distinctly unproud of my actions that evening. I didn't notice that it had gone midnight. The phone rang three times and Dan answered, his voice strangely breathless.

"Everything okay, Dan?" I asked.

"Fine, just fine," he answered, sounding a little annoyed and definitely very flustered.

"Can I speak to Beth, please?"

He didn't answer.

Then I heard my best friend on the phone. Equally breathless and flustered. And that's when the penny dropped.

"Oh Jesus, I've not caught you mid-shag, have I?" I laughed down the phone.

"Something like that," Beth answered.

"Christ, look, I'll go. I just wanted to tell you, you're a rock."

"Are you drunk?"

"Long story, Beth, and I don't want to kill your vibe. Away you go and get laid. I'll talk to you tomorrow."

"Are you coming home?"

"I don't know, I'll get back to you tomorrow. Night, honey."

The truth was I wasn't exactly sure where home was any more.

17

Beth

Seduction. I used to be fabulous at it. I had a drawer of saucy little numbers from La Senza or, for special occasions, from Agent Provocateur. Dan's favourite had been a pair of knickers which tied at the side. They were cream lace, almost paper-thin. He said they made for easy access. I would wear them with a matching cream lace plunge bra and hold-ups.

I would go the whole hog. Candles, wine, rose petals on the bed, a blindfold if I was feeling particularly adventurous. I promised myself on our wedding day that I would always make the effort – so I'm not sure when it changed exactly.

All I know is that I found myself on Day 14 of my cycle walking into the living-room and announcing to Dan that it was "time".

He was sprawled out on the cream leather sofa, his tie loosened, his shoes off. His eyes were glued to the TV, a bottle of Stella Artois in his hand. Keeping his gaze on the TV, he asked: "Time for what?"

129

"You know. Time for you to perform." I tried to keep my voice light, but with every second that passed my optimum fertility was dropping. I eyed the bottle of beer and tried to keep my patience. This wouldn't help matters at all.

He glanced up. I wiggled my hips, but even I knew my look of dressing-gown and thermometer waving in my hand wasn't exactly erotic.

He sighed (again) and stood up, walking towards the bedroom with the look of a condemned man about him.

I moved to kiss him, to try and inject some romance.

"Look, babes, I'm really tired. Can we just get this over with?"

The words hurt. I wanted a baby, but I wanted the experience of making that baby to be memorable for the right reasons. I didn't want to look back at the moment of conception and think that it was just a chore for Daddy Dearest.

I tried to smile. "C'mon, baby. That's not the attitude." I loosened his tie further, slowly unbuttoning his shirt, while I kissed his neck.

I felt his body respond, his breathing change just that little bit and I felt myself relax. It was okay, he wanted this after all.

Things were just getting hot and heavy when the phone rang. I begged Dan not to answer it, wriggling my hips beneath him in a bid to distract him, but he reached over my head and answered it anyway – putting me on the phone to talk to Aoife.

Did he not realise how important this was?

Finishing the call as quickly as I could, I turned to where he sat on the side of the bed. I wrapped my arms around his neck, rubbing my hands across his strong chest. "Where were we?" I purred.

"Is Aoife okay?"

"Sure she is." I said, trying to drop the subject of my best friend and her train-wreck of a life. "Let's not worry about Aoife just now. Let's worry about us."

"You didn't tell her Jake had called to the shop."

God, why couldn't he just drop it and move back to the more important matters?

"No. She sensed we were, erm, busy, and said she would speak to me tomorrow."

"Do you think you should have told her?"

It was clear this was going nowhere fast. "Dan, look, can we talk about this tomorrow? If we miss this window of opportunity, we will have to wait another month."

"And that would be so bad?"

At that point I stood up and stormed to the bathroom, but before I could slam the door I heard the door of the bedroom slam as Dan walked out, stealing my thunder.

I sat down on the warm floor and wondered how on earth I was going to pull back from this. I didn't want to let another month pass. I couldn't, I wouldn't, but I couldn't exactly force myself on him either.

God, why wasn't this easy? We had spent all the years we dated trying not to get pregnant and now that we wanted it more than anything else, why did it have to be so damned hard? I just wanted to be pregnant. We were doing everything right. It wasn't bloody fair.

I stomped to the kitchen, still naked, and opened a bottle of wine, knocking back half a glass in one go which caused me to splutter. Tears sprang to my eyes, mostly due to the choking, and I slammed the glass down on the worktop while I tried to catch my breath.

"Are you okay?" Dan asked, walking into the room.

"Yes. No. I don't know."

"I know what you mean."

"Glad someone does," I managed with a half smile.

Dan walked towards me, wrapping his arms around me and pulling me close to him. He kissed my forehead and I allowed myself to fall into his body. He kissed me again, on the cheek this time, and then softly on the mouth. I responded – this time because I wanted to, really wanted to.

We made love there and then, right in front of the fridge, and then we went to bed and slept spooned together and I tried, desperately, not to think about the fact that I hadn't had the chance to prop a pillow under my hips after the deed to ensure our best chance at conception.

18

Aoife

Two summers ago, when I wasn't pregnant and when Jake and I were still in the relatively first flushes of our "relationship", we went shopping with Beth and Dan.

It was an amazing, glorious summer day. The sun was splitting the roofs, as Anna would say. There was a general quietness to London, everyone seemed to be lost in a glorious chilled-out summer vibe. We had closed Instant Karma for a week – something we did every year to get holidays over and done with – and spent too much time in beer gardens and on roof terraces soaking in the sun and the smog.

On that particular day we decided to take the train to the coast for a picnic on the beach. We would buy wine and beer and get tipsy as the sun set before bedding down in a local B&B for the night.

We were giddy with excitement as we traipsed around Waitrose filling our basket with delicious treats for our seaside repast. Beth and Dan walked ahead of Jake and me. Beth's hair was tied back, a green summer dress and white flip-flops making her look as though she had just stepped out of a French catalogue. Dan was sun-kissed, a smattering of freckles across the bridge of the nose making him look almost boy-like. And yet, he was all man. His T-shirt clung to his toned chest, his three-quarter-length trousers showing off his tanned legs and feet. If he hadn't been like a brother to me I would have fancied him.

That said, I only had eyes for Jake with his rugged jeans, his tatty T-shirt, his sunglasses on top of his head. He oozed sex appeal. I looked at him and could almost feel every part of his body on my own and it sent shivers down my spine despite the heat.

Beth and Dan looked almost virginal in comparison. But as we walked, I saw it. It was a split second, a casual touch, a nothing gesture but it chilled me. As Dan walked beside Beth, he placed his hand gently and tenderly between her shoulder blades while staring at the nape her neck. His hand moved slowly down to the base of her spine, where it rested for a few seconds, before he kissed her cheek. To most casual observers I'm sure they looked like a loved-up couple sharing your average tender moment. To me, that touch symbolised everything that was missing from my own relationship. My heart sank and I fought to get rid of the lump in my throat.

Dan loved Beth. He worshipped her. He wanted her body and soul. Jake wanted me in body only.

I tried for the rest of the day to shake the thought from my head. I clasped my hands in Jake's a few times, waiting for a tenderness in his reaction. As the day turned to evening, the embers of our beach fire burning out, he walked toward me, wrapping his arms around my waist as I stood staring out at the water. This could be my tender moment, I thought. He started singing softly. I closed my eyes and leant back toward him, letting the words of "Tupelo Honey" wash over me. I could feel his body against mine, the warmth of his skin and his breath as he sang just for me and in the moment I thought I had my victory.

"Let's get back to the B&B," he whispered. "I'm horny as fuck."

I woke to the sound of Maggie's cries. She seemed to be increasing in volume on an almost daily basis. The noise cut through the furriness of my brain and I buried my head under the pillow to ease the pain. My tongue was stuck to the roof of my mouth and from my under-pillow cave I could smell my morning breath. I wasn't sure if it was that precise aroma or the eight vodkas in quick succession that were making me feel queasy.

I had flashbacks. Moments of clarity from the night before. Had Jake really phoned? Had I really leaked breast milk in the bar? My face burned at the memories.

I could hear Anna carry Maggie down the stairs and I felt a confusing mixture of relief at the fading of the noise and guilt that I had now let my aunt watch my baby for two nights in a row. I pushed the feelings quickly to the back of my head. I had bigger fish to fry, as the old cliché goes. Today was the day of reckoning – again. I had to decide whether to stay in Derry and sort this out for once and for all, or go back to London and sort out the situation with Jake.

Neither seemed a particularly appealing option, especially with the hangover I had, but I longed to be in Jake's arms again. I wanted to give him a chance to do right by us. Sure, I knew there was a possibility he wouldn't, but maybe he had changed. After all, he had phoned me. I hadn't phoned him. He wanted to call round. It was my own damn fault for coming to Derry. I knew something like this would happen.

And yet, I knew if I walked away now from Anna and everyone I would cause irreparable damage to my family. I knew it could be salvaged if I stayed. Anna's kindness the previous night had shown me all was not lost, and my father, God love him, he was prepared to try.

No, Anna was right. I was a mother. I had to be sensible. I had to decide which I thought had the strongest chance of working. I had to stay in Derry. All I had to do first was sleep until the marching band left my head and my stomach stopped churning. It was eleven when I woke again. The house was quiet bar the almost inaudible babble of the TV from the living-room. I got up, showered and dressed and made my way downstairs.

"It lives," Anna smiled. "How are you this morning?"

"Better now than I was at eight. I'm sorry, Anna. I was a real feckwit yesterday, but I've decided to stay and sort this out. If you don't mind?"

"Of course I don't mind," She smiled, standing up to kiss me. "Now sit down with this gorgeous little woman of yours and I'll make some tea and toast and then we will go about making this all better."

I nodded.

My phone rang shortly afterwards. Beth's name flashed up on the screen. I had a sudden embarrassing memory of hearing her sex noises over the phone the previous night.

"Beth, I'm so sorry," I mumbled as I picked up.

"You weren't to know," she answered. "Sorry for not being more with it. Are you okay? Are you coming home?"

"I'm going to stay on for a bit."

"Good, glad to hear it."

"Jake phoned," I said, slipping it casually into our conversation. "He wants to see us."

She paused before answering, "You don't really want to see him, do you? Not after everything?"

"Beth, you know I do. He has a daughter now. He has a right to see her."

She sighed – the deep sigh of someone who had sat with me for countless nights over the last nine months while I wailed like a hormonal banshee over the unfairness of it all.

"Anyway," I said, deciding that changing the subject was the best approach for all concerned, "how's work? Do you miss me?"

"You've only been gone two days," Beth laughed, "but of course we miss you. Matilda is beside herself with loneliness."

"She'll take the right hump with me over deserting her."

"Do you know then when you might be back? I could tell her and put her mind at rest"

"It might be a while," I answered. "I have to do this properly."

"Okay, honey, I understand. But don't be too long, Elena Kennedy is busting her designer knickers to get a look at young Maggie. And I miss her desperately too."

"She misses her Auntie Beth as well," I added and we said our goodbyes.

That was that then. I was in Derry and I was staying until I was no longer the black sheep of my highly dysfunctional family.

Anna was the list-making queen. If there was anything at all in this world you needed to plan, then Anna was your gal. I suppose she had to be. She needed to be super-organised after Uncle Billy died. Maeve had been only eight and Anna had to juggle working full-time with raising Maeve and trying to keep Billy's business afloat.

She managed nicely on the business front for five years – largely due to the efficiency of her lists – before selling and making enough to buy her council house outright.

Once Maggie had fallen back to sleep, Anna called me to the kitchen where she sat at the table, two cups of tea in front of her, and a notebook and pen at the ready.

"Right, my dear. Let's sort this out," she said, sipping from her cup. "What are your priorities while you are here? Let's list them and formulate a plan."

She looked so serious that I had to bite back the giggle that was threatening to burst from my mouth.

"Okay then," I said, adopting my serious business face – the one I use when a client describes a colour scheme in vivid yellows and purples or something equally horrendous. "Well, I suppose the first priority is for me to phone Joe and apologise for last night."

"Good start," Anna nodded.

"Then after that, well, it's Mum, isn't it? I want her to want to get to know Maggie. I know she's pissed off with me, but I don't want her to take it out on my baby."

The words "my baby" felt strangely alien to me.

I meant what I said about my mum. Sure it would be nice to have her welcome me back into the fold with open arms, but as she hadn't done it in thirty-one years I doubted she was about to change the habit of a lifetime.

"Well, I think we need to get you over there again. Or maybe the three of you could meet in a neutral venue – somewhere you can talk without getting all hot-headed."

I thought about looking offended but decided not to bother. If there was one thing that I and my mother did well, it was get hot-headed. It made for a fun time for all during my teenage years. Joe and Daddy would head out together on the pretence of getting some fresh air. The truth was they just wanted away from the two screaming banshees we became. It was strange really – my mother, the epitome of deportment and etiquette, screaming at me like a drunken fishwife.

"What next?" Anna asked, interrupting my thoughts.

"Erm, spend some time with Dad. I want him to feel proud of me again."

"I don't think you will have too much trouble there, love. Your daddy never was one to hold a grudge. Sometimes I don't understand how he and your mother ever got together."

"Opposites attract," I muttered.

"Right. Anything else?"

"Would it be unchristian to say 'Wipe the smug and superior look off Jacqueline's face'?"

"Well, yes," Anna said, a look of mischief in her eyes, "but let's do it anyway."

She scribbled away for a few moments and then handed me the sheet of paper.

"Right, my dear, this is your mission, should you choose to accept it."

Every task was underlined and marked beside a day and time. Between tasks, she had set aside time for me to rest, to spend with Maggie and to get some fresh air.

"You look awfully pale, sweetheart," she said, reaching over and pushing an auburn curl from my face.

"That'll be the hangover, Anna. Don't worry about me, I'll be fine."

"I'm sure you will. Now, on you go and phone Joe while Her Royal Highness sleeps and I'll do this list out properly. I'm sure I have some highlighter pens somewhere."

★　★　★

Joe answered after two rings. He was obviously in efficient mode this morning.

"Hey, big bro," I started, figuring if I kept it light-hearted he would be less likely to go off the deep end at me.

"Aoife, how's the head?"

I couldn't really tell what mood he was in from his voice. Was it that he had just given up on me?

"It's better now. Look, Joe, I'm sorry. I've been a fecking eejit. I'm going to make this better – with everyone. I promise. I'm going to show you all I can do this."

"I'm glad to hear that," he said.

"I mean it, Joe. It's going to be different."

"Okay, Aoife, I believe you."

I could hear his smile from the other end of the phone. He always did like to humour me. I knew I would have to show it, not just say it.

As the lady from *Fame* says, this was where I was going to start paying, in blood.

I hung up and dialled Mum.

"McLaughlin residence," a very polite voice answered.

"Mum, it's me."

"Aoife," she said, flatly, all airs and graces gone.

"I thought maybe we could meet up," I started.

"I'm very busy, Aoife. I'm doing the flowers at the chapel today."

"Maybe I could call up, show Maggie where her granny and granda were married."

I heard a sharp intake of breath. I don't know if it was at the notion that I would dare show my unmarried mother of a self in the House of God or that I had referred to her as Maggie's granny.

"I'm not sure, Aoife. The chapel is very cold these days. Father Forbes has cut the heating bill. The baby might get too cold."

It was not lost on me that she didn't use Maggie's name.

"She'll be all wrapped up warm. Her pram is really very cosy," I continued.

"Aoife, maybe another time. We have the Bishop coming to say Mass this weekend. There's lots to be done. I wouldn't be able to give you the time of day."

I knew there was no point pushing it. She was ashamed. Making her feel that shame more acutely by arriving at the chapel with my baby in tow wouldn't help her forgive me. I felt tears spring to my eyes.

"Maybe I'll call round to the house later then, Mum?"

"Maybe. I'll phone you when I'm back. Honestly, Aoife, I've so much on."

She hung up and at that moment Anna appeared with a colour-coded chart at the door.

"Ta-*daa*!" she announced, twirling around.

I burst into tears.

Fecking dirty bastard hormones.

Anna glanced down at the phone in my hand. It didn't take psychic ability for her to realise by the look on my face that whoever I'd just spoken to hadn't been receptive to whatever it was I said.

"Was that your mum?" she asked and I nodded, letting out a snottery sob.

"Now come on. No one said this was going to be easy, but our family aren't quitters and I'm not going to let you fall at the first hurdle. Get up, get your coat on and put that wain in her car seat. We are going for a wee drive."

"But it's not 'go out for a wee drive' time," I said, staring at her colour-coded chart.

"Read the small print, sweetheart," she said and sure enough there at the bottom, in her cursive writing was an addendum: "*All activities are subject to change for whatever reason Anna deems fit.*"

I let out a laugh, and looked at the strong, amazing woman in front of me. How was it possible she was in any way related to my mother?

We got in the car and drove to Moville, a seaside down on the Donegal coastline with a breath-taking scenic walk.

"We need to get some colour in your cheeks," Anna said, assembling the pram in the car park. "We'll have a walk along here and then stop by the chipper for a bag of chips clattered in salt and vinegar when we are done."

"Won't Maggie get cold?" I asked, slipping on my gloves.

"Sure she's snug as a bug in a rug in there. She'll be fine."

"Mum thought she would catch pneumonia from being in the cold chapel."

Anna rolled her eyes. "Your mum always was a fecking drama queen."

We started our walk, along the familiar concrete path of my childhood. The sky was dark and heavy with the late February clouds. The sea swirled before us, grey and commanding, and it dawned on me how my situation meant nothing – not in the grand scheme of things. I glanced over to Anna, saw her staring out at the water and knew she felt the same.

"I used to come here all the time when Billy died," she started. "The house seemed really claustrophobic, so I would strap Maeve in the car and the two of us would walk along here together. Or I would get a sitter and come down here myself. I would take a seat over there," she said, pointing to the old changing rooms, "and stay for hours, just staring out at the sea. When it was really windy. When it all felt too much it was great. I could scream out to the waves and let it all out."

I imagined her, sitting there alone and I felt a tear spring to my eye.

"You know," she said, moving closer to me as if she were about to impart some big secret, "one night I was here wailing and moaning when I heard an old man shout out. I damn near gave him a heart attack. He thought the banshee was coming for him."

She laughed, linked her arm in mine, and we walked on. "It's amazing what you can survive – what you can laugh about later." We walked on, feeling the breeze whip around our faces for half an hour before turning and walking back to the Foyle Hotel where we ordered two coffees and I started to feed a now wide-awake Maggie.

"She's just precious," the waitress cooed.

"She sure is," Anna answered.

"You do right to be proud. My mammy is the same with my wee man. She loves being a granny too," the waitress said before walking off.

"Jesus Christ, she has me a granny and there was me thinking I didn't look a day over twenty-one, Lord save us," Anna laughed with a wink.

"Get used to it. You might be the only granny this wee one ever knows."

For the first time my heart didn't sink at the thought.

19

Aoife

We were just running a bath for Maggie, the papers of our food from the chippy now in the bin, when we heard the door open.

"Let me see her, where is she?" a high-pitched and excited voice shouted around the house.

"Upstairs, love!" Anna called and we heard what sounded like a troop of elephants thunder up the staircase and into the bathroom.

Maggie, relatively non-responsive to anyone or anything until now, opened her eyes wide and gazed straight at Maeve as if she were totally mad.

"Oh. My. God. Aoife, she's totally class! She is amazing! Can I lift her?"

Maeve, always the whirlwind, didn't wait for my reply before lifting Maggie up over her head and twirling her round.

"Maeve Mary O'Donnell, would you calm down!" Anna chided, failing to hide her pleasure at seeing her gorgeous daughter. "The wain will throw up on you, and besides weren't you supposed to call around yesterday?"

"Okay, I'm sorry, I'm sorry," Maeve answered breathlessly. "It's just she is so gorgeous. Well done, Aoife! I bet the father is a pure ride."

I nearly choked and Anna nearly had a coronary.

"Maeve, that's enough of that talk!" her mother scolded.

"It's okay," I laughed. "He's not bad as it happens. Just a complete arse, but pretty hot in the looks department."

"You can tell," Maeve enthused. "I mean you are quite pretty, but she is a wee stunner." She looked at Maggie, tickling her tummy. "Yes, oo are, yes, oo are! Oo are so gorgeous!"

"Careful, Maeve, everyone will wonder if you're taking the notion yourself," I chided.

"God no. I love babies, but not for me, not yet. I can't even look after myself. Fair fucks to you, Aoife!"

"Language!" Anna said, her voice raised.

"Sorry, Mammy, I'll calm down, honest."

But it wasn't in Maeve's manner to calm down. She was a one-woman whirlwind and at twenty-three showed no signs whatsoever of calming down into adult life. I have to say, I admired that about her.

"I'm starved," she said, distracted from Maggie by her rumbling stomach, "I'm away to get a sarnie. See you three babes in a few minutes."

You couldn't help but smile when Maeve was in the room and at least now, in this space, I felt totally accepted and loved.

I smiled at Anna. "You should be very proud of her."

"What, with that language? Her father would be spinning in his grave!"

"Sure she does no harm. It's nice to see her so confident and happy."

"I suppose. I shouldn't complain," said Anna. "Now let's get Miss Tissy here a bath."

I sat back and watched her hands tenderly wash my daughter, the gentle way in which she wet her hair and soaped her down and I felt contented for the first time in a long time.

Just before I went to bed, I phoned Mum. She may have put me off seeing her in the church, but seeing Anna and Maeve together – their effortless bond – made me realise that I couldn't walk away on this relationship.

She answered the phone, her voice tired.

"Mum," I started, "I'm going to bring Maggie around tomorrow morning. I'll bring the buns and we'll see you around eleven."

She made to protest, to come up with some excuse, so I said a quick goodbye and hung up. I was not going to give her the chance to tell me no, or to shun me again.

Then I phoned Beth, just to check on the shop and Matilda. She sounded tired too.

I was sure the pressure of taking care of the business, with just Heather for company, was getting to her. A few of the clients she was dealing with were very demanding. That and keeping everything else ticking over was bound to be stressful.

It was clear that I couldn't spend forever here in Derry, not when the business needed me, so I made a resolution to myself that Mum would listen to me the following day. Now all I had to do was think about what exactly I was going to make her listen to.

Tired as I was, those thoughts played on my mind throughout the night. As I got up to feed and change Maggie, I looked into her darkest blue eyes and thought of all the things I was going to have to tell her granny come morning.

Things about me, and Jake and my life in London. Things about sex. Things about getting pregnant and being pregnant and then not being pregnant any more. Things that any normal daughter should talk to her mother about (well maybe, with the exception of the sex thing). It troubled me.

I wasn't a victim. Not in the traditional sense anyway. Yes, I hoped Jake would fall in love with me but, while he didn't, I enjoyed the down and dirty – the pure filthy no-holds-barred passion of him. Being Catholic and Irish, I know I'm not really supposed to admit to that but, my God, at times the man made me feel like the most sexually irresistible woman on the planet.

The first time I met his friends, I'd made an effort. My hair was glossy, curled and hanging loosely around my face. I wore a white cotton gypsy-style top, with a red flowing skirt which swished around my tanned ankles and made me feel so very feminine.

It was a hot summer's day and when I walked into the pub, and took off my cardigan, I felt Jake's eyes on me. His friends nodded, smiled and said hello, but Jake just looked at me, his eyes dark with lust and I felt a surge of warmth in the very pit of my stomach. I walked to him, kissed him gently on the cheek and said my hellos. I felt in control as I walked to the bar to get a glass of wine. I could almost sense him walk up behind me, and then I felt him wrap his arm around my waist.

"How are you?" I said.

He took my hand, moved it downwards to his crotch and I could feel him, hard and hot, and although he didn't speak any words, I knew he wanted me there and then.

If I'm honest, I wanted him too. I wanted him so much it took my breath away and as we stood staring at each other in that busy bar I could hear and see nothing but him.

We shagged in the toilets that night. It was hardly high romance, but it was passionate. I'll give him that. Jake did passion well. Perhaps though, thinking about it, my mother never needed to know about that particular episode.

Feels Like Maybe

I woke hot and flustered, the thought of that first encounter with Jake replaying in my mind. Was it really only ten days ago that I promised myself I would never, ever touch another man again? My God, I still had to wash myself down with warm water when I peed to stop the stitches stinging – how could I even contemplate sex? And what good would it do me anyway when I had no man willing to oblige?

No, I had to clear those thoughts from my mind pretty damn quick smart. I had a mother to see, and I was pretty sure she had a sensor that could tell if I'd had any impure thoughts in the preceding twenty-four hours.

My mother is the queen of routine. Her mornings start the same, and vary only depending on whether it's a Sunday (Mass) or Tuesday or Friday (the *Derry Journal* is out).

On those days she's out of the house that wee bit earlier. If it's a Sunday, she leaves just in time to get the front pew in the chapel she has lovingly spent the week cleaning.

If it's a *Journal* day she is down at the newsagent's before nine – just so she can see who has died or who has been up in court. The morning is never complete for Mum without the latest gossip. As a teenager I'd hear her rattling about as I tried to sleep in – my duvet pulled over my head. At six forty-five the bathroom door would slam and by six fifty she'd be downstairs and the familiar whistle of the kettle would screech up the stairs, invading my sleep.

By five past seven, after a battering of cups and plates at a level that would have woken the dead never mind a stroppy teenager, she would holler up the stairs at me and Joe to get ready for school. We were always ready half an hour early. This gave us time to do our chores or, if she was feeling particularly close to God, a quiet round of the Rosary.

By the time 10 o'clock came, she would have the house spick and span and be sitting down to her second cup of tea, some daytime telly or a read of the paper.

I knew, then, if I timed it just right and arrived with Maggie in tow at about ten thirty (enough time to clear away the cups and dust down the biscuit crumbs) she would be free to give us her undivided attention.

At the same time, the thought of having my mother's undivided attention was not something I relished. It rarely proved a positive experience.

Taking a five-minute break from my feelings of impending doom, I nipped upstairs and phoned Beth once again.

"Instant Karma, Beth speaking. How can I help you?"

"Hey, babes," I started, "promise me you will give Matilda a good home if my mother kills me and buries me under the patio. Likewise, promise me you will visit me often if I kill her and bury her under the patio."

Beth laughed. "You'll be fine, honest. Look, you have dealt with worse than this. Remember the time Janet Hetherington went off on one because she wanted forest green in the dining-room and you ordered sage? You talked her round then. If you can manage that, you can manage anything."

"You have a point, but she could be bribed with the promise of a complementary water feature to Feng-Shui her room a little. I wonder what I could bribe my mother with?"

"You've got Maggie. You don't need to bribe her any further. How is my little treasure anyway?"

"She's lying here on the bed beside me, cooing at nothing. I can't believe how much she is growing, Beth. She more pudgy than wrinkly these days."

Beth sighed. "Sweetheart, you are so lucky."

"Yep, a single mother with a family who hates her and an ex who doesn't want to know. I'm the luckiest gal on the planet," I deadpanned, then I looked at my daughter – this bundle of pink.

150

"I know, Beth. Honestly, I know I'm lucky. I'm sorry if I don't show it all the time."

"I'm sure it's hard work too. Look, Aoife, someone has just come into the shop. Heather is on her coffee break so I'll have to go. Good luck with your mum."

When we arrived at my mother's house, I saw my father's car was gone. There would be no safety cushion this time.

"Do you want me to come in with you, love?" Anna asked, sensing my discomfort.

"Nope, it will be fine. I think it's best I do this alone."

I lifted Maggie and we walked to the door. Even though I had a key, it felt wrong to use it, so I rang the doorbell. My mother simply nodded at us when she answered the door – opening just enough for us to come in and then returning to the living-room where she sat on the sofa. There was a fire burning in the hearth, but there was little warmth in the room. Maggie started to whimper. A quick look at the clock let me know it was time for her feed.

"You don't mind if I feed her, do you?" I asked.

"The kettle's in the kitchen and the glass jug is beneath the sink if you need to heat a bottle."

"It's okay, I'm breast-feeding," I replied, discreetly latching a hungry Maggie onto my boob.

My mother looked stunned. "I wouldn't have expected you to breast-feed," she said eventually. Knowing my mother, she would have expected me to leave the child to her own devices and forage in bins.

"It gives her the best start," I answered confidently.

"It takes more than breast milk to give a child a good start," she said, nose in the air.

If I bit my tongue any harder, I was pretty sure I was going to bite the damn thing right off.

"Yes, Mother. It takes loads of love, and I have that to give."

"How will you manage?"

"To love her? Easily."

"No, how will you manage your career and a baby. A baby needs her mother."

I fought back the urge to laugh. My mother may not have worked when we were little, but I couldn't hand on heart say she had been there for us.

"I have childcare arranged. There is a crèche close to the shop." There was an audible intake of breath at the word crèche.

"I've been down and spent the morning there, Mum. They seem very lovely."

"It wasn't like that in my day," she muttered.

"Yes, well, I have to support us and I can't do that and be with her all the time."

"If you had a partner you could."

"Really? Gosh, where do I buy one of those, Mum?" I couldn't hide the annoyance from my voice any longer.

"No need for cheek," she answered, feigning upset.

"I'm not being cheeky, Mum, but if I could have a partner don't you think I would have one? I didn't choose to do this alone."

"Didn't you? Sleeping around like a tramp."

It stung, thinking that was how she saw me. To think she knew so little of me she believed I would just casually sleep around.

"I wasn't sleeping around. We were together for three years."

"And you never brought him home? Give me a break, Aoife, and stop your lies for once."

"I'm not lying, and is it any bloody wonder I wouldn't bring him home to this?"

I would have got up and stormed out at that stage, were it not for the fact I had a baby attached to my left boob. Damn. I couldn't even do dramatic exits any more.

20

Beth

They call it the two-week wait. I logged onto my computer and onto the website which had become home over the last year and a half. Logging in I typed a message. I knew my 'friends' online would understand. At least I could talk to them. They didn't know my name. They didn't know who I really was. To them I was just Betsy Boo – a woman who was on day 15 of her cycle and trying once again to get lucky.

I wasn't alone when I logged on. They understood. They got why this was so totally consuming. And when it got too much, I'd allow myself to lurk on the parenting boards. I'd read the pregnancy stories and birth stories and see people move from expectant mothers to loving new mums and I would promise myself that one day I would be posting the stories of my labour and birth and regaling all those people with stories of my baby's first feed, first trip out and first time sleeping through the night.

I was so prepared for when it happened that I was able to

provide lists of must-haves for Aoife when she went into hospital.

It was too early for symptoms. I knew that, but then again some people say they just know, don't they? They feel different. Life changes at the moment of conception.

"We did the deed last night," I typed. *"Keep your fingers crossed. Babydust to all."*

It was twee, of course it was. Babydust to all. If only it were a matter of a tiny sprinkling of fairy dust.

I was reading through the latest pregnancy announcement when the bell over the door tinkled again. I heard Heather greet the customer, and a familiar voice said hello back.

Stalker Man was on the scene.

"Crap," I muttered under my breath.

"Is the owner here?" he asked Heather and she nodded in my direction.

"How can I help?" I asked, maintaining my most business-like face.

"I just wanted to apologise for being so snappish with you the other day," he said. "You were right, I was wrong to interfere. You probably think I'm some kind of mad stalker person."

"Not at all," I lied. "Apology accepted. And I'm sorry too. It's been a bit of a mad month."

"With the new baby and all?"

"Exactly."

"Is your friend not back yet then?"

"No. Not yet. A couple of weeks, I think."

He nodded and I realised I'd done it again – revealed personal details that I really shouldn't have.

"Anyway," he said, "I'll be off. I just wanted to apologise. I run the new gardener's and florist's on Gardiner Street by the way. Here's my card, if you ever need a gardener to help with any of your projects."

"Gardiner Street? Well, you've got the location going for you anyway!" I offered and shook his hand, staring at his name, Tom Austin, embossed in italic writing on his card. "And again, sorry for being rude the other day."

"It's forgotten," he said and left.

"Ooooh, who's he?" Heather cooed. "He's dreamy." She stared out the door after him.

"You'd be best to stay away," I warned. "He's a little weird."

I sat down again with the pretence of working on another mood board, but instead finished typing my post onto the internet site.

21

Aoife

Mum stared at the clock and I stared at Maggie's head. The silence was almost unbearable.

"It's not what you think, you know," I said eventually. "We really were seeing each other for three years. It just never reached the stage where I could bring him home."

"You were embarrassed by us then? Now that you have your fancy life in London."

Her words dripped scorn. Couldn't she see the irony of her accusations? It was she who was embarrassed by me.

"No, Mum. It wasn't like that. He never loved me. I thought he did and I was foolish. I didn't plan to get pregnant. It just happened and when it did he ran for the hills. I was hoping he would come round, that he would be there for us, and that's why I put off telling you. That, and I knew you'd be mortified."

She took her eyes from the clock and looked at me and my child. It should have been a heart-warming scene – a new mother breast-feeding her baby. She just shook her head.

"I thought more of you, Aoife. I always knew you were flighty, but this? I thought you would have more sense than to get yourself in trouble."

"Things happen, Mum, and I'm just trying to make the best of the situation."

I took Maggie from my breast, her eyes heavy with sleep and put her on my shoulder to wind her. Looking at my mother, I knew I had to make this right for Maggie if no one else.

"Do you want to hold her? You can wind her if you want."

"Best you do it, Aoife. I'm out of practice." She got up to put the kettle on. Walking to the kitchen she turned back, stared at us both and said: "I hope she doesn't give you half the bother you've given me."

I think it was about then that the red mist descended. A day before, I would have wailed and cried about the injustice of it all, but suddenly this wasn't funny any more. Give her bother? I'd never given her a day's bother in my entire life.

Walking to the kitchen, rubbing Maggie's back, I demanded: "What do you mean 'bother'?"

She looked a little stunned. She was used to my tears, but not to this.

"Now, come on. You know. You've always been a little high maintenance."

"In what way?" We weren't going to skirt around the issue this time. We were going to get to the bottom of this if it killed us.

"You know, just wanting stuff, demanding stuff, whingeing."

"No, mother, I don't know. I've never wanted anything or demanded anything. I went to school. I did my best and as soon as I could I got the hell out from under your feet and I've not been back under them since I was eighteen. I've done very well for myself, thank you, without demanding anything."

"Now, Aoife, we both know that's not true. As a child you were the clingiest urchin in the street. You were always in my face, looking for attention, for hugs, for approval. I couldn't turn sideways without you there."

Her words floored me, because much as I may have actually been a needy child, surely the whole point was that I was a child at the time and she, for my sins, was my mother.

"You weren't supposed to turn sideways without me, Mum. You were my *mother*, you were supposed to be there to reassure me."

"All the time? Why couldn't you just have got on with things like Joe? He was never the bother you were."

"Oh yes, the golden child – still living five minutes away and expecting you to iron his shirts!"

"Both Joe and Jacqueline are very busy, you know."

I had overstepped the mark. By criticising her son and heir, I had put her on the defensive.

"God love them," I said, with a healthy dose of fake sincerity. My brother and his wife wouldn't know busy if it bit them in the arse.

"Enough, Aoife, there's no need for that tone."

"The way I see it, Mum, there is every need for that tone. What has Joe got that I don't? Why do you care about him so much more than you care about me?"

"You're talking rubbish, Aoife, whining again, looking for affection."

"Is that so bad?" My voice was wobbling now. "I'm your child for God's sake!"

"You're a grown woman and you made your bed and you might as well lie in it."

I wanted to swear. I wanted to lash out. Years of anger and frustration were welling up inside me. Instead Maggie burped, loudly, bringing up most of her feed.

As I walked out of the room to change her, I heard my mother mutter: "You should have given that child a bottle."

I took Maggie upstairs to what used to be my bedroom and sat there wondering if my mother had been right? Was I a demanding child? I remember being desperate for a sign that she actually did love me. How ironic – that was the very thing that turned her against me all the more.

As I changed my wriggling child into her clean clothes, I heard someone come up the stairs. I braced myself for Part Two of my battle with Mum – no doubt I was using the wrong brand of nappies and the wrong size of clothes for Maggie.

Instead the door creaked and Dad was standing there, looking at Maggie with a faint smile across his face.

"She's a wee smasher," he said.

"I know," I answered. "I wish Mum thought the same."

"She'll come round," he said, sitting down on the edge of the bed, taking Maggie's tiny fingers in his strong hands.

"Why does everybody keep saying that? You, Joe, Anna, Beth. You all seem to think that she will thaw but I don't think that's possible."

"Your mother is not the witch you think she is, Aoife." He lifted Maggie, cradling her in his arms as if she were a delicate piece of china.

"Was I a needy child, Daddy?" I looked straight at him.

A look of confusion spread across his face. "What do you mean?"

"Did I crave attention? Was I always on at you two?"

He paused, taking a deep breath. "What makes you say that?"

"Mum. She said I never gave her a moment's peace."

He sighed. "Aoife, your mother doesn't always mean what she says."

"Well, what does she mean then? I've spent the last umpteen years trying to figure her out and the only conclusion I can come to is that she simply doesn't like me."

"She loves you, Aoife. She loves you so much. She has only ever wanted the best for you."

"She has a funny way of showing it."

"And you have a funny way of showing her you love her back," he said.

And the man had a point. I expected love from my mother. I expected unconditional love from her because it was my birthright as her daughter, but I'm not sure I ever offered it back.

When I was a young girl, I did everything with my daddy. It was an accepted fact in our house that it would always be me and Dad against Mum and Joe. That's how it always worked, even down to teams for Trivial Pursuit. Now my father was telling me Mum had loved me all along and Mum was telling me I'd never given her a minute's peace. It just didn't add up.

"I don't understand," I said simply.

"Let's go for a walk," Daddy replied.

We wrapped Maggie up and put her in her pram. My father insisted on pushing. It stunned me. Two days ago he could barely look me in the face and now here he was pushing Maggie, his chest puffed up with pride.

I linked his arm and we walked towards St Columb's Park.

"Your mother only ever wanted the very best for you, Aoife," he began. "When she had Joe, she wanted so desperately to have a little girl. I can't begin to tell you how happy she was when she had you. You were an awful baby. Colicky, crying all the time. Your mother was exhausted. I mean, Joe was still a toddler – and a wee demon of one at that – and you, well, you would never settle down for her. You had her squealed out during the day."

I blushed, as though I felt responsible somehow even though I was only an infant at the time and my crying was hardly on purpose.

"I would come home and find her exhausted, the house a mess, and you know your mother – the house was never a mess. You would be there, screaming, your wee legs curled up tight to your tummy and I would lift you and the crying would stop. Your mother was beside herself. All day she had walked the floors with you and nothing would appease you and all I had to do was smile and you would start gurgling."

"I always was a daddy's girl," I smiled.

"And it broke your mother's heart," he answered and I felt guilt swell up inside me.

"I didn't do it on purpose."

"I know that," he soothed, "and your mother knows that now, but she was addled with hormones back then. You must know what that's like." He nodded at Maggie. "All she could see was that she didn't get the dream daughter she'd hoped for and you seemed to love me more than her."

I didn't know what to say, so I said nothing. I just looked at my father, amazed at this story – horrified that I'd managed to push my mother away from me at such a young age without even trying.

"I'd say, knowing what I do now, she was a bit depressed. Post-natal or whatever they call it these days," my father added.

I could hardly believe I was hearing my own father talk about post-natal depression. Men didn't talk about such things – and sixty-year-old Derry men most certainly didn't.

"Of course in those days, it wasn't talked about as much as now. Funny really, half of Derry was on anti-depressants and tranquillisers due to the Troubles. They would share their wee Roche 2s and 5s like they were Smarties, but no one talked about what it felt like when your baby cried all night. It seemed insignificant when half the town was being blown to smithereens. The upshot was that your mother felt she had failed with you and she shut herself off. It wasn't fair on either of you."

"Has she ever talked to you about it?"

"God no. You know your mother. She would die if she knew we were having this conversation." He started to blush. "I was watching the *Loose Women* one day and they were talking about it and the penny dropped. I don't normally watch it, but I was waiting for the news, you know." He spoke quickly, his embarrassment written all over his face and I wanted to hug him and tell him how I loved him from the bottom of my heart. But he walked on, rabbiting to himself about daytime telly as he went.

By the time we turned and started heading for home, I didn't know what to think any more. Part of me wanted to make it up to Mum in some way.

It made more sense to me now – how she shunned me, how she didn't want to be hurt. Even though I knew she had to be over it by now, I knew why she couldn't handle me bringing a crisis – especially a pink tiny baby one – to her door and I wanted to make it right.

But, on the other hand, I knew what it was like to have a tough time with a baby. Being a single mum wasn't easy – I knew that the day Maggie was born. Coping with the crying and the nappy changes – the relentlessness of it all on my own – hadn't been easy and no, I hadn't been perfect as a mum by a long shot but I knew that I would do my best to make it up to my daughter. I wouldn't hold it against her for her whole damn life.

Dad opened the door for me and I pushed the pram up the steps to the hall.

"Make sure you leave that thing out there – I've hoovered!" Mum hollered. I wondered momentarily if that "thing" she was referring to was me, Maggie or the pram. No, I chided myself. I must not think negative thoughts. It was not her fault.

We walked into the room and she was sitting staring at the TV, which wasn't even switched on.

"Nice walk?" she asked my father, her gaze never meeting mine.

"It was lovely," he said. "Maggie seemed to love the fresh air."

"She's two weeks old. She'd love anything," Mum sniffed and went back to watching her imaginary television programme.

My resolution to be nice and play fair was wavering further. I took a deep breath. "Would you like to hold her, Mum?" I had to stop myself from qualifying my offer with reassurances that Maggie wasn't at all colicky like I had been and that she wasn't likely to send her into a tailspin.

"Maybe in a wee while, Aoife. I'm going to put the kettle on."

She was doing that a lot when I was about.

"Sure I'll do that, Mum. Here, you really should hold her. She's asleep and no bother at all."

"Look, you know me. I'm fussy about my tea. I'll hold her in a bit."

I could feel tears pricking at the back of my eyes. I knew now why Mum had been hurt, but she shouldn't take it out on Maggie who had done nothing in her life to hurt my mother.

"She doesn't bite," I blurted out and Mum looked shocked. "I'll make the fecking tea so just sit down and hold your granddaughter." My voice had adopted a menacing tone and Mum sat down without further argument.

I handed my daughter into her stiff arms. It was a strange feeling. On the one hand I wanted my mother to accept Maggie and me, and on the other the thought of placing my precious little bundle into the arms of this woman who had shown me little or no love throughout my life made me feel very uneasy.

"Hold her properly, Sheila," I heard my father say and she cuddled Maggie closer to her. "Doesn't she look like Aoife did when she was little?"

"I don't really remember," my mother said, flustered. "I suppose so."

I sat down, the tea forgotten, my heart aching with the news my mother didn't even remember my newborn stage.

Mum looked up at me. "What do you think, Aoife? Does she have a look of the father about her?"

"A little. He's a bit baldy too." I laughed nervously, but Mum didn't join in.

She may have been holding my child. She may even have looked as though she was actually starting to thaw out her ice-cold exterior and enjoy it, but I was under no illusions whatsoever.

22

Beth

Dan had offered to take me out for dinner. Who was I to argue? I had been hanging drapes in Karl's guest bedroom when my mobile jumped into life.

"Hey, gorgeous," he soothed down the phone. "How are you?"

"All the better for hearing your voice," I answered. I liked these moments – moments when it felt for all intents and purposes as if we didn't have a care in the world.

"Fancy going out tonight? I can get us a booking at the new Thai place if you're up for it?"

I looked at my watch. It was gone four and the light was starting to fade. There wasn't much more we could get done here anyway at this stage.

"I look a bit of a sight," I warned him.

"I'm sure you look amazing," he replied, winning an extra couple of brownie points for his efforts. "Will we meet at six?"

"Perfect," I said, hanging up.

That would give me time to get back to the shop and check in on Heather. I could even nip upstairs to Aoife's flat and run a brush through my hair and change my top. I always kept a spare set of clothes at her place, just in case.

Pulling the blinds closed on the old sash windows, I stepped down from the ladder and packed away my bits and pieces for the night. Dinner sounded lovely and Dan sounded so relaxed. He hadn't managed to sigh once in the course of our conversation. I was delighted with the improvement in his mood.

Driving back through the traffic, bumper to bumper in the rush hour, I tried to force myself to relax. There was no need to feel stressed. Everything was happening just as it should. The two-week wait and all its constant symptom-spotting could go hang for tonight. I was going out with my man and we were going to enjoy ourselves. A small voice in my head told me that if I was pregnant this month then I'd better make the most of nights like this anyway. God knows once Junior came along there would be no more heading out for dinner at an hour's notice. No, it would all have to be planned. Perhaps Aoife and I could baby-sit for each other. That could most definitely work. I smiled and pulled into my parking space, noting that the lights were still on inside the shop. I knew I should trust Heather but there just wasn't the same bond there as Aoife and I shared. I wasn't sure she wouldn't just lock up early and bugger off home, turning away whatever potential clients would pop in late in the afternoon.

I walked in to find Heather closing down the computer, the cash register already cleared of its measly takings. Aoife always said she didn't know why we needed a register – people rarely actually purchased things in the shop, tending to book appointments instead – but I had insisted on an old-fashioned push-button machine in brass. I loved it – in fact I loved everything about this shop. With a jolt I realised it was just about the only place I was happy these days.

"Is it okay if I nip off now?" Heather asked as I unzipped my jacket. "It's only that my tube train leaves in five minutes and I want to nip in for a pint of milk on the way."

I nodded absentmindedly and she left, leaving me to lock the door behind her. I sat down on the daybed and surveyed everything around me – the opulent silks, the rich tapestries, the scented candles and the colourful prints. Everything in this room signified that I was a success. To the outsider I had a life to be envied.

"I will think positively," I said aloud, trying to convince myself. From the corner of my eye I could see Matilda staring down at me from her perch on the shelf. "I don't know why you're giving me that look," I said. "I know, I know. I'm a very lucky person indeed."

I still felt lucky when I walked into the restaurant and saw Dan sitting at the table, a glass of white wine before him. He looked tired, stubbly and manly. His tie was loosened a little, his top button was undone. His hair was messed up a little, short blond tufts stuck up like a scruffy schoolboy. I smiled to myself. He really was gorgeous and it amazed me we had been together fourteen years. We had seen each other grow up, supported each other through college and helped each other achieve our dreams. And I still fancied the arse off him. With Dan nothing was impossible, I reminded myself as I walked over to him and kissed him full on the lips.

"Not that I'm complaining," he grinned, "but what was that for?"

"Does there have to be a reason?" I smiled sitting down. "I'm absolutely starving," I added, picking up the menu and scanning it quickly.

"Do you want me to order you a drink?" Dan asked, trying to get the waitress's attention.

"Just water for me," I said, adding quickly "because I brought the car."

We both knew the real reason was that during the two-week wait I tried where possible to avoid alcohol just in case I was pregnant, but it caused less friction if I just brought the car and we pretended everything was normal.

Yep, when Dan and I were together, nothing was impossible.

23

Aoife

"Did you know?" I asked.

I was sitting in Anna's living-room. Maggie was sleeping soundly beside me and I stared into the fire as I asked the question.

"Yes and no," Anna answered. "Your mum and I haven't ever really been close and you know her, she doesn't talk about feelings. It wasn't really done."

"But you knew something was up?"

"I could see she seemed to be struggling a little with you. But I was only a teenager myself. I didn't really get how hard it was. I just thought that's what everyone with a baby and a toddler went through."

"But she wasn't like that when it was just Joe?"

"God, no. She was like the cat that got the cream. You would have thought no one ever had a baby before – she used to sicken us all bragging on about him."

Some things never change then, I thought to myself. She still bragged about him. I felt bitter that her depression hadn't affected her feelings towards him. He had escaped it all scot-free. The fecker.

"Don't take it too personally, Aoife," Anna said and I snorted with laughter.

"How could I not take this personally? This is a mother not loving her daughter who just so happens to be me. There is no other way to take it."

"But she does love you. She has just never learned how to show it."

On the day I packed up my bedroom and almost all my worldly belongings, apart from my Kylie and Jason tapes which I had since outgrown, my mother had not shown any emotion.

Daddy drove me to the airport, ready for my new life at Manchester Uni and Mum sat tight-lipped in the front of the car. I don't quite know what I had expected. Perhaps some tears? Perhaps she should have pressed a crumpled letter into my palm and told me to read it once I had boarded the plane? Perhaps it would have contained an outpouring of love so poetic and meaningful that I would have sobbed loudly the whole way to Manchester and told the world I had the best damned mammy ever.

As it turned out, she hugged me, loosely. Her lips pursed in a cat's arse of a pout, brushing my cheek.

"Take care, Aoife," she said. "Don't be making a holy show of yourself or me."

She hurried me on through security and I only glanced back once, to see my father waving at me, tears in his eyes. Mum was nowhere to be seen. I imagine she had gone to get the car so she could get free parking for leaving within twenty minutes of arriving.

I cried on the plane that day, but it wasn't because I felt loved. It was quite the opposite.

As I lay in bed that night I thought about it all. I tried to put those last few weeks in some kind of perspective. It was almost too much to get my head around. Three weeks before I had been this single (albeit pregnant) businesswoman leading a pretty darned successful life in London. One of the presenters of GMTV had even asked me to give her a quote for a refurbishment of her city crash pad. And now here I was, lying in Anna's floral spare room, my daughter beside me, and dealing with the knowledge that my mother never really loved me because I cried a lot.

I stared at Maggie and I couldn't resist lifting her from her Moses basket and cuddling her close to me. I didn't know what the future held for us. I didn't know that she wouldn't one day become a mad colicky screaming brat and that my head wouldn't explode and I'd get an awful dose of depression myself.

But I knew that if I did, if that did happen, I'd do my damned best to sort it out and not let it fester for years.

I felt sad for my mother, sad for her experiences but also bloody angry. Mothers are not supposed to act like that. In thirty-one years she hadn't sorted her head out. What made me think that she would now, just because I was a mother myself?

"You look tired, love," Anna said as she poured me a cup of tea. "Did this little madam keep you up all night?"

"She was as good as gold. Just two feeds and went straight back off after." I cooed down at Maggie. Was that a hint of smile on her face or just wind? I liked to think it was a smile. "But yes, I am tired. I've been thinking a lot of things through."

"Your hormones are all over the place right now, but I promise you all of this will get easier. Don't give in to bad feelings. You are dealing with a lot, but stay strong and give it a little time.

I nodded. "I'll stay a week."

"Or two," Anna said. "You know this house will be lonely without you."

I smiled, reaching out for her hand. "You'll never be lonely, Anna. Sure I'll never be off the phone. How else am I going to learn how to be the best mammy in the world?"

She smiled, and lifted her chart.

"Now," she said with a wicked grin, "I know you aren't going to like this, but Joe phoned earlier. He wants us to come over for dinner with him and Queen Jacqueline tomorrow."

"Can I change my mind about leaving?" I deadpanned.

"What, and not fulfil the 'wipe the smug grin off Jacqueline's face' part of the chart?"

She had a point.

Driving into Joe and Jacqueline's perfect estate (or should I say 'housing development' as estate was just "so working class" according to Jacqueline), I could almost smell the money. Sure enough it was just buttons compared to the financial dealings of our clients in Richmond, but compared to me and my flat above the shop this was luxury living.

The lawns were all perfectly, uniformly manicured. The hint of frost on the grass made it all look just so ethereal and dreamy. This was luxury living, Derry style, and my mother was hugely proud of how well her son had done.

Parking in my brother's driveway, in front of their double garage, their brand-new people carrier, I breathed in deeply.

Dinner with Joe and Jacqueline – my idea of hell – and yet, I knew if I was to make the most of this time at home at all I would have to face my demons, and demons don't come any bigger or nastier than my sister-in-law.

Anna lifted Maggie from the car while I straightened down my top. I'd done my best to look presentable but there was no way that I would have been able to fit into the one or two designer items that I owned from my pre-pregnancy days. However, I reminded myself, it was a miracle I wasn't still wearing my maternity clothes.

I pushed a stray curl behind my ear and walked to the door, glancing down at my daughter and praying she would behave herself for the next two hours.

I rang the doorbell and Jacqueline answered, in a perfect cream linen suit, standing on her cream carpet with her cream walls surrounding her. I wondered if she allowed her child to touch her or anything around her for fear of him leaving a mark.

"How absolutely delightful to see you," she chimed and both Anna and I made an unconvincing "Hmmm" sound in unison. "Do come in, but could you leave your shoes at the door?" she said before walking ahead of us up the hall towards the kitchen.

"The decontamination chamber is on your left," Anna stage-whispered in the same clipped tones Jacqueline used, "and your sterile overalls are in the vestibule to the right."

I bit back a giggle as I kicked off my shoes and donned the slippers available, and continued to the kitchen where Jacqueline had taken a seat at the breakfast bar. Odhran was sitting on the floor, piecing together a puzzle, and Joe was wearing an apron emblazoned with the words "*All this . . . and he cooks*" while he cooked up a storm on their cream range in the middle of their cream Shaker style kitchen.

Whatever I thought of my sister-in-law, she obviously had the two men in her life trained well.

"Odhran, look who's here!" Joe cheered and his son looked up – rather blankly – at me. In fairness it had been a while since he had seen his Auntie Aoife and I was a stranger to him. He looked at Anna and smiled, running to give her a cuddle, and then peeped his head over the edge of the car seat.

"My mummy has one of those in her tummy," he said proudly as Jacqueline smiled beatifically, one hand resting on her growing bump.

I fought the urge very hard to reply: "Yes, but your mummy's baby has horns and answers to the name of Damien."

"Yes, that's right," Jacqueline said. "Mummy and Daddy are having another little baby together, aren't we?"

She was smiling, but she was spitting pure venom. Mummy and Daddy. Another baby together. Bitch.

I started to hope there would be no sharp cutlery on the dining-table or I wouldn't be responsible for my actions.

"So," Jacqueline said as she took her place at the top of the table, "Mum tells me you're going to be going back to work quite soon."

"Your mum? How does she know?" I stuttered.

Jacqueline laughed, throwing her head in exaggerated glee. "Oh sorry, when I say 'Mum' I'm talking about your mother. Joe and I decided it would be nice for her to have me calling her Mum after all these years. After all, I'm like a daughter to her."

I looked at Anna who shrugged her shoulders to let me know she hadn't been aware that my mother had in fact developed maternal instincts towards someone other than me.

"That must be nice," I said.

Jacqueline grinned. "Oh, it is. She was absolutely delighted."

Yes, Jacqueline was like a daughter to my mother, the daughter she never had.

Joe cleared his throat and walked to the table where he set down a roast chicken and started to carve. For the briefest of seconds I wished I was the chicken.

We survived the dinner, but simply because I soon realised that having a baby could have its benefits. Shortly after dessert I made my excuses that I really had to be going because I wanted to get Maggie settled down for the night.

"But don't you want a wee look at our spare room?" Jacqueline had asked.

"No, we'd rather sleep back in Anna's. All our things are there."

"No, I don't think you understand me," Jacqueline said. "I was wondering if you could come up with a few ideas for our nursery."

I looked at her, giving her a kind of death stare, and then turned to Anna. "Come on, Auntie Anna, I'm really, really tired now."

And we left.

No doubt this would not curry favour with my mum (or should I say Jacqueline's mum?) but I didn't care. For the love of God, I was a new mother, I didn't need this annoyance. I had enough annoyances in my life as it was.

The following week passed in a flurry of sameness. Joe and Jacqueline didn't invite us back to their cream house and my mother didn't thaw. She would hold Maggie and occasionally coo in her direction but she felt no more affection for her than she did the neighbour's dog. She felt even less for me. She would talk to me, be courteous even, but the conversation rarely extended beyond the weather. If she saw me wince as I tried to latch my daughter on to my breast she would mutter about bottles. If a nappy needed changing she would leave the room or encourage me to go upstairs to do it. We didn't even have the usual safe topic of my work to turn to. I wasn't doing anything at that moment to make her proud. There were no yoga rooms to talk about, no TV presenter homes to boast to her neighbours about. There was just me and my baby and the problematic lack of a partner.

We went through the motions – me trying to engage her in conversation, her answering in monosyllabic sentences, and all the while my mind was thinking of that lack of the partner and the fact that if I could go home, Jake could well be waiting to see me. God, I wanted to see him. I wanted to make at least one aspect of my life better.

When my two weeks were up, and my progress no further forward, I went back to London and for all intents and purposes it felt as if I was going home. Yes, I cried when I kissed Anna goodbye. I didn't relish the thought of doing this alone. I had become used to her support. I had loved that she had taken Maggie overnight on several occasions to allow me a good sleep. When I was feeding, she would bring me glasses of water to make sure I stayed hydrated and when the hormonal rages came, she would hug me while I cried and help me feel more human.

She was Maggie's surrogate daddy and I felt secure with her. I just wasn't sure how I would manage without that help – but I knew I would have to as chances were I was going to be alone for a long time.

I couldn't rely on Anna my whole life and I had to face it that the majority of my life was waiting for me back in London. So with mixed emotions of fear, excitement, dread and relief I boarded the plane.

24

Aoife

The High Street seemed really noisy that first morning. Maggie had woken me at six thirty demanding to be fed and once I had satisfied her hunger I decided it was high time to satisfy my own. I showered and dressed, pulling my hair back in a pony-tail and scraping a little make-up onto my face. Once I was ready I dressed Maggie and we set out for our walk up the road to Mrs Morelli's.

We had got home quite late the previous night. Although Dan had offered to pick us up from the airport I'd braved a taxi. If I had survived my mother for seventeen days I could certainly survive a half-hour run in a London cab.

It had been blissful to step through the doors of the shop. Everything was reassuringly the same. The daybed still sat in the corner, a purple shot-silk throw cast over it, scatter cushions making it seem all the more inviting. The same prints and paintings hung on the wall and the same display of trinkets sat on the large wooden dresser. Of course Matilda was there, illuminated by her usual light, smiling down at me.

"Nice to see you too," I muttered as we made our way past up to the flat.

Beth had obviously been round earlier. My fridge was stocked with fresh milk, cheese and ham and there was a freshly bought crusty loaf on the worktop. A king-size bar of Galaxy sat beside it with a scrawled note. *Thought you might need this. Will chat in the morning. Can't wait to see Maggie. Love you both (Auntie) Beth xx"*

Walking into my living-room, my gorgeous, eclectic, messy living-room I felt myself breathe out for the first time in two weeks. I would deal with Jake come morning, but for now I was going to sleep and enjoy it. I was home.

The March air whipped about us as we walked up the street for breakfast. I might not have solved all my problems in Derry – hell, I might not even have solved any of them – but I definitely felt a little bit more in control now.

As I reached Morelli's, a man, the same man who had seen me snivelling like a wet hankie two weeks before, walked in front of me and opened the door.

"Here you go," he said, holding it for me to push the pram through.

I smiled a thank you before quickly moving to my seat. My face reddened at the memory of that last encounter. I had been all snotters and ugly tears – not to mention I hadn't showered or washed my hair in a couple of days and my body had been leaking fluid from every orifice.

He walked to the counter, momentarily glancing back at me and smiling, and I realised he had more than likely remembered our last encounter too. I was about to crawl under the table to hide when I heard Mrs Morelli's unmistakeable Italian accent boom towards me.

"Eeva, you are back, and you have the *bella bambina* with you!" She walked towards us, her hands outstretched to welcome me into a hug. "Stand up so I can get a look at you," she ordered and I obeyed, because let's face it, it would take a braver woman than me to argue with Mrs Morelli. "My goodness, Eeva, you look wonderful! But you are fading to nothing. Quick, I'll get you a Full English now!" She shouted to her husband to put on the house special before turning her attention to Maggie, who was wide-eyed with wonder at this magnificently matronly woman. "She is so big, and you are so small," she said to me. "You are obviously, you know, breast-feeding, yes?" She squeezed her own buxom bosom at this statement and I heard a snort of laughter from the man at the counter. I gave him my best glare and he at least had the decency to look embarrassed. Much like myself, if I'm honest.

"Yes, I'm breast-feeding," I responded, "at least until I go back to work."

"Yes, it has been very busy at your shop. Poor Beth has been there day and night. She looks worn out, poor thing."

"I'm sure she's fine," I chided. "At least she gets a good night's sleep each night! But I'll talk to her anyway."

"You know I worry about you girls," Mrs Morelli said, sitting down for the long haul. "So tell me about Ireland. Was your mama okay with the news?"

"She is coming round," I sighed. "Taking her time about it, but she will get there in the end. I just couldn't stay away from here forever. I needed your breakfasts for starters," I smiled, as the much-maligned Mr Morelli set a plate of bacon, sausages, eggs and toast in front of me.

"This looks delicious," I said, tucking in.

"And I thought the Irish fed you well," Mrs Morelli said. "Nothing beats a Full English, eh?" She rubbed my cheek as if I were a baby myself, and stood up to get on with her day's work.

At the same time the man at the counter lifted his takeaway coffee and pastry and made for the door.

"She's right, you know. You do look amazing now."

And he left, while I sat there, mouth gaping open, sausage speared on my fork.

A hoot of laughter sounded, this time from Old Man Morelli. "Eeva, I think he likes you!"

I shook my head, but I didn't speak because, for probably the first time in my life, I was speechless.

The one thing I could give Jake was that he did always tell me I looked amazing. Even when I had just woken up and my auburn mass was in dire need of the frizz-eaze and my face had creases from the pillow, he would look at me, his eyes filled with desire, and say: "Shit, Aoifs, you are the mutt's nuts!"

Perhaps some women would have preferred more poetic language, but the mutt's nuts worked for me. Despite his aspirations to be the next George Michael ("although, obviously not gay" as he would deadpan to hoots of his own laughter time and time again) when it came to lyrics and when it came to straight talking he called a spade a spade – and indeed a dog's testicle a dog's testicle.

It had therefore been a long time, nine months to be precise, since a man had paid me such a compliment.

Having eaten my breakfast, I walked home. So I looked amazing? I wasn't sure I bought it. Not now anyway. Carrying Maggie up the stairs, barely even registering the fact that Beth wasn't at work yet, I placed her in her crib and stood in front of the mirror to size myself up.

Here I was. Average height. Hair, admittedly quite shiny thanks to washing it the day before. Skin, relatively clear – the post-baby break-out finally clearing.

I had to say it, my breasts looked magnificent beneath my jumper – all firm, rounded and exceptionally womanly. I am woman, hear me purr . . .

Stomach – could do with some attention, but thankfully my just-washed (Size 14) jeans still had a bit of stiffness about them which hugged in the worst offending areas.

Bum, not bad – still, I hoped to get back down to a Size 12 but I'd just given birth. I had to give myself a break.

All in all, not bad. So why I did what I did next is beyond me entirely. Instead of leaving that general impression of 'not bad', I stripped down to my underwear. After all, if I truly looked amazing then surely some man, somewhere, would some day want to see how truly amazing I looked in my pants.

Face and hair were both the same in my semi-naked state, so I started my analysis with the chest area. My heavy cotton nursing bra strained to hold in my heaving chest, veiny and blotchy with the trauma of breastfeeding.

In the coolness of the room my nipples should have been standing proudly to attention through my reinforced bra, instead two white discs – breast-pads – covered them, giving me the appearance of a nippleless Barbie Doll. If only I had her waist. Further down, I saw a map of reddish stretch-marks creep up over the top of my belly-warming passion-killer pants. No, I couldn't face my thongs and bikini panties just yet, so my comfy for pregnancy M&S Size 16 baggy, saggy white full briefs completed the look – almost.

Further down, an unkempt pant moustache of hair crept out the side of my briefs, showing a neglected bikini line.

And then, just when I thought it couldn't get any worse, I started to laugh and it all started to wobble. Yep, this was me.

I was fecking amazing.

I heard the bell above the door ring downstairs and expected Beth to come thundering up the stairs, so I threw my clothes back on – went back to looking 'not that bad' – and cooed at Maggie. "Auntie Beth is here!"

Her face lit up, a smile, most probably wind, danced across it.

However the stairs remained quiet and I wondered had I imagined the tinkle of the bell.

I walked to my door. "Hello?" I called, suddenly panicking that perhaps I'd forgotten to lock the door behind me in my haste to get naked in front of the mirror, that the man from Morelli's was in fact an axe-murderer who had come to finish me off. Matilda was proving to be a very inefficient guardian angel. There was no reply, and I called again. My mind was whirring. I knew I shouldn't go down the steps. Not unarmed anyway.

"Hello, anyone there?" I called a third time and a tiny, desperate voice called back.

"It's only me!"

25

Beth

I didn't have any symptoms that month. No sore boobs. No metallic taste in my mouth. No cramping low down. I had discussed my symptomless state on my website with what Dan referred to as my imaginary friends and we had wondered if my lack of symptoms could in fact be a symptom in itself.

This was different. This felt different because there was nothing there to allow me to convince myself a fertilised egg was bedding in for the summer. Why I allowed myself to get my hopes up then is beyond me.

Each morning I would look at my calendar, counting down those 14 days and mentally ticking each of them off. Technically after 11 days I could buy a First Response test and give it a whirl, but I didn't want to. I wanted to hold on to the dream that this could be it for a couple of extra days. I could be strong when I wanted to be. I could hold off until the day my period was due and if I did that then I wouldn't be jinxing yet another month.

It was funny how I had these routines and superstitions. I liked to think I did everything the same each month, but if I'm honest I always varied it a little because perhaps each little variation held the key to our success.

I'd tried to stay calm, not to read anything into anything but when I posted on the web about my experiences a flurry of support messages flooded through.

"Good luck, Betsy-Boo. This has to be your month," one wrote.

"Keeping everything crossed for a 'positive' outcome for you," wrote another.

I allowed these posters to raise my hopes – even though I knew from bitter experience it was unlikely that all the good wishes in the world would make a blind bit of difference to me and my dodgy womb.

Then it was Thursday, and I lay listening to the rain beat off the window pane. Dan was sleeping still, his body wrapped up in the duvet, his face crumpled by the pillow. He looked kind of troubled, so I reached over and kissed him lightly on the cheek. He muttered something almost inaudible and rolled over, pulling the duvet over him.

I padded out of bed and to the window where I looked out to see the grey sky looking down on the cars which drove past on their way to work and school. By now Aoife and Maggie would be home. I looked forward to seeing them. It had surprised me just how much I had missed my best friend. I suppose it hadn't really been a surprise that I missed her daughter. My heart fluttered a little at the thought of cuddling Maggie close to me and breathing in her gorgeous baby smell, feeling the softness of her skin. It was a bittersweet feeling. When holding her the hole in my heart started to close over just slightly, but I knew the moment I handed her back to her mother – and saw the look that only they as mother and daughter could share – that my heart would hollow out again.

I sighed and walked to the bathroom to run the shower.

Glancing in the mirror I saw a tired face stare back at me. I was pale, my blonde hair hung limply around my face which was still puffy from my night's sleep. I splashed some water on to my face and stared again at the mirror which was starting to steam up. I could do this, I could get through today.

I started to strip off, peeling off my pink vest top and my stripey pyjama bottoms. There it was. The blood.

Another month gone. Another failure. Another fucking disappointment to pile on the disappointment. My lack of symptoms – how could I have been so stupid to think they could have meant anything other than the fact that once again my body had let me down. I felt my stomach start to cramp and my heart start to break.

I looked again, hoping I was wrong. I hoped there was nothing there. I couldn't see this again. I didn't want to do this again. I couldn't feel like this again.

Tears started to slide down my face. Hot angry tears as I stood there naked in the steamy bathroom. A sob, which I had buried down for the past few weeks, erupted from my throat and I fell to my knees. This was not fair. Why could this not happen for us? Did I not deserve this? Had I done something wrong? Was I a bad person? The sobs came thick and fast as I sat there, knees curled up to my chest, fist in my mouth to muffle the sound of my crying. I rocked back and forth, like a demented escapee from a madhouse.

I'm not sure how long I sat there, but when I looked up Dan was standing in the doorway looking at me with a mixture of pity and what I could only read as contempt.

"Yes," I snarled. "It's all over for another month. But hey, nothing is wrong. We are both perfectly fucking capable of having a baby, aren't we?"

I didn't mean to hurt him. I didn't mean to lash out, but I couldn't help it. Why should I be the only one to sit on the floor, tears pouring from me along with all traces of my dignity?

"It's not my fault," he said, a note of resignation in his voice.

"So it's mine then?" I shouted, standing up, shaking with rage, disappointment and hurt.

"I didn't say that."

"But you thought it. You fucking thought it, didn't you?" I gestured widely, knocking the glass of water which had been sitting on the window ledge crashing to the floor. The noise reverberated around the room, but it wasn't enough to bring me to my senses.

"I didn't think it," he said calmly.

"Don't lie to me, Dan. I've seen how you look at me. I've seen how you look at Aoife, who got pregnant at the drop of her knickers, and I know you blame me."

"Get a grip," he said, still calm – almost resigned to my outburst.

And before I realised just what I was doing I had gone too far. I slapped Dan, square across the face.

He stared at me with shock in his eyes and I stood there, amid the broken glass, shaking and crying.

"This can't go on, Beth," he said. "I can't do this any more."

"Oh fuck off then! Do a Jake – except at least he managed to get his girlfriend up the duff!"

"Enough, Beth," Dan said, his face reddening not only with the imprint of my hand but now with anger. "Enough. Enough. Enough! What the hell has happened to you? I can't be with you like this. I can't do this every month."

"I said leave then," I answered, but my voice wasn't quite so angry now. My rage was fading and being replaced with pure and deep fear. I'd done it now. I'd pushed him too far.

He looked at me, and in that moment I realised just how pathetic I must have looked to him.

"I'm sorry, Dan, I'm so sorry!" I reached out to him, longing for him to hold me in his arms and to comfort me. I longed for him to tuck me into bed and bring my chocolate and Nurofen and rub my stomach until the cramps subsided.

He didn't respond. He didn't pull me to him. He just turned away.

"Have your shower, Beth. I have to go to work. We'll talk about this tonight."

26

Aoife

I don't to this day understand why I didn't hear that she was crying. I ran back to the bedroom, lifted Maggie from her crib and went downstairs – a grin across my face, eager to see Beth's reaction to my pudgy gorgeous growing baby girl.

She was sitting there, on the daybed, the shutters still down outside and her face soaked with tears. Mascara coursed down her cheeks, her lipstick was smudged and she looked as if she had been on the drink all night.

In hindsight, my walking into the room, grinning like a buck eejit, shouting "Ta-*daa*!" was poorly timed.

I almost dropped Maggie with the shock of seeing Beth like that. Yes, she was a soppy cow who cried at the drop of the hat but these were proper heart-sore tears.

This was not because she had stubbed her toe or left a collage at home – not this time.

"Jesus, are you okay?" I said, rushing over to her, trying to hug her and hold on to Maggie at the same time.

She sniffed, nodding her head.

"Are you sure?" I asked.

She nodded again, between the gasping sobs.

"Really sure?"

At that she shook her head and caved in towards me, sobbing onto my shoulder. Maggie, alarmed that for once the wailing wasn't coming from her, or me for that matter, joined in and I sat there completely bewildered, soothing them both.

When the avalanche of tears started to dry Beth stood up, walked towards the counter and started pulling tissues and make-up from her bag.

"Heather will be here soon. I can't let her see me like this." "What's wrong, Beth? Did you have a row with Dan? Are you sick? Have you gambled all our money away so that we have to go on the game? Because frankly my body's not up to much these days."

"Nor's mine," she said dejectedly, wiping her streaked make-up off.

Confusion must have been written all over my face as she turned to me, took a deep breath and said: "I'm fine, honest. It's just a horrible bout of PMT. You know what a wreck I am when my period arrives." Her voice wavered a little.

"You sure?"

"I'm sure," she replied, slicking on some lip-gloss. "Now let me see my gorgeous girl."

And Beth was back – happy, smiley, reliable Beth.

I would be lying if I said the episode didn't unsettle me. All sorts of scenarios ran through my head, especially the thought that perhaps something could be up with her and Dan. I liked things to be nice and simple in my world. My mum was forever to be strange, Anna was forever to be kind and squashy to hug and Beth – Beth was always, absolutely always supposed to be deliriously in love with Dan.

I'd spent time with this couple, from the days when they would snog in public and perhaps even feel each other up because they were just so young and in love they couldn't help it, right through to the stage where they bumped along nicely together, the shining example of what I wanted in a relationship.

Surely I had to be getting this all wrong. Maybe Beth did just have horrendous PMT. After all, Mrs Morelli had told me just how tired she was lately and the shop was exceptionally busy. I promised myself to do more. When Maggie slept I could saunter down the stairs and help Beth with ideas for schemes and proposals. I could answer the phone when necessary, freeing up time for Heather to accompany Beth out to clients.

I wasn't ready to give up this most precious of times with Maggie just yet – and if I'm honest I wasn't physically up to giving my maternity leave up for good – but I could eek a bit of time out for Beth – surely that was the least I could do.

When Maggie was sleeping, I lifted her monitor and walked down the stairs to tell Beth of my plan. She was sitting at her desk, staring into space. Mrs Morelli was right, Beth did look tired.

"Hey, sweetie, are you okay?" I asked.

"I'm always okay," she said, still staring. "How are you?"

"Grand."

"So was Ireland really that bad?"

"It wasn't the worst. I mean I didn't really expect much from Mum and she delivered that not very much for me."

"She'll come round though."

"Aye, some time in the future I'm sure she will. I don't really want to think about it too much though."

And I didn't. While I felt as though a giant weight had been lifted off my shoulders when I made the decision to come back and get on with my life, there was a wee part of me screaming inside that it wasn't fair. I pulled up a seat beside Beth and sat down.

Beth would usually have started chattering away by now, telling me everything from what went on at her latest appointment to what Dan had for tea the night before, but she sat, still staring, twiddling a sample of fabric in the fingers of her left hand. Her eyes were dark, shaded circles showing just how much she had been crying.

"You might hate me for asking this," I started, "but is everything okay with you and Dan?"

"You would love it if it weren't, wouldn't you?" she snapped. "Ever since you split up with Jake you can't abide to see me happy, but sorry to disappoint you, Aoife, everything is just fucking peachy, thank you."

"I didn't . . . I wouldn't . . . I can't believe . . ." My mouth flapped open and closed, no sound coming out.

Of all the shocks of the last year, this was perhaps the biggest. I just could not believe for one second that Beth would think I intentionally wished her and Dan anything other than happiness. Tears stung in my eyes and I was just about to launch into a snottery sobby chorus of why it was exceptionally unfair of Beth to even let that thought cross her mind, even for one wee tiny second, when the bell above the door pinged and Beth jumped to attention for our customer. I, on the other hand, walked back upstairs and sat with my head in my hands, wondering what the hell had just happened.

The night Beth and Dan had got engaged, I had cried buckets of happy tears. Jake had been quite worried at one point and kept telling me to pull myself together. I doubt I have ever been so happy for two people. They deserved to be together and to have the best that life could offer them.

Beth and I had guzzled champagne and giggled over the ring all night while Jake had taken great joy in referring to Dan as the condemned man.

Every detail of their wedding had been discussed at length on the daybed, from the chair covers to the fairy lights twinkling overhead at the marquee. Dan had joked that I knew so much about the wedding that it was a wonder Beth hadn't invited me on the honeymoon with them.

"No offence, Irish," he had said, nuzzling into Beth's neck one night, "but I want the future Mrs Jones to myself for those two weeks."

"Apart from all the phone calls I'll make," Beth had giggled.

"Who said you'll have a chance to get near a phone?" Dan had countered with a cheeky grin and the two of them melted into each other's arms.

And that's how it always had been and my stupid grin in response to their general in-love-ness had always been there.

I didn't want them to split up. I wanted them to be happy but I didn't think any more, or even one wee second, that everything was just fucking peachy, thank you.

The kettle was boiling when I heard a knock at the door and then Beth's voice call out, asking if she could come in for a chat.

I grunted a response – not very adult of me, I'll admit – but I had to show her how hurt I was.

"I'm sorry," she said as she walked into the kitchen.

"And so you should be. How could you think such a thing?"

"I don't. At least I don't think I do. I don't know what I think any more."

"Beth, please talk to me. Whatever it is, it can't be that bad."

She shook her head, opened her mouth as if she was about to say something and then shook her head again. "I'm just really tired, Aoife. I never realised how tough running this place on my own would be."

"But you have Heather?" I offered, lifting an extra cup from the cupboard and dropping a tea bag into it.

"She's a nice enough girl, but the words chocolate and fireguard

195

come to mind. She just doesn't get my vision the way you do, Aoif."

"Look, I've been thinking," I said, adding the milk to the cups. "I'm going to help out more. Maggie is still sleeping a stupid amount of the time, and there is no reason why she can't sleep in her pram and I can answer the phones, do a little ordering or help you discuss projects."

Beth nodded. "That would help. God, how pathetic am I? I can't even cope with running the business on my own for a month."

"No harm in asking for a bit of support, sweetie. God knows I've had your ear bent enough over the last year."

I handed her a cup of tea, and she smiled a watery half smile.

"Can we please be friends," she said, "and can you forget what an awful bitch I was just then?"

"Of course, Beth." I answered, and all was right with the world again.

So we sat down and I launched into chapter and verse about my pant moustache and the growing bags under my eyes from the lack of sleep.

Later that evening, when Beth had gone home and I had managed to survive another breast-feed without having someone to run and fetch me water and chocolate, I decided it was time to stir things up.

It had been approximately thirty-seven minutes since I'd allowed a thought of Jake to run through my head so I knew it was time for action. I was back in London. He was, I guessed, also in London and there was no reason therefore in my mind why the pair of us could not be in London together. He had a right, nay an obligation, to meet his daughter and I too had a right to stand over him looking 'not bad' and boasting about how magnificently we were coping without him.

The only fly in the Sudocrem was that I kind of needed Dan to do that initial bit of detective work for me again. I had sent a text to Jake as soon as we had touched back down on English soil and so far had heard nothing, but I knew Dan would at least be able to get a message to a third party who could in turn contact Jake and get him to pull the finger out and come over and see us.

However, given that I was now concerned that Dan could well be in the same highly emotional state as Beth, I didn't want to act as though I didn't give two flying fecks. I would have to approach this carefully indeed.

I picked up the phone and dialled Dan's number. He answered, his voice as chirpy as always.

"Hey, Dan. It's Aoife. How are you?" In my best Denise Richards from *This Morning* caring voice.

"Hey, Irish," he said back, not a hint of emotional turmoil in his voice. "Nice to have you back. Things are fine here, busy as always, you know the *craic*."

Dan loved the word *craic* and used it whenever he could. In fact he was one of the few English people who could use it without sounding as if they were trying too hard. Dan would not use the word *craic* unless things were okay in his world.

I was now more confused than ever. In fact, I was so confused that his jovialness kind of threw me. I had planned to have my sympathetic head on my shoulders for the duration of this phone call. Now it would seem I didn't need it. Perhaps Beth was just overtired after all.

"So, Dan, you probably know why I'm phoning."

"Before you start, sweetheart, I spoke to Jake this morning. He's off in Germany at the moment, but will be back in a few days. He does want to see you – but I'm saying this as your friend, remember what a wanker he is. You don't have to see him if you don't want to."

"He's the father of my child, Dan. He has rights."

"Any man who can walk away from his child has no rights in my mind," Dan seethed.

"Imagine you saying that, in your big Fancy Dan lawyer's office!" I smiled. "What would your bosses say?"

"Just my opinion, Aoife. You, and Maggie, are better off without him. He's a fecking gobshite."

Bless Dan's little heart, he could even swear in Irish. "I know, Dan. But we need to sort this out. There is so much unfinished business between us, not least Maggie. All I've ever wanted out of this is one more chance to chat."

"Okay, I'll tell him to ring you and make the appropriate arrangements. I can be there, Beth can too, if you want. You don't have to do this alone."

"Thanks, but I'm a big girl now and as my darling mother has said, I've made my bed. I might as well lie in it."

"Well, you know where we are if you change your mind."

I smiled. It was nice to feel loved, but that nagging feeling still wouldn't go away. "Dan," I asked, "is everything okay with Beth? She seems a little down today."

He sighed, one of those bottom-of-your-boots sighs that let you know without doubt that you are about to be lied to. "She is fine, Aoife. Just tired."

"You would tell me if something was wrong? I mean, I know I'm a hormonal time-bomb at the moment, but if there is anything I can do?"

"She's just tired, Aoife, honestly. She needs to take it easier."

I knew not to push it any more so we said our goodbyes and I realised that I was officially done with maternity leave. Beth needed me almost as much as the wee woman sleeping in the Moses basket did.

27

Beth

I was perhaps losing the plot. I rubbed my eyes, staring at the computer screen again and again without seeing what was glaring at me from the screen.

I had managed to offend Aoife, break a glass, throw a mental hissy fit and slap Dan. Jesus, I had slapped Dan. Did that make me a husband-beater? I have never raised my hand to him ever, ever before. I have never raised my hand to anyone. I can't explain it. A red mist descended and I wasn't in control any more. This was not right. Nothing about this was right.

I was used to getting what I wanted and what I worked for. I grew up relatively privileged – my own room, my own phone, my own car when I turned seventeen. But my parents had also taught me to work hard to reap rewards, so I did it. I played the good girl. I studied hard, worked hard and I got my rewards. I had my business, my flash car and my gorgeous apartment. I didn't feel guilty about what I had because I knew everything was hard won.

So why now, when I was working hard at it and doing everything the right way, wasn't I getting the one thing I really wanted?

I wanted to stomp my feet with the unfairness of it all.

I had hit him. I can't believe I had hit him. He was the one person I didn't want to hurt. He was the one person who knew how much I wanted this and he was the one person who wanted it just as much as me. I couldn't have felt more wretched if he had come and hit me himself.

His eyes had been so cold as he walked out of the flat. I had seen it creep in. I had seen the sympathy waver and the contempt increase. This was no good. This was not how it was supposed to be. Dan was supposed to be my rock and here I was pushing him away.

"You stupid fucking bitch!" I chided myself, a little too loudly and just in time to see Tom Austin standing in front of me, a quizzical look on his face.

"Jesus, do you never knock?" I blurted.

"I didn't think I needed to knock in a shop," he smiled and I felt myself blush.

"Well, can I help you?" I stuttered, trying and failing to hide my embarrassment.

"I just wanted to ask if you could put some of my leaflets in the shop. Business is a little quiet given the time of year."

I nodded. "Okay, if you advertise us in return."

"It's a deal," he said, outstretching a strong, rough hand to me. I noticed there was a single-stem ivory rose in his other hand – and I started to blush even more furiously.

"I'm married, you know," I said, shaking his hand.

"That's lovely," he said, his face once again a picture of confusion.

I glanced downwards at the rose and his face reddened.

"Oh this," he said. "Erm, sorry, but could you leave this for your friend? The one with the baby? I saw her in the coffee shop earlier so I know she is back. I thought she could do with a little confidence boost."

If ever there was a moment when I wished the ground would open up and swallow me whole, or that aliens would abduct me, or that the world would come to an end in a cataclysmic explosion of immense proportion – that was that moment.

"Of course," I stuttered. "I'll give to her later. She's upstairs with the baby now. Her baby. She has a baby. But you know that, you saw the baby. But she's not married. Not that you have to be married these days. Well, she would have loved to be married but . . ."

Tom was laughing now, a hearty laugh that cut through my babbling and made me laugh uproariously too.

"You have a very pretty smile," he said.

I grinned back at him, just before looking over his shoulder to see a rather unimpressed Dan standing in the doorway.

"Dan," I said, ignoring the fact that the first thing I should be saying to him was sorry, "this is Tom, the mad stalker guy I was telling you about."

Tom looked at me, laughing all the harder which of course made me take a fit of the giggles I couldn't quite shake.

"I mean, the gardener. He is the gardener – from Gardiner Street – isn't that good? Imagine? I wonder if there is an Instant Karma Street?"

"Are you drunk?" Dan deadpanned, and the laughter that had been pouring from me stepped up a notch.

"I'm sorry," Tom said. "It's my fault. I came to ask this lady, who I'm guessing is your wife, if she would display some leaflets for my business."

Dan glanced down at the rose, his eyebrow raised just that little bit.

"Oh this," Tom said "is for the lady who lives upstairs. The one with the baby?"

"The one with the baby," I repeated as tears of laughter coursed down my cheeks.

28

Aoife

The sound of laughter intrigued me. Maggie was having a little kick about in her Moses basket so I lifted the monitor and padded down the stairs. When I opened the door I saw Beth and a stranger – no, not a stranger, the man from the coffee shop who told me I was amazing – laughing as if Dan, who looked pissed off, had just told them the funniest joke in the world. I glanced at Matilda – she seemed to have a sly smile on her face.

They didn't notice me at first, and I stood and watched them. It was such a stark contrast to earlier when Beth had been almost inconsolable with misery. It dawned on me it was a stark contrast to how Beth had been generally over the last few weeks, or maybe even months.

Coffee Shop Man noticed me first. He stopped laughing, but kept smiling and put his hand out to Beth's shoulder to let her know someone else had entered the room. The gesture seemed to make Dan look even more pissed off.

"Is everything okay down here?" I asked.

Beth and Mr Coffee Shop nodded, red-faced, while Dan said nothing, choosing to stare at his shoes instead.

"Hi," Mr Coffee Shop said, waving a single ivory rose in my direction.

I was confused, very confused. I felt as if I was walking into some weird and sick soap opera where nothing made sense any more. Was there something going on between Beth and this handsome stranger? Did that explain what I had seen earlier that day? My brain was running at ninety miles a minute, jumping to every conclusion in the book. I must have looked demented as I stared from one to the other of them, trying to make some sense of it all.

Both Beth and Mr Coffee Shop started laughing again, and Dan looked on completely bemused.

"Could someone please, for the love of God, explain to me what is going on?" I demanded.

"I haven't a bloody clue," Beth squeaked while Mr Coffee Shop rested his hand on the counter, using the other to rub his aching ribs.

"This man, Tom, is here to drop off some leaflets and give you a flower apparently," Dan interjected, his face like thunder. "And as for Beth, well, I don't bloody think she knows anything any more. She certainly doesn't know how to act like a grown-up."

With that he turned and walked out the door.

The laughter stopped.

All I could do was stand and stare, open-mouthed.

The man with the rose, Tom, blushed and said he would call back later. He put the rose on the counter and I noticed a petal fall to the floor and blow across the room as the door opened and closed and he left.

"Do you want to tell me what's going on?" I eventually said to the top of Beth's head as she sat gazing at the floor.

She looked up, her eyes watery, and lifted a pencil and began to draw.

"I have a lot of work to do, Aoife. Why don't you go and see if Maggie is okay? I'm sure I heard a little squeak there."

"Beth, what is going on?"

"Nothing. Nothing at all. Everything is fine. There are no problems. There is no reason for anything not to be perfect so if you don't mind, I'll just get on with this."

I looked at her, silently imploring her to open up to me, then glancing at Matilda imploring her to intervene, but the silence continued. I sighed, lifted the rose from the counter and carried it upstairs.

Something very weird was going on and I didn't like it one bit.

I walked to the kitchen and took a tall glass from the cupboard and filled it with water. Sitting it, and the rose, on the windowsill I wondered what on earth had just happened. Why was a virtual stranger giving me a flower and what the hell was going on with Beth and Dan?

Texting Dan, I told him he could talk to me any time. I then sent the same text to Beth before sitting down and holding Maggie close to me, enjoying the warmth of her. I breathed in her soft, baby smell and kissed her head. It felt okay, in that moment, to have one person at least who would always love me and who I could protect as best as I could for as long as I could.

It was a good thing I wasn't waiting for Beth to come and apologise because five o'clock came and went and she didn't come anywhere near me. I heard the door rattle and the shutters come down and looked out the window in time to see her pull off in the car.

This had been the strangest of days and just for a moment – and trust me it was the briefest of moments – I almost wished I was still back in Derry. At least it made sense there. Sort of.

I gazed at my phone. I hoped for a text from Beth, or Dan, or even Jake. It mocked me silently, peeping into life only once at ten with a message from Anna wishing me sweet dreams. I already missed her desperately.

Maggie woke, mewling softly, and I walked to the kitchen to get a glass of water to have by my side while I fed her. The rose was there, its petals open wide. Yes, this had been a very strange day indeed, so I did what I always did in such circumstances – lifted the phone and called Anna. Unusually she wasn't in and I found myself talking to her answerphone.

"Anna, it's Aoife. I just wanted to have a wee chat. Maggie misses you dreadfully. I kind of miss you too. Things are a bit mad here. I'm going to go back to work. Don't worry, only part-time and I'll be able to keep Maggie with me. Oh, and I got a rose from a handsome stranger. It's gone ten thirty, so I'm off to bed soon but call me in the morning if you get a chance. Love you."

I hung up and settled down into bed. Maggie was lying beside me, staring at the lights of the ceiling as if they held some great magical power, and I nuzzled into her neck for a kiss.

I felt all at sea. First of all I'd come back hoping to see Jake only to hear he had cleared off to another country. And then Mr Coffee Shop had told me I looked amazing in Morelli's that morning. That would have been enough excitement for one day without the worry that Beth and Dan were on a hiding to nothing and the mysterious appearance of the rose. Then again maybe Tom really did just want to advertise his business through us – nothing as likely to gain a bit of free publicity as a healthy dose of flirtation and flattery.

It felt nice though. It really did. I enjoyed having a man look at me with a glimpse of respect and, dare I say, lust in his eyes. I hadn't had anyone look at me like that in a very long time. After Jake left I immediately fell into such a fit of depression that any man who so much as glanced at me had been met with a look that would kill dead things. The horrors of morning-sickness hadn't done much for my feminine glow either. At best I looked like all the blood had been drained from my body, at worst I would open the shop with my hair scraped back from my face which was beaded with perspiration from a fresh vomiting session, and my eyes ringed with dark circles, a result of insomnia and floods of unending tears. By the time the shock of Jake doing a runner had left me, I was the size of a house and, trust me, the last thing any man looks for in a new relationship is an in-built third party to add to the dynamic. The only man I had been intimate with in nearly a year had been my doctor – nicknamed Shovel Hands – and that internal examination was truly an experience neither me nor my poor fandango wished to repeat any time in the near future.

And that's not to say my fandango wasn't screaming "Please, for the love of everything pure, don't even think about touching me ever, *ever* again!" but a flutter in my heart was leading me to think that I wanted something with a man again, be it a hug, a friendly chat, a mind-blowing bonk or even just an ivory rose . . .

Jake had never bought me ivory roses, despite knowing they were my favourite flower. He had never bought me flowers at all. In fact, he wasn't one for presents. I always pretended not to mind – after all he wrote songs for me or dedicated covers to me during his gigs. Surely that was more romantic and I was all about the romance – and the wild, passionate sex that we had night after night.

God, I missed sex! But what I missed more was companionship and that feeling of belonging to someone or something greater than just me. However imperfect it had been, my relationship with Jake at least made me feel part of something and now I just felt lonely. Maggie let out a little squeak, almost a giggle, and my heart splintered just a little. Of course I wasn't alone. But then again seeing her, her eyes the mirror image of her father's, I felt confusion sweep over me.

I needed to see him and I needed to see him soon. Dan said he would be away a "few" days. I wondered how long a few meant. Was it three? If it was then one of those days was already done and perhaps it would only be two days until I saw him again. I lifted the phone to dial Beth and Dan's number but then, remembering the scene in the shop earlier and the icy atmosphere between them, I hung up.

God damn it, why was no one home when I needed to talk? I lifted Maggie and walked around the flat, feeling uneasy and unsettled. When we walked into the kitchen and I saw the rose, for just a second I thought I might phone Tom. Surely his number had to be on the leaflets downstairs. I didn't know him from Adam but surely that wouldn't matter? He did, after all, think I looked amazing and if he did think I looked amazing then surely he wouldn't mind a phone call from me at 10.30pm?

I padded downstairs, my daughter in my arms, to Beth's desk, and I noticed her computer was still on. I shouldn't have looked, but then again I always was a nosey fecker and I couldn't help it. Clicking on the screen, I was about to enter the world of Betsy Boo and her imaginary friends.

29

Beth

The flat was in darkness when I came home. I don't know what I expected. I hoped he would be there, but I kind of knew he wouldn't be. I had hoped I would walk in and he would envelope me in his arms and tell me it was okay. Instead I walked into a cold and dark room. Flicking on the lamps and the gas fire I made myself a cup of tea and curled up on the sofa.

A sickening feeling filled me. Maybe he wasn't coming back, ever. I still couldn't believe I slapped him. I swear I felt my hand sting and my cheeks burn at the memory. It just felt as if everything was going wrong.

The light was flashing on the answerphone and so I pressed play, hoping but again not expecting, Dan to have left a message,

"Beth, it's Mum. It feels like ages since we've had a chat. I'm just ringing to tell you I miss you and I really want to see you soon. I'm tired of my only daughter giving me the cold shoulder. Call me back."

In those few seconds, I realised how much I missed my mum.

I didn't want to push her away any more. I was tired of pushing people away so I lifted the phone, dialled her number and waited to hear her voice. The phone rang, but there was no answer – just an answerphone for me to talk to – but when the beep came I couldn't speak. There was a lump in my throat, choking me, and I couldn't say all the things I wanted to, so I hung up feeling more wretched than before. Funny, I hadn't thought that possible.

This was bad. I felt worse than the time I cheated on a maths class test and had the teacher tell me how proud he was of me, when I knew it was all a lie. I had pretended on that occasion too that everything was perfect. But I was tired now, tired of pretending everything was perfect with Dan and me. I didn't care if the doctors said nothing was wrong, something was clearly very wrong and I was going to get answers. I would demand the Clomid he had talked about prescribing me. I would opt for whatever test they could offer. I would do whatever it took.

That is, I would if Dan would let me. At the moment I didn't even know if he wanted me at all. He could be out finding someone else right now – some gorgeous young thing with wide child-bearing hips and a uterus in perfect working order. Someone who didn't ever slap anyone around the face, no matter how much they irked them.

I switched on the computer and logged on. It was time to tell the girls that Betsy Boo wasn't pregnant this month. They would understand. They would be able to comfort me and tell me I wasn't going mad. Then again, maybe I was just fooling myself about that too. I switched it off almost as quickly as I had switched it on and climbed into bed hoping that if I fell asleep I would wake up and find Dan beside me.

I was sixteen when I first kissed him. It wasn't a remarkable story.

It was the college disco and I'd had a vodka and coke, stolen from my mum's drinks cabinet. I was a little drunk. Dan has teased me about being a cheap date ever since. "Back for Good" by Take That was playing and I was pretending that I hated them when the truth was that if Robbie Williams had walked into the school assembly hall at just that moment I would have completely lost control of my faculties.

Dan was gorgeous. All the girls loved him. He was one of the cool kids, but he worked hard. We all knew he was going to make it big one day and every one of us wanted to be on his arm when he got there. I couldn't believe it when he walked over to me and asked me to dance.

I had been standing there, cool as could be in my distressed denim jeans, white T-shirt and Rachel haircut from *Friends* when he walked over, hands in his pockets, floppy fringe hanging over his eyes and I felt my heart-beat quicken and my mouth dry and I was sure I would throw up, or choke, or spit or faint and do something so stupid that he would walk away and I would become the laughing stock of the entire college.

"Wanna dance?" he asked and those two words (or is it three) changed my life forever.

I did want to dance and we moved awkwardly together, not sure where to put our hands or how close to stand or what to do with our lips. I remember staring at his mouth, willing him to kiss me but being terrified at the same time. What if I was no good? What if he was no good? What if he slobbered and in that one sloppy kiss-moment destroyed my illusions of him, or what if he pulled away at my shoddy sixteen-year-old effort?

With his hand resting at the small of my back and his fringe tickling the top of my head he leant forward and I tilted my head towards him, our mouths meeting in a gentle, wonderful, sexy kiss that sent every one of my three-and-a-half-million teenage hormones into overdrive.

We were pretty inseparable after that. Of course everyone said it wouldn't last. We were much too young. When we went to university the vultures would start circling. We were definitely not going to survive the time apart.

But it was true for us: absence *did* make the heart grow fonder.

I was smug about it, I'll admit. We had the perfect relationship and I always, always felt one hundred per cent secure in what we had. On those lazy boozy nights out on the piss with Aoife, I never looked at another man. I never felt the need. I had everything I wanted and while I didn't mind going on the hunt for a man for Aoifs, that's all it ever was.

Those few years, when we had stolen weekends crammed together in a single bed for hours on end, only getting up to order a pizza or open another couple of bottles of beer! It was a far cry from the life we had now with our perfect apartment complete with designer drapes, Italian leather sofas and John Rocha Waterford Crystal to drink our wine from.

Funny, life was simpler then. We were happier then – with nothing but each other. It hurt me to admit it but it seemed now as I lay in bed waiting for the turning of his key in the lock, that that wasn't enough any more. Without a baby – our baby – nothing was enough.

I closed my eyes and pulled the duvet up over my face, fooling myself that I could fall asleep. "It's not bloody fair," I muttered as hot tears ran down my face. "It's just not bloody fair."

30

Aoife

As it turned out Beth's imaginary friends weren't all newly wed bridezillas gossiping about the soaps and the latest fashions in Zara and Ghost. They were women who were obsessed with babies and trying to get pregnant and ovulation, basal temperatures and egg-white cervical mucus, whatever the holy fuck that was.

My head was spinning. Betsy Boo was one of them – one of those faceless women who had posted month in and month out about their quest to get pregnant.

Tears poured down my face as I read of her disappointment each and every month. When the tears stopped they were replaced by horror at all the things I'd said – all the times I'd chided her about her childless life, all the times I'd teased her about getting a move on or her eggs would shrivel up to nothing. For all I knew they were already shrivelled up.

And when the embarrassment lifted, the anger set in. She was my best friend. How could she not share this with me? Didn't she trust me? Was I not really her friend? Were the past ten years of living and working in each other's pockets all a big fat lie? For God's sake, I was a mother now. Surely if anyone could understand what she had been going through it would have been me?

Slamming closed the laptop I paced the length of the shop. When had we relocated from Richmond to the Twilight Zone? Things could not get any messier or any weirder if they tried their very hardest.

Putting my life into perspective, things were at the very best eventful and at the very worst completely mental. Here I was, a mother of one, with an ex-partner who wanted to see his daughter and a new mystery man telling me I was amazing and giving me flowers for no apparent reason. And then there was my mother who never really loved me – well, not enough anyway – and my brother who lived so far up his own arse he could brush his teeth from the inside. And him and his perfect wife were about to produce yet another perfect child to make their perfect life more fecking perfect while my best friend, who clearly now desperately wanted to have a baby – and whose life I had thought was perfect – was going through hell and not telling me because I was either too damn selfish to be relied on or she just didn't think I had a right to know.

And I was standing in a closed shop at eleven o'clock on a Wednesday night, telling all this to a fecking statue of an angel called Matilda who, by the sly look on her face, seemed to find it hilariously funny.

As if on cue, Maggie started to whimper and I joined in. Walking upstairs, I held her in my arms and wished with every part of me that I could hit the pause button and catch my breath.

Thankfully Maggie settled quickly – amazing what a good boob can do – and I looked down into her eyes and realised just how hard all this must have been for Beth. All those times she held Maggie, wanting a baby of her own.

I wanted to call her, but Lord knows if she would be available to take my call or if she and Dan would be having a deep and meaningful encounter. I stared at my mobile, willing a text message to bleep from her telling me she was okay, and at the same time trying not to lift it and text her myself just to tell her how fecking mad at her I was.

Beth didn't show up for work that following morning. I was lying sleeping, blissfully enjoying a snooze after dealing with the early morning feed, when I heard a god-awful clatter from downstairs. The shutters of the shop were being pounded in and just at the stage where I was about to lift the phone and call in the local constabulary, it burst into life itself.

"Hello?" I asked, cuddling my daughter to me as if that simple gesture would protect me from what I imagined to be a serial killer battering at my door.

"Aoife, it's me, Heather. I've been standing outside for twenty minutes. It's bloody freezing and Beth isn't answering her phone. It's gone quarter to ten. Can you ever let me in?"

"I'll be right down," I muttered, climbing out of bed and slipping into my furry dressing-gown which made me look kind of like the Abominable Snowman. Typical, the one morning I had no trouble switching off the voices inside my head and falling back to sleep, Beth didn't show up and I had to let Heather in.

I stumbled through the shop. It felt weird, perhaps even wrong, to be standing in the shop amid the samples and lush fabrics in a fluffy nylon dressing-gown with baby sick down the front.

I turned the key and opened the door to let Heather in. She was a strange blue colour, as if her waif-like stature couldn't take the pressure of standing outside in anything lower than 15 degrees Celsius for anything more than ten minutes.

"Thank God. I was starting to think I would never feel my toes again," she said, pushing past me and huddling against the radiator. "Do you know where Beth is?"

"Erm no. I haven't heard from her."

"It's unlike her to be late."

I nodded, wrapping my dressing-gown closer around me and glancing down. I was wearing my furry slippers. I thanked God there was no mirror in the kitchen, I dreaded what my auburn mop was doing right at that moment.

"She has been a little stressed out lately," Heather said, walking into the small kitchen and switching on the kettle. "She flipped out at the Rodgers' place on Monday because the paint looked a shade too dark on the wall. I told her it was fine and she shouted at me what would I know about fine."

Heather looked at me, her doe eyes almost misted over, and I know she wanted me to tell her that Beth must have been having a bad day and not to take what she said seriously, but all I could do was nod again – my mind racing.

This was not like my friend. She was normally so laid back. Nothing ever phased her. When she fell asleep while pulling an all-nighter over her final-year project, she simply woke with a smile on her face and declared that she must have needed the rest. While I would have freaked out and spent an hour crying and hyperventilating, Beth had just got down to work and finished the project with fifteen minutes to spare.

When she was getting married and the baker phoned her three days before the wedding to tell her he had forgotten to make her cake, she laughed it off. "If that is all that goes wrong with my Big Day I'll be doing brilliantly," she cheered in her posh English tones before phoning her florist and asking her to make a gorgeous display to decorate a Marks and Spencer cake and no one ever noticed it wasn't the £400 original she had planned for.

Beth was one of life's problem-solvers, so to lose the head over a shade of paint unsettled me. Not that it took much to give me that sick feeling in the pit of my stomach any more.

Heather was sipping from her cup of tea when the phone rang. "That will probably be Beth now," she said and I nodded, walking to the counter.

"Hello, Instant Karma," I said.

"Aoife, darling, how are you?"

At the sound of Anna's voice, her warmth and the sheer love in the way she called me darling, I felt myself wobble a little.

"I miss you," I said in a small voice and Heather looked up at me with a sad little look on her face. Beth and I were once her idols. We were the coolest interior designers Richmond had and yet now here was me in my Frosty the Snowman dressing-gown, a strange odour which was either perspiration or sour milk emanating from me, while Beth was missing in action.

"Can I call you back in five minutes?" I asked and of course that was okay with Anna – because let's face it everything was always okay with Anna and that was why I loved her so much.

Before I called her back, I checked my mobile. No texts from Beth and none from Dan either. Usually I got some sort of explanation if Beth was taking a day off, but not today.

I went upstairs, sat down and dialled Anna's number.

"Sweetie, I'm worried about you," Anna soothed.

"I'm grand," I lied,

"You're lying," she countered.

"Just a wee bit," I offered.

"Come on, sweetie. You know you can tell me anything."

"Ach, it's just I thought coming back here would be easier and it's not. Things are very bad with Beth. Oh Anna, how could I not have known?"

"Not have known what?"

"She's been trying for a baby with no luck. And she doesn't know I know, but I found her posts on an internet forum. She's had tests and everything but she still can't get pregnant and it's tearing her apart. How could she not have told me?"

Anna took a deep breath. "Sometimes people keep secrets for all sorts of reasons known only to them. All you can do is pick up the pieces when they eventually let you in."

Touché. Anna was a sly fecker when she wanted to be and she always got to the point.

"But what do I do now?" I asked. "Do I confront her?"

"Well, the problem with that, darling, is that she'll know you were checking on her. She obviously didn't want you to know or she would have told you. How would she feel if you told her you were reading her innermost thoughts on the internet?"

"Hmmm. You have a point. But how can I not confront her? How can I have this knowledge and not share it? I can't pretend not to know, Anna, can I?"

"If you want to protect your friendship then you are going to have to try. You know more than most that people deal with things when they are good and ready to."

But how long would that be?

In my case I had held my secret close to me for eight months. In my mother's case, she had yet to talk to me about the secret of her depression or openly admit that she had never bonded with me. She had yet to accept it. Lord only knows how many of us were carrying around secrets at any one time, wondering whether there would ever be a right time to tell people about them, or hoping the time would come when they wouldn't need to be a secret any more. I had been waiting for Jake to come back and make it right. It dawned on me that my friend was probably waiting for the day she could tell me she was pregnant and then inform me of the horrible journey she had been on over the last couple of years. And of course then it wouldn't matter because she would have her happy ending.

Looking around my flat, at the absence of Jake's clothes thrown over the sofa the way they once had been, and at the picture of my parents – my father smiling, my mother stony-faced – I realised that not everyone got their happy ending. Even Anna – happy, bubbly, gorgeous Anna – didn't have a happy ending. She still wore her wedding ring and, even though she didn't admit it, I knew there were still nights she went down to Moville and wailed at the sea, giving passing men out walking their dogs in the dark heart attacks at the thought the banshee was coming for them.

"Are you okay?" she piped up over the phone.

"Anna, I really love you," I said and wished with all my heart that we didn't live so far from each other.

We said out goodbyes and I got dressed. I could hear Heather bustling about downstairs, but no matter how much I strained my ears I could not hear the phone ring, or the bell above the door ring and Beth shout her usual hellos.

Realising I had to do something to stop myself going completely doolally, I strapped Maggie in her pram (the fancy Bugaboo that Beth – infertile Beth – had lovingly bought) and went for a walk.

The air was fresh, a slight frost thawing on the footpaths as we walked. I looked down at my daughter, encased in her snowsuit, a white dummy getting the battering of its life in her mouth and for a second I felt jealous. How nice would it be to only have to worry about dummies and boobies and snowsuits?

We walked while my brain tried to come to terms with all that was going on and we walked right up Gardiner Street until I found myself staring in the window of Austin Flowers.

Tom was inside. I could see him through the door wrestling with some Cala Lilies and assorted greenery. He seemed engrossed in his work and I wondered what his story was. Here was this man – this very handsome man – and he had taken to hanging around our street – our shop – and telling me I looked amazing. He was singing to himself as he tied some raffia around a glass vase, and I came to the only conclusion that a modern woman living in the posh part of Richmond could. He was clearly gay and he clearly wanted Beth and me to be his fag hags. When he told me I looked fabulous, it was obvious he was just one of those guys who liked to tell women – all women – they looked amazing.

And we were his dream girls when you thought about it. We had a shop full of hand-painted silks and luscious wallpapers. We were attractive (well, we were, especially Beth) and I had a baby he could no doubt pretend was his own on some level. We could help him and his new business and he could help us. I blushed crimson when I thought about how I'd had found myself staring at his manly hands the previous day, but then I smiled. I could do with a gay friend. We could be like Julia Roberts and Rupert Everett in *My Best Friend's Wedding*. He could be the one to dance with me when Jake married someone else and make it all better.

I was about to turn and leave, walk on back towards Morelli's for a hot chocolate (me) and a breast-feed (Maggie), when Tom looked up and waved at me. He smiled and he certainly didn't look very gay – but then what does 'gay' look like anyway? I may have grown up in Derry but I should not let my parochial upbringing get in the way of my perception of others.

I smiled back, waving.

He walked to the door. "Come in for a chat," he smiled. "I'm just finishing this order and then maybe I can treat you to a cup of coffee."

"That would be nice," I replied, looking around me at the shop decorated in plush creams, golds and purples. "You must tell me who your designer was so I can have them bumped off."

"I inherited most of it from the previous owner," he said. "The floristry side of things was hers too. I'm just finishing off a few of her standing orders before I concentrate entirely on the gardening."

"Austin Gardens doesn't have quite the same ring, does it?" I said.

He laughed, walking to the kitchen and switching on the kettle. "I'm afraid the coffee won't quite be to Morelli's standard. I only have instant."

"Instant will be lovely," I shouted to him. "With just a drop of milk, please."

Maggie started to wriggle about, letting out a ferocious hungry cry.

"You don't mind if I feed her here, do you?" I called, stripping off her sleeping suit and sliding my T-shirt up to unclip my breast-feeding bra.

"Not at all," he said, clattering about, before appearing again. "Do you need me to heat a bottle for you or any . . ."

He stood, his mouth gaping open at me, his eyes fixed on my boobs which in fairness to me were barely exposed. The nipple at least was completely clamped in my daughter's mouth.

I sensed his embarrassment. Funny, I hadn't thought he would have minded. I didn't think for one second that he would be one tiny bit interested in my boobs or that he – being a modern man – would have a problem with breast-feeding.

"Sorry, I didn't think you would mind," I said, probably emphasising the 'you' too much.

"No. I don't . . . I just wasn't expecting . . . you're fine . . . here's your coffee," he bumbled before turning and walking back into the kitchen, his face red as the roses in the bucket by the door.

Maybe he wasn't as gay as I first thought.

I knew I had to salvage this, and quick. "Tom, sorry. I'll go if you want!" I shouted at the door.

"No, it's fine. Carry on. I have a design here for a garden I'm landscaping. I'll just work on it until you're finished."

And that was how I ended up sitting, boobs out, in a florist's/gardener's on Gardiner Street at the exact moment Elena Kennedy walked in.

"Oh my darling Aoife!" she said, moving closer to me and stroking Maggie's cheek (and very nearly my boob) while she air-kissed me. "Oh, this little one is darling! Absolutely precious. How wonderful to see you here! I didn't know you knew Tom, He's marvellous, isn't he? He landscaped our garden last summer and he does all the arrangements for our little soirées. He's quite the catch, you know," she winked.

"Erm I don't really know him. I just called in to say hello."

The unspoken words "and I decided to get my baps out in front of him for I no longer have any shame after baring my fandango for anyone who wanted a look at the hospital" hung in the air between us like a bad smell.

"Well, he is wonderful. You should really be recommending him to your clients."

I decided to nod in response. Everything I thought of saying would involve some half-baked innuendo about bushes or getting dirty or something equally embarrassing.

I took Maggie from my breast, covered myself up quickly and called to Tom that he had a customer, and he walked out, the same flustered look on his face.

"Elena, nice to see you," he said, casting a furtive look in my direction.

"Yes, and I see you've met Aoife. Great girl altogether, isn't she?" Elena replied.

I blushed and was about to make some comment about how I wasn't all that great really, when my phone beeped and I saw a message from Beth flash up on screen.

"Where are you? I'm at the shop. Need to chat."

"Sorry. But I really have to go. Tom, we might get that coffee eventually. Sorry for the embarrassment. I can assure you I don't usually get my boobs out for a man before the first cup of coffee."

Blushing furiously, I beat a hasty retreat to the shop for the conversation with Beth where I hoped she would tell me all about her struggle to conceive a child and our friendship would be back on an even keel.

31

Beth

I heard the door click shut shortly after 2 a.m. and I heard Dan stumble through the flat, knocking the ceramic bowl off the hall table, toppling to the floor and swearing as he tripped on Lord only knows what.

My heart had started to thump, waiting for him to come in and talk to me. I wanted him to tell me how angry he was and how I had hurt him. I wanted him to make me hurt the way I had hurt him. It didn't matter that I was hurting in my own way – it only mattered that he got his revenge on me for saying those horrible things and hitting him that morning.

I prepared myself to say sorry as many times as it took, but I needn't have bothered because within a few minutes I heard the door click shut to the spare room and Dan swear as he stubbed his toe on the bedstead.

It was strange how I knew every inch of this apartment. I could recognise every noise, identify every piece of furniture, where it was and the level of swearing it incited from my husband when he stumbled into it after a few too many pints.

I thought I knew him too. I thought I knew every thought process in his head, but I obviously didn't.

When I was sure he was asleep – when I heard the snores – I got up and cleared up the smashed bowl, wrapping it in newspaper and throwing it in the bin and then I sat on the sofa watching nonsense until eventually I fell asleep.

When I woke up I could hear the traffic move outside the flat. The door of the spare room was still closed, the sound of Dan's snoring still seeping through into the living-room. I stood up, stretched and felt empty. Dan and I had never gone to sleep on a fight. We had always talked it through and yet now, here we were, two people on different sides of a closed door, not knowing what the other thought or wanted.

I made a pot of coffee. It was my silly little peace-offering. I brewed it in the coffee machine, biting my nails and glancing furtively towards the spare-room door every five minutes. I buttered some croissants, put them with the cafetière and two mugs on a tray and walked into the room.

"Dan," I called gently. "You're going to be late for work. I've made coffee."

He looked at me, and momentarily I saw the love he had for me in his eyes. But then it was as if he had remembered yesterday – remembered that I'd slapped him square across the face, that I'd blamed him for not getting me pregnant, that I'd failed once again to give him a baby – and he rolled over.

"I'm not going in today. I've already let them know. I'll get some coffee later, after you go to work."

"Well, I'm not going in either," I said petulantly. I could be a stubborn bitch when I wanted to be.

"Good for you," he said, pulling the duvet up to his cheek.

I left the tray with its mugs and croissants on the bedside table and went back to the sofa where I took up my position of staring at the TV again. I wanted to go in and demand that he talk to me, but I figured he held all the cards now and I would be unwise to force his hand. I realised then how lonely I was. I couldn't talk to Dan, nor could I talk to Aoife. She wouldn't understand. Kids had never been in her game plan so how could I expect her to understand my obsession?

I couldn't phone my mum. She didn't know either and she would kill me for keeping this a secret. The only people I could tell were those "friends" I had online and what would they say? Surely any sympathy they had for me would dry up as soon as they read how I'd slapped Dan and pushed him away. No, it was becoming clearer and clearer to me that I was in this on my own.

After I'd showered and made a cup of instant coffee (the cafetière not having returned from Dan's lair) I decided to take affirmative action.

I phoned my doctor's surgery and made an appointment. I know it had only been eleven months since our tests had come back clear and fine – and that Dr Browne had told us to go home and relax (yeah, right) for at least twelve months before coming back for more invasive testing, but I needed to do something.

I no longer had faith that it was just going to happen, and if it did, what would the cost be? What state would Dan and I be in by the end of it? I secured an appointment for the following week for an initial assessment. All I had to do now was persuade Dan to come along. And, of course, persuade him to talk to me in the first place. That would be a better start perhaps.

I was hanging up the phone when he came into the room, bleary-eyed.

"The coffee is cold," he muttered, eyeing my steaming cup with the jealous look of a hungover man in desperate need of a caffeine fix.

"I left it an hour ago," I replied, trying not to snap.

"Sorry," he replied and that annoyed me.

He wasn't supposed to say sorry. That was my line. I was supposed to get in there first to make it all better. Now my sorry would seem a little stupid in comparison – as if I was just trying to keep score.

"I'll make you a fresh cup," I said, walking to the kitchen.

"There's no need," he called after me.

"It's okay. I don't mind. I was going to the kitchen anyway," I lied.

I poured his cup and walked back. He was sitting on the sofa – on exactly the same spot where I had spent the lion's share of the last ten hours. I handed him the mug and hovered nervously.

"We need to talk," I said.

He nodded and I felt tears well up in my eyes. God damn it. How was I going to get through the conversation when I was crying already, before we had even started?

I knelt down in front of him. Usually at this juncture he would say something entirely inappropriate like "while you're down there," with a cheeky wink, but he just looked at me and I could see my sadness reflected in his eyes.

"I'm so, so sorry," I said. If I had started to explain exactly what I was sorry for – how much I was sorry for – I feared we would be there all day, so I just repeated the line over again. "I'm so sorry."

"I know."

"I don't want to lose you."

He shook his head, trying to form the words and I searched his expression for any clue as to what he was going to say.

"I don't want to lose you either," he said, "but if I'm honest I'm afraid that I already have."

It was my turn to shake my head. How could he think I would leave him? But then hadn't I admitted to myself that he alone was not enough any more? Could I make it enough? Could we be happy without that missing link I'd wanted all these months? He wanted it too. I knew he wanted it. He'd helped choose the names, he'd found Dr Browne. Could we live together without achieving our goal?

"I've made an appointment with Dr Browne for next week. I'm going to ask for the dye test, and for Clomid. I'll ask for anything it takes to make this work."

"I need you back, Beth," he said, taking my hands in his. "I need you back to make this work. Can we give the pregnancy effort a break? Even a month?"

"But I've made an appointment!" My heart lurched at the thought of giving it a break. I didn't want to give it a break. I didn't want to waste a month for nothing.

"You can change the appointment," he said.

I wondered how he couldn't hear the thumping of my heart in my chest. It was almost deafening and yet he seemed oblivious.

"But we might as well go!" I implored him. "It will take a while to set up tests and everything anyway and then we can forget about it for a while."

"Beth, please. Before this destroys us."

He was pleading now, his eyes filled with tears, and I wanted to make it all better. I wanted to nod and agree just to make him happy but my heart was breaking at the thought of not even trying to get pregnant for a whole month. It was as if the pain of getting my period next month was hitting me now. I was grieving already for another unconceived child.

I couldn't talk to him, but I didn't want to walk away. So I just sat there, staring into space and listening to my husband crying.

I'd never seen Dan crying before. Well, I lie, he did shed a tear when England got kicked out of the last World Cup but that was more down to the eight bottles of Stella Artois and male pride than anything else. I'm not saying the emotion wasn't real, but it didn't make me want to cry too. It didn't tear at my heart like these tears. It may be unpatriotic to admit it, but when England got kicked out of the World Cup I felt relieved. I would have my husband back.

I suppose all he wanted now was me back, but I don't think I even knew who "me" was any more. I knew I was obsessed. I wasn't blind to that obsession. I could feel myself mull over every twinge, every symptom, every book and website on conception that existed. While at clients' houses, I would have imaginary conversations in my head where I would tell Dan I was pregnant and he would cry – happy tears this time. For two weeks out of every four I would stroke my belly that little bit when no one was looking, just in case. I wouldn't climb ladders, or lift heavy sample books or eat soft cheese, or drink alcohol or take Nurofen, just in case. If I'm honest I would push Dan away for those two weeks in case the very act of sex – that which was supposed to foster our love – might damage our mythical baby. I had consumed so much Folic Acid and Pro-Natal that I was sure I rattled when I walked. Could I switch that off? Could I let that go – even for a month?

I didn't know.

All I could do was turn to Dan once again, pleading back at him with my eyes. "I'm sorry, Dan. I'm so, so, sorry."

"I know," he said.

And we held each other in silence but with so many thoughts racing through our minds, for what seemed like forever.

"I'll go with you," he said eventually and I sobbed – loud gasps racking my body.

"Thank you! Thank you!" I cried, as he kissed my head.

"But do one thing for me, Beth. No more secrets. We aren't going to avoid your mother until you are pregnant. We aren't going to hide from Aoife any more while you tear yourself apart every time she makes some jibe about us getting our skates on."

"I don't know, Dan . . ."

"Well, I do know. I've watched you tear yourself to pieces all through her pregnancy and you aren't going to do that any more.

Beth, Aoife loves you. She won't judge you. We can't keep this to ourselves any more. It's tearing us apart."

"It's tearing me apart."

I put my head in my hands. He had just offered to come to the appointment with me, and now he was asking this one thing of me and I wasn't sure I wanted to tell. It was as if saying it out loud would make it real. As it stood, I could contain it because only Dan, me, Dr Browne and some "imaginary" friends on the internet knew that we couldn't get pregnant despite there being nothing wrong with us. If I said it out loud to Aoife – super-fertile Aoife – it would make it more real than I wanted it to be. But if I didn't tell her then Dan would be angry at me.

"Okay," I nodded and he kissed me gently.

"It will be okay, Betsy," he soothed. "We will get through this."

I really, really hoped he was right.

32

Aoife

Heather had gone out to see a client by the time we reached the shop. I was sure my face was still blazing from the embarrassing exposure of boobs to Tom Austin, but I forced those thoughts to the back of my head because Beth needed me now and perhaps this was the time when she was going to reveal her big secret.

I wondered how I should react, given that technically speaking I knew her secret already. I didn't want her to know that I had been snooping but I always was a lousy actress and an even worse liar. When other teenage girls could have managed to sneak out of the house with make-up concealed in their schoolbags I would blush so furiously that my mother – with her radar for teenage fibs set to high – would suss something was up and stare at me in such a way that I would blurt out my sad little secrets without her even having to confront me.

As I walked back to the shop I practised a variety of facial expressions. I could do shocked, I guessed, perhaps even outrage at not being privy to this information before. I could do sad. And from the slightly wary look of strangers walking past me as I pulled those expressions, I could clearly do 'mental' down to a tee.

Beth knew me really well. Surely she would see through whatever it was I was trying to pull off. She always was able to tell when I was fibbing. She said there was a second or two's pause before I spoke which gave me away every time.

The first time she had experienced the 'pause' hadn't been long after we'd met. As two eighteen-year-olds out on our own for the first time and feeling a little like fish out of water at our very big university we had found each other and clung on for dear life during our first few weeks in Halls. I had arrived in Manchester knowing no one. The girl from school who was supposed to be my roomie had failed to get the requisite grades to get on her law course, so I found myself alone in a room which bore more of a resemblance to a prison cell than the stylish student digs I had been dreaming of. I set about making it more homely, trailing in remnants of material bought from the local fabric suppliers and setting up my sewing-machine in the corner to batter together some curtains.

I had been sewing merrily one night when a knock came to my door. I opened it to find a tall blonde firing me rather dirty looks.

"I'm Beth," she stated in her plummy southern English tones. "I'm in the room next door. I wondered if you could possibly keep the noise down."

"Noise? It's only my sewing-machine!" I answered and in comparison my Derry accent sounded loud and brash. If I'm honest I sounded like an extra from a dodgy film about the Troubles.

"It's eleven thirty," she said, "and I'd like to get some sleep."

Looking down at my watch, I saw that she was right. Shit, how had it got to be so late?

"God, I'm sorry," I said. "I got carried away transforming the room. I'll stop now."

"Thanks," she said, smiling now and looking instantly less scary as she glanced around my room at the swathes of material and piles of lifestyle magazines. "You're not on the interior design course, are you?"

"Yes, I am."

"God, so am I. Look, I'm sorry for stomping in here. You must think I'm a real stick in the mud."

"No, you're fine," I mumbled,

"And you are a liar," she laughed.

I found myself smiling back and I reached out my hand. "Beth, I'm Aoife. Nice to meet you."

Nothing had been able to get past Beth since that day so I knew that even with my best face-pulling antics, it was unlikely that she wouldn't figure out I'd been snooping on her. In fact, oh my God, maybe she already knew and that is why she was summoning me back to the shop? Shit! Did I log her computer out? Maybe she remembered leaving it on, so by logging her off I'd left a trail of clues back to me being a nosey fecker. Arse! I wondered if I could blame Heather. I mean, Heather was kind of disposable anyway and . . . no, I couldn't think like that. If there was one thing I believed in it was the power of the Karma Fairy to come and bite you square in the arse if you messed anyone else around. No, there would be no pause needed, I was just going to have to throw myself at her mercy and hope she'd forgive me. I wondered, as I walked along, if I could blame my addled hormones. I mean it had only been four weeks since I'd given birth – surely I was allowed some momentary lapses of judgement, but then again, feck, wouldn't it be highly insensitive of me to blame pregnancy hormones when Beth was trying to get pregnant and couldn't?

No, much as I had wanted Beth to tell me this news herself, this was now scary. If I was being honest about it, it was even more scary than my first post-baby poo and that was perhaps the scariest experience of my entire life.

I suddenly wanted to turn around and run home, but then again running home involved running through the shop and past the kitchen where I could hear Beth pottering about.

Maggie started to whimper, a cry I recognised as a baby in need of a fresh nappy, and at that Beth walked out to face me.

"Aoife," she started and my face started to blaze. She walked towards her laptop and closed the screen shut. "We need to talk."

I opened my mouth to chat but I wasn't sure what to say, given that after all I was standing in front of her now bearing the one thing in my arms that she wanted with all her heart, and I hadn't even wanted this little creature in the first place.

Damn. How could I have said all those things? My mind flashed back to a conversation we'd had over at Ivory Towers when I was fourteen weeks pregnant and puking my anatomy on a regular basis.

"Why would anyone do this?" I'd moaned. "God, there's no dignity. There is no joy, no maternal glow. There is just me, getting fat – despite throwing up every single thing I've eaten over the past ten weeks. And then this, this . . . creature . . . will come out of me and demand my attention for ever more and I'm not ready for it, Beth. I don't want it. I don't *want* this fecking little parasite!"

Beth had nodded and hugged me, holding my hair back from my face as I threw up but she didn't say anything and now I knew why.

She walked past me, as I busied myself changing Maggie's nappy on the daybed, and locked the shop door, dropping the window shutters and turning off the main lights. Only the glow of Matilda's light and the fairy lights on the willow branches beside the bed illuminated the room.

She sat down, gazing at Maggie. Miraculously she didn't retch at the stench. I noticed her mouth open and close. I knew she was trying to find the words too and yet I couldn't reach out and talk to her and tell her I understood. At the end of the day. I didn't understand and I was never likely to.

"Aoife," she began, "I need to tell you something and it's not going to be easy for me. You'll probably be really pissed off at me, but I need you to hear me out before you respond because I'm hoping you'll understand once I've told you the full story."

I looked at her and our eyes locked in that moment. There was so much between us now. This massive secret and all the hurtful and horrible things I must have said about babies and getting pregnant without realising what I was doing and, of course, there was my daughter.

Beth glanced down at the squirming pink ball on the bed, now trying to reach her hands to her mouth, her perfect blue eyes open wide and gazing at the twinkling lights.

"I can't get pregnant," Beth said.

"I know," I answered, before I even realised what I was I saying.

"You know?"

"I found out last night. I'm sorry, Beth, you left the computer on and, well, you know what a nosey baggage I am and I looked and I'm sorry – but, Beth, why didn't you tell me?"

She looked down at Maggie again and then back at me, tears in her eyes. "How could I have told you, Aoife? With all you were going through?"

"I would have helped. I would have been there for you."

"Aoife, you weren't even there for yourself. You didn't need our problems and then, you see, I thought it would go away. I'm young. I thought that given a matter of time I would get pregnant too and we could do this together."

"I would have liked that," I said. "I'm sure your turn will come, Beth."

"I wish I was sure. Oh Aoife, it's been twenty-four months of trying. We've had tests, blood tests, sperm tests, checks that I'm ovulating, and they can't find a reason why I'm not pregnant and yet we're not and it's been killing me!"

I took her hand. I didn't know what to say. All the thoughts that were swimming through my head were hopelessly insensitive and patronising. I could tell her to relax, but I guessed she had tried that. I could tell her this motherhood malarky was not all it was cracked up to be, but looking at Maggie lying on the bed I knew it was more, so much more, than I could ever have imagined and my heart broke just a little bit for my friend.

"I'm sorry."

Those two words were all I could muster and then I started to cry with her. I reached out, hugged her close to me and we sobbed together. I stroked her hair, soothing her the best I could – but I didn't know how to take away her pain.

After a while, we decided to move up to the flat and I made us a cup of tea. Beth told me all about it. It was as if now that she had started talking she couldn't stop and two years of frustration and hurt poured out.

She told me all about her decision to start trying for a baby. She told me how Dan had been so excited and they had wandered about in a daze, lost in each other as they shared their little secret. They weren't just making love any more. They were making a baby and every time they walked together, and saw a mum-to-be rub her stomach or a father push a pram they would share a secret smile. That would be them some day soon, they were sure.

And then her period came, and kept on coming. Six months she could cope with, she told me. That was fine. She just thought it was taking its time but then when it reached a year – and she watched my belly swell – something in her snapped. They went and had tests, which gave them no answers and they were sent away again to keep trying.

Life had become hard. Dan and her, the couple I thought were the most in-love and together couple in world, were having a hard time. My friend – my gorgeous supportive friend who had rubbed my swollen feet and gone to antenatal classes with me – had been going through her personal hell.

I started to cry, wailing and moaning that I was the most god-awful bitch in the entire world and she must hate me, really hate me for being such a baggage. If we had been the owners of a ceremonial sword I would have thrown myself on it. All we had though was a letter opener with a mother-of-pearl handle, and it was quite blunt and I didn't really fancy throwing myself on a blunt antique so I cried some more.

I couldn't understand how life could be so cruel to some people. What had Beth or Dan done to deserve this? Where was the reason in all this? And yes, maybe it would happen for them sometime but what if it didn't? I could not be so blithe as to assume everything would work out perfectly because life did not always have fairytale endings. Look at me, a single, frumpy mother of one clinging onto the hope that when Jake came back it would all work out. Look at Anna, widowed in her mid-thirties and having never found love again. And then there were jammy bastards like Joe and his perfect Jacqueline who seemed to have it all and revel in their success even though they wouldn't know hard work if it came up and bit them square in the arse.

"I wish I had known," I muttered through my tears.

"It wouldn't have made a difference," Beth said, a note of resignation in her voice. "And to be honest, I thought if I didn't say it out loud it wouldn't be true. We didn't tell anyone, Aoife, not you, not my mum. No one. The only other people who have a notion of what we are going through is our doctor and the nurse who helped with the tests."

"So what now?"

"We're seeing the doctor again and asking for more tests. We have to do something, Aoife. It is tearing us apart and that is so not what I want but at the same time I can't rid myself of the notion that I want – no, I *need* – a baby. I need one so much that it hurts. I have a physical urge to feel my own child in my arms. I see you, Aoife, when you don't think I'm looking, I see how you look at Maggie and I see how she looks back at you. I see how she fits into the crook of your arm as if she was made for it. I see how her little eyes open and dart around when she hears your voice because she knows you are her mother and I want that for me and Dan."

"I want it for you too, darling, and please God you will get it but in the meantime you have me and this little one to keep you busy. I know this might be shit timing, and perhaps you don't want to hear this – feel free to tell me to butt out or to fuck off or whatever – but, Beth, would you and Dan please do me – us – the honour of being Maggie's godparents?"

She nodded, tears flowing, and I knew that no matter what, I would be there for my friend and she would be there for me and there would be no more secrets.

"Well, darling, how was your day?" Anna's soft lilting tones soothed down the phone.

"You wouldn't believe it if I told you," I said, curling my feet up under me on the sofa and sipping from my mug of tea.

Beth had not long gone home and, after feeding Maggie, I was settling down to a cuppa and a couple of chocolate biscuits while I winded her on my shoulder.

"Try me," Anna laughed. "You'd be surprised at just how open-minded I can be."

So I regaled her with a rerun of the whole day, from my exposed breasts in Tom's shop to the chat with Beth.

I had not expected Beth to be so open with me – not now after all these months of her not telling me anything. But it made sense now. The whole episode with Dan in the shop, the emotion on his face. It made sense and they still loved each other, they just had to remember that and work through it.

"I've asked her to be godmother to Maggie," I told Anna. "She was so delighted. I didn't know how she would take it, but she was over the moon. We both had a good cry over it."

"That's lovely, darling," Anna said, but I knew her well enough to sense the hesitancy in her voice.

"What is it, Anna?"

"Your mum."

"What about her? Still the devil incarnate?"

"Now, now, Aoife. You know she isn't that bad," but still I could sense the smile in her voice. "No, she mightn't be too happy with your choice of godparents."

"But Beth is Catholic. Surely she can't have a problem with that?"

"She may be Catholic, but she's not Joe. Your mum was telling me she was hoping Joe and Jacqueline would get asked."

"Jesus no, and have the pair of them look after Maggie if something happened to me? I'd be afraid they would lock her in a cupboard under the stairs and make her do all their housework like a modern-day Cinderella."

"I know, pet. I tried to tell your mother that you might have your own notions, but she got herself all excited about it."

I felt a headache start to throb just behind my right eye. Rubbing my forehead, I sighed. "Well, I suppose I should be grateful she's interested in my child's future at all, even if it is only down to a latent hope that I'll snuff it and the Sunshine Twins will raise my child as their own."

"I don't think she'd wish any ill on you, she just wants her day in chapel."

"God bless her cotton socks," I sighed, before saying my goodbyes.

How is it that even the most innocent of gestures, carried out

239

hundreds of miles away from Derry, cause such ructions? This time it hadn't even involved unprotected sex with an irresponsible wannabe rockstar.

Then again, in for a penny, in for a pound. Today had already been so mind-blowingly surreal that phoning my mother and dropping this latest bombshell couldn't possibly make it worse and the way I saw it was that I'd be better off getting all this over and done with so that tomorrow, like Scarlett O'Hara said, could be another day.

The phone rang its standard three times.

"Hello, McLaughlin residence."

Ah, Mum and her gorgeous phone voice. My headache moved up a notch.

"Hi, Mum, it's me, Aoife." I don't know why I felt the need to tell her my name. I guess I never believed she would recognise my voice without further clarification. In truth I was delighted every time she didn't follow that clarification with "Aoife who?".

"Aoife, how are you?"

"I'm fine, Mum. How are you? How is Dad?"

"We're both doing well, considering." There was a sniff.

"Considering what?" I asked, although I knew I shouldn't have bothered.

"Well, you know we're both still getting over the shock of little Maggie. Don't get me wrong, she is quite adorable in her own way but well, a shock is a shock."

I rolled my eyes. It had been almost three weeks since she'd found out about my daughter. How long exactly was she planning on milking the shock factor? And as for my darling daddy, he was long over it. Just that morning I had received a parcel in the post of a teddy bear to Maggie from her doting granda.

"Yes, well, it was a bit of a shock to me too, Mum."

"Mary Ferris tells me every child is a blessing. So I suppose I've to be grateful for that. After all, it's not like you were sixteen like that wee cuddy down the road who is walking about, bump wobbling in one of the crop-top thingies, like she has no shame."

"Yes, Mum. But don't forget her child is a wee blessing too."

She sniffed again.

"Speaking of blessings," I started, "I've asked my friends Beth and Dan to be godparents."

"Oh, Aoife! Joe was kind of hoping you would ask him."

If I had money to spare I would have bet every penny that Joe, God love him, hadn't even thought about acting as godparent for my child. He would be much too busy fussing over his own unborn child and how absolutely perfect he or she would undoubtedly be and how they could fit into his perfect cream world.

"Well, maybe next time," I muttered, even though I know it was cruel to wind my mother up to such an extent.

"Sometimes I wonder where I went wrong with you, young lady," she chided before making her excuses and hanging up in a fit of pique.

As far as conversations with my mother went, it was one of the less painful ones.

33

Beth

A godparent. Godparents. Dan and me. Standing in a church, promising to protect and love Maggie and help Aoife raise her to feel loved, secure and blessed.

I wasn't entirely sure how I felt about it. Of course I adored every adorable baby crease of Maggie, but was Aoife only asking me because she thought we would never have kids of our own?

I tried to shake the thought from my head. This is why I hadn't wanted to tell anyone. I could handle insensitive comments from people who genuinely didn't know any better, but I wasn't sure I could do sympathy. But then, as I told myself, who else would Aoife have asked? I must not try to convince myself she is only asking me because she feels a duty of care to my fragile mental state.

I cooked dinner for us – steak with garlic potatoes. It was Dan's favourite and I was still trying my damnedest to make up for that horrible domestic-violence incident. I opened a bottle of red and poured two glasses before setting them on the dining-table beside our balcony doors. Looking out at the rain battering against the windows, I longed for the summer. Maybe none of this would feel so weird, so dark and depressing, when the sun was shining.

We would have a lovely meal and then, when it was all done, I would tell him how we were going to be godparents to the most beautiful little baby in the world.

On cue the door opened and Dan walked in, sexy with a six o'clock shadow and his tie loosened around his neck.

I smiled, walking towards him.

"I've cooked us dinner," I announced as he dropped his briefcase to the floor.

"Is there enough for three?" he asked, stepping aside to allow Jake Gibson to walk in with his trademark swagger and smile.

I tried not to say it. I tried to keep the words, the look of utter horror from my face but I failed miserably.

"You have got to be fucking joking," I said.

"Beth, nice to see you," said Jake with his usual smarmy smile.

Dan just stood there. His shoulders shrugged and his eyes pleaded with me not to say too much more.

"Can I help you with dinner?" he asked, darting his eyes towards the kitchen.

Jake walked to the table and lifted a glass of wine, gulping it back as if it were apple juice and slumping down on the sofa like he owned the place.

I looked at Dan and he raised his eyes, pleading with me to follow him. I set my wine-glass down and traipsed in behind him, slamming the door probably too loudly behind me.

"Calm down," Dan started before he turned to look at me.

"This had better be good, Daniel Jones. I thought we agreed that man was not welcome in this house ever again."

"He called to my office. He said he needs to talk about things. Much as I wanted to tell him to fuck off, he deserves a hearing. He says he's going to change."

"Yeah, right."

"He wants to see them both. And Aoife wants to see him too. He spoke to her a few weeks back."

"Yes," I said, "a few weeks back. And then nothing. He has a daughter who is almost a month old and he has spoken to her mother once. Am I – are we – really supposed to believe that him being in their lives will be a good thing?"

"No, Beth, but as I've said before, it's not our decision to make. Much as we might love Maggie, she isn't our responsibility."

"Well *that*, Dan, is where you're wrong," I said indignantly. "Aoife has asked us to be godparents and that means that Maggie is our responsibility in a roundabout way and the part of me that is responsible for her doesn't want that dirty bastard anywhere near her."

Dan rubbed his eyes. He looked so tired and fed up of everything and yet the part of me that wanted to make it all better was overruled by the part of me that was utterly disgusted by the creature sitting on my sofa.

Dan walked to the stove and started checking the dinner. "This should go three ways," he said.

"Dan –" I started.

"Beth, we can give him dinner and then we can kick him out. We can be there to pick up the pieces if and when it all goes wrong with Aoife, but we can't stop it from happening. They are linked now. They have a child and he might be a bastard, but he is Maggie's daddy and you don't want that child to turn around to you in ten or twenty years and accuse you of denying her a relationship with the man who gave her life."

"Jake didn't give her life. He gave her sperm. It's hardly the same thing."

"It's very much the same thing. Trust me," he said, a wounded look on his face, and once again, even though I had not touched him, I knew I had slapped my husband – my gorgeous, sexy, tired husband – square across the face.

245

"Okay." I said. "I'll put out another place setting."

It galled me to sit across the table from Jake. We had been so close once and now every time I looked at him I felt betrayed. I felt betrayed not only for what he had done to Aoife, but what he had done to Dan and what he had done to us as a foursome. It had been perfect, or thereabouts, until he walked out on my best friend and shattered everything about us. All those nights out drinking, dancing, shagging, laughing. All those day trips to the beach, all those nights watching the sunset, drinking cold beer and chatting about what it would be like when we achieved our dreams and had become successful. Aoife and I would design rooms for stars of TV and music, who Jake would introduce us to because he would, obviously, be on the A-list. And Dan would be a high-flying lawyer negotiating his cousin's record deals. We would holiday in the Seychelles and Milan and spend lazy weekends poking through the Paris antiques market choosing trinkets for our shop which we would then keep for ourselves.

But he smashed that dream, and I just didn't know that I could ever forgive him.

We made small-talk. The usual topics of the weather, the pollution levels in central London, the congestion charges and who was shagging who and where came up. I smiled through gritted teeth and resisted the urge to spear him straight in the head with my fork.

"So how've you been?" he asked, gazing from Dan to me and back again.

He had been in our house for an hour now and had not once mentioned his daughter.

"Oh, just fine," I answered.

"Same old, same old," Dan chimed in. "You know – work, work and more work. Things are going really well."

"Great. Things are looking up for me too," he grinned. "My latest demo is getting a lot of hits on My Space and there are a few interested parties."

We'd heard all this before, of course, and had long since stopped believing it. But then again, knowing the bastard that Jake was, now probably was the time that his life would take off – just as everything in ours was crashing and burning.

"Great," said Dan.

"And what about you, Beth? Work busy?"

I bit my tongue. There was no way to answer this without telling him what an utter shit I thought he was for leaving my gorgeous best friend in the lurch, which of course had left me in the lurch in the business sense. Dan looked at me, his eyes pleading with me not to say something which would cause friction.

I smiled. "Same as always."

I was ultimately very pleased that I resisted the urge to ping a garlic potato into his smug and selfish face.

He downed two glasses of wine – wine that cost £15 a bottle – and sat back declaring the dinner I'd cooked as "decent scran".

"Glad you liked it," my husband replied, as he rose to his feet with the remaining dishes. "I'll put the coffee on."

And that left just me and Jake alone in my living-room, sipping wine and pretending everything was okay. The only problem with that is that I was all out of pretending everything was okay.

"So . . ." he said.

"Buttons," I replied with the stock response from my childhood.

"What?"

"You said 'so', I said 'buttons'. Sew buttons. Geddit?"

He raised an eyebrow and smiled. "Look, Beth, I know you think I've been an awful bastard."

"That would be the understatement of the year."

"Just remember, you only know one side of the story."

I nodded. "Would that be the side of the story where you played around with Aoife for nearly four years, made her believe you loved her, got her pregnant and walked out before the pee could dry on the testing stick?"

"I never said I loved her."

"You were with her for almost four years, Jake. You practically lived in her flat. You went everywhere together. You ate her food, drank her wine, slept with her every night and spent her money. She could reasonably have assumed you loved her."

"I'm not the kind of man who falls in love," Jake said. "I'm like the bloke in that Status Quo song – 'The Wanderer'."

I snorted, because this was all utterly ridiculous. Jake was a grown man. He was thirty-two. He knew as well as I did that, whether or not those three words had passed his lips, Aoife was entitled to think they had a future together.

"Look, I wasn't ready for a baby," he added. "She caught me on the hop. Can you imagine what it's like to be told out of the blue you're going to have a baby?"

"No," I said, my heart lurching, "I can't imagine that one little bit."

"Well, then you get it then, don't you?"

"No, Jake, I don't. There are things in life you can't just walk away from and your own children are among those things. You helped make that baby, the least you could have done was stayed around to see her come into the world. What you did was the lowest of the low."

"Well, I'm going to change all that now, aren't I?" said Jake, defensively.

"Well, unless you are Superman I doubt very much you have the power to fly around the world so fast you manage to turn back time."

"I know that, but I can make it better. I'm going to see Aoife and do right by her and the baby."

"Maggie," I said. It irked me to hear him call her "the baby". She was so much more than just "the baby".

"I want to be a part of her life and of Aoife's too if she will have me."

My heart sank. Once again I'd managed to fuck up. I wanted him to clear off forever but it seemed I had talked him into taking responsibility and going back into Aoife's life. I might not have been the cleverest woman in the world but I knew that particular scenario was not going to end well.

"She's doing okay without you," a voice from the kitchen said.

I looked around at Dan.

"You've done enough damage, Jake. Why don't you just leave Aoife and Maggie be. They don't need you."

"I've changed," Jake replied and I heard myself snort in unison with my husband.

"I don't care if you believe me. I'll prove it. I can be a father, and a responsible partner."

"But you don't love her . . ."

"Who said that?" Jake asked with a sly grin.

"You said so yourself!" I could no longer hide the exasperation from my voice.

"No, I said I never said the words. That is completely different – and anyway, there is more to life than love, isn't there?"

No, I thought, looking at Dan's stricken face, there isn't.

34

Aoife

My phone rang at 3 a.m., just as Maggie was settling back down to sleep after her feed. The ringing woke her and she was as unimpressed as I was. But much as I would like to be the kind of person who can ignore a ringing phone, I have always been too nosey not to answer. Even though it was most likely to be some drunken eejit looking for their girlfriend or boyfriend, there was a wee part of me that instantly was convinced it would be a call from home telling me someone was dead or dying. Soothing an irate Maggie on my shoulder, I answered.

"Hello?"

"Aoifs. It's Jake. I'm outside, can you let me in?"

I knew instantly he was drunk. Maggie's crying stepped up a decibel and I rocked her gently. Looking down at myself, I realised I was in a right state. I was tired, wearing my old maternity PJs which now sagged unattractively at the stomach. My hair was greased back off my face and my daughter – our daughter – was screaming her lungs out and, oh yes, pulling her knees up to her tiny belly letting me know that an almighty rumble was not far away.

"Aoifs!" he called again.

I felt myself well up. I wanted this meeting to be on my terms. I wanted the upper hand for once but if I didn't let him in now, maybe I would have lost my chance.

I opened a crack of the window and shouted to him that I would be down in a minute. He looked up, bleary-eyed, and unsteady on his feet.

"She's got a great set of lungs, doesn't she?" he shouted. "Takes after her old man!"

A part of me really hoped that wouldn't be the case.

I walked down the stairs, the rhythmic movement settling Maggie into an uneasy slumber, and opened the door.

He was leaning against a lamppost, staring at his shoes. And then he looked up. He was almost beatific – his deep blue eyes, his stubbly face and his smooth head.

His full lips – oh, how I loved those full lips! – parted and he said: "Let me in, Aoifs. I'm dying for a slash."

He followed me up the stairs and for the first time since knowing Jake I was uncomfortable with him walking behind me, getting a good look at my post-baby butt and that made me walk all the faster.

"You know where the bathroom is," I said as he darted down the hall.

Shaking with nerves, I placed our daughter back in her Moses basket in the bedroom and sat on the sofa waiting for him to come back.

"Thanks for that, Aoifs," he said, sitting down and stretching out on the sofa. "I was bursting."

I nodded. "So?"

"Buttons," he replied, and fell about laughing as if it were the funniest joke in the world.

I should have known I would get no sense out of him – not in that state anyway. But I persisted for a good twenty minutes before I gave up.

"You wanted to talk," I said.

"Yes, but you know, Aoifs, I'm shattered. Can't we talk in the morning?"

My heart sank further. In fact I started to worry it was going to sink right through my feet and land splattered on the daybed in the shop below.

"I'll call you a taxi," I said, reaching for the phone.

"Well, I was kind of thinking I could sleep here," he slurred.

His eyes stared at me, pleading with me to let him into my life again, and even though I wanted him to leave, I couldn't bring myself to say the words.

I lifted a throw and tossed it in his direction and then I walked out of the room, head held high, before crawling into bed and crying myself to sleep.

I woke at six to feed Maggie and he was still sleeping, snoring heavily. I woke again at eight and he was still sleeping. I fed Maggie, showered and dressed and still he slept. I felt like a caged lion, unable to do whatever I wanted or needed. It was Saturday. The shop was closed. Beth wasn't going to come and force open the shutters and climb up the stairs to me for a natter. I was here with my own thoughts. The flat suddenly seemed stifling. Looking out the window, I saw the sun sitting over the roofs across the street. It was going to be a gorgeous day, one of the brisk and sunny March days which signal the end of winter. I wrapped Maggie in a blanket and went downstairs. I let myself out into the musty old yard at the back of the shop. In the warmer weather Beth and I would sit on the wrought-iron fire escape and drink wine, ignoring the concrete around us. I pulled a cushion from the shop and set it on the stairs before sitting down with my daughter in my arms.

I glanced at my watch: it was gone ten. Still a wee bit too early to call Beth on a weekend. She and Dan usually spent the morning in bed before she went out to see clients in the afternoon. Given everything I'd uncovered this week, I certainly did not want to be the person to put demands on their couple time.

I had barely slept. My dreams had been filled with memories of Jake and our courtship. And no matter what lovely moment I'd recalled, the dreams always turned back to that moment when he turned and walked out on me just as I told him he was going to be a father.

And yet it had been a tonic to see him. It felt good to be in the same flat, the same room as him. Good and comfortable. I wished, for just a second, that I could turn back the clock just for one day to have that time with him again. I didn't want to wish Maggie away. I just wanted a taste of my old uncomplicated life for just one day. Just one lazy morning shag. Just one afternoon in the pub, lost in each other. Just one night watching him sing, listening to his voice and knowing it was for me.

But looking at my girl, of course that wasn't going to happen. I had to make the most of what I did have. I hugged her close to me, singing "Twinkle Twinkle" to her and rocking slowly back and forward. Being with Jake felt comfortable but this, this gorgeous closeness, felt natural. I didn't need to play games with my daughter. I was me and me was good enough. She couldn't talk yet, but I knew if she could she would tell me she loved me. And I wouldn't have to earn that love, it was there in spades.

I sat there for a short time, until it got a little chilly and I got tired of the view. There was only so much staring at concrete you could do with a month-old baby on your knee and only so many verses of "Twinkle Twinkle" you could sing. I made a mental note to learn more nursery rhymes. Surely there was a class, or a book or an online resource I could use. I snorted to myself – of course – there was always Beth's online resource. I'm sure those motherly types knew every nursery rhyme going. There was, I knew, no point in asking my mother. She didn't do nursery rhymes. They were "twee and juvenile".

Walking back to the flat, the first thing I noticed was the absence of snoring. The second was the smell of stale beer. The third thing I noticed was Jake pulling on his trousers and buckling his belt. It was all too familiar.

"You wanted to talk," I started, a feeling of panic rising.

"I do," he said, sleepy and sexy, "but I have to be somewhere. You shouldn't have let me sleep so late . . ."

"I thought you needed it. You were out of it last night."

"Look, I'll come back later and we'll talk. Promise."

And he was gone. And it was only then that it dawned on me he hadn't even looked at the baby in my arms.

"Don't let the fucker hurt you, sweetheart."

You've got to love Auntie Anna. Always to the point. Her first reaction to my news that Jake had stayed over (on the sofa) and would be returning later, was to let rip a series of expletives so vitriolic she would need to spend a month in confession for it.

"I won't, Anna. I'm stronger now," I said with conviction, although in my head I wondered what exactly he wanted to talk about. Could he have come to his senses? Yes, well, I knew he hadn't looked at Maggie as he left but he probably didn't want to have that grand meeting with her when he was rushing out the door to something. He would want to do it right – savour the moment. I made a mental note to dress her in the gorgeous wee romper from Next I'd picked up in Derry for his return visit.

"Aoife, are you there?"

"Sorry. I was a little distracted."

"It's no wonder but, darling, I know you think you're stronger but chances are your head is still pretty messed up. I remember after I had Maeve, my head was mince for months. I thought I was losing the plot. I made all kinds of rash decisions. I even threw a chair at poor Billy once."

I laughed a little, to hide my discomfort. "I'll be fine, Anna. You don't have to worry about me. And anyways, aren't I too scared of you to do anything stupid?"

"Damn right, lady. I'll be on the first cheap flight to London to kick your arse."

I held the coffee cup in my hand while Beth rocked Maggie back and forth. Mrs Morelli bustled around us, tidying up the shop and getting ready to go home. She was kind enough not to lift the coffee cups from us and shoo us out. Perhaps she knew this was proper serious conversation.

"I'm sorry. I should have phoned and warned you but I didn't actually think he would just show up like that. He was pretty wasted by the time he left ours and I knew you would be sleeping . . ."

Poor Beth looked distraught.

"It's fine, Beth. You weren't to know he would actually go through with it. He hasn't really gone through with anything much in his life lately – unless you count his super-successful music career." I was proud of myself that I managed a snort at that point. Perhaps I was stronger than I thought.

I sipped from my cup and she looked down at my daughter. For the first time I could see the longing in my friend's eyes and it almost took my breath away. I felt a bubble of emotion try to force itself up from my throat and quickly I patted it back down. Beth didn't want this sympathy. Support? Yes, but tears and pity? Never. And besides, if I started to feel sorry for her would it mean that I believed it was never going to happen for her? I didn't think I could allow myself to contemplate that.

"Promise you won't let him hurt you," Beth said.

"Why does everyone keep saying that?"

"Who's everyone?"

"Well, Auntie Anna, and you . . . and Anna . . ."

"It's only because we care about you," Beth offered.

"I know, but I'm a big girl. I'm able to protect myself."

She glanced down at Maggie again.

"And I'll protect her too, Beth. I won't let anyone hurt her," I said.

"I'm glad to hear that."

Jake had phoned to say he would call over after eight. I fed Maggie and showered for the second time that day. For the first time in what felt like years, I shaved my legs and the suspect bikini area.

I didn't want him to want me, but I wanted him to know what he was missing. Not that he would get to see the delightful topiary in my pants, but I would know it was there and it would make me feel stronger in myself. I would feel like a proper woman and not just a bruised fandango with leaking boobs.

I even put some make-up on, dusting some bronzer along my collar-bones and between my breasts. Not that he would see my breasts. No way.

I dressed in nice underwear, wearing a thong for the first time since early pregnancy and a lilac lace Elle MacPherson nursing bra. I pulled on some indigo boot-cut jeans and a V-neck white T-shirt. I wanted to create the alluring, but not slutty, look of a woman ready to tramp on the heart of the man who had trampled on her heart.

Not that I was going to let him see just how much he had trampled on my heart. No way.

★   ★   ★

Maggie was sleeping when the doorbell rang and I was halfway through a glass of Pinot Grigio to steady my nerves. The TV had been on for some time, but if pressed there was no way I could tell you what was actually showing on it. It seemed I had been lost in a blur of memories, hopes, fears and promises that I would be strong – that and running around cleaning, tidying, hiding packets of nappies under the chairs.

I opened the door and saw him walk up the stairs to me. He looked up and he broke into his trademark smile. He seemed impressed.

"Wow, Aoifs! You are looking good. Motherhood obviously suits you."

Yes, by the way his eyes were drawn to my swollen breasts I could tell he was very, very impressed with just how much motherhood agreed with me. I pulled my arms across my chest, but not quick enough to stop that frisson of excitement in my core at having him look at me with lust in his eyes.

"Come in, Jake," I said, lifting a glass from the kitchen and walking back towards him. Automatically I poured him a glass of wine and sat down beside him. "Your daughter is sleeping in the other room."

"I'll see her after we talk," he said and I wondered for a moment how he could resist the urge to run straight in to her and scoop her up into his arms. "I want to see you first." And he looked deep into my eyes.

Oh, I could sense this wasn't going to end well. Someone was going to be hurt by the time this was over and, if the pounding of my heart was anything to go by, it was going to be Anna and Beth.

I tried to speak, honestly I did, but the words just wouldn't come out. So I sipped my wine and met his gaze again.

"I really was a bastard. Wasn't I?"

"Something like that," I muttered. I noticed he was still staring at my breasts, and I caught myself looking at his hands – his strong, passionate hands which could leave me trembling. No, I reminded myself inwardly, this is a very, very bad man who hurt you and left you to give birth alone in a strange hospital.

"I'm sorry," he said, putting his glass of wine on the floor and reaching out for my hands. "I should have given you more of a chance. I just freaked out. I wasn't ready for a baby."

"Wasn't?" I repeated, as a small flicker of hope lit in me that perhaps a leopard really could change his spots.

He smiled. "I'm ready to have you in my life again, Aoifs. I've missed you." His subtle glances downwards at my breasts became less subtle and I took a deep breath.

"Jake, you can't just walk in and out of my life when you want. This is about more than me and you now. I have a daughter. *We* have a daughter."

He stroked my hand. "I know that, Aoifs."

"Well, she is my number-one responsibility now, Jake, not you."

"Hey, I understand," he said, running his forefinger gently along my wrists, circling erogenous zones I had long since forgotten about.

My breath deepened and my head spun. I wasn't sure what was happening. This was not the Jake I knew and hated, or loved, or cried myself to sleep over. This was some strange creature who was showing empathy and concern and telling me he wanted me in his life.

Me. He was ready to be in my life again.

But he didn't say our lives. Me and Maggie – the McLaughlin girls. Mother and daughter.

"Do you want to hold her?" I asked, withdrawing my hand from his and standing up.

"My mum always said never wake a sleeping baby," he replied, reaching for my hand again.

"She sleeps a lot, Jake, and you don't have to wake her to hold her."

I walked away, aware he was watching me as I left, and lifted our perfect little girl into my arms. Not sure whether or not I could trust him not to hurt her, either physically or emotionally, I walked back into the room and handed her to him. He sat down, cradling her in his strong arms. I expected him to look awkward, to look disgusted, but he looked for all intents and purposes as if he had done this a thousand times – as if the crook of his arm was made for the curve of her spine.

Tears sprang to my eyes.

"She's a cracker, isn't she?" he said, looking back at me.

And it was in that moment that I knew no matter what we would always be a family. He was her father and no amount of me wishing him in her life or wishing him out of her life was going to change that. We three were intrinsically linked.

He began to sing, crooning so quietly I could barely hear it. The words were so familiar and yet I'd never heard them sung like this before – like a ballad. This was our song, but now it was his and Maggie's and my heart melted just as it did every time Jake Gibson walked into my life and, just as with every time he walked in, I started to fool myself that he would never walk back out again.

"Signed, Sealed, Delivered". Surely that had to mean something?

I walked to the kitchen just to steady my nerve, looking out the window at my concrete garden – into the blackness – and I tried to quell the thudding in my chest. I stood there for five, maybe ten minutes and then I walked back into the room. Jake had placed Maggie back in her Moses basket and was staring into the bottom of his wine-glass.

"Don't you think she looks like me?" he asked eventually.

"Yes," I replied, looking into his eyes and seeing the same slope of nose that I had seen on Maggie's face, the same shape of eye, the fullness of lips.

I realised I might already have had too much to drink. Damn pregnancy – makes you a fecking lightweight.

He looked at me then, at my boobs *and* my face, and he reached his hand to my cheek. The roughness of his skin felt sublime against my face and my eyes closed as I drank in the feel of him. I had missed this. Missed him.

"Aoifs," he said, only it was more of a gentle moan and he reached towards me, brushing his lips against mine.

My whole body felt alive as I responded, slowly at first, tasting him, feeling him respond in turn. It had been nine months – nine very long and very lonely months – since I had been kissed by Jake Gibson and every part of my body felt suddenly alive.

In fact some of my body felt a little too much alive.

It was with a mixture of alarm of "oh holy fuck, what is this?" that I realised that not only were my nipples standing proud (which I expected) but they were also leaking breast-milk all over my pristine cotton T-shirt (which I did not expect).

I could sense his hand move toward me and much as I wanted and needed him to cup my breast in his hand and do with it what he wanted, I just couldn't.

"Stop," I said, pulling back from him and trying to focus on the room around me. "Stop."

35

Beth

The drive to my mother's house had been an odd experience. I don't think either of us could switch off all those horrible little thoughts that were running through our minds.

I knew that just as we were powering down the motorway, Jake would be sitting in Aoife's flat, chatting to her – possibly even cuddling Maggie. My Maggie.

If I asked Dan once if it would be okay to call Aoife just to see how things were going, I asked him a thousand times. But he just told me, over and over, that it would be prudent to wait until she phoned me.

"Aoife's a big girl," he said again, like some New Age mantra.

And then again, we had problems enough of our own. We had to face my mother and Dan had made me promise to come clean about our problems conceiving. It's not the ideal conversation you want to have with your mother over the lamb roast on a Sunday, now is it?

While my mother and I had a gorgeous friendship, there was still a part of me that could never be comfortable discussing my ovaries and my sex life with her. Even in my late teens I used to turn an attractive shade of beetroot if I needed her to get me some "women's things" when my period arrived. So to discuss my desire to conceive a child seemed somehow wrong. But then, surely if anyone understood how nice it was to have children, then it would be my mum. She'd had three of us and, according to family legend, would have had a whole heap more if my father hadn't put his foot down.

I think our house became a sort of halfway house for waifs and strays because of that. Both my sister and brother had brought friends home almost every weekend while they were at university and, while I studied a little bit further away, I generally came home accompanied by an Aoife totally gobsmacked by our lifestyle.

I'll admit, we had it nice. We were spoiled materially, but much more importantly with love and I wanted so desperately to share that with my own child.

"Your mum will be fine with this, you know. You haven't actually done anything wrong," Dan soothed.

"I know, and I know it means she might lay off the 'when are you going to make me a grandma' comments for a while, but I can't help but feel she will be disappointed in me."

"That's daft, Bets. You know that."

I looked at him, his eyes staring straight ahead at the road as he drove. "I just want to have your baby so much."

"Remember you said that when you're threatening to cut my balls off in the delivery room."

"I can assure you I will never, ever threaten to cut your balls off. They mean too much to me."

"Even if they can't give you a baby?" he said, staring onwards – afraid even to glance at me, even for a second.

"Even if we never have children and I'm stuck talking to no one but you for the rest of my life," I answered – and, actually, I started to realise I wasn't lying this time.

Still, I wasn't going to give up on this just yet. Not when we had our appointment to look forward to on Thursday.

Dan pulled the car onto the driveway, the gravel crunching below the wheels as we drove to the front door. Floodlights illuminated the front of the house and I could see the lights on in the dining-room and lounge. Mum was obviously cooking dinner – any excuse to show off her eight-seater dining-table which was a bit grand and ornate for my liking but was her pride and joy.

I had yet to convince my mother to let me "do" her house. The closest I got to an Instant Karma makeover was a revamp of my old room, where Dan and I slept when we visited.

I stepped out of the car just as my mother opened the big red front door and smiled beatifically at us.

"Oh darlings, it is so nice to see you! It has been much too long."

She walked towards me and enveloped me in a hug and I breathed in her comforting scent of fabric softener mixed with Chanel No. 5.

"It's nice to see you, Mum," I muttered into her, before she released me from her hug and made for Dan.

"You really shouldn't keep our daughter away from us like this," she scolded. "We've missed you both. Come in, grab a drink. Dinner will be ready in ten and then you can fill me in on all your news."

We looked at each other. Without speaking I think we both realised what that meant, and neither of us wanted to give the family indigestion talking about our issues over the desserts.

Dan carried our overnight bag upstairs while I hung up our coats and poured myself a glass of wine. Sitting on a stool at the kitchen island, I watched my mother strain pasta and put the garlic bread in to bake.

"It's nothing fancy," she said. "Just pasta with garlic bread and salad. I haven't had a chance to get down to Waitrose."

"I'm sure it will be lovely, Mum," I said, reaching for a sliver of cheese from the board she had prepared for after dinner.

"You look tired, Beth, and a little pale. Have you been working too hard?"

"I always work too hard," I said with a wry smile. She looked a little worried and I reached out and touched her hand. "I'm fine, Mum. Don't fuss. Things are a bit crazy with Aoife and the baby and all, but honestly I'm okay."

"And how is Aoife and the gorgeous Maggie? I must get up to see them. I would have been up before now but I didn't want to gatecrash on you and Dan when you both work so hard."

"Maggie is beautiful and Aoife seems to be taking to motherhood like a duck to water. I have a few pictures in my case. I'll bring them down after dinner and show you."

Mum took a sip from her wine-glass. "Funny, I never saw Aoife as the motherly type. I always assumed you and Dan would be parents long before she settled down."

I nodded. Now was not the time for this conversation.

"I think she thought that too, Mum, but sometimes things don't work out just as you would think."

Dan walked into the room and kissed me lightly on the top of the head. "Pauline, can I help you with anything?" he said.

"Ooh yes. Can you toss that salad while Beth runs and get the pictures of Aoife and Maggie. I'm dying to see them."

Dan rolled his eyes at me. We both knew babies were going to be the main topic of conversation while we were here – but we had been kind of hoping to do it on our terms and not my mother's.

"There will be time to see them after dinner, Mum," I said. "I'll go and set the table. Dan will toss the salad and you can pour my gorgeous husband here a glass of this fine Chardonnay."

"Yes, dear," Mum said, lifting a wine-glass from the cupboard.

"Your dad should be here any minute and then we can eat."

"Thank God for that. I'm starving," Dan said. "That daughter of yours hasn't fed me today."

My father – a burly man who to outsiders looked reserved but who actually had a heart of gold – arrived some ten minutes later, just as I was polishing off my first glass of wine and pouring my second.

He walked in and smiled before kissing me gently on the top of my head in much the same way my husband had done.

"How are you, princess?" he asked. "You look pale. Are you working too hard?"

I smiled. "I thought Mum was supposed to be the worrier! I'm fine, Dad. It's been a long week and I'm looking forward to a day off tomorrow. For tonight I'm just going to eat, drink and be merry,"

"That's my girl," he said, patting me on the shoulder before sitting down in front of the glass of wine waiting for him.

"So why has it taken so long for you to bring my daughter down to see us?" Dad asked Dan.

"I've been pushing her to come down here for weeks, but you know how it is. Something always gets in the way and work has been mad for both of us, especially since Aoife went on maternity leave."

"Aah, Aoife. How is she? Has that cowardly bastard of a father lived up to his responsibilities yet?"

I felt Dan blush. Even though it wasn't his fault – even though Jake was an independent adult – Dan couldn't help but feel somehow responsible for introducing him to Aoife in the first place. I squeezed his hand under the table.

"Aoife doesn't need him to raise her baby," I said. "She's doing a great job."

"Of course she is. You two girls are wonderful at everything you turn your hand to," Dad said. "And won't it be great when you and

Dan here have your own baby? Aoife will have been there and done that first. She's a great girl."

It was my turn to grimace – just a little – not enough for anyone other than Dan to notice and it was his turn to squeeze my hand gently under the table.

Whatever happened to the days when we used to play footsie under the table? Now we were reduced to supportive hand-squeezes. I couldn't help but smile wryly. Maybe if there was more footsie and less "handsy" we would be pregnant by now.

"She is indeed a great girl," I said as my mother walked in carrying her salad and garlic bread.

I knew it was going to be a night of wine and good food. Did I really want to ruin it with news of our problems?

No, that could wait till the morning, I told myself as I tucked in. It wasn't like anything was going to change between now and then anyway.

Dan and I curled together in the wrought-iron bed in my freshly designed room. The dinner had been lovely and for the most part we had managed to steer the conversation away from babies. For all his encouragement to be open with my folks, I knew he was reluctant to actually say the words "We are having problems having children" out loud. I turned around to look at him, his face silhouetted in the dark room, and I gently traced my finger along the line of his jaw. I don't know how I could have been so blind to it before. He was worried that this was all his fault just as much as I was worried it was mine. These new tests we would have might get us some answers but they might not be answers we wanted to hear. It was okay-ish thinking no one and nothing was to blame. How would we manage if we found out differently?

I stared at the clock. It had gone five. I was suddenly so thirsty that I knew there was no way I was getting back to sleep without first drinking a long cold glass of water to quench my thirst. Slipping out of bed and into my dressing-gown, I padded down to the kitchen and poured some water from the fridge.

As I drank, I wondered how Aoife was. Please God she had sent Jake packing and he would clear off on some half-baked dream again sometime soon. I didn't want him getting his hands on my goddaughter. At the thought of the word "daughter" I sighed and drank deeply from my glass.

"You okay, darling?" my mother's voice called out.

I looked up to find her standing poised with one of Dad's golf clubs in her hand as if she was about to take a swing for me.

"Jesus, Mum, what on earth are you doing?"

"We're not used to having people about any more," she said, blushing furiously. "I forgot you and Dan were here and when I heard someone rattle around in the kitchen I thought we might have had burglars."

"I'm sorry," I laughed. "I didn't think I had been that noisy."

"Don't fret. I wake at the drop of a pin these days. The rattle of the ice-cubes would have done it."

"Can I pour you a glass too?"

"Ah, go on. Let's be devils!" she laughed, passing me a tall glass for her water. She sat down on the stool opposite me.

I marvelled at how her perfectly coiffed hairstyle seemed to have survived what little sleep she had managed.

I rubbed my eyes and drank some more. "I really need to realise my limits when it comes to wine. I'm going to regret that in the morning."

"You only live once and, besides, once you have kids you won't be able to manage it any more. Enjoy yourself now while you still can."

At that, I burst into tears – watery, gulping sobs that racked my body and made my mother adopt a very concerned look indeed.

"Darling, what's wrong? Is it me? Damn it. Your father has told me I need to stop badgering you and Dan about having kids. It's just, well, you know I'd love to be a grandma. But you do it in your own time, sweetheart. I'm not one to butt in to your life. I'm really sorry if I've upset you."

"Oh Mum," I cried, "I'm so sorry. There's something I need to tell you."

36

Aoife

"I kissed him. Or more he kissed me. Anyway we kissed, and I'm sorry, but nothing else happened. I promise. God, I'm embarrassed to tell you this, but my boobs, well they started leaking and then I wasn't quite in the mood any more."

"Thank Jesus and the wee donkey for your leaky boobs," Anna answered, her voice thick with concern.

And there was me thinking the story of my leaky boobs would have raised a smile, or maybe even a wee laugh from her.

Nada.

"I know you don't approve," I started, "but I think he may actually have changed."

She snorted.

"You should have seen the way he looked at Maggie. He was totally besotted with her."

"So he stayed then? Despite your leaky boobs? Just so he could get to know his daughter a little better and maybe change a nappy or two?"

I rolled my eyes at the phone. I had fully expected this to be hard work, but not this hard. Then again, I knew what I was about to say sounded a little pathetic.

"No. Well, he stayed for a bit and then he had to go. He's in the studio today and he needed his sleep."

"Aoife, you deserve better." Her tone was harsh. It reminded me of that night I went out and got wasted in Derry.

"You don't know him, Anna," I said.

"I know enough of him. You are an intelligent woman. I know he's Maggie's daddy but you don't really believe him now? If he really cared he would have stayed, or he would have called sometime in the last nine months. He can't just walk in and out when he wants to."

"But I loved him," I said.

"That's the first sensible thing I've heard you say all day, young lady," Anna said. "If you are saying you 'loved' him then there might just be hope for you yet."

We finished our call and I wrapped Maggie up and headed for the park at the top of the street. Anna was right, of course she was. I knew that, but love wasn't always about being sensible, was it? When he had kissed me last night I had wanted him. I hadn't cared about how much he hurt me. I just wanted the perfect life we could have together – like we had before he walked out on us. I couldn't see that it was so wrong to want that.

And it would make life easier at home. Perhaps not with Anna, who at this stage was probably fashioning a voodoo doll of both Jake and me to attack with pins. No, knowing Anna she was probably making a chart detailing how and when she would tear us apart – and then she would make the voodoo dolls.

But my mother, chances are she would be delighted. After all, the shame would be gone. Sure it was a bastard that we hadn't managed to get married before our daughter was born, but Mother would soon forgive us for that once I phoned her and told her to buy a hat and head down to Veronica's for a Mother of the Bride outfit.

There was a spring in my step as I walked through the paths of the park until slowly, like it always did, that sinking feeling returned. I'd always had that sinking feeling with Jake. In fact, when I thought of how he used to make me feel, I'd forgotten just how far my heart could sink with him. It had always been that way. I'd always been waiting for the axe to fall and for the next humiliation to be heaped upon humiliation.

The first time I saw him I'd been blown away. He had been on stage singing, moving his hips, eyes closed in the spotlight.

People had been chatting all around us, enjoying their pints and glasses of wine, but all I could see was him. I told him that once and he had laughed it off, saying that of course all I could see was him – who else in that bar would have been looking at anyone else but him?

But yet he must have seen something in me he liked, because between sets he sat by me, bought me drinks and talked to me like there was no one else in the world that mattered. And it wasn't as if he couldn't get attention when he wanted it. Women swarmed to him. Like flies round shite, Anna would no doubt say. I realised those swarming women came with the territory. It would have been foolish and the cause of much heartache not to. Both Beth and Dan sent gentle warning signals to me.

"He's not the settling-down type," Dan drawled in a faux American accent, while nuzzling into Beth's neck.

"Not like ma sugar plum," Beth drawled back, and we all laughed.

Because at that time, in those early weeks and months, there was no way I even considered settling down with Jake. He was to be a bit of fun, which I know is terribly un-PC, but that is all I was interested in. Work was going well and while I wouldn't have said no if Mr Perfect had come along and whisked me off my feet, I wasn't openly seeking anyone. I just wanted someone to have a few drinks with, maybe a little rumpy pumpy with (well, in fairness, maybe a lot of rumpy pumpy with) and if anything more came out of that so well and so good.

But when I met Jake first – when I saw how women flocked around him and how he in turn responded to them – I resigned myself to the fact that he was not a keeper. I'm not sure when I changed my mind. Maybe it was after four months when we were still together and people started referring to him as my boyfriend. Maybe it was when he was still there at six months and I realised I missed him when he wasn't around. Or maybe it was on our year anniversary when he crooned to me from the stage and announced to a crowded room that I, Aoife McLaughlin, was his number-one girl. So despite my best intentions not to fall under his spell, I did, and all the while I hoped he was falling under mine too. Seems my magic appeal – my allure – was on the blink though because he didn't.

"Or did he?" I muttered aloud. "Now he's back telling me he's missing me and wanting to be with us – as a family. Everything I've cried for, prayed for, hoped for over the last nine months, no matter how much I cursed him!" And so it should have been simple, but all I felt was utterly, utterly confused.

"It's the first sign of madness, you know," a voice from behind a tree called out.

I glanced up, realising I'd been talking to myself as I walked at full speed around the park. I saw a familiar head look out from behind the tree trunk and my face turned even redder.

I looked at Tom Austin with a mixture of embarrassment and indignation at being caught ranting to a pram and said: "I was talking to the baby."

"Good at relationship advice, is she?" he said, dropping the secateurs from his hands and dusting off his gardening gloves on his trousers.

"What are you doing here anyway?" I said, pulling a strand of stray auburn hair back from my face.

He looked down at his hands, at his gardening tools and looked back at me, a sly smile on his face.

"Well, maybe you should just get on with it then?" I said. "We wouldn't want to disrupt you."

I started to walk off, hopeful that I could pick up my pace again quickly, when he called after me.

"Aoife! Wait!"

I turned to see him walking towards me. I didn't need this now. I just wanted to walk and clear my head and figure out what the hell I was doing with my life.

"Look, I'm sorry. It seems I always make a complete tosspot of myself whenever you are around."

"S'okay," I sniffed.

"Is everything all right with you?"

"Trust me, you don't have time to hear this story, Tom. It will be dark in a couple of hours and it looks like you have work to do. Best leave it for a Bank Holiday or a month when you have nothing better to do." I managed a small smile.

"I have time if you need to talk," he said. "Look, I know you don't know me from Adam, but if you need to sound off to someone I'm pretty willing to bet I give better advice than a baby."

"Thanks," I said, and I genuinely meant it. "Look, I'll let you get on with your work, but I'll keep your offer in mind."

He smiled, and went to walk back to his spot behind the tree while I turned to start my walk again. But then, a strange thought popped into my head. Tom really could be a sounding board for this. He had no vested interest in me. Sure he thought I looked amazing, and yes admittedly he had already seen my jugs but unlike everyone else he had no reason to judge me or Jake. Yes, this could definitely work.

"Tom?" I called and he turned around, looking a little surprised. "Would you like to come round for dinner tonight? Perhaps I could do with someone to talk to."

A broad smile spread across his face. "I would like that very much, Aoife. I'll see you around eight."

I walked on and suddenly I realised I was more confused than ever. What the hell was I doing? Inviting a stranger – a male stranger – into our home? What would Jake think about it? Should I even care what Jake thought about it? And it wasn't as if Tom was a love interest, was it? He was a friend who had offered to listen and, with Beth up to her eyes in her own problems and Anna making her voodoo dolls, friends who were prepared to listen were in pretty short supply.

It dawned on me at that moment that it was entirely possible I was losing the plot altogether. "Oh Maggie, I feel sorry for you. You deserve a better mammy than the likes of me."

She gurgled and burped, smiling contentedly at me and I wondered for just a second if she was laughing at me.

When I got home I fed my daughter and then began to scan the cupboards for something suitable to cook for Tom and our strictly platonic, sounding-board dinner date. The problem was, having been away in Derry for the lion's share of the previous month and having spent the rest of the time surviving off chocolate biscuits and cups of milky decaffeinated coffee, the cupboards were bare. I was looking at some lonely jars of pasta sauce – which I was pretty sure had been there since before I moved in – and a few tins of soup. The fridge was a veritable wasteland with some wilted ham and a brown lettuce. I made a mental note to do one of the online shopping thingies when I got the chance, but that was not going to help me tonight. I doubt Tom would be satisfied with some chocolate biscuits or a cup of formula, so I started to dig through the phone book for the number of a takeaway. Yes, it was cheating but this was yet another one of those occasions when having a baby meant you couldn't just jump in the car and head to M&S for some ready-to-cook delight. I hadn't found the nerve to try the car seat in my Beetle yet and I wasn't about to try now – not without Beth to help me anyway.

I straightened the throws on the sofa and switched on the lamps. It was only then I noticed the light flashing on my answerphone. I pressed the button, waiting for Anna to admonish me further or Beth to tell me how things were going down at home with her folks.

Instead it was Jake, in a very uncharacteristic middle-of-the-afternoon call. I never expected to hear from him, ever, during the day – not even when we were officially a couple.

"Hey, babe," he drawled. "Hope you and Mags are doing okay. Look, babe, I know I said I would call over tomorrow night but it's not going to happen. I have a gig lined up. I'll call you when I'm free. Was great to see you last night."

I sat down, lifted a chocolate biscuit from the packet on the side table and took a large bite. Perhaps Jake hadn't changed at all. And her name wasn't Mags. It was Maggie. That irked me. It really fecking irked me. Jesus, was the word Maggie too hard for him to manage?

I finished the biscuit with the second bite before looking at my watch. Tom would be here in just over two hours, which was a good thing really as now I really, really needed to talk.

How had I come to this? How was it that it was a Sunday afternoon and the only people I had to talk to were a six-week-old baby girl and a man I had met only a handful of times and who, to all intents and purposes, was a complete stranger to me.

I lifted Maggie from her Moses basket and laid her down on her play-mat. Her little legs kicked with such determination and her eyes tried to focus on whatever they could. She seemed a little lost, and I knew how she felt so I knelt over her, singing to her softly, and she caught my eye before her wee mouth broke into a huge gummy grin. Her first gummy grin. I moved closer and kissed her cheeks, breathing her in through my tears of happiness. Someone loved me – unconditionally and in spite of my dreadful singing.

★　★　★

By the time Tom arrived I had worked my way through every emotion known to man and a few new ones I was pretty sure I had just invented right there and then in my Richmond flat on a Sunday afternoon. My eyes were rimmed red with tears – confused tears of both happiness and sadness and my CDs were scattered around the floor. I had taken them all out and treated a smiling Maggie to a musical history of my life, randomly playing a minute or two of each song before switching to the next song and the next memory. I had at least managed to feed Maggie and now she was lying in her vest ready for her bath which I had planned to do before Tom arrived. Then again, I had also planned to have the flat in decent order and dinner ordered.

Instead he was met with Meltdown Aoife – a tired mess of a thing reminiscent of that first time he had seen me in Morelli's.

"Are you okay?" he asked, and I snorted, that mixture of a laugh and a cry that pretty much summed up my mental state.

"I have to bath the baby," I added and he nodded, following me up the stairs and into the living-room.

"Can I do anything to help?" he asked.

"Just sit down," I said, a little gruffly, lifting Maggie up and heading for the bathroom. Softening, I added: "Make yourself at home."

Fair play to him, he had the decency not to look either

horrified, terrified or disgusted. From the little he knew of me, I guess he knew such behaviour was pretty much par for the course in my world.

I ran the tepid water into the baby bath and added some Baby Organics bath milk. I kind of wished I could climb into the sweet lavender-smelling water myself. I gently washed my daughter and then, as her eyes grew heavy, I gave her one last feed, kissed her gently and put in her Moses basket. For the first time since she was born, I prayed over her.

I sat watching her, for maybe twenty minutes. I watched the gentle rise and fall of her chest, the fluttering of her eyelids which was either the by-product of her sweet milky dreams or wind, and I stroked her cheek as if she were a china doll. Then I gathered myself together and walked into the living-room, fully expecting Tom to start lecturing me about my bad manners. It seemed people were lecturing me a lot this weather.

He wasn't there, but from the sounds and smells coming from the kitchen I knew he hadn't left.

"I hope you don't mind," he said without looking up as I walked into the kitchen. "I nipped out while you were bathing Maggie and bought in a few pieces for dinner. I'm not much of a cook but I'm guessing from your cupboards you aren't a gourmet cuisine type of gal. I wasn't sure what you liked, but I figured you can't go wrong with chicken, so I've put a few breasts on to roast and the potatoes and veg should be ready in about half an hour." He glanced at the clock on the kitchen wall and then at me.

There was only one question I could ask him: "Why?"

"Well, you don't want your potatoes lumpy. I hear you Irish are fussy about your spuds."

"No, Tom, why? Why are you doing this? Why are you here?"

"I suppose you're looking for an answer more in depth than 'because a strange woman asked me while I was working in the park'?" he asked, and I blushed.

"Well, yes. I know I asked you. But why the dinner? Most men would run. Why do you care?"

"Sit down, Aoife," Tom said, ushering me out of my own kitchen and handing me a glass of fizzy water. "I wasn't sure if breast-feeding mums could drink wine, so I thought this would do," he explained.

I sat down, feeling as if I was in some weird and wonderful twilight zone.

"I've not really been honest with you," he started.

I wondered momentarily if this was when he admitted he had been worming his way into my life so that he could kill me and chop me up to make some human brand of fertiliser for his gorgeous gardens. Could Tom Austin be a modern-day Sweeney Todd?

"So be honest with me, Tom, because it really feels as if no one has been honest with me for a long time."

"We have a mutual friend," he said. "Elena Kennedy. She told me about you when I said I was opening the shop near Instant Karma. You know yourself how Elena likes to talk, so I'm sorry but I know a lot of your story. I know about your ex and how he ran out on you and, to be honest, I thought your life sounded like a bit of a train-wreck."

I smiled, a watery mascara-streaked smile.

"Elena asked me to keep an eye on you. She thinks you are something pretty special, you know. Anyway, that first day I saw you in Morelli's it didn't take me long to figure out who you were. I guessed there couldn't be too many auburn-haired, Irish girls with new babies on the High Street and, if you don't mind me saying so, it seemed obvious to me that your life *was* a train-wreck. But I've seen you get stronger and I've seen how you care for your little girl and how you seem to care for your friends. But I can see you are floundering a bit and as I had promised Elena to keep an eye out for you, well – here I am. I've no agenda, Aoife. I'm just doing a favour for a friend and now that I know you a little bit more I think you could do with a friend."

"No one has ever cooked me dinner in this flat before," I muttered, because I couldn't bring myself to thank him for watching out for me. I was supposed to be a strong, independent woman and not need anyone watching out for me. But I did need it and even if it had only started as a favour to someone else (who I would most likely kill the next time I saw her, and then offer her body parts to Tom as fertiliser), it was still nice.

As it turned out, Tom Austin was a pretty good cook and an even better listener. It made me suspicious of him because surely there had to be something wrong with any man who seems to be quite wonderful at everything he turns his hand to? He served our dinner and once I pulled myself together enough to stop snivelling into it, I told him all about Jake and our near-miss the previous night.

"Do you think he really has changed?" Tom asked, sipping fizzy water from his wine-glass.

"I'd love to think so – for Maggie's sake. She deserves a daddy."

"It takes more than a roll in the hay to make someone a daddy," he said.

"I know, but you can't change the biology and he's not all bad. We had some good times. Damn it, we had some great times!"

"But was it really a relationship? From what you and Elena have told me it was just that – good times."

I blushed. Did Tom Austin and his perfect cooking and perfect listening think I was the perfect slut? Did he think I was some kind of nympho gagging for Jake?

"I did love him," I said, staring into his eyes because yes, while Jake Gibson was a fantastic lover who made me feel alive with his every touch, for me anyway it was all about true love. I loved how he made me felt physically but, more than that, I loved the excitement of life with him. I got off on the buzz of his gigs. I loved how he could make me feel like the centre of attention when he was in the mood and I had believed, genuinely believed, that even though he didn't tell me he loved me I didn't need those three little words to prove that what we had was worth it.

Tom didn't reply. It was as if he was waiting for me to explain further – to justify how I, a seemingly intelligent woman, could fall for such a ne'er-do-well as Jake.

"It was a different lifetime. I wasn't looking for forever with him, definitely not at first, but then as things carried on, I fell for him. And I loved the lifestyle – our lifestyle."

"So he treated you well then?" Tom asked, with a raised eyebrow. He knew the answer – he didn't need me to explain.

"He cared for me in his own way . . . but, Tom, if you had seen how he looked at Maggie and if you had heard all the promises he made, then trust me you would be tempted to give him a chance yourself."

"So why are you dithering then, Aoife? Why, if you believe what he told you last night, are you not with him now?"

"He's busy tonight."

Tom rolled his eyes. "And if he wasn't? Would you have run off into the sunset with him?"

"Well, that would certainly make my mother happy," I sniffed.

"But would it make you happy? Do you believe he could make you happy?"

"Yes ... no ... I don't know."

Tom had the good grace to smile. "You really are mixed up, aren't you?"

"I never pretended to be anything other than mixed up, Tom."

He topped up my glass, more of the fizzy water. "So why would your mother be so happy to see you with Jake?"

I looked at the clock. It had gone ten. There was no way I was getting into that conversation tonight. I needed at least five minutes' sleep before morning.

Tom left about an hour later, after we'd spent some time surveying and making plans for our yard.

"I'll check in with you tomorrow," he offered and I shrugged.

"You don't have to, Tom. I appreciate you listening but I'm sure you have better things to do than listen to me and my problems."

He laughed, and I realised what a beautiful smile he had. "Look, Aoife, you know how it is uncool for us men to watch soaps? Well, your life is better than that – and I can't wait for my next instalment."

He reached over and kissed me on the cheek, staring into my eyes as he stepped back, and a new kind of confusion flooded through me.

37

Beth

Mum had looked stricken when I told her that for the last two years we had been trying and failing to conceive her much-longed-for grandchild. She sat back on the kitchen stool and rubbed her eyes with her hands.

"Oh Beth, I'm so sorry. No wonder you've stayed away. I've been an awful, awful mother. God, when I think of all the things I've said to you, all those comments. Oh darling, you must really hate me!" She started to cry and I went to her and hugged her.

"Of course I don't hate you, Mum. You weren't to know."

"But to not tell me, darling! You must have been so angry with me not to tell me."

It never crossed my mind she would react in this way. "No, Mum. No, you don't understand. I wasn't annoyed at your comments. Yes, they hurt but that wasn't your fault. I didn't tell you – we didn't tell you – because we were coming to terms with everything. But you know what, Mum, I think I've accepted it now. I've accepted that there is a problem and it's not going to just happen for us, and that's okay."

"My poor darling! You must have been through hell."

She moved to hug me again and I put my hand up to stop her. I'd had my cry now. If I cried any more I was afraid I wouldn't stop.

"I'm okay, Mum," I tried to reassure her. "We'll see our consultant on Thursday and see what he has to say."

She sighed, sitting back down. "And do you know what he will do?"

"I don't know. More tests, I guess. But we know I'm ovulating and we know that Dan's okay, you know, down there." I blushed again. I could barely believe I was talking to my mother about sperm. Specifically my husband's sperm. I would prefer my mother didn't know he had any.

"So you've got him wearing boxers and eating all the right foods and everything?"

I raised my eyebrow.

"Don't look at me like that, Beth. I read magazines. This is more common than you think."

"I know, Mum. I know it's common," I said, shaking my head, but sometimes, when faced with Aoife and her amazing procreational abilities, it didn't feel common at all. I mean, for God's sake, Aoife threw up one pill – one pill – and bam, sperm, egg, baby. Job done.

Mum continued: "Look, I know it must be lonely. I know you must feel like the only person in the world who has ever tried and failed to conceive a baby, but it really is more common than you think. There was an article in *Marie Claire* about it just last month. Wait there, I'll run and find the copy."

"Mum, there's no need," I said as she disappeared out of the room.

Well, at least she knew. And Aoife knew. It was all out there in the open now and thankfully the pair of them had taken it well.

They hadn't stared at me with unwanted sympathy, they'd just got on with it.

I heard her run down the stairs and then she re-entered the kitchen, *Marie Claire* under her arm and a rather sheepish-looking husband behind her.

"Your mum has told me," Dad said, his face blushing as crimson as my red pyjama trousers. "Princess, whatever it takes. Whatever money you need. Whatever we can do, we'll help you through this."

I smiled, weakly. God only knows what Mother had told him. Knowing her, she'd even revealed Dan's sperm was A-okay. And I definitely did not want my daddy to know anything about sperm. No way.

He came over and hugged me, an awkward middle-class kind of a hug which radiated embarrassment but a certain sense of duty.

"And Beth, if it turns out that you can't have babies, sure we can always buy one of those ones from one of those eastern countries or the like."

At least that made me laugh, but for the life of him my father couldn't understand why.

We chatted for a little longer and then, all of a sudden, I felt tired. The kind of tiredness that only comes when you have truly been unburdened. There might only have been a wee glimpse of it but as I climbed the stairs to bed, *Marie Claire* under my arm, I felt – just for a split second – a little glimmer of hope.

I climbed into bed, spooning myself against a still sleeping Dan and fell into the most restful sleep I had had in about a year.

When I woke he had gone. The sun was streaming through the Roman blinds, casting a shadow across the room and from a quick glance at the height of the sun in the sky I realised I must have been asleep for a long time. I looked at the clock by the bed and saw it had gone eleven. Ordinarily this would have me sitting bolt upright and jumping at the day, but not today. Today I felt relaxed and I allowed myself to sink back down into the pillows and close my eyes again.

When I woke for a second time, Dan was beside me, cup of tea and bacon sandwich in hand. I had a sense he had been there for some time and as I opened my eyes he reached over and kissed me gently on the forehead.

"Morning, Betsy," he said with a smile.

"Hey, you."

"So you told your parents then?" he said, rubbing his hand gently along my arm.

"I did."

"And they were fine?"

"They were fine but most of all, Dan, I was fine. I'm sorry. You were right. We should have told them a long time ago. We had nothing to be ashamed of, and I'm sorry for all I've put you through."

He put his finger to my lips – in an act so tender and delicate that I felt my heart leap in my chest in the way it had done all those years ago.

"For better or worse, Beth," he said and then he kissed me.

38

Aoife

"So there were two kisses then?" Beth asked, as I curled my feet up under me on the daybed and opened our second packet of Jaffa Cakes.

"Well, I don't know if Tom's counts as a kiss," I said through a mouthful of biscuity goodness.

"Did his lips touch your anatomy?" Beth said with a wicked smile.

"Well, yes, but it wasn't a snog. Jesus, I sound like a fourteen-year-old talking about snogs! Surely there must be a more acceptable way to discuss a curt with a member of the opposite sex."

"Curt, I like that word," Beth laughed, practising her best Derry accent. In our thirteen years of friendship she had mastered an impressive repertoire of Derry phrases, and curt, Derry teenage slang for snogging, was her current favourite. "You could always say embrace," she added.

"I think I'll stay with curt!" I answered. "Anyway, we were talking and, Beth, I have to tell you he's a great listener. Things just happened. I don't even know how." I touched my fingers to my cheek, to the exact spot where his lips had made contact. "But I'm sure it was just a friendly kiss and I'm sure that's all I want it to be," I said with a false confidence.

"And what do you want from Jake? Please tell me you don't want him back, not after everything he has done!"

"Why does everyone keep saying that?" I sighed, cramming a full Jaffa Cake into my mouth.

"Because we care about you," Beth said.

I rolled my eyes in what I admit was a very childish gesture. I was rewarded for my childishness with a Jaffa Cake hurled directly at my head.

"He destroyed you, Aoife, and he walked out on Maggie."

"But he didn't. He didn't walk out on Maggie. Yes, he left me and he left a positive pregnancy test, but he didn't leave her. He came for her and you should have seen how he looked at her – like she was the most precious thing in the world!"

"So where is he now? Where was he yesterday when you were dining with Mr Austin? Where is he today?"

"Working," I said, and got up to put the kettle on. "Things are starting to happen for him."

It was her turn to roll her eyes. I realised this conversation wasn't going anywhere positive.

"Anyway, Tom is calling around later to look at our yard," I said in an effort to avert a crisis.

"Just look at it?" she said, a smile letting me know I had been successful.

"No, we were out there last night after dinner and he said it had a lot of potential as one of those gorgeous little city gardens. I don't know why we never thought of it before but now that I have Maggie I can't help but feel it would be nice to have somewhere to sit out in the summer. Not to mention, Tom said he would do it at a knock-down price if we showed it to clients looking for a similar makeover. Everyone's a winner!"

"And you get to spend more time with Tom," Beth said, eyebrow now seemingly permanently raised.

"Yes, I get to spend more time with a friend."

"Whose kiss on the cheek makes you all flustered."

Perhaps it was time to start talking about Jake again.

Beth had seemed more like herself that evening. I couldn't quite believe the transformation in her and yet, at the same time, I had a flash of guilt that I hadn't really realised how unlike herself she had become over the last few months.

I know that as excuses go mine was a pretty damn good one. I mean, how was I supposed to keep a track of her moods when my own were all over the place, while oestrogen and progesterone and whatever else was coursing through my veins at a rate of knots? But all that aside, she was my best friend. I had known her for thirteen years. I should have noticed her light dimming a little. But at least now I could see it brighten again. I could put all my problems, worries and concerns aside for just a few moments and be thankful for that.

And then I would go back to thinking about Jake and Tom, but Jake mostly with occasional thoughts of Tom and that softest of kisses on the cheek. At the end of the day, when Jake kissed me (and used his tongue) I'd known what his intentions were. He wanted me. I knew that and I knew I liked it. There was a familiar stirring in me and I knew – leaky boobs aside – that if he kissed me again I would be powerless to resist.

As for Tom. He was sweet and kind. He planted nice flowers. But his kiss was just a friendly one.

"It didn't mean anything," I said to Maggie as she gazed into my eyes, trying to convince myself I meant it.

Tuesday was always going to be a bit of a strange day. First of all I had agreed with Beth to take Maggie with me when I accompanied her on a visit to Elena Kennedy's pad. Apparently Elena's boudoir was now "dated" and she wanted a new look for the spring. We couldn't complain really – the woman was one of the sole reasons Instant Karma had stayed afloat in the early, dodgy years and thanks to her connections we were kept busier than we could really manage.

And then Jake was going to call round. He could finally slot us in – and I'm sure it was in the hope I could "slot him in" in return.

Packing Maggie's industrial-sized baby bag, I told her of our plans. "First we are going to see the lovely, Mrs Kennedy. If you could manage to look really, really cute and not throw up or do one of those big skittery poos of yours or squeal your head off, that would be grand. I've only brought three changes of clothes, so please keep that in mind. Feel free to sleep, my angel, too, any time you want."

I kissed her head and wondered if anyone in the world had hair as soft and downy as hers.

As I started to strap her into her car seat, the phone rang, making her jump out of her contented doze and scream blue murder.

It was Perfect Jacqueline. "Hi, Aoife. Goodness, Margaret doesn't sound too happy there, does she? Is it colic? It sounds like a colicky cry to me. Odhran had it for a bit but only after I ate out one night. You are eating properly, aren't you? It's very important when you are breast-feeding."

"Hi, Jacqueline, how are you?" I said, choosing to ignore her barbs.

"Well, actually, I was phoning to ask when you might be

available to do the baby's nursery. Time is ticking on."

I rolled my eyes. "But surely you are only about eighteen weeks gone? There's a lot of time."

"But you know your brother, Aoife. He likes things sorted long before time."

I knew that was a blatant lie. Joe was a typical man. He didn't give a flying feck if things were done on time or late. All he cared about was his work, his beer and the footie.

"But surely the baby will be with you for a couple of months first?"

"Six actually, or maybe seven. You know you're supposed to keep them with you for six at least? I hope you haven't put Margaret in her own room yet – she's much too young."

"Maggie is fine and she is with me," I answered tersely. "But then surely if Baby is going to be with you for six or seven months there is no rush at all."

She sighed. I swear I heard her eyes rolling. "You're being quite unhelpful, Aoife, and my hormones are all over the place. You should have more consideration."

"Jacqueline, my baby is barely six weeks old. I'm on maternity leave *and* I'm in another country. What exactly do you expect me to do?"

"No need to get shirty!"

"That's where you're wrong. There is *every* need to get shirty. Every bloody need in the world!" And at that I slammed the phone down with such strength that the number two bounced off and flew across the room.

"Feck," I said and, now more than just a little flustered, I lifted my daughter, still screeching in her car seat, and headed downstairs to meet Beth.

Waving to Heather, who was lost in the most recent edition of *Heat* magazine I climbed into Beth's car and set about ranting about the god-awful pain in the arse my sister-in-law was.

"Why don't you tell your mother to have a word?" Beth asked with a smile and the thought of my mother having a word with the daughter she never had made me laugh.

"Forget about it, Aoife. Don't let the madwoman annoy you. She's a hundred miles away, what damage can she do?"

★ ★ ★

Elena Kennedy's house was a thing of beauty and I'm not just saying that because Beth and I have redesigned it about twenty times over. A mixture of neutral and accent colours, bespoke furniture, gorgeous lighting, all tied together with a theme which brought the outdoors in. When you walked into Elena Kennedy's hall you felt your stress levels fall immediately. It was the jewel in our interior design crown and if I had the money I would buy it off her and live in it myself. It was the house of my dreams and why she wanted to tweak it any further was beyond me.

"Aoife," she purred as she walked down her marble staircase, "so very lovely to see you and your gorgeous little girl again. Come through the lounge. I have a little present for her."

I followed her through to the living-room, perhaps my favourite room in the house. The walls were off-white, with natural wood flooring and distressed furniture surrounding a grand marble fireplace. Her chaise-longue had been a rare find – one we had made on a weekend trip to Paris on a booze cruise. We had wandered around some of the markets on the Sunday morning, eyes bleary with our hangovers, and I had spotted the piece in the window of a shop. Yes, it needed a little makeover – some tender loving care – but I could see the potential and it had become my favourite ever find.

I sat down on it, lifting Maggie from her car seat and pointing her away from the rich fabric I had used to recover it and towards the more washable floor.

Elena lifted a small, blue bag from the console table and handed it to us.

"It's only something small, but hopefully you will like it."

I opened the gift bag to find a stunning Tiffany rattle and a gift envelope.

"I hope you don't mind, Aoife," she said as I opened the card, "but I've set up a little trust fund for Maggie. It's not much but you girls do so much for me, I wanted to do something special for her."

The something special was to the tune of £2,000. Approximately £1,995 more than Maggie's own granny had spent on her.

I could barely believe my eyes. "Elena, it's a gorgeous and generous gesture but it's much too much. Really, we couldn't possibly accept this."

"You don't have to accept it. It's for Maggie, not for you."

Her tone was such that I knew not to argue. Much as I respected Elena and her custom, I knew she was not the kind of person you wanted to get on the wrong side of.

Perhaps then it was the wrong time to mention her asking Tom to keep an eye on me.

"So I hear you had dinner with Tom Austin on Saturday," she said, lifting Maggie and holding her against her ridiculously expensive Dior shirt. Seems she had no such qualms about raising the topic of her interference in my life.

"We did indeed," I answered, "and it was lovely."

"Hope you don't mind my meddling," she said with a sly grin.

I shook my head, perhaps unconvincingly. "Not at all. Tom seems like a very nice person. I'm sure we could be great friends."

Beth snorted – which I thought was rather unprofessional and a little bit disloyal to me.

"Yes, well, we'll see," Elena answered, rocking Maggie gently.

It seems this was another discussion in which Elena did not want to be argued with.

Elena Kennedy liked to follow trends. She had heard many reports of Megan Park and her beaded cushions and wraps. This was the new look she wanted for her bedroom in hues of ethnic greens and creams. I tried to explain it wouldn't tie in with the rest of the house but she wasn't to be dissuaded. If her bedroom looked well, she would follow this with the guest room and the kitchen.

"If you're sure," Beth said, not bothering with measuring up the room as we almost knew the figures by heart.

"Dear hearts, I am always sure about everything I do," Elena said and signed off yet another cheque to us.

At least if no one else in Richmond or the wider area ever wanted an interior-design firm again, we would be safe with Elena.

We called into Morelli's for coffee on the way back to the shop. Beth ordered a latte while I reluctantly stayed with my decaf.

We were just biting into our gorgeous homemade biscotti when the door opened and Tom walked in.

"We really have to stop meeting like this," he smiled, staring somewhat pointedly at the empty chair beside Beth.

I would have ignored the hint, but Beth smiled and pulled it out. "Have a seat, Tom. I'm sure you're exhausted from lugging plants around all day."

"Actually today I was putting together some displays for a wedding. Not quite so macho," he answered, sitting down and lifting the coffee menu from the table.

I glared at Beth across the table and she smiled back.

"So Aoife tells me you are going to transform our sad little yard into a gorgeous city-centre retreat?"

"Well, I'll give it a go. There's so much you can do with it. It's a great little suntrap – perfect for fragrant plants and flowers. It could be a real treat for you both."

"Well, it will be more for Aoife really, won't it?" Beth said. "I mean she'll be around more than me."

"Not really," I interjected. "It will be there to benefit all our businesses."

Mrs Morelli bustled over with a cappuccino for Tom. "I don't know why you look at the menu every day, Mr Austin – you always order the same thing," she smiled.

He glanced in my direction. "I guess I just know what I like."

I wasn't surprised when I got the phone call. A little disappointed maybe, but not surprised. I had got home from Morelli's in plenty of time to clean the flat, have a shower and even shave my legs – all the while praying fervently that Maggie would stay sleeping. I lit some scented candles, blow-dried my hair and spritzed on some Chanel No 5. I was just putting in my earrings when the phone burst into life.

"Hello?" I answered.

"How could you?" came the reply. No "Hello". No "How are you?". No "How is Maggie?".

"How could I what?" I asked, running through possible offences against my mother – apart from the obvious child-out-of-wedlock one which I thought we had already dealt with.

"Don't play the innocent with me, missy," my mother retorted. "I don't know where I went wrong with you, Aoife, but you are not the child I reared."

I had to bite back a response that she would hardly know the child she reared as she never spent more than an hour at a time with me, but instead I tried – in vain – to think of what the holy feck she might be going on about.

As she slammed the phone down, it dawned on me. Perfect

fucking Jacqueline. That is what happened.

Immediately I lifted the phone and called Anna. "Has my mother been on the phone to you today?" I barked. It had been my time not to say hello, or ask how she was, or how Maeve was.

"Oh, indeed I have had the pleasure. She is not happy at all."

"Is it because I didn't book an immediate flight to designer Her Highness's nursery?"

"I think her exact words were 'I can't believe our Aoife would be so selfish as to leave Jacqueline in a state like that'."

And thus began the Big Freeze. All the work I had done rebuilding our family and getting along with my mother, despite her obvious dislike of me and my child, had been for nothing. In one fell swoop I was frozen out. I was sure that if I listened hard enough I could hear Jacqueline cackling madly from across the Irish Sea.

My evening was rounded off nicely – and when I say nicely I mean horribly – when Jake rang and announced something had come up and could he possibly reschedule for the Friday.

"Give Mags a kiss from me," he crooned while in the background glasses clinked and music played. "Love ya, babes."

Well, at least he said he loved me – and he didn't even ask for a blow job afterwards.

39

Beth

Dan had booked the morning off work and Aoife was going to help Heather in the shop. I felt a little guilty asking her to work but she assured me it was something she wanted. It would help her take her mind off the Big Freeze with her mother and her ongoing confusion over Jake and his arsey behaviour.

Why she was confused baffled me. This was typical Jake. He had always been like this and always would be like this. Dan had rolled his eyes as I explained this to him for the 150th time that morning.

"Betsy, you were happy enough for her to be with him before she got pregnant," he said as he put on his tie. "And yes, I know he is an asshole but you have to let this be between the two of them now." He ran a comb through his hair.

I felt tears spring to my eyes and I knew it was a terrible overreaction, but my nerves were on edge. We were going, in the matter of an hour or two, to be one step closer to having, or not having, a child of our own. I had so wanted to be proactive with this but now I was scared.

I swallowed a few drops of Rescue Remedy and took a few deep breaths. Dan looked at me, concern in his eyes, and came and wrapped his arms around me.

"Look darling, this is one of those times where we have to accept the things we cannot change, change the things we can and have the wisdom to know the difference."

And I wondered just which of my major life crises he was talking about.

As he drove across town, I gazed absently at sample books and catalogues, looking for something just perfect for Elena Kennedy's bedroom. At least I could lose myself in this. It was one of the things Aoife and I agreed on most. When all else failed, we could lose ourselves in creating magical, restful and unique rooms. Each new project was a new challenge and we promised each other that the day it felt like a chore was the day we would close the business and try something new.

But we had been going for eight years now and if anything I was becoming more obsessed and in love with what we did. The first few years had been tough, admittedly. Dan had been working his apprenticeship in the law firm and bringing in a pittance of a wage while we didn't have the money to set up a shop and relied on word of mouth and my clapped-out Mini to get us out and about. It was only when my parents, seeing how well we were doing, had gifted me the lease to Instant Karma that things really started taking off. Since then we had transformed dozens of rooms (and not all of them Elena Kennedy's), from dining-rooms to conservatories, lounges to bedrooms, kitchens to nurseries. I loved the nurseries most. The promise of all that was to come was so breathtaking that I would spend hours trailing shops and suppliers for the perfect room for that new little life. As I thought of all the baby rooms I had decorated, and how I had yet to decorate a room like that for our house, the tears sprang to my eyes again.

Shove the notion of a few drops of Rescue Remedy. I necked the bottle.

I knew from the forums I had been using what to expect of this appointment. Even though we had the blood tests and I underwent some glorious internals twelve months ago, we would have to basically go through it all again and if we were lucky we would also get offered a dye test to see if my Fallopian tubes were blocked. If I pushed it, I could ask for a laparoscopy too, in case there was something inside me that was stopping me getting pregnant.

Dan had already produced a sample for testing twelve months ago. He hadn't enjoyed his experience, wanking into a cup over a seedy magazine in a sterile hospital room. He never trusted the lock on the door. All had been fine with him though. His swimmers were strong, plentiful and very mobile. We had also been able to ascertain that there was nothing in me which killed them off – which was fortunate. Dan had laughed out loud when Dr Browne told him that some women's insides are not suitably habitable for sperm. "Typical of you women," he said between hoots of laughter until Dr Browne assured him it was most certainly no laughing matter.

A lot can change in twelve months, so chances are Dan would have the chance to get acquainted with the little plastic cup again and I would get to experience the joy of stirrups and some man checking out my foof at close range.

I took a deep breath, closed the catalogue and stepped out of the car. Taking Dan's hand, I walked up the three steps to the large glass door which was etched with our doctor's name.

A cheerful receptionist greeted us. The wall behind her was covered with pictures of smiling babies and smiling parents. Products of Dr Browne's fertility expertise no doubt. I felt hope bubble up inside me.

"Beth and Dan Jones," I said. "We have an appointment at two."

The cheery receptionist looked down at her computer and smiled back up at us. "Sure. The doctor will be with you in a few minutes. Take a seat. Can we get you anything?"

I bit back the urge to say "A baby would be nice" and replied that no, we were fine. Dan again found it hilarious that we were offered tea or coffee when we visited the doctor. For what we were paying for the appointment we should have been offered champagne and caviar, I had replied. It would be worth it though. Dr Browne had a remarkable reputation – he had even been on the *Lorraine Kelly Show* a few times to talk about all his miracle babies.

We sat looking around us, sharing furtive glances. Across from us sat a young black couple with worn faces. They were looking down at their hands which were clasped together in worry, or was it hope? I couldn't quite tell. Beside them sat a smiling woman with a gently swelling tummy. She was reading a copy of *Pregnancy and Birth* and she had that motherly glow about her. I recognised it from Aoife all those months ago. It was as if a light had been switched on inside her. I swallowed down a sob and took a few deep breaths. I wanted that.

"I wonder if they're trying to work out our story?" Dan whispered in my ear as I grasped his hand à la the couple across the room. "I bet they're trying to figure out how long we've been trying and all our intimate details."

I looked at him with a weak watery smile. I couldn't speak. I couldn't join in his chit-chat because there was nothing much that could be said now. I bloody hated waiting-rooms.

Dr Browne, an amiable man in his mid 50s with speckled grey hair and those little half-moon glasses, walked into the room and glanced around. Spotting us, a warm smile broke across his face: "Mr and Mrs Jones, do come in."

We followed him, like errant schoolchildren being sent to the headmaster's office, and sat down. If we thought the reception was overkill on the happy baby photos, Dr Browne's office was a revelation. Surely it wasn't possible for a man to have helped so many children come into the world? After our last visit Dan had joked that the good doctor must cut pictures out of catalogues and pretend they were all down to him. In the eleven months since, the number of pictures seemed to have doubled.

"Now, Mr and Mrs Jones, what can I do for you?" he asked, looking down at a file on his desk, which I could only assume held our most personal of details.

"Well, we first saw you about eleven months ago," I said. "We had been trying to conceive for a year then, but with no joy. We had tests and you were happy enough that I was ovulating and that my husband's sperm was up to scratch. But well, it's eleven months on and we still are not pregnant and, well, we want to be."

Dr Browne scratched his chin, read a little more of our file and looked up. "I see. And your cycle has been as before?"

"Yes," I answered, lifting my charts out of my bag. "I've been charting my temps and egg-white cervical mucus. These are the charts. It would all indicate I'm ovulating."

He nodded. "And I'm guessing from this chart that the star stickers stand for the times you have had sexual intercourse?"

I felt myself blush. Sticking little stars on the chart to keep track of when we had done the deed had seemed like a good idea. Dan had even joked I was rating his performance depending on the colour of the stars. Gold was a great shag, silver was a quickie and any primary colour indicated a "doing it because we're ovulating" fumble. We had laughed about it, but now it seemed more than a little embarrassing. They never made charts like these on *Blue Peter*.

Nodding in reply to Dr Browne, I bit back my embarrassment. "Yes. We aim for as often as possible on or around ovulation. I know some people say you do it on alternate days, but we thought we would give it the best chance."

He nodded. "And after intercourse, do you take any special measures?"

"Well, for the last ten months I've been putting a cushion under my hips to tilt my pelvis. I'll stay that way for fifteen minutes before we do anything else."

Dan stayed quiet throughout, something which I think wasn't lost on our doctor.

"And you, Dan? How are you finding this?"

"I'm doing all I can," he answered. "Beth here has me on a diet designed to optimise my sperm production. I'm there to have sex every time she is ovulating. We're doing everything the books say we should do." His voice started to wobble and I reached for his hand. Beneath his confident, sexy lawyer exterior Dan was a shy man and discussing his virility was clearly killing him.

Sex was supposed to be intimate, between two partners. Not between two partners, a doctor and wall full of smiling, gummy babies.

"Right then, what we will do at this stage is arrange a few more tests. I can put you on the NHS waiting list but you know that could be two or three months."

My heart sank, two or three months was much, much too long.

"And if we go private for the tests?" Dan asked.

"Well, we could get you in next week. What we want to do is a dye test. Which is basically to flush dye through Beth's uterine cavity to see if there are any blockages."

"And what about a laparoscopy?" I asked. In for a penny, in for a pound.

"I'm not sure that's justified at this point," he said. "I would be inclined to wait for the results of the dye test first and see if that gives us any more clues. I'd also like to order some blood tests from you both – and, Dan, could you supply another sample for testing just to make sure the old results are still accurate?"

Dan nodded. "Whatever it takes. And we'll have the test next week. Anything that gets us closer to having our baby."

Dr Browne sat back in his chair, took off his glasses and rubbed the bridge of his nose. "I think it's only fair I tell you that these tests don't mean we will find out what is stopping you conceiving. Sometimes things just don't happen and there isn't a reason. The best thing you can do is go home, spend time with each other and try to stay relaxed."

Dan squeezed my hand, but all I could think was that I didn't really know how to do relaxed any more. I was okay today because we were doing something positive, something in the direction I wanted to go. And it was the first fourteen days of my cycle. My descent into madness wasn't due to start happening for at least another week and then – who knows? Last month I slapped my husband . . .

I took a deep breath. Relax – I had to relax.

We gave our blood samples, and Dan performed in the special room with the special magazines and the little white cups. Bless him, he walked out looking flushed and a little embarrassed – and I wanted to protect him from all this.

Then again, next week I would be lying with my legs splayed and strange devices inserted into my foof in what I knew, from my internet forum, to be an uncomfortable and unpleasant procedure. The best-case scenario would be that they would find out that something blindingly obvious and easily fixable was causing the problem – and we would do what we could to fix it. The worst case was that something would be properly big-time wrong – a blockage, an infection, something which could mean our journey to natural parenthood was over.

We drove home in silence. Dan stared at the road while I pored over the catalogues, turning down corners and dreaming up a dream room for Elena. Aoife and I were due to talk about it tomorrow and brainstorm our ideas and I had to be on my game, no matter what else was going on in my head.

We got home, walking through our communal hallway and lifting the post from the table. Amongst the usual junk mail and bills was a package with familiar writing. Mum. I would know it anywhere. We went upstairs and, as Dan put on the kettle, I opened it to find a multipack of loose boxers for Dan and an ovulation kit for me.

I didn't know whether to laugh or cry so I did what everyone would do after such a stressful day. I poured a large glass of wine for me, opened a bottle of Becks for Dan, filled our bath and begged him to climb in with me.

As I wrapped my legs around his waist in the soapy water and kissed him hard on the lips I whispered: "Does this count as relaxing?"

40

Aoife

I woke up at five thirty to rock-hard boobs, a crying baby and a magazine page stuck to my face. Peeling it off, I sat up and lifted Maggie into bed with me. Latching on, she started to guzzle hungrily, her eyes drooping with satisfaction. My own eyes drooped with exhaustion.

Luckily I was able to settle her again but then, as I changed my bed sheets and wandered about in a half-asleep daze, it dawned on me that it was now Friday. Jake would be over later and we could finally sort this out – one way or another.

I was also going to discuss Elena's bedroom with Beth while Maggie had her morning nap and Tom had promised to call over and look at the yard in the afternoon.

It was going to be a busy day, so I crawled back under the covers, switched off the lamp and did my best to fall back to sleep. Suddenly everything seemed too loud, the ticking of the clock, Maggie's baby snores, the rumble of my own stomach (I had been in starvation mode before seeing Jake again) so by the time nine o'clock came and Beth rattled on the shutters of the shop I had taken on the appearance of the living dead.

She called up to the flat, her voice light and breezy. Somebody had obviously had a good night's sleep. She had texted me to let me know all had been okay at her appointment with the fertility specialist – it had obviously taken a weight off her mind.

"Morning, my princesses!" she called. "Are you ready to get some work done? I've brought coffee and bagels from Morelli's. Mrs Morelli says you need to eat more. You're much too skinny, apparently."

I walked to the doorway, cradling Maggie to me, dressed in my finest faded tracksuit bottoms and an old maternity top. Beth looked up at me and started to laugh. As I walked down the stairs, she laughed harder and harder.

"Yes, I know it's not exactly haute couture, but we aren't actually going out, are we?" I chided, putting Maggie in her bouncy chair, which was the latest addition to our treasure trove of knick-knacks.

"I think I've found the perfect scheme for the windows," Beth said, staring at me oddly, a smile still on her face.

"Well, share then."

"That," she said, pointing to my cheek where my slobber had obviously transferred a print from a magazine, "is perfect."

Once I'd washed my face and Beth had stopped laughing, we sat down to work. Maggie was happy to watch us from the sidelines. It was nice to work together, and it was nicer still to chat freely about work, about Maggie, about life. It seemed a long time since Beth had been so free and easy about everything. Heather, God love her, even smiled a couple of times. It must have been hard on her, I realised, to work with two such hormonally imbalanced women.

"I think this is starting to shape up nicely," Beth said. "Elena will be impressed, although I think we really need to let her have a look at these prints. You know how fussy she can be."

I nodded just as the doorbell sprang into life and the woman herself walked in.

"Morning, ladies. I just wondered how you were getting along?" She was in her sports gear, her lithe body – sculpted to within an inch of its life by her punishing exercise regime – suddenly making me very aware of my own jelly belly and my oversized smock top.

Breathing in, I sat taller.

"We have some good ideas here, Elena," said Beth. "Why don't you take a seat and have a look?"

She was already crouched down in front of Maggie, cooing at her while my daughter smiled appreciatively back. That's my girl, I thought, keeping in with the rich folks.

I stood up to offer my seat and she glanced at me.

"Oh goodness, Aoife. That's not your best look, is it?"

It crossed my mind that Elena, her bluntness and my mother would get on very well together.

"She *is* still on maternity leave, Elena," Beth said. "This commission is a special favour for you."

Elena smiled. "Well, I am honoured, but she still needs to smarten herself up a little more."

Was I not in the room any more?

Elena flipped open her mobile phone and hit a speed-dial button.

"Maria, Elena here. Could you bring a few things over to Instant Karma? Yes, new mummy, size 12 to 14, I would say. Smart casual, maybe something a little sexy too and, Maria, bring some of those magic pants things. She needs a little help around the tummy area."

I stood, mouth gaping open. First Elena had sent a mysterious gardener to keep an eye on me. Then she had given my daughter an overly generous present and now she was dressing me. It all felt a little weird. I looked to Beth for some sort of silent signal that I wasn't losing the plot and the bemused look on her face offered me some form of comfort.

"Elena, seriously. There's no need for this."

"The way I see it, Aoife, there is every need," she answered calmly. "Now show me your ideas for my bedroom."

Maria – a pleasant girl in her mid-twenties wearing a pair of those very stylish heavy framed glasses and a silky neck scarf – arrived about an hour later. She bustled into the shop laden with carrier bags and air-kissed Elena. Looking at me, Heather and Beth, she then looked back at me again.

"This must be the new mummy," she said.

Yes, it was that obvious.

She unloaded her bags, revealing gorgeous wrap dresses, slouchy jeans and body-skimming T-shirts, not to mention some impossibly high heels and a pair of pants which started just below the bra line and extended to just above the knee.

"Just one question," I said. "How on earth do you pee in those things? My bladder is weakened considerably these days."

"You'll manage," Elena answer. "Now off and get changed and come back down when you look more like the old you."

I nodded. For some reason I could not speak up to Elena, no matter how much I wanted to tell her to butt out. Her heart (and wallet) were in the right places.

I came back down a while later, having tried on this and that, in the wrap dress which disguised my jelly belly, and with my hair swept up in a smooth chignon.

"Now that is much, much better," Elena said, glancing at her watch.

Beth seemed to have a smug kind of smirk on her face now but my reticence about telling Elena to butt out also extended to asking my best friend what on earth she was smirking about in front of our number-one client.

"Right," I said, casting a glance at a now-sleeping Maggie, "have we decided between the extra wardrobe or the dressing-screen?"

"I'm not sure," Elena said, glancing at our mood boards. "I love the wardrobe, but I'm not sure I need it – but then the screen would just be for decoration, wouldn't it?"

"That's what we are all about, Elena," Beth said, sipping from her coffee cup and glancing over my head at the door.

I turned around in time to see Tom walk in with his folder and smile directly at me.

"Aoife," he said before looking at the other two women in my company.

I smiled back and in spite of myself I felt a little flutter.

He was handsome. Feck that, he was sexy in his own way. He was standing in rugged jeans, a white T-shirt and a Barbour jacket. His face was sun-kissed even though it was only March and freezing outside. For a second – only a split second – we were the only two people in the room. I was then aware of Elena standing up and running to share an air-kiss with him.

"Tom, how gorgeous to see you here today! How are things? Are you here to work? Doesn't our Aoife look fabulous?" She stared at me and I felt like a child being shown off in her Sunday best to a proud granny.

"She always does," he said, looking straight at me, and I heard Beth giggle in the background.

Swinging round, I looked at her and she looked at Elena and then shrugged her shoulders back at me.

Oh. My. God. The new clothes suddenly made sense and I realised that Elena had not only sent the handsome gardener to look out for me but she was trying to pimp me out as well. And my best friend was in on it – Elena must have filled her in on the scheme while I was upstairs.

I didn't know why Elena was doing this. I didn't really care at that stage. I was suddenly so very tired of everyone thinking they owned a piece of me. A seven-week-old baby was enough to be going on with.

"If you will excuse me," I said, mustering as much dignity as I could, "I've recently had a baby and I'm very tired. I'm going to go upstairs now and have a sleep. Beth, could you finish off with Mrs Kennedy and then have a chat with Tom about the yard?"

I stumbled upstairs, returning downstairs just once when I realised Maggie was still down there in her bouncy chair. Fuck the lot of them.

I had stripped off my fancy new wrap dress, and slipped on my pyjamas when a knock came to the door.

"Go away!" I yelled. "I'm going to sleep."

"Aoife" a voice called out, "please let me in!"

It was Tom.

When I didn't answer the handle turned, the door opened cautiously and there he was.

"Are you okay?" he asked.

I looked at him rather blankly. "I'm not quite sure. I think Elena Kennedy may be trying to pimp me out to you. She brought all these clothes over today. I might just be her latest project. *We* might just be her latest project."

He blushed. "I thought something odd was going on. When I came in today and saw you looking so – well – dressed up."

I had the good grace to laugh. "Are you trying to say I usually look like shit?"

"Not at all," he said, his cheeks reddening further. "You look good to me all the time, but today you had a certain something."

"It was the magic pants," I muttered and sat down, aware that the magic pants were now gone, replaced by belly warmers and cosy jammies.

Tom sat down too and rubbed his eyes. "Look, I think she has our best interests at heart."

"Yes, but what does she know about our best interests? I'm so messed up, Tom, you know that. Jake is coming around tonight and he wants to try again. Elena knows how much I love him. So, much as I'm flattered, I'm not really in a position to be in a relationship with anyone else."

Tom smiled a sad smile. "Aoife, much as I'm flattered, neither am I. My divorce has only just been finalised. I just want to make a fresh start. That's not to say that if I wasn't so messed up I wouldn't be interested in you. I would be, but it's not a good time for me either."

"Elena never said you were divorced," I said, my face flushed with embarrassment.

"No, she wouldn't. She likes to pretend my ex never existed. I don't talk about Kate much so I imagine Elena thinks I'm ready to move on."

"But you aren't," I said, more of a statement than a question.

"I don't think so. I'm too busy just trying to hold my head above water. I'm relatively new to the area. I lived down in Devon with Kate. When we split up I wanted a fresh start so I moved up here and started doing some freelance work – a few gardens here and there. I met Elena and when I finally decided to set up shop in Gardiner Street she told me all about you. She said we could work together and she told me you might need a friend."

"I've been horrid, haven't I?" I said.

"Don't worry," he said. "I feel pretty pissed off myself. As I said, I like to keep myself to myself and I don't like my every move to be watched by anyone."

"Her heart is in the right place, I suppose," I said.

"You're probably right, but nonetheless we're both here now feeling very awkward and I guess that probably means any chance we did have at a friendship is blown."

By the tone in his voice I knew he wasn't looking for me to assure him otherwise.

313

We sat in silence for a few seconds before he spoke again.

"I suppose I should go downstairs. They'll be thinking we're making mad passionate love up here," he said with a wry smile. "Are you going to come down?"

"No, I could do with a sleep," I replied before seeing him out and going to bed to dream about making mad passionate love with Tom Austin.

"I'm sorry, Aoife," Beth said as she perched on my sofa. "I thought you might enjoy a bit of flirtation and when Elena told me she was dressing you up because Tom was coming over, I thought you'd be delighted. It's quite romantic really."

"But no one asked either me or Tom if we wanted romance," I said. As I saw Beth raise her eyebrow and smile, I added: "Which, by the way, we don't. I'm happy. He's happy and besides, in case you had forgotten, Jake is coming over later and I'm pretty sure we're going to be talking about getting back together."

Beth sighed. "Aoife, are you sure that is sensible?"

"He is the father of my child," I said, "and I still love him."

"Elena was right," she said as she walked out of the room. "You seem to want to make yourself as miserable as possible."

"Do I crave misery?" I asked Anna, as I rubbed Maggie's back, trying in vain to release an elusive burp. It seemed I spent most of my life these days either clamping her on to my boobs or rubbing her back for dear life.

"What are you on about?" she answered, vaguely amused.

"Am I a misery guts? Do I love drama? Am I, to put it finely, turning into my mother?"

Anna laughed, her throaty laugh ringing down the line. "Have you been drinking?"

"No, I'm serious, Anna. Help me out here."

"What has you asking such a buck-stupid question?"

"Something Beth said today. One of our clients said she thinks I crave misery. From Beth's storming out of the room, I'm thinking Beth agrees with her."

"I think you two need your heads banging together," Anna said and I could tell she was vaguely amused by the whole sorry scenario.

"Anna, please, I need you to be honest with me. Am I a misery guts?"

"We all have our bad days, pet, but no, if you want me to be honest I don't think you are any more miserable than the rest of us miserable feckers."

I changed position slightly, and resumed rubbing.

"Now your mother," Anna continued, "there is one miserable beggar. I saw her today – bumped into her in Foyleside – and she was wearing a face like she'd just had a slap. I asked what was up and she answered 'Ach, you know,' and nodded like I'm meant to be fecking psychic or something."

"It'll be the Deep Freeze she's talking about no doubt. Her letdown of a daughter," I sighed.

"Aoife, pet, you need to realise, your mother doesn't need people to do anything to make her do her best Pauline Fowler impression. She was made that way."

"But nonetheless, Anna, I do give her all her best material."

"And God love her, the woman wouldn't know suffering if it came up and bit her on the arse."

The change in her tone was subtle, but I noticed it immediately.

"Are you okay, Anna?" I asked.

She paused and replied: "Not really, love, but you don't need me being a misery guts. Not when you are enough of a sour-head yourself."

There was an air of forced jollity to the end of her sentence. It didn't fool me one bit.

"Anna, what's wrong?"

There was another pause and then I heard her sniffle. Next thing she was crying softly.

"Anna, you're scaring me now. What's wrong?"

"Nothing, pet. Only it's the anniversary of Billy's death. I should be over it by now, but it catches me unawares sometimes. God, he was a right royal pain in the arse when he was alive, but I would give anything to have him bug the shite out of me for one more day."

We talked on. She cried and I soothed as best I could, which wasn't much given the distance and then she hung up, promising me that she wouldn't drink herself into oblivion. She said instead she would probably just take a drive down to Moville and howl into the wind for a bit.

After I hung up, I texted Maeve and told her check in on her mum. At least that was something positive, but I wished there was more I could do.

Billy was a larger than life character. Being that my relationship with my mother had been on the shoddy side, I spent a lot of time at Anna's, and Billy was always there to make me laugh and chat with. I was nine when Maeve was born and by the time she reached five or six, I became the regular baby-sitter.

Anna and Billy were always out at one thing or another and the pocket money came in handy. They would come in from their business functions or nights in the pub and sit at the kitchen table cooking loaves of toast and brewing pots of tea and we would chat into the wee hours before I would crawl up to bed in the spare room.

I may only have been fifteen or sixteen, but they treated me like an adult.

I used to be envious of them, of the love they so clearly shared. Every time I visited, there was a new card or a new gift on the mantelpiece. Each made public declarations of love – *"To My Soulmate"* – *"To My One and Only"* – and I could never resist snooping at the handwritten messages inside.

Some of the cards were from Anna, the majority were from Billy and I hoped and prayed with all my heart I would find a man who would love me the way he loved her.

Billy died in a car accident. There had been snow showers and his car had simply glided off the road and into a brick wall. He had died instantly. I was with Anna when the police called to the house to break the news. I sat in shock, my heart thudding in my chest, my mouth dried, as I saw Anna collapse to the floor and scream out in raw, animal pain. I watched as the policewoman lifted her to her chair and then I ran upstairs to make sure Maeve was still asleep. If I'm honest with myself, I think I ran away because I could not bear to see Anna in so much pain. I'd seen people react on TV like that – to fall into a screaming rage at what had just happened – but I had never seen my Anna act like that, and I wanted to block the sound of her cries out of my ears.

I sat on my bed in the spare room, hands over my ears, rocking back and forth until the door opened and my father walked in. And then he held me in his arms while I screamed until my throat was sore.

"Could the message be, '*Thinking of you. Love you loads. Aoife*'?" I said to the helpful florist on the other end of the line. (Not Tom, in case you wondered. Tom didn't do Interflora.)

I then hung up and set about bathing Maggie and making sure she was looking her absolute cutest for when her daddy would arrive. Jake was due to be here in just over an hour and I wanted to make sure both mother and daughter were looking their best.

Once Maggie was bathed, dusted in baby powder and put into her finest sleepsuit, I jumped in the shower myself before dressing in the new slouch jeans and tunic top Elena had left behind. Sure, Jake may not have been the person she intended me to wear the clothes for, but needs must. After spending an afternoon lost in the memories of Billy and Anna, I felt a need just to hold someone close – and if Jake were to walk into the room and reach out for me I knew I would fall into his arms.

When the doorbell rang, I almost tripped over myself to get there. Jake stood, a wide smile on his face, his sunglasses perched on his balding head and a bunch of carnations in one hand.

"Hey, babes," he said, walking past me, passing the flowers to me like a baton in a relay race.

"Hey," I said back, following him upstairs.

"Is Mags in here?"

I bristled at the use of the word Mags, but chided myself. Sure he was allowed to have a pet name for her. He was her father. Her daddy – that gave him a right to call her just about anything he wanted.

He walked in to where she was sitting in her bouncy chair and lifted her.

"Careful, mind her wee head," I said and he lifted her to his shoulder.

"She's great, isn't she?" he said.

He smiled at me and I felt myself relax a little. Sure he had run up the stairs to see her, and run past me to get there, but now that he was there and we were our little family unit again, I knew it would be okay.

He walked around singing to her, smiling at her and proudly telling me how much like him she was.

I sat down and waited for him to ask me how I was. I waited some more and then I went to the kitchen to put on the kettle for me, and open a beer for him. I lifted a vase from under the sink and filled it with water for the carnations. I tried my best to ignore the reduced price sticker on them. It's the thought that counts.

When I walked back to the living-room he was sitting with his feet on the sofa, our daughter back in her bouncy chair and the TV blaring *Tonight with Jonathan Ross* across the room.

As I handed him his beer he glanced at me: "Cheers, babe," he said before turning his attention back to the interview on screen.

As I sat down, he looked at me again.

"Not drinking, babe?"

"Erm, no. I'm still breast-feeding." I flushed slightly at the mention of breast-feeding – perhaps because of the last unfortunate leaking nipples incident or perhaps because this man and me were basically all about good sex and any sexual word at all – even breast out of context – was enough to send me into a fit of excitement.

"Right," he said and went back to watching TV.

I sat for a while, sipping my tea and nibbling delicately at a digestive biscuit, before I couldn't hold it in any more.

"Jake, are you okay?"

"Fine," he said, reaching his empty beer bottle towards me in the international sign language for "get us another one, love".

I got up and left my cup by the sink as I took another bottle from the fridge.

Handing it to him, I said: "Are you sure you're okay?"

"Yes, Aoifs, I'm sure. Why are you asking?"

I could hear the annoyance in his voice. "Well, I thought we were going to talk some tonight?"

"What about?" he said, turning towards me while keeping one eye on the TV.

"The last nine months perhaps?" I said, my voice a little harsher than I had intended.

"Look, Aoifs, what's to talk about? I went away and worked, you had a baby and here we are now."

"But where are we exactly?" I asked.

He rolled his eyes. "Here, babe. We are right here in this room. Isn't that enough?"

I didn't want to beg him to tell me he loved me. I didn't want to ask him to tell me he was going to be there for me and Maggie. I wanted him to say it without prompting but I knew by the way this conversation was going that wasn't going to happen now. The damage had been done and we were slipping into dangerous territory. This was the same territory I had lived in for three years together when I longed for him to tell me he cared, when I asked him over and over again like someone who had no self-respect.

Anna never needed to ask Billy. She never needed to talk about a missing nine months. She was never fobbed off with phone calls because he was too busy. They were a partnership.

We were nothing.

We were just two people who admittedly had amazing sex together, but we weren't two people who were meant to be. Not even the gorgeous little bundle of pink in the corner could change that.

"I think you should leave, Jake," I said, with as much strength as I could muster.

He stared at me, open-mouthed. "What are you on?"

"I'm not on anything, Jake." I said, steadying my hand against the sideboard to stop it from trembling.

"Aoife," he said, using my proper name for perhaps the first time ever, "I've come here to see Maggie, and you."

"I know, and you've seen us and now I really, really think you should go."

In spite of myself I felt tears spring to my eyes.

"But c'mon," he said. "This is nice, isn't it?"

"I don't know what 'this' is. But it isn't what I want or deserve – and it certainly isn't nice."

He lifted his jacket and left and I knew then, finally, that I would never feel him kiss me again.

I sat down, lifted Maggie to me, and waited for the torrent of tears to follow.

To my surprise they didn't.

I lifted the phone and called Anna again. When she answered, her voice a little stronger than last time, I told her I loved her. "I know today is tough, Anna, but you were so, so lucky to have Billy. You were so in love. You just did all that loving in a few years."

"I know, darling," she said.

"I've told Jake to go," I said. "He'll still have access to Maggie. Just none to me."

"Are you okay?" Anna asked.

"Fine," I said, my voice starting to break just that little bit, "but the next time I'm in Derry can you drive me down to Moville some evening? Me and the sea need a little time alone."

41

Beth

When Aoife phoned I knew something was wrong. Mostly I knew something was wrong because I had been so horrid to her earlier that she wouldn't have phoned me unless she really, really had to. I hadn't meant to be mean to her. It was just that sometimes I wanted to shake her and make her realise that people were looking out for her.

When she had gone to get changed in the shop, Elena and I had talked.

"You probably think I'm nuts," Elena had said casually as she sipped from the cup of chamomile tea I had made for her.

I smiled noncommittally. The wrong answer and we could lose our best customer and, I had to admit, I liked having Elena around. She added a certain something to our lives, even it was only impetuous acts of generosity such as this.

"Well, I suppose I am a bit nuts. But I see something in Aoife that reminds me of me when I was her age. I didn't know where I was going or what I was doing and I got in with the wrong kind of man too."

She was clearly in confessional mode and I sipped from my coffee, pushing the sample catalogues to one side and settling down to listen.

Elena suddenly looked wistful. "God, I loved him, and when he broke my heart – which was always going to happen at some stage – I was so devastated I lost all sense of me. It took me a long time – too long – to find myself again. And it was ten years before I met Gerry and realised I was worth loving. I don't want that for Aoife. She deserves to be happy and Maggie deserves to have a proper family."

"You've a very kind heart," I answered.

She smiled. "Some people think I'm an interfering old bat and I probably am but I just want to share some life experience around. God knows my two aren't a bit interested. The two boys couldn't wait to get away to university and they haven't really looked back since. I always wanted a daughter," she said wistfully. "When I look at Aoife I know what will make her happy. I know she needs someone to take care of her."

"And you think Tom could be that person?"

She sighed. "I'm not sure. I thought so, but you know Tom has his own problems. He has been hurt and I know what could make him happy too. I just need them both to see it."

"He's divorced, isn't he?" I asked, leaning forward, hoping I suppose to hear that someone's life was more of a train-wreck than mine.

"I'm not sure of the details," she said, "but he has been hurt. I'm not saying he is still in love with her – but whatever happened, well, I don't think it was how they hoped things would pan out."

"I don't suppose anyone thinks bad things will happen," I said, my heart sinking.

"He was devastated when he moved up here. I had to give him a good talking to, you know," Elena said. "I told him he wasn't ever going to get any business worth talking about looking like he had been dragged backwards through one of his own hedges. He took his time, but he is getting there, I think."

"Perhaps he isn't ready for a relationship though," I said. "I'm not sure Aoife is either – much as I would love her to find a man who actually cared about her." I sighed. "You do know that Jake is back on the scene – Maggie's daddy. He says he wants her back. He doesn't act like he wants her back, but she wants to give him a chance."

"God," said Elena, "I hope we can make her see sense."

"I think she needs to see it for herself," I said.

And then Aoife was back, looking gorgeous, just in time for Tom to walk into the shop.

I knew Aoife didn't like people meddling in her life. She was a stubborn so-and-so, but looking at Tom's face when he saw her (and ignoring the fact that he was quite possibly on the rebound) I thought it might just be possible that we could engineer a romance between the pair of them.

But, of course, it took a mere five minutes for that positive frame of mind to slip as Aoife seemed to twig what was going on and all hell broke loose. She stormed upstairs and Tom followed later. He had a face like thunder as he walked up the stairs, after (quite bravely) telling Elena her interfering wasn't appreciated, and his demeanour had not improved much when he came back downstairs a short time later and left with a curt goodbye.

I thought Elena would have lost her cool, but she smiled at me as she left.

"Trust me, Beth, there is time for this to work out yet."

Of course, I didn't trust her, so I went up to talk to Aoife and then I'd told her she loved misery.

Dan had laughed when I told him the story. "You know what they say," he said, ducking for cover. "Misery loves company."

"Thanks for the support," I mock-huffed.

"Look, Betsy, we've talked about this a hundred times. Aoife needs to make her own choices and you and Elena interfering isn't going to make her change her mind. You know how stubborn she is. The more you try and push her away from Jake, the closer you're going to push her to him."

I nodded. Dan was more than likely right.

So you could have knocked me down with a feather when she phoned and told me she had kicked him out once and for all.

I left the dishes in the sink and Dan sitting alone at the table and drove straight over to see her. It was strange that my feelings were mixed. For the past few weeks all I could do was wish that this moment would come – the moment when Aoife would finally kick that no-good layabout out of her life once and for all – but then I knew this would have been tough for her. I had to remind myself not to break into song and dance when I saw her.

Letting myself into the shop, I climbed the stairs to the flat and opened the door. "Aoife!" I called out, walking into the living-room. There were candles burning and a CD of cheesy eighties ballads was playing in the background. Calling her name again, I noticed a small auburn-headed figure lying on the rug, a glass of wine at her side.

With her eyes closed, mascara streaked down what had clearly been a beautifully made-up face, she was singing at the top of her lungs that she wanted to know what love was.

I felt my heart swell with love for my gorgeous, tuneless friend.

I walked over and sat beside her, pouring a glass of Chablis for myself, and then I did what every best friend should do in such a situation. I gave her a hug and started singing, just as loudly and just as badly as her.

"Are you okay, sweetie?" I asked eventually.

Aoife wiped her nose on the sleeve of her cardigan and nodded. "He's no good, is he?"

I shook my head.

"And he was never going to treat me well, was he?"

I shook my head again.

"And even though I'm probably never going to have sex again and spend my life obsessing about Maggie and then fall apart when she leaves home, this is the best thing I could do, isn't it?"

I nodded.

She cuddled into me and I held her for a while as she cried, and then sang again with her about Broken Wings.

When the singing had finally subsided, I asked her what had happened.

"You were right, Beth, when you said I was a misery guts. And no, that doesn't mean I fancy Tom or anything or that I appreciate what Elena has been up to behind my back, but it made me think. I deserve more than that. I want what Anna and Billy had. I want what Elena and Gerry have. I want what you and Dan have."

Funny, I thought as I hugged her. It had been a long time since it had crossed my mind that anyone could be jealous of what Dan and I had. Perhaps it was time for an epiphany of my own. Physically we might be faulty goods, but emotionally we were pretty solid.

As I crawled under the duvet on the sofa later that night – too tipsy to drive home – I lifted my mobile and dialled Dan's number.

"Hey, sexy," he answered, his voice husky from sleep.

"Hey, yourself."

"You okay, Bets?" he asked, his voice deep with concern.

"I'm fine, Dan. Just fine. I love you. I just wanted to let you know."

"I love you too, babe."

"Don't forget it," I added.

"I won't."

"Promise?"

"For better or worse," he answered and even though we were a few miles apart, and just disembodied voices down a phone line, I felt closer to him in those few moments than I had done in a long time. It was possible, I thought as I drifted off to sleep, that I felt closer to him than I had ever done.

42

Aoife

I woke up to a thumping headache, a furry mouth and a crying baby. As I changed Maggie's toxic nappy and heated a bottle of formula I had flashbacks to the night before. I – me, Aoife McLaughlin – had told Jake Gibson to leave. He would have access to his daughter – I wouldn't deny him that – but I was no longer his to pick up and drop down whenever he wanted.

I had done that. It had been on my terms. This time yesterday I was planning on making a go of things with him again, of letting him be my significant other and now it was done and dusted. Forever. My head was swimming. I wasn't sure it was a result of the two bottles of Chablis Beth and I had demolished the night before or whether it was because I could not quite believe what I had done.

And yet, a wee part of me felt proud. For the first time in my entire relationship with Jake I had called the shots. I felt empowered. I felt almost as if I should be singing a Gloria Gaynor song or shouting about Girl Power.

I smiled, holding Maggie to me, and then set about making breakfast for me and Beth.

"Morning, sleepy!" I shouted into the living room.

"Go away!" she called back, and I smiled again.

It reminded me of our student days, mornings cooking fryups after nights on the lash. We would dig out whatever we could find, frying half a loaf of bread and topping it with baked beans to bring us round from the night before's excesses. And then we would walk to college, where we would do our best to stay awake and alert through lectures before whiling away long afternoons in the art studios putting designs together. Of course when we were students I didn't have a baby crying through the night or demanding a half-hour burping session when all I wanted to do was lie down and sleep.

"Come and get it while it's hot," I called, slicing the sausages in half and covering them in ketchup.

I looked around as Beth walked in, her hair stuck to the side of her face. Rubbing her eyes she said: "Why did we open that second bottle?"

"*We* didn't open it." I laughed. "*You* did, you insisted on it. You said it was for medicinal purposes."

She grimaced before taking a bite out of her sausage sandwich. "I'm not sure I'm going to make it through the morning."

"You'll be fine. We've had worse hangovers than this."

"God, woman, *you* seem fine. Do you have an invincible liver or something?"

"Trust me, my liver is suffering," I said, "and so is my head and my stomach and my heart a wee bit too but I think I did the right thing and that makes me feel a little better."

I was so glad that Beth had never told me "I told you so" or cheered at the news Jake was no longer going to have a place in my affections, but I could tell from the sly smile on her face that she was happy.

"I'll try not to be a misery guts any more," I said.

"You bloody better not," Beth answered, clinking her orange-juice glass against mine. "One miserable bitch is enough between us."

"You aren't miserable," I soothed.

"Oh Aoife, you are and always have been a god-awful liar."

I spent most of that day curled on the sofa on one of what I had taken to calling my "maternity leave" days. I stayed in my fluffy robe and just cuddled, soothed and played with Maggie. When she slept I slept, when she ate I ate, when she gurgled I gurgled back at her. It was blissful. For the first time I didn't look at her and only see her father stare back at me. It was as if I had been given a degree of freedom by making my choice. And I fell in love with her. Perhaps, I realised, I had been living in a bubble for the last few weeks, unable to allow myself to fall so madly in love with her and now I was doing it. It's not that I hadn't loved her before, because I had, but now I realised that motherhood allowed you the glorious pleasure of falling in love a bit more each and every day.

As we sat there, mother and daughter together, a strange urge came over me. I wanted to speak to my mother. Perhaps I was on a forgiveness high, but now that I had made peace with myself, I wanted to make peace with my mother too.

Dialling her number I listened to the phone ring and then heard her familiar voice doing the usual McLaughlin residence thing.

"Hello, Mum, how are you?"

"Fine," she answered. "I'll just get your dad for you."

Maybe I would try again another day.

As it started to get dark, I dressed and wrapped Maggie in her softest fleece blanket before strapping her into her pram and we set off for a walk to the park. My hangover had subsided and I knew all I needed now was a good blast of fresh air to tire me out enough to enjoy a good night's sleep – if Maggie would let me have one.

I loved chattering to Maggie in her pram, loved how she was now starting to react to things happening around her, not to mention how her face would brighten up when she heard my voice.

I knew that at seven weeks old her interest in my running commentary on the trees, cars and streetlights was probably minimal but I chattered anyway. I didn't care if people thought I was a crackpot, chatting to her and pulling funny faces.

"Oh look, Maggie, it's a cat. A cat says *miaow*! And there's a doggy. A doggy says *woof*! Do you see the pretty lights? See how they sparkle? Yes, they are pretty and so are you. Yes, you are!"

"They say talking to yourself is the first sign of madness," a voice behind me said.

I turned, startled, to see Tom.

"I'm not talking to myself although it's debateable whether or not I'm going mad," I said.

He smiled.

"Anyway," I continued, "what are you doing out this evening? Do you make a habit of jumping out of bushes at random women because I have to say that, if you do, I'm pretty sure you would score quite high on the madness scale yourself."

"I didn't jump out of a bush," Tom said.

"Not this time maybe, but you do seem to have a habit of appearing out of nowhere."

"Aah, Aoife, you've uncovered my secret. I'm a superhero. Gardener Man!" He flexed his muscles and I couldn't help but laugh.

"Look, Maggie, look at the big eejit!"

"Eejit," Tom replied. "I like that. Eejit Man – perhaps that will be my new persona."

"Well, for what it is worth I think you would make a pretty fine Eejit Man."

"I aim to please," he said with a bow. "But seriously, in case you do go spreading rumours that I'm a nutcase who stalks women on the streets of Richmond, I'm not. I was just walking back from a job, as it happens. It was a nice evening, so I thought I would grab some fresh air. If you want I'll walk you back to the shop."

"That would nice," I said with a smile. "You never know who you might meet on these walks. Maggie and I could do with a superhero to make sure we get home okay."

"Eejit Man at your service!" said Tom and we set off together.

Eejit Man walked me home. He even offered to push the pram some of the way and being that some of the way was uphill I let him. I suppose, to people looking at us, we would have looked very much like a proper family. He would have looked like the proud daddy and I was playing the role of the stunningly beautiful wife and mother. (Well, a girl can dream, can't she?) The conversation was easy. We talked about our days – mine cuddling Maggie, his laying a rockery. I left out the bits about the Big Freeze with Mum, the hangover after my night drinking with Beth and of course all that nasty business with Jake. I don't know what, if anything, he left out but it wasn't lost on me that we all have our own secrets that even the people who see us day in and day out know nothing about.

"Hopefully the night air will have tired her and she will sleep well for you," Tom said and I yawned.

I wasn't sure if he was talking to Maggie or me. We reached the shop and I invited him in for a coffee. It seemed the mannerly thing to do.

"I'd best be off home, Aoife. I'm aching and in need of a long, hot Radox bath to soothe these muscles."

I tried to ignore the shiver of excitement that ran through me at the thought of Tom and his muscles, reminding myself that I did not need a man to complete me. I was an independent woman. And besides, even if the urge was there to drag Tom upstairs and run a bath for him (and lump in there beside him), he didn't need, or want, me.

"Well, thanks for walking us home," I said, letting myself in the side door of the shop.

"It was a pleasure," he said with a bow and headed off in the direction of Gardiner Street.

I watched him as he walked off – and wondered was he the person he really said he was? He seemed genuine and decent, but I couldn't help but wonder why someone like him would be interested in befriending someone like me. Sure I'd heard Elena's story, but that just didn't ring true. Someone like Tom Austin could have women flocking at his feet. I mean he was a handsome, successful, single businessman and he always had flowers. What more could a woman want?

I thought of Jake – of our raw animal passion – and how he made me feel and I realised that if I could take the two best things about these two wonderful men and mix them together I would be on to a surefire winner.

When I opened the door to the flat, the light was flashing on my answerphone. I pressed the button.

"Aoife, it's Anna. Can you call me, please?"

I smiled as I settled down to give Maggie her last feed of the night. Anna would have her flowers by now, she was probably phoning to say thank you. I made a mental note to call her back once Maggie was settled. Of course, Tom had been right, the night air had tired us both out and after I put her in her Moses basket, I closed my eyes and drifted off.

★ ★ ★

I woke to the shrill ringing of the phone. As I tried to open my eyes, Maggie started screaming in a bid to drown out the opposition. My back was aching from lying on the sofa and as I reached for the phone I knocked the lamp over, shattering the coloured glass on the wooden floor. "Shit. Feck. Hello?" I muttered.

"Aoife, it's Anna."

"Hang on, Anna, I've just knocked over the lamp."

"Aoife, I need to talk to you."

"Sssh, Maggie," I said, lifting her from her Moses basket, trying to quieten her down. Of course the closeness of her screaming mouth to my ear didn't help.

"Anna, I'm sorry, Maggie has woken. I'll call you back in five."

"Aoife, please, this is important."

There was an urgency in her voice. I don't know how I hadn't picked up on it before.

"What's wrong?" I said, rocking Maggie on my shoulder, the pace of the rocking increasing with the pace of my heartbeat.

"You need to come home, darling. I've booked flights for you and Maggie first thing from Stansted."

"Anna, you're scaring me. What's wrong?"

"It's your mum, darling. She's in hospital. They think it's a heart attack. She's very ill, sweetheart, I tried to phone you earlier. I left a message . . ."

She chattered on, but I couldn't hear her any more. My mum was sick. The same mum who hadn't spoken to me in the best part of a week over a stupid fecking nursery and she was ill. She could be dying and I was here staring at a broken lamp and listening to my baby wail on my shoulder.

"Are you okay?" Anna asked, her voice breaking.

"I'll see you in the morning," I answered, my voice weirdly robotic – as if it was saying what it should but I couldn't think about what we were discussing. "I've things to do, Anna. Keep me posted. I'll see you in the morning," I repeated.

I settled Maggie and set about packing our stuff. Bottles, bibs, baby-gros. Nappies, dummies, wipes. A few pairs of jeans for me, a new toothbrush from the cupboard. I threw it all in the case with neither grace nor style. The clock ticked loudly as I worked, and I thought of how my daddy and Joe would be with Mum now. How Jacqueline would be holding my mother's hand and weeping over her sick body. I felt sick, sore and tired. For the first time in my life, I truly understood what that expression meant.

"Damn you," I muttered under my breath. Angry that the last words I'd shared with Mum, just that afternoon, had been stilted and awkward. She was my mother. My mum. My mammy. "Damn you," I said again and fell to the floor sobbing.

I didn't really sleep that night. I dozed occasionally on the sofa, getting up occasionally to stare out the window or at the clock in the kitchen. At about three I went downstairs for a one-to-one with Matilda. I'm not sure if I was imagining it, but her usual sly grin was gone and she seemed to look almost sorry for me.

"I know she's a baggage," I muttered, "but she's my baggage."

I could hear Tom's voice in my head telling me that talking to myself was the first sign of madness, and it crossed my mind that there was a distinct possibility that I was in fact losing it. I had thought about phoning Beth earlier and getting her to come round, but I figured she had dealt with enough of my crises lately. Besides, I was really going to be leaving her in the shit soon enough, wasn't I? There was me promising to do more, and be there for her more and there I was fecking off back to Derry again – just when she needed me most. She would need at least one day, if not two, for the dye test. She had been hoping I would keep things ticking over at the shop but now I was going to let her down. That started a whole new bout of crying.

By the time morning finally came I was almost hallucinating with tiredness. My eyes were out on stalks from crying, my cheeks scourged red from a waterfall of tears. As soon as it was acceptable to do so I phoned the hospital at home to check on my mother.

"I'm her daughter," I blubbed as the nurse told me that Sheila McLaughlin remained in a critical condition.

"I'll get your father or brother to call you when they get a chance," she soothed.

I told her there was no need. I would be on a plane in a matter of hours and be there myself. If there was going to be more bad news, I would prefer to be on home soil to hear it.

At ten past eight I phoned Beth. I needed to leave shortly afterwards and I guessed both Dan and her would be up by now.

"Beth, I'm sorry," I started before breaking down yet again.

"What's wrong?"

"I have to go home. My mum is sick. They think it was a heart attack. She needs me."

"Oh, Aoife! Can we help? Have you booked flights?"

"Anna has taken care of everything. I fly out at eleven."

"Can we drop you to the airport?"

"No, honestly, it's fine. I have a taxi ordered. I'll be fine. I just need to get home, Beth. She needs me."

Beth's voice started to wobble a little. "Of course she does, darling. Go home, take care of your mum and we'll see you soon. Stay in touch. I'll light a candle beside Matilda for her and hope for the best."

"Thanks," I choked and hung up just as the taxi beeped its horn outside.

"Come on, Maggie, time to go home," I said, lifting our suitcase and heading down the stairs.

43

Beth

"Is something wrong?" Dan asked as he straightened his tie.

"Aoife's mum is sick – a heart attack. She has flown home to Derry to be with her. It sounds serious."

"Shit," said Dan. "Is there anything we can do?"

I shook my head. "She said no. Oh, Dan, I hope her mum is okay. I don't think she could bear it if anything happened. Not now when she is getting in control of her life."

I sat down at our table and took a deep breath. Today was going to be tricky enough but now I would be worrying about Aoife and her mother as well.

I'd only met Sheila twice, once when I went back to Derry for a week one summer when we were still at university, and again at graduation.

She had marked my card from early on. When I had greeted her as Sheila she had sniffed. "You can call me Mrs McLaughlin," she said, putting a coaster under my glass of water and straightening the cushion at my side.

"Sorry, Mrs McLaughlin," I said. "It's nice to meet you."

I could see why Aoife thought her cold and aloof, so when she became pregnant and decided to keep the news from the folks back home, I kind of understood. In her position I would have been in no rush to tell my mother either. Funny that – how different things were. If I told my mother that I was pregnant she would dance a merry dance and take a full-page ad out in *The Times*.

But having said all that, I knew Aoife loved her mother. Even though there had been a Big Freeze lately, she had returned from Derry a few weeks ago sure that some sort of slow progress was being made. She told me she'd had a conversation with her father which had explained a lot and when she spoke of Sheila now there was sometimes the oddest hint of affection.

With the exception of Jake, and now Maggie, and indeed me, there was little that Aoife was openly affectionate about. If she was nice about her mother, it meant she really, truly cared about her.

And, just as with the last nine months of her life, there was little I could do to help her. That was a shit part of growing up into responsible adulthood, I thought, not being able to take the pain away from friends. Now I just had to sit back and watch what they went through without being able to run to a teacher, parent or youth club leader and demand they make it all better.

Then again, if I was still a teenager, I very much doubt I'd be getting ready to go to a doctor to have radioactive dye flushed into my uterus.

Yes, it would nice to have someone to make it all better for a while.

Dan kissed the top of my head. "I'm sure Aoife will be fine.

Hopefully her mother will be okay, but there's nothing you can do about it now, Betsy. Let's go to our appointment. I'm sure Aoife will phone you if she needs you. If you really want we can try and get you over there to help her, but we should really keep this appointment."

I nodded.

Dan sat down opposite me and took my hand.

"It will be all right," he said, "and if it isn't all right then we have options. This isn't the end of the world for us."

I nodded, grateful for his tenderness. Who knew what was ahead. I certainly didn't. Maybe we would be fine and we would just have to continue our monthly dance. Maybe we would need IVF or some other intervention. And maybe, although I'm not sure I wanted to contemplate it just yet, if all that failed we could adopt. We would make great parents. There were children out there who needed a happy home and we could be the people to provide it. But for now, I didn't really want to think about that. I wanted to think about my baby. Our baby. I wanted to feel the nauseous waves of morning-sickness. I wanted my trousers to tighten and my bra to get uncomfortable. I wanted to buy trousers with elasticated waistbands or those funny tummy panels which go up under your boobs. I wanted to curse heartburn and drink Gaviscon by the bucketload. I wanted to feel those first magical bubbles Aoife had spoken off. And I wanted them to get stronger and stronger and turn into thumping great kicks. I wanted to gasp, hold my tummy and say with a smile "That was a big kick." I wanted to sit on the Tube and rub my bump and when I got home I wanted Dan to rub Cocoa Butter cream into my stretching tummy and laugh as it jumped about. I wanted my waters to break in Tesco and I wanted to make a frantic call to Dan telling him "It's time." I wanted to suck on gas and air and cringe as a doctor did an internal. I wanted to watch the contractions ebb and flow on the monitor by my bed. I wanted to swear at Dan and tell him he was never, ever getting near me again before pushing with all my might. I wanted to hear a moment's silence, a pause for an intake of breath and then a shrill cry. I wanted the midwife to tell us we had a son or a daughter and then hand him or her to me and for me to cuddle my baby – our baby – close and look at my husband and see love in his eyes like nothing I had ever seen before.

It was the most natural thing in the world to want, wasn't it? And if I had to switch that off, I would switch it off – but I didn't want to yet. Just please, God, not yet.

Dan was holding my hand while a dazzling white light shone between my legs. I felt drowsy – just a little sedated. I was told this procedure wouldn't hurt. I had been assured it was no more painful than a smear test, but to be honest I'm not the biggest fan of smear tests anyway.

"We'll inject this dye now, Beth. It might feel cool, but it shouldn't be anything more than uncomfortable."

I looked at Dan and he stroked my hair. His eyes told me this would be okay, so I breathed deeply as my uterus was filled and cramps started to take over. Breathing through the pain, I bit back tears. This was all for the greater good, I told myself.

It was over quite quickly, and I was given a couple of painkillers. I dressed, my legs wobbling slightly, and Dan and I took our seats in Dr Browne's office for the results. We didn't talk, because there was nothing either of us could say that would make a difference.

"Right, let's have a look at what we have here," Dr Browne said, his face giving nothing away.

I took a deep breath and crossed my fingers.

44

Aoife

It was sunny when we arrived in Derry. People were smiling all around us, happy to be home. They stood, three deep, at the luggage carousel vying for pole position to pick up their bags and get out onto prime Irish soil, and down the road for Dohertys' baps, a strong cup of tea and a copy of the *Journal*. I stood, my baby in a sling at my chest, willing them to stop their cheery chatter and get out of my way. I wanted our bags too, but not for a happy reunion with Derry's finest traditions. I wanted to get out through the arrivals' doors and see Anna. I wanted her to tell me everything was okay and then to whisk me off up the road to the hospital where my mother would be sitting up in bed, telling everyone to stop making a fuss and that she was perfectly fine, thank you.

I switched my phone on: no messages. Surely no news was good news. But then again, would they have left a message on the phone to tell me she was gone? "Hi, Aoife, it's Joe. Mum's dead.

Call me back!" No, they wouldn't do that. They would wait to tell me in person. A sob bubbled up my chest, the pain of it doubling me over. People looked at me, annoyed that I was disturbing their joyous homecomings. One wee woman walked over and put her arms around me. "There, there, dear," she soothed, "it will be okay." She didn't ask what was making me cry, which I was grateful for, she just offered me a crumpled tissue and stood beside me until the carousel whirred into life. "God bless, sweetheart," she said as I lifted off our cases and headed for the white doors that would bring me to Anna.

Anna, Maggie and I drove in silence to the hospital. I stared out the window at how the landscape of my home city had changed. There were large shopping developments, dual carriageways – a modern city. Why had I not noticed this a few weeks ago? As we drove I felt a certain longing for Derry of old, with no shops to speak of. It was a boring place but a safe place. My mother wasn't sick in the Derry of old.

We parked at the hospital and I strapped Maggie back into her sling. Walking towards the doors I hesitated.

"You're not keeping anything from me, are you, Anna? I'm not going to walk in here and find her already dead or anything? I don't think I could bear it."

Anna rubbed my arm. She looked tired, I thought. "No, Aoife, I'm not keeping anything from you. Your mother is very sick but she is alive."

Walking into the ward, a frazzled-looking nurse gazed at my bundle in her sling.

"She can't really be here," she said, with disdain.

I tried to fight back but I couldn't, so Anna stepped in for me once again. "My niece has just arrived on the plane from London.

This is Mrs McLaughlin's grandchild and we are going to see her. I'll take the baby then, but she has a right to see her granny in the circumstances."

For the briefest of moments it looked as though the nurse might continue with her protest, but I guess she knew better than to argue with Anna and she waved us on. We walked up the corridor. I looked in every door, at old-looking people lying attached to wires and machines. Tired-looking relatives sat by their sides, not even aware that a complete stranger was looking in at their grief and worry. As we walked closer I saw a small, pregnant figure walk out of a door towards me. Her hair was tied back and in need of a wash, her face was pale and her linen trousers were a wrinkled mess. She put her hand to her face, streaking her make-up, but even though she looked as unlike herself as she had ever done, I knew that I was looking at Jacqueline.

"Aoife!" she wailed, running to me. "Thank God you're here. We've all just been falling apart. Come in!"

I don't think I had ever seen Jacqueline show emotion. Even on her wedding day she remained as cool as a cucumber as if an unplanned smile or stray tear would crack her perfectly made-up face. I put my arms awkwardly around her, Maggie squirming as Jacqueline pulled me close.

"Come on, Aoife, we should go in," Anna said gently.

I'm not sure which sight shocked me more. It may have been the small, deathly white woman lying in the hospital bed or it may have been the sight of my brother – the perfect atheist – on his knees with a pair of Rosary beads in his hand, or it could have been my father, crying as if it was his heart that was broken and not my mother's.

What do you say in such a situation, I wondered. "Hello," seemed too glib, and wailing wouldn't help anyone. I didn't think anything I could have said would have helped so I walked towards the bed, squeezing Joe's shoulder as I walked past.

Daddy looked up at me, his face almost as gaunt as my mother's. His expression only changed when he caught sight of his granddaughter cradled into me.

"Oh Aoife, I'm so glad you're here!"

I grasped my mother's hand. Her fingers felt cold and bony. Her skin seemed paper thin. If the rhythmic beeping of the heart monitor by her bed had not been telling me otherwise, I would have sworn she was already dead.

Dad stood up and I fell into a hug with him. It was strange – the role of parent and child strangely reversed. I was comforting him. I was the strong one for now, and believe me I was weakening by the minute.

I'm not sure I've ever really understood the relationship between my parents. At times I wondered if they were together simply because my mother wouldn't have the shame of a marriage break-up over her. There was nothing intrinsically wrong with their relationship, but there was never any sign of passion.

Then again, I don't think I would want to see any passion between my mother and father.

Hugging my father now though, it dawned on me that he loved her. He really loved her. The thought of our conversation in the park, when he told me how she had suffered when I was little, flitted through my mind. He was fiercely protective of her. He had helped her and encouraged her every step of the way to love me. She might have been a complete cow to me, but to him she was his life. And to Joe, and yes, even to Perfect Jacqueline, she was the centre of the family. If anything it was strange that I was here – my eyes puffy with tears – when all I'd ever done was tell everyone just how much she drove me to distraction.

When he released me from his hug, I asked the one question I knew that I had to.

"Is she going to be okay?"

Joe looked up. "She needs an operation, a triple bypass. They're concerned about whether or not she will survive the procedure but it's her only chance."

I nodded. Her only chance. It was then the room started to swirl and I felt a tingling creep up the back of my neck, over my head and over my eyes until all I could see was black and all I could feel was my leaden body falling towards the floor.

★ ★ ★

I woke in a hospital bed. For a moment I thought I was doing a *Dallas* and the last two months had all been a dream. Instinctively I reached down to my stomach – no, no bump. Maybe it had all been a dream. Suddenly I felt bereft that my daughter might have been nothing more than a figment of my imagination.

But that, of course, didn't explain why I was in hospital. I lifted my head from the pillow and felt dizzy at once so I slumped back down. I rubbed my eyes, aware now of the drip in my hand and of the person sitting beside my bed reading a magazine.

What was Anna doing in London? This was all getting a bit too Twilight Zone for my liking.

"Anna?" I said.

"You're awake then?" she said, looking up. "As if it wasn't enough your mother being in hospital without you fainting on us too. The doctor says you're low on iron and a wee bit dehydrated."

It was starting to come back to me now. My mother, my fainting, my daddy . . . oh God, my baby . . . hadn't she been in her sling when I fell?

"Maggie?" I gasped.

"She's fine. You fell backwards so she wasn't affected at all. She's with Jacqueline. To be honest, I think Jacqueline is glad of the distraction."

"My head . . .?"

"You hit it as you fell."

At least that explained the headache.

"And Mum?"

"They're taking her down to theatre soon. The doctor says half an hour on that drip and some iron tablets will have you right as rain so just rest now. You've had a bad shock, darling." Anna reached over and kissed me on the forehead and I grabbed her hand.

"I know I'm always giving out stink about her," I said, "but I do love her even if she is a bitch. I want her, need her, to be okay."

"I know, darling. I feel the same."

Perfect Jacqueline behaved perfectly with Maggie. To my shock and surprise she even managed to call her Maggie and not Margaret. She fed her for me, winded her, changed her nappy and got her off to sleep without so much as a whimper and then she took her home to look after because she "knew more about babies than Maeve anyway".

Although Anna had to pretend to be outwardly offended at that, she admitted later it was true. Given half a chance Maeve would have taken my child to the pub with her to show her off as the latest must-have fashion accessory.

That left just me, my dad, Joe and Anna in the waiting-room. We paced up and down, drank too much coffee and said very little. I couldn't really handle thinking or talking at all. My mind was whirring. In an operating theatre not far from where I stood someone was cutting into my mother's chest, spreading her ribs and trying to save her life. Perhaps she was already gone and they were arguing amongst themselves as to who would be the unlucky doctor to break the news. I didn't envy that job. I think I would be rubbish at it. I'd start crying with the family no doubt.

And then we would have to plan her funeral. Should I bring Maggie? Was she too young? Would it be appropriate to breast-feed in a chapel? My mother would turn in her grave at the thought.

If she was dead, that is. Which she wasn't, I reminded myself. Not that I knew anyway. Bizarrely I had an urge for a cigarette. Ironic really, given that I'd spent the morning in cardiac intensive care. Leaving my family to it, I walked downstairs, stopping at the shop to buy some cigarettes, before going out of the door away from the prying eyes of disapproving nurses and doctors and lighting up.

I hadn't smoked in a year. And even then it had only been on very drunken nights. I hadn't smoked properly since I left college ten years ago. I supposed though it would be a bit like riding a bike: you never forget. Lighting up, I watched the smoke swirl over into the afternoon air and breathed deeply, the hot smoke catching the back of my throat and making me cough before the hit of the nicotine took hold and I felt myself relax.

This had been a weird day to say the least. I thought of the drip that had been in my arm and felt a dull ache start. I wondered for a moment if it had hurt before the thought of it crossed my mind or if I was being a complete hypochondriac, feeling pain simply because I knew I had been in the wars.

As I smoked, breathing in deeply, I thought of my mother fighting for her life. Why was nothing ever simple? I knew that was a selfish thought but just when I had finally realised that Jake Gibson was not my knight in shining armour my mother had to go and nearly die on us. Selfish bitch.

I chided myself. Right now she could be dying, her soul hovering over me watching me smoke my sneaky cig and hearing my inner most "selfish bitch" thoughts. I shuddered, throwing my butt to the ground and stubbing it out. It was time to go back in, but just as I headed to the doors again I remembered that today was the day Beth was due to have her dye test. Regardless of what was happening to me and my mother now, I couldn't let my best friend down again. I hadn't been there for her before, so I was damn sure I was going to be there for her now.

I switched on my mobile and dialled her number.

"Hey, Bethy," I said, a strange monotone emotionless voice coming from my mouth. I wasn't sure how to play this. Too upbeat and I risked offending her if it had all gone wrong, too downbeat and she would be worrying about me and not herself. And she needed to put herself first for once.

"Hey, Aoife, how are you? We've been worried sick. How is your mum? Are you okay?"

"Never mind me, how are you? How did the test go?"

"Well . . ." she started.

45

Beth

If I'm honest, I didn't quite know how I felt or how I was supposed to feel. We knew that hundreds of couples, hundreds of women, had heard the same diagnosis and faced the same uncertain future.

I wasn't sure if I felt relieved or annoyed to learn that my tubes were clear. If they were damaged we would know what we were facing. But they weren't and in a strange way I felt we were no further forward. There was no one to blame – no clear road to follow. The doctor had smiled when he told us that they were clear but we had left in silence.

"It's good news, isn't it?" Dan said as we drove off.

"I suppose."

"What do you mean, you suppose? The tests are clear. You are ovulating. Your insides are healthy, my sperm is top notch apparently – so it's good, right?"

"I suppose," I said again.

I knew Dan wanted a baby – our baby – but he was tiring of this roundabout of emotions and trying and cycle days. Would he lose all sense of urgency over it now that there was officially "nothing wrong"?

Sensing him tense beside me, I forced myself to take a deep breath. "Of course it's good news. There's nothing stopping us now."

When we arrived home I changed into my gingham PJs and curled on the sofa. Dan brought me a glass of wine "to celebrate", when all I really wanted was a cup of tea and a hot water bottle for the cramping.

I lifted the laptop and went online. The girls on my forum would understand the mixture of relief and disappointment that was coursing through me now. I should have felt delighted, but I felt strangely numb. Why, if everything inside me was clear and blockage-free, was I not pushing a Bugaboo down the High Street already?

As I typed my message, pouring out my thoughts and feelings in a way I never could to Dan, Aoife, my mother or any other living soul, the phone rang.

"Hey, Aoife," I said, "how are you? How is your mum?"

But she didn't answer, instead turning the topic of conversation away from her and her mother and onto me. Even in this crisis, she didn't want to talk about her mother and normally I'd have shooed away her concern for me but I needed to talk about it.

"The tests are clear," I said. "So we're back to waiting a few months to see what happens and then considering some interventions."

"Are you okay with that?" Aoife asked, her voice laced with concern.

"I don't know, Aoife, to be honest. I don't know what I was hoping for. Maybe I wanted them to find a problem, maybe I wanted them to find a baby. Gosh, I don't know."

"You poor pet," Aoife soothed and I felt a surge of guilt.

Her mother could be dead for all I knew.

"And your mother?" I asked.

"Fighting." Aoife sighed. "She's in surgery now. She's very sick, Beth. They aren't sure her heart will survive the strain of the operation. Jesus, Beth, she might die. And no doubt it will be my fault for causing her all this bloody stress."

I found it hard to sleep that night. I tossed and turned, drifting off occasionally to a variety of weird dreams. As I got up to pee for the one hundredth time, Dan pulled me close to him.

"Hey, fidget bum," he said sleepily, spooning me against him.

"I'm sorry, did I wake you?"

"Only a couple of times," he teased. "Are you okay?"

"I can't switch my brain off."

He laughed. "I didn't know you'd switched it on."

Digging him in the ribs, earning a loud "Ouch" from him, I smiled in the dark.

"Watch it, Jones," I said. "I have friends in high places."

He kissed my hair. "You wouldn't do anything to get rid of me, would you?"

Turning towards him, curling my leg over his, I stroked his jawline. "Not a chance, mister."

"Irish will be fine, you know," he said, folding his hand over mine. "She's tougher than you think."

"I know."

"And you're tougher too," he said, kissing me, softly at first, and then deeper.

Somehow, in that dark room, I started to believe again I would be fine too.

It felt odd opening up the shop knowing that Aoife and Maggie weren't upstairs. I wasn't going to hear her thumping about, or Maggie's lusty cry beckoning her mummy to feed her.

Heather arrived shortly after and started tidying around. We were due new stock later and Tom was planning to start work on the yard. It was going to be busy.

I checked my mobile for any signs of a text from Aoife – any word on how her mother was doing – but it remained silent. I looked at Matilda, the same Mona Lisa smile on her face as always, and I offered up a prayer for the cold and aloof Sheila and her beautiful, loving daughter.

The bell above the door pinged and Tom walked in.

"Morning, ladies," he said, and Heather descended into a fit of girlish giggles.

Rolling my eyes, I offered Tom a cup of coffee before he started work.

"Sure," he said, looking over my shoulder at the stairs which led to Aoife's flat.

"Is she not about then?" he asked.

"Didn't she let you know? She's gone back to Derry, Tom. Her mum took sick a couple of days ago and she left yesterday morning."

"Will she be okay?"

For a moment I wondered if he was asking about Aoife or her mum, but deciding it must be the second I shrugged my shoulders. "From what I can gather, it's pretty touch and go. I'm waiting to hear from her any time now."

"Poor thing," he said, lifting his tools and walking towards the yard.

It seemed he didn't want a cup of coffee after all.

"He's okay, isn't he?" Heather asked, staring after him with a lustful look in her eyes. "Do you know if he is single?"

I knew he was technically single, but something told me he wasn't available.

46

Aoife

"The next twenty-four hours are critical."

I was a bit of an *ER* addict and I was well used to hearing those words. But I never thought I would hear them in relation to my mother.

She had survived the operation, but she needed life support to allow her body to recover, and even then, we were warned, she could crash at any time.

At any time doctors could flood into her room and stick paddles on her chest, shout "Clear!" and shock her back to life. It would be kind of exciting if it wasn't so serious.

I sat up and rubbed the small of my back. My boobs were the size of watermelons, aching from not feeding my daughter in twelve hours. Dad and Joe were sitting staring at their shoes. Anna was looking out the window. I felt a bit like a spare piece – an extra in the scene. Sipping from the bottle of water Joe had brought up from the staff canteen for me, I looked at my watch – it was 2 a.m.

I wondered how Maggie was. I felt an urge to be with her, to hold her. This was strange: on one hand there was my mother who needed me and on the other a defenceless little baby.

"I think I need to go to Maggie," I said, standing up.

"She'll be settled for the night now with Jacqueline," Anna said, "but in any case you should be taking it easy. How about we get you home for some sleep? It's been a long day."

My father nodded, as did Joe, and I felt I couldn't resist. I was tired and all I wanted was the comfort of Anna's uber-floral bedroom.

"I'll leave my mobile on," I said. "Let me know if there's any change."

When we got home I had a shower, expressed some milk for Maggie and fell into bed. I didn't sleep the best though, if I'm honest. I had weird dreams where Beth gave birth to my mother while Tom Austin looked on with a broad smile across his face.

In the morning I woke early and went to the kitchen. Anna was already up, drinking tea and saying the Rosary.

"It's not like you to pray," I said, rubbing her shoulders as I walked past.

"I figure it can't hurt," she said. "Every little is bound to help."

"Just like Tesco," I said, absently dropping two slices of plain bread into the toaster for breakfast.

Anna smiled, and went back to her prayers. I listened, comforted by the rhythm of the Rosary and the slow clacking of her beads. A candle was burning on the windowsill, offering up a silent "intention" for my mother.

I buttered my toast and sat down, waiting for Anna to finish so that we could make whatever plans necessary for the day ahead.

"Sorry, love," she said when she was done, "I should have said – I've phoned the hospital and your mother has made it through the night."

I instantly felt like a complete fecking eejit that I hadn't asked before stuffing my face with buttery toast and hot tea. Pushing aside the remainder of the slice, even though the butter had melted into the bread just how I liked it, I sat upright.

"We can head to the hospital as soon as you want," I said. "I'd just like to call and see Maggie first." I cradled my arms around my body instinctively. I hadn't been apart from her for so long before and it felt as if a part of me was missing.

"Of course, darling, but I want to let your dad and Joe get back for some sleep as soon as possible. They've been there all night."

I nodded and set about getting ready for the day.

I tried to remind myself that Jacqueline had been quite nice yesterday after all and that chances were she would be minding Maggie a lot for me while my mother battled for her life and I had to let all the past hurt and insecurity go.

Anna rang the doorbell and Odhran ran as fast as his chubby legs could carry him down the hall, grappling with the key in the door like an overexcited puppy.

"Hello, hello, hiya, hiya!" he chimed, jumping up and down.

"Odhran, calm down," I heard Jacqueline chide as she walked towards the door, my baby in her arms, and let us in.

Odhran immediately made a break for freedom towards the street. I can't really say that I blamed him.

For a second I stood and watched, amazed that he could run so fast before something clicked in me that perhaps the middle of the street was not the safest place for a toddler. I tore after him, grabbing him to me and turned to find Jacqueline with her hand over her mouth, a look of terror on her face. Anna lifted Maggie from her which I figured was wise, given that to even the most casual of observers, it looked as though Jacqueline was about ten seconds away from dropping my child square on her head.

"You wee fecker!" she squealed at her son, her face red with a mixture of relief and fury.

It seemed her perfect facade was falling by the minute.

When we had calmed down, poured a cup of tea and ensured Odhran was in a safe place with his Thomas the Tank Engine toys, Jacqueline apologised for her outburst.

"You know I wouldn't normally use language like that. I'm just a little tired and no, Aoife, that's nothing to do with your little lady. She has been a dream. Makes me eager to meet this little one." She rubbed her tummy.

I held Maggie close to me, eager to lap up the compliments. For once in my life I'd done something worthy of my sister-in-law's approval.

"I suppose you should be going," Jacqueline said, looking at the kitchen clock.

"You're right," I said, "but if Anna doesn't mind, we'll just have a quick look at that nursery of yours first to see what kind of space I'll be working with."

Jacqueline smiled, squeezed my hand and thanked me. "This means a lot, Aoife. You always make such a good job of things."

Mum had a bit more colour in her cheeks when we reached the hospital. Daddy on the other hand looked pale and exhausted and Joe wasn't far behind.

"I'll run youse both home," Anna said. "I don't think you're in a fit state to drive and between Sheila and Aoife we've had enough McLaughlins in hospital for one week."

Too tired to argue they followed her and left me alone with my mother, her eyes still closed, painkilling medicine and saline running into her and God knows what running out. Her hair was a mess, matted to her head and the pillow, and I thought how she would hate it. This was a woman who never missed her Saturday morning blow-dry and set for love nor money. I reached into my bag and took out my own hairbrush, before standing at the top of my mother's bed and slowly dragging it through her hair just as she had done for me when I was little.

Now I remembered all those mornings where we had our battles of wills – me demanding she leave me alone and I liked the knots in my hair, and her saying I would look like a scarecrow going out of the house like that. When we had exhausted our shouting she would spray a mix of conditioner and water in my tangled auburn fizz and as gently as possible pull the comb through, singing the songs of Connie Francis as she went. It would take all of "Lipstick on your Collar" and half of "Stupid Cupid" before I was free to go.

As I stroked her hair a memory came back to me. I remembered the time when she only thought I was asleep. I was lying on the sofa, off school with measles, as she talked to her friend – stroking my hair as she did.

"I would hate it if anything happened to her," she had said. "I couldn't be without her for the world."

I knew what she meant.

"She's a fighter, you know," a short, dumpy nurse said to me as she came to check all the tubes and wires.

"Stubborn as a mule," I nodded, realising for the first time that I wanted that bloody stubbornness to work in her favour.

"She's doing very well, love. Don't give up hope. Where there is life there is always hope."

"Thank you," I said and continued brushing, soothing out the knots, straightening the gold and grey.

When Anna arrived back I had finished. I was sitting holding my mother's hand and staring out the window.

"You okay, pet?" she asked.

"Grand. Just thinking a lot."

"I know what you mean," she said, sitting down beside me.

"Have we been really horrible to her all these years?" I asked, not looking at her.

"Probably a wee bit," Anna said. "But listen here, Aoife, just because your mother is ill that doesn't mean she's suddenly a saint. She's a hard woman to live with and she doesn't always show herself in the best light, but I'd like to think beneath it all her heart is in the right place."

I looked at her, thinking of her choice of words. "I bloody hope so after all this," I laughed in spite of myself.

Anna smiled. "You know what I mean, cheeky. Maybe this is the wake-up call we all need to put things in perspective. We'll get this all sorted out once and for all."

What neither of us said was that we hoped we would get the chance.

My mother opened her eyes the following day. She looked around the room, disorientated and unsure of herself, and reached a hand up to my face. I kissed her hand, and she pushed my hair behind my ears.

"That's better," she said, before wincing with the pain.

She always had preferred my hair behind my ears and if I'm honest with myself it did look better that way.

She looked around again at four pairs of expectant, red and tired eyes and said:

"Jacqueline, where's Odhran?"

I stepped back from the bedside, heart breaking, while she chattered to the people she loved most in the whole world.

We drove home in silence. If I'm honest a part of me – just a small part, mind – hated my mother more in that moment than I ever had. I had spent two days wailing, praying, being away from my child, and did she care? Did she fuck! Why I thought she would change – that there would be some deathbed epiphany was beyond me.

"She's not herself," Anna said, staring forward.

"Oh yes, she bloody well is," I muttered and stared back out the window.

We continued our journey, saying nothing.

When we got home I carried Maggie upstairs. She was fussing and squirming – annoyed at me for leaving her for a couple of days and for bringing her to this strange country again where she wasn't the absolute centre of attention.

"Come on, baby! Be good for Mummy."

I jiggled her, holding her close, waiting for her to latch on to me and relieve my aching boobs and realise she still loved me, but she arched her back and screamed.

"Oh for fuck sake," I said – a little too loudly – and laid her in her cot and let her scream while I cried my eyes out.

By the time I lifted her to my breast again, her face was as red as mine, her eyes as sad as mine and I continued to cry as I latched her on and she fed. As her eyes grew sleepy, the guilt kicked in. I had let her down – but then again was it any wonder? I didn't know how to be a mother. No one had ever shown me.

When she was fed and winded, I lay down beside her on the floral duvet and closed my eyes. I was just drifting off to sleep when my phone beeped to life.

"Hi, Aoife. Tom here. Beth gave me ur number. Hope ur mum is ok? Take care. x."

I realised I hadn't even thought of Tom, or Jake, in the last few days but now that his name was there in front of me I felt a pang. It confused me. I didn't know him, I reminded myself. We had only met a couple of times, but there was something about him which made me feel comfortable sharing my secrets with him.

I lifted the phone and dialled his number.

"Hey there," he said and I found myself smiling. "How are you, Aoife?"

"Okay," I fibbed, my voice wobbling. God, he really was going to think I was a complete lunatic.

"Really?" he asked.

"No," I stuttered.

"Is it your mum?" he asked, full of concern, and I started to sob.

"Oh I'm sorry, Aoife, I'm so sorry. If there is anything I can do. Flowers for the service, anything?"

"She's not dead," I stuttered. "She's just a bitch!"

There was a few seconds' pause and I could hear him take a deep breath. "Right, okay. Well, I'm glad she's not dead but I'm sorry she's a bitch. Is there anything I can do to help?"

"It's enough that you listen to me," I sniffed.

"Aoife, I will always be here to listen to you. Us two hopeless cases have to stick together."

"I don't think you are a hopeless case, Tom," I smiled. "You, Mr Successful Businessman in your fancy London shop."

"Right, is that coming from Ms Successful Businesswoman with her fancy London shop *and* a gorgeous baby girl?"

"Point well made," I smiled. "I'll stop feeling sorry for myself if you stop referring to us both as hopeless cases."

"Promise," Tom said and I could hear his smile. "You are a very strong person, Aoife. I know that about you. You will get through this, and when you get back I'll take you out to dinner to celebrate."

"I would like that very much," I smiled and we said our goodbyes.

★ ★ ★

When I woke from my sleep – to the sound of Maggie crying in my ear – I saw that it was six forty-five and time for hospital visiting. I would have to make the effort. Even though I didn't want to. My mother would, no doubt, not even care if we made the effort. Brushing my hair, pushing all the loose tendrils behind my ears, I sighed. Then I dressed Maggie in something suitably prim and proper that I knew her granny would like. I had to put my anger behind me because I had learned over the past few days that even if she drove me to distraction I would be lost in my own way without her.

She was my mammy. Complete fecking bitch that she was, she was still my mammy.

When we arrived at the hospital, my mother looked just as small, just as weak, but at least now her eyes were open and, although tired, she made an effort to talk to me.

"Aoife," she said, looking at the bundle of pink in my arms, "you've brought the baby, I see. So you thought I was going to die too, did you?"

I wanted to assure her that no, I was always completely sure she was going to recover but that would be a lie that I just couldn't keep up with. My heart – never mind hers – had been ripped out the last few days, causing me to think of everything in my life and reassess it.

"Yes, Mum," I said, stepping forward, "I thought you were going to die."

My mother looked aghast.

"You shouldn't upset her," a well-meaning but fearsome nurse said and it took me a moment to realise that she was talking to me.

I looked at my mother, saw her clutching her chest, and saw her crying.

363

"You all thought I was going to die. You wanted me to die!" she called to me, pointing a bony finger at me.

"No. No, I didn't," I croaked. "How can you say that? How *dare* you say that?" My voice grew angrier.

"You've never cared, Aoife," my mother said through her tears and the nurse took me by the arm and led me out of the room.

"We can't get your mother upset, dear. Not in her condition."

I looked down at my daughter, asleep in her sling. I thought of the last two months and every damn thing I had been through and I wondered who cared about whether or not I was upset? Nobody gave a damn. How could my mother think that?

I turned and walked out of the ward, down in the lift, out into the fresh air and gulped lungfuls of it down as my heart thumped in my chest. How could she ever think that? I looked up and saw Joe walking towards me, a broad smile across his face.

"Lovely day, isn't it?" he chimed, the worry lines smoothed on his brow. His mammy was going to be all right. His world was back to how it should be.

I shrugged, trying to smile but grimacing instead.

"Aoife, what's wrong? Is Mum okay? Jesus, tell me she's okay . . ." The colour drained from his face and I reached to steady him.

"She's fine, Joe. Don't worry. Back to herself."

"Thank God for that," he said, sitting down on the bench close to the door. "So what's wrong then?"

"I caused this, didn't I? This stress. I made her sick."

He shook his head. "You're being daft."

"Am I? Seems Mum thinks I'm the cause of everything that went wrong with this family ever. I know I've made mistakes, Joe. I'm not perfect – and I'm not saying Maggie was a mistake either before you start getting notions on you."

He shook his head. "I never said that."

"But I did handle this whole thing wrong, and I've apologised for it. I want to make amends. I've been trying to make amends. I don't want Mum to keep hating me. She drives me mad but when I thought she was dying . . ." My voice wavered. "I just wish she could like me – accept me even – for who I am."

He stood up and hugged me, awkwardly admittedly as he tried not to squish Maggie.

"You didn't make her sick, Aoife. She's high maintenance. She always has been. And trust me, with a wife like Jacqueline I know high maintenance when I see it. She didn't have a heart attack because you had a baby. She has spent her whole life getting tied up in knots over stupid little things, so she was always going to be a candidate for something like this."

I was astounded. I couldn't believe he had come out with these verdicts on his wife and his mammy. But then I just sighed, enjoying the hug from my big brother.

"Look, Aoife, go back to Anna's. Spend some time with your daughter. Have a sleep if she will let you. All this will seem easier to deal with when you're rested."

I nodded and headed back to Anna's house where I went to bed even though it had only just gone eight.

The following day I got up, feeling rested, and headed to the hospital again with Maggie. As we arrived I looked in the door to her ward and saw her sleeping. There were no flowers in her room, and just a couple of cards. She looked small and lonely and I thought how scary it must have been to feel as if her life was coming to an end.

I had been standing there for about five minutes when my father walked through the doors at the end of the corridor, carrying a cup of coffee. He looked older too. "Fair shook" as my granny would have said.

"Is she still sleeping?" he asked, and I nodded.

"Good, she needs her rest."

"So do you, Daddy. You need to keep your strength up."

"Aye, Aoife. You are probably right, darling."

He sat down on the low chairs at the end of the corridor and gestured at me to join him. "Might as well stay out here while she's sleeping. The heat in there would knock you out."

We sat for a few moments in companionable silence before I started to speak. "Daddy, what happened? I know Mum had a heart attack, but what actually happened?"

He sighed. "I had gone for a walk, darling. Your mum was doing her ironing, you know what she's like. I don't know what happened exactly, I just know when I came back she was sitting on the floor against the door, the colour of death. Her skin was clammy. Aoife, she looked fierce. She was clutching her chest, she couldn't even speak. I thought I was losing her." His eyes misted over and I squeezed his hand.

"I don't know how long she was there. I dread to think what she was going through – how scared she was. I never want to see her go through that again."

I squeezed his hand tighter. "Poor mum," I said, a certain resolve building inside me.

When my mother woke I was holding her hand. She looked at me, a little confused, as I kissed her cheek. It felt alien to be so close to her, but I wanted to let her know that despite her very best efforts I did care about her.

"Yes, Mum," I started, "I thought you were going to die and it scared me. I love you. I don't want to lose you. I want to make whatever is wrong with us right and I think we need to start again now."

I stood up and took Maggie from my father's arms and laid her in the crook of my mother's arm. Maggie cuddled in as if that crook was made to hold babies. My mum stared at me in silence for a moment, then looked at Maggie and back at me.

"Don't make the same mistakes I did, Aoife. You don't need me to go over it all – we both know what happened but I did love you. I do love you. Don't let this little one question your love for even one moment."

I nodded and leaned over onto the bed to embrace her and Maggie, making sure I didn't hurt her, and we sat there for a long time – saying nothing but for the first time ever enjoying the fact that there would be no more awkward silences.

Once Mum was off the critical list, I had some tough choices to make. We knew she would be convalescing for a while and, God love my father, while he was a decent sort he wasn't really the kind of person to play nursemaid to anyone. He would always have one eye on the clock, wondering what the weather was like on the golf course, or what time he could get away to the pub for a pint of Carlsberg.

He told me that there was no need for me to stay, but said it in such a small voice that I knew he was hoping against hope that I would.

When I told him I had no immediate plans to return to Richmond, the look of relief on his face was a picture.

"Come and stay at home, Aoife," he pleaded. "It would be nice to have you around."

I thought about it, for all of maybe two seconds, but declined. "Daddy, the last thing Mum will need when she is recovering is a young baby in the house. I'll stay with Anna, but I'll be over every day, I promise."

He nodded. He understood that while things had no doubt

changed entirely in the last few days between me and my mother, my staying at home would be likely to kill her entirely.

And besides I had grown quite fond of Anna's floral spare room. My only concern was that when I eventually did make it back to London my designs would reflect this new obsession. Could I, I wondered, interest Elena Kennedy in a 1980s' Poundstretcher Chic transformation?

Now the only thing I had to do was break the news to Beth – who only a week ago I had promised to help by returning to work early from maternity leave. I wasn't sure how she would react. Well, in fairness, I knew how she would react. She was Beth. She took things on the chin. She understood how important it was for me to be there for my mother and she wouldn't do anything to make me feel bad about that. She wouldn't need to. I would do a good job of that myself.

"I'd better get this over with then, eh?" I told a cooing Maggie as I dialled the number of the shop.

"Instant Karma. Heather speaking, how can I help you?" a sing-song voice answered.

"Hey, Heather, it's Aoife. Is Beth about?"

"Oh hang on, she's out in the yard with that hunky gardener man," Heather answered. "I'll bring the phone out to her."

I could hear her clip-clop on the wooden floors of the shop, the tinkle of the bell above the door and Tom's low, earthy laugh.

"Beth, it's Aoife on the phone."

"Hey, gorgeous!" said Beth. "How are things? How is your mother getting along?" Her voice was laden with concern and I felt rotten that I was just about to land her in it.

"She is getting better, but slowly," I started. "Look, Beth, there is no easy way to say this. I'm going to have stay here for a while. They need me and Mum and I are making inroads into making things better between us."

She paused, while she fixed a smile on her face I imagined, and answered: "Aoife, do what you have to do, but you will be missed."

"It might be a week or two, maybe more, but I will be back," I offered.

"Take as long as it takes."

I wished I could jump down the phone line and hug her.

"And Beth, could you do me a favour? Can you run upstairs and empty my fridge? I'm pretty sure I left some milk in there that will be growing legs by now, and feck knows what state I left the place in. And, if you can, can you see if I have any messages. Jake is probably wondering where on earth his daughter has disappeared to. And, Beth, could you tell Matilda I was asking for her?" I said this last one lightly and of course she replied that she would.

"And Tom says hi," she added. "The yard is looking wonderful. He's done a wonderful job, even if he has been a little down in the dumps lately."

I wanted to think there was some subtle romantic subtext to what she said – that he was missing me – but maybe she was just talking about roses and herbs and him being a typical grumpy man.

47

Beth

If I was to say that I wasn't hacked off to the bottom of my bottom that Aoife was staying in Derry I would be lying. I understood, of course I did, but the thought of holding the fort in sunny Richmond with only Heather for company was enough to drive me to drink.

As I poured a glass of wine and sat down in our transformed yard at Instant Karma I thought about how much I was going to miss her.

"Penny for them," Tom said, sitting down beside me and sipping from the wine he had brought to celebrate finishing the garden. Dan had promised to join us later with a Chinese and a bottle of bubbly.

"Nothing and everything," I said, taking a drink and looking out over the lavender, jasmine and rosemary now gracing a raised flower-bed beside the iron steps.

"This smells fabulous," I said, nodding to the flowers.

"It will be even better in the summer," Tom said. "Hopefully Aoife will get some use out of it."

"I'm sure she will," I smiled. "And I'm sure clients will love it too. It should generate some work for you."

"Let's hope; it's been quiet lately," Tom said, staring out across the yard.

It seemed to me there was something on his mind but I wasn't sure if I was the person who should be asking what that was. I didn't really know him after all. We chatted each day when we met – mostly laughing over the fact I thought he was a mad stalker when we first met – but I wouldn't say we really talked. Chat was very, very different to talking. I knew that more than most. I had kept my mouth shut for the past umpteen months and nearly driven myself mental in the process. All that time, I guess, I had been waiting for someone to read my mind (or my ovaries) and ask me what was wrong in a way that I knew I could trust them implicitly with my feelings and darkest secrets.

"Penny for yours right back," I said, sitting back against the railings and stretching my legs out in front of me. It might only have been early April, but there was a hint of warmth in the sun which felt glorious after the long, cold winter.

"For my business? A penny would be a fair price," Tom said miserably.

"Is it that bad?" I said, trying to sound concerned but failing to hide the shock in my voice.

He sighed. "Well, not really. It's starting to pick up but I long for the day when work will walk in off the street and I can give up the damn floristry and concentrate entirely on gardens."

I smiled. "I didn't think the floristry quite suited you."

"No, not my thing. It's not very manly, is it? Every woman I meet seems to think I'm gay because of it."

"So you want to meet a woman then?" I said with a wink.

Tom blushed and while I was very much a married woman who

was exceptionally happy with the very gorgeous man she was married to, I couldn't help but find Tom Austin – in that second – more than a little attractive.

"I don't know," he said. "I swore off women a while ago – in a completely non-homosexual way, of course. I was married," he continued, "and it all ended horribly."

"I'm sorry," I said.

"Don't be. If we had stayed together any longer than we did I'm pretty sure we would have killed each other. We wanted the same thing but it just wasn't going to happen and we spent a lot of time resenting each other. In the end we broke it off as friends rather than keep going as partners and start hating each other. It was shit, but it was for the best in the long run."

"I'm sorry," I repeated, wondering if he could actually in that moment read my thoughts. He just smiled. "I know how you feel," I said and took a deep gulp of my wine.

"Oh, I doubt it," Tom said. "I'm infertile. You've got to love the irony really. People think because I'm a florist I'm less of a man in some way – when it doesn't even take working with flowers to emasculate me."

My heart started to thump and I tried to speak. I honestly tried to say something but the words wouldn't come.

"When we first had problems Kate said she still wanted me and we would work through it. We talked about adoption, even had assessments for fostering but in the end she had to be honest with herself. She wanted her own baby and she met someone who could give her that. I don't blame her. I was angry, but I want someone to want me for me and not what I can or can't give them."

"I *know* what you mean," I said again, and Tom looked at me, realisation dawning as he heard my tone of voice. "We are trying, but it's not happening. We've been trying for two years and we've had all the tests. There is nothing wrong. You've got to love that, nothing wrong – so where is our baby?"

"I hear you," Tom said and clinked his glass against mine.

A bottle and a half of wine later, we had discussed the ins and outs of our lives, and had moved on to our hopes for the future.

"And you are happier now then?" I asked him, wondering could it ever be possible to be happy knowing that you were never going to be a parent and that because of that very fact your other half didn't want to know you any more.

"In theory? Yes, I suppose. It gave me the impetus to move up here and set up in business but I'd be lying if I said I didn't miss the companionship I had with Kate, even if, by the end, most of the time I wanted to kill her."

"So you want companionship now?"

He looked at me. "Beth, I know you and Elena are scheming to get Aoife and me together but who's to say I wouldn't make the same mistakes with her that I made with Kate? Except with Aoife it wouldn't just be her, it would be Maggie too and that's a big responsibility. That's someone else's child – I can't hurt her if it goes wrong."

"But in theory you are interested in Aoife then?" I asked with a wicked glint in my eye, the wine making me giddy.

"In theory. She is a nice girl. Slightly mad, very quirky, delicious accent," he said – with his own wicked glint – before adding, "but only in theory and now that you and your mysterious womanly ways have made me confess all my sordid secrets, you'd better tell me what was on your mind after all."

When Dan arrived an hour later, Tom and I were drunkenly toasting our futures.

"Baby," I called out enthusiastically, "come and see the yarden! That's what we are calling it. It's a mixture between a garden and a yard. A yarden. Geddit?"

"Your wife, sir, is a genius," Tom said. "We're going to start a new business. Yardens R Us."

I burst into uncontrollable giggles. "Will you be our mascot, honey?" I said, wobbling towards Dan and wrapping my arms around his neck. "We were thinking we could dress you up as a gnome or something."

"Are you drunk?" Dan asked, smiling broadly at me.

"Only a little. We were celebrating the garden."

"Yarden!" Tom called out, adding, "I'm very sorry, Dan, for plying your wife with alcohol. I assure you my intentions are entirely honourable."

"Apart from the bit about wanting to sleep with Aoife," I teased and he laughed.

"You are a piece of work, Beth, you really are," he said.

"Yes," said Dan, kissing the top of my head. "She really is a piece of work, and I love her to bits."

"Really?" I said, staring into his eyes.

"Really," he said back.

"I think I'd better be off," said Tom, kissing me on the cheek. "You can keep me some of the Chinese for tomorrow."

And then he left, and Dan and I christened the yarden and made love between the sensuous scented flowers and gently glowing candles.

We slept in Aoife's flat that night. After our outdoors session we came back in and ate our Chinese in her flat before I emptied the fridge, watered her plants and checked her answerphone. I wasn't surprised to find Jake hadn't called. He might have looked at Maggie as if she completed him, he might have promised both Dan and me that his intentions were honourable towards his daughter, but I knew he wouldn't have called. He would never be the kind of man to be tied down to anyone or anything, even if that anything was his own child. I sighed, and curled up beside Dan on the sofa. Yawning, my hangover starting to kick in, I snuggled to him and closed my eyes.

"Can we just sleep here tonight?" I muttered sleepily.

"'Course we can, darling," he said, kissing my hair. "Anything you want."

The following morning, green with the after-effects of two bottles of Pinot Grigio, Dan and I walked up to Mrs Morelli's for a cooked breakfast before we started work.

"Beth, you look tired, my darling." Mrs Morelli said, filling my coffee cup and feeling my head in the way a mother would to check the temperature of her sick child.

"Over indulgence, Mrs Morelli. Too much wine and fattening food."

"Are you sure?" she smiled. "Have you something to tell me?" She rubbed her tummy and raised her eyebrow.

I managed to keep my composure. Seems if you are a married woman of a certain age it's fair game for people to assume you are up the duff at any given stage. I'd become used to it over the last two years. It always smarted a bit, but I'd realised that people didn't mean to be insensitive and for the most part I could handle comments such as these.

"No, afraid not, unless it's a baby bottle of Pinot Grigio," I smiled, as Dan reached for my hand under the table. I squeezed his hand back, in the universal sign language for "I'm okay, really".

As Mrs Morelli bustled away, clearly unconvinced by my hangover, I realised how lucky I was to have Dan sitting opposite me. Just a few weeks ago we had been at breaking point and now, even though we were no further forward, we seemed to have found each other again. I doubted the guilt about hitting him would leave me, not yet anyway, but with it came a deeper love for a man who could stand by me when I was being as horrid to him as I possibly could be.

I was a very lucky lady indeed.

By twelve noon I was on my third bottle of Lucozade and seriously considering sending Heather back down to Morelli's for some bacon sarnies. The hangover did not seem to be abating at all, which made it all the more galling when Tom Austin walked in smiling and looking a picture of health.

"How can you not be hungover?" I asked with a hint of disgust in my voice. "You didn't even have the Chinese."

"What can I say? I'm a man, I can hold my drink. Constitution of an ox."

I smiled. "Don't give me that, Mr Austin – you were like an old woman spilling her guts out after a couple of glasses of wine."

"Which is sort of why I'm here," he said.

I looked at him and the small hand-made sign he had made for our garden, advertising his business. "So you don't want to talk about the 'yarden' then?" I teased.

"Well yes, but Beth, if you could manage not to tell Aoife about those things I said last night I would really appreciate it," he said.

I nodded.

"Seriously, Beth. Okay, you know I'm interested in Aoife, but let me take this at my own pace, please?"

I nodded again. "If you promise to at least send her a text or something."

He promised and I thought about the fact that, just ten minutes before, I had sent my best friend a text myself, letting her know the local gardener had taken a shine to her.

Tom really should have called over earlier if he wanted to keep things under wraps.

48

Aoife

Tom Austin liked me. In an official way. And Jake hadn't phoned. Not even once. I sat on my mother's eiderdown, staring at the fresh flowers I had arranged for her on the dresser and digested this information which had just arrived via text from Beth.

I shouldn't have been surprised that Jake hadn't called, and I wasn't upset for me. But I felt for Maggie. She should have a daddy who loved her, just like my daddy loved me.

And as for Tom, well, I didn't know how to process that information. He was scared of getting hurt or hurting me, Beth said, but just a week ago he had told me he was not looking for love in any way, shape or form.

I sighed. Was I interested in him? Of course I was. He was handsome, funny, tender – his gentle kisses on my cheek made me feel cherished. He listened to me, talked to me and he wasn't afraid to push a pram. He was everything Jake Gibson wasn't – everything I never thought I deserved. Jake had chipped away at

379

my confidence. I could see that now. Even though I had thought he cared, even though he had jumped my bones at every given opportunity, he hadn't cared at all. I realised that the night I had spoken to Anna about Billy. I had realised that when Tom had kissed me on the cheek, not expecting a blow job in return. Sighing I stood up and returned to my hoovering, If my mother was to come home in a day or two, I wanted her house to be as perfect as possible for her. Looking at the walls, seeing that they needed a lick of paint I decided to call past the DIY store and pick up a few new bits and pieces for her. Maybe it was time my mother saw just how great an interior designer I could be.

I visited the hospital with some colour charts and a cheery Maggie – who despite being a source of shame to begin with – had taken a real shine to her granny. In turn Odhran had taken a real shine to his baby cousin and to all intents and purposes we looked like quite the happy family. There was even an uneasy calm between myself and Jacqueline, which Anna was struggling to come to terms with.

"I'll have to bin the voodoo dolls then," she had quipped, before we left for our afternoon visiting.

I had smiled. "Don't worry, Anna, you're still my most favouritest relation in the whole world. I doubt very much me and Mrs Jacqueline McLaughlin will ever be the best of friends, but it's nice not to be at war."

"I dunno – I like a bit of war myself," Anna said with a sly smile.

"I'm sure there will be plenty of war in our family in the future," I said. "We can never stay quiet for long."

Now, sitting on my mother's bed I looked around at my family and smiled. Mum was looking brighter – still pale, her hair thinner, her hands still wiry – but brighter all the same, as if a burden had been lifted off her shoulders. Although she didn't have the strength to bounce Maggie on her knee, she curled her arms around her on the bed and with Odhran on her other side she told them a magical story about Finn McCool and the Giant's Causeway.

As she spoke a memory stirred of times when I was child that she would sit me on her knee and tell me the same story.

How strange was it that I had blocked out so much of the happiness that must have existed in my childhood? I knew it wasn't perfect, but it didn't seem it was half as bad as I remembered. Hopefully my mother was having the same sort of epiphany and that I wasn't as bad as she remembered either. Even though I knew that in my teenage years in particular, I had been a wee fecker.

When she finished her story, I showed her the colours.

"Just choose what you want, Mum. Joe and Dad are going to help me do the room. Beth is going to send over some fabrics from the shop and we can make it really nice for you coming out of hospital."

"Oh, the neighbours will be jealous," Mum smiled. "Imagine the likes of me getting a fancy makeover by a London designer. Very posh."

"It's only a coat of paint and some new curtains, Mum – don't get overexcited. I don't want you giving yourself another coronary."

"Still, it's designer paint," Anna smiled, squeezing my hand.

"It's so nice that we are all getting along," my mother added. "It does my heart good."

We all smiled – cheesy, corny Kodak smiles like people who had gone to the very edge and come back miraculously but knew we could go there again at any time. That was the nature of families, I suppose.

"Do you know what would make me really happy?" my mother said before mopping her brow.

She was starting to act dramatic so I knew instinctively this was going to be a biggie. She was going to ask me to sign Maggie up for the convent, or an arranged marriage, or make me promise to stay in Derry and never return to the sinful hole of London. She coughed lightly, rubbing her chest – her stitched-up and bandaged chest – and looked at me.

"Aoife, it would make me very, very happy if you could have Maggie christened while you are back home. I'm sure Joe and Jacqueline would agree to be godparents and it would make me very proud to bring Maggie up to the chapel to meet everyone."

I was gobsmacked. My mother finally accepted my daughter enough to want to bring her to her chapel to meet the priest and she hadn't asked me to wear sackcloth and ashes. This was major. This was acceptance at the highest level.

"And, you know, Anna can even bring her new man to the party," my mother said, and I wondered if I was going to collapse and find myself in a hospital bed for a second time.

"New man? New Man? Anna, I think you better start talking and now, missus," I said as we loaded Maggie into the car and set off for a drive down to Moville for a walk along the waterfront.

"I could kill your mother," Anna muttered, strapping herself in.

"And you who had the cheek, the brazen cheek, to tell me off for keeping Jake schtum. You are in big trouble," I teased.

"Look, Aoife, it's nothing. Well, it's early days. I've only just told Maeve and she's coming to terms with the fact her mother is still an attractive woman who may one of these days have sex again."

I blushed but not as furiously as Anna. "Well, all I'm saying,

Anna, is that if you do have sex again then please be careful. We don't want any other illegitimate children in this family," I smiled.

"That shop has shut a long time ago," she laughed, "and don't worry, I've no intention of jumping into bed with anyone. Christ, I wouldn't remember how. I'm not sure I haven't healed over down there."

"So tell me about him then," I said.

"Ach, Aoife. I don't know. I still feel strange about it all. I know Billy has been dead a long time, but I know that no one will ever fill his shoes. I'd be lying though if I was to say I never get lonely and John, that's his name, helps me feel slightly less lonely. We met at one of those god-awful weekends for bereaved and divorced people. Your mother made me go – she said I was spending too much time sticking my nose into other people's lives and not enough into my own. I was going to tell her to go and fuck herself but Maeve persuaded me it couldn't do any harm."

"So you went?"

"I went and met him. He's two years older than me. His wife died of cancer three years ago and his children are grown up. He's a nice man, Aoife, and he makes me laugh again. I didn't intentionally keep anything from you – I just wanted to get it right in my head before I said anything to anyone."

"It's okay. I understand where you're coming from."

"So you don't think I'm an evil bad person for seeing someone?"

"Ach Anna," I said, squeezing her hand, "of course not. Although I am quite jealous that you have more of a prospect of a good shag than me!"

We giggled together.

"It's nice to have you home, Aoife, maybe you should think about moving here full-time."

I laughed harder. "No, Anna, I couldn't do that. My life is in London now. I still love Derry and you know I love coming home to see you but I have a nice wee life happening there and I can't turn my back on that. And besides, Beth would kill me."

"And this would have nothing to do with any men you may or may not be interested in yourself?" she asked with a wink.

"Most certainly not, although I promise if there is a stage when there is something to tell you about me and my love life and any prospect of anything remotely resembling a good shag then I will tell you and not keep him secret."

"You better not, missy," she said.

Now that the secret was out, Anna felt no shame in leaving Maggie and me alone in her house while she went out to the cinema with her new beau. We sat, the pair of us, still somewhat shellshocked by the events of the last week, looking at each other. Maggie gurgled contentedly and I wondered did I detect a wee Derry twang in her babyish bubble-blowing.

"Let's go for a walk, toots," I said, strapping her into her pram. Now seemed as good a time as any to get that walk through Creggan I had been planning over and done with.

It's strange to walk through the streets of your hometown and not really know anyone. Of course it had been so long since I actually lived in Derry that should my old school mates or neighbours walk past me I doubted I would have recognised them. It seemed odd to me to hear people talking in Derry accents, even though it was the same as my own. I had grown so used to hearing the sound of a London voice and mixtures of glorious accents from all round the world. I thought of Mrs Morelli – for all intents and purposes my surrogate mammy – and smiled. The closest we got to Italian culture when I was growing up was Fiorintini's ice-cream parlour on the Strand Road. I remembered my parents taking me and Joe there after our First Holy Communions. We were allowed

Knickerbocker Glories filled to the brim with jelly and ice-cream while my parents would share a plate of chips saturated in vinegar. We would look at the pictures of Rome and Pompeii on the walls and imagine travelling there some day.

However, with my mother and her refusal to ever leave Ireland, we never got much further than Buncrana for a day trip. I wondered now that she had come to the edge would I be able to persuade her to take on a new challenge and come to London to visit me?

As I pushed the pram up Broadway I felt a kinship with where I grew up, but I wanted so much to mix my two lives, old and new, together as much as possible.

Walking up past the chapel, sitting down at the playpark, I lifted my mobile and dialled Beth's number.

"Hiya," Dan's voice answered.

"Hey, you, is your gorgeous wife there?"

"Why does no one ever want to talk to me?" he teased. "Irish, a man could get a complex."

"Dan, you know I love you and if you weren't married to my bestest friend I would be jumping your bones right now, but I'm on my mobile, freezing my arse off in a park in Creggan and I'd love very much to talk to Beth before my jaw freezes over and I lose the power of speech."

"I should be so bloody lucky," he laughed and called for Beth.

"Hello," she groaned down the phone.

"Are you okay, sweetheart?" I asked, my high spirits replaced with concern.

"Ach, you can blame that shit Tom Austin for getting me drunk last night. I must be getting old – I certainly can't hold my drink in the same way I used to – I've been throwing my guts up all day."

The me of old would have teased Beth about being pregnant – luckily I stopped myself in time before I made an unforgivable gaff.

"Tell me about it," I said. "Two wine gums and I'm anybody's this weather. Look, Beth, I'm phoning for a reason. Mum wants me to have Maggie christened back here. Is there any way you and Dan could make it over? It will be in a week or two – enough time for mum to be out of hospital – but it would mean a lot."

"Of course we'll be there," Beth said, her voice choked with emotion. "I wouldn't miss my darling girl's christening for the world."

"Are you okay?" I asked.

"God, yes, just got the emotional hangover now. You know what it's like for old birds like us. Have a couple of drinks and spend the next day like a paranoid and emotional wreck."

"The joys of aging," I said before telling her I loved her and hanging up.

As I wrapped my coat around me I thought about how life changes as you get older. Twenty years ago I would have been haring about on these climbing frames in the middle of winter with not a coat on my back and now, in April, walking back to Anna's, I started to have illicit fantasies about woollen mittens and a nice furry scarf.

"Better not stay in Derry too long," I told a sleeping Maggie. "I appear to be turning into your granny."

When we got home I settled my daughter and made a cup of tea. My phone beeped to life and I lifted it.

"Thinking of you. Come home soon, Tom x"

As I curled on the sofa, cupping the warm mug of tea in my hands, I started to feel nice and fuzzy all over. No, there was no way I could stay in Derry forever. There was too much waiting for me back in London and I dialled the number of that very thing that was waiting for me.

"It's nice to hear your voice," I said, sitting back and sipping my tea.

"Yes," Tom said and I could hear the smile in his voice.

"Elena Kennedy would be delighted we're chatting so much."

Tom laughed. "I saw her yesterday actually. She was asking if we had been in touch. I was tempted to tell her we were having cyber sex every night."

I laughed, but my face reddened at the thought of any kind of sex with Tom. I chided myself. We were just friends. He was just my Eejit Man. I was here nursing my ailing mother. I could not be having impure thoughts about the gardener.

There was an awkward silence. I imagined for a moment that Tom was having the same thoughts as me and my face reddened further – the heat spreading to all sorts of places in my body.

"So how's business?" I squeaked.

"Oh, busy. Would you believe I had to turn down a floral order today because the garden business is picking up? I have three yards to transform for next week."

"Yes, Beth told me the yards were taking off."

He was quiet for a moment. "God, we got drunk last night. I hope I didn't make an eejit of myself." His pronunciation of eejit wasn't quite right but I appreciated the effort. Then it dawned on me he might well be having regrets about telling Beth his feelings for me were growing.

"Well, Beth never made any mention of eejitness, so you might just be safe."

"I don't think I'm safe around you at all, Aoife. Not one bit."

49

Beth

I crawled into bed within an hour of getting home. I was dog tired and the Lucozade had failed to lift my hangover. Rubbing my tired eyes and sipping tea from my oversized cup I switched on my laptop. There was much too much work to be done for me to go straight to sleep. Besides, Dan wouldn't be home for another hour at least and I wanted to see him before I went to sleep. It surprised me how I missed him when we were apart, even just for a day at work. You would have thought that after fourteen years we would have had enough of each other. Aoife has mocked us of course. "Love in a bucket," she called it. Of course I had to ask her what the hell "love in a bucket" meant and when she assured me it was a good thing I did smile kind of smugly back in her direction.

No, I would definitely be staying awake until Dan came home, I thought, before setting to work to polish off Elena's costings and proposals.

As I typed, I realised it had been a week since I had logged onto my internet forum. It wasn't that I didn't want the support or the advice of the girls who I had spent the last two years chatting with, it was just that by now I wasn't sure I had anything left to say.

I had spent two years getting mine and their hopes up, then dashing them, telling them nothing was wrong, then perhaps it was, then no, everything was fine. I'd had enough babydust thrown at me to last a lifetime and, if I'm honest, it was hard now. There were women on there who were on their second pregnancies while I still waited for my first. Dan had been right, I had to let go of it for a little while. The dye test had shown nothing was wrong, so maybe it was just a matter of trying desperately to relax and see what happened.

Nonetheless I clicked on, just to see how the girls were getting on. I found a message for my attention.

Betsy Boo,
How are you? We haven't heard from you since the dye test. Hope you had good news, hon. Sending babydust your way.

I tried to type a response but to be honest, I just couldn't be bothered. Sighing, I returned to costing Elena's transformation and thought about how I was going to break it to Dan that we were going to Derry in just over a week and a half to stand as Maggie's godparents.

Just then the phone rang and my mother's cheerful voice said hello.

"Hi, Mum," I replied. "How are things?"

"Never mind me, Beth, how are you, darling? Have you been taking those pre-natal vitamins I sent you? I was talking to Mrs Sedgewick today and she was telling me her Caroline had trouble conceiving and then she tried some supplement or other . . . hang on . . . I wrote it down here somewhere . . ."

"Mum, you haven't been telling all and sundry about us, have you?" I said, trying to keep my cool. The hangover was certainly affecting my mood and I felt I could snap at even the most minor indiscretion, never mind my mother sharing the intimate details of my fallopian tubes with the local gossip.

"Darling, it's nothing to be ashamed of. I was reading in the *Sunday Times* last weekend how many more couples will experience fertility difficulties in the coming years. Assisted conception is going to be the norm."

I was in trouble now. My mother clearly had her research and development head on and would not stop now until she knew everything there was to know about fertility issues. Who needed Dr Browne when Mummy Dearest was on the case?

"Mum, I'm really tired. Can we talk about this tomorrow?"

"Oooh, you don't think you could be . . . you know?"

"Mum," I said, exasperated beyond words, "no. I just had a few drinks last night and I'm suffering for it today. I'm fine and barren, remember? No babies here."

"No need to get snappy, Beth," my mother replied and I felt guilty. I should have known when I told her that she would go into overdrive like this. She was a classic fixer and now that she knew that A) we actually wanted to produce her much-desired grandchild and B) we were actively trying and failing to do so, she would do everything in her power to make it happen.

Most of the time I loved the fact that my mother was a fixer. If ever I had a problem I never thought long about running to her for help. She got the job done, but this was different. I just wanted her to listen this time. I knew she couldn't find the answer, so I wanted her just to stop trying and then maybe we could all just let what was going to happen do it in its own time.

"I'm tired, Mum. Sorry. I'll ring you tomorrow."

I hung up and switched off the laptop, snuggling down under the covers and switching on the TV to watch *Coronation Street*. I was asleep within minutes.

"You're getting old, Mrs Jones," Dan said, climbing into the bed beside me.

I looked at the illuminated alarm clock and saw it had gone nine.

Dan looked as exhausted as I felt.

"Sorry, babe, I was wrecked."

"I know how you feel," he said, snuggling down beside me. "I think we could really do with a break away."

"Funny you should say that," I smiled. "I know of the perfect place."

Dan hadn't been to Derry before. He was of a generation who was too terrified to even contemplate a visit to Northern Ireland in case he was blown up, shot or sprained an ankle dodging bullets. When we first met Aoife he would listen, eyes wide in fear, as she told stories of her childhood. Of course, Aoife being Aoife, she embellished widely. Although we soon told Dan that we'd only been winding him up I'm not sure he believed us and any time I suggested a trip back to see Aoife's family he would shrug his shoulders and say he was busy.

"Go on and make a girls' weekend of it," he would say, and I would smile.

"There's a ceasefire, you know," Aoife would tease and of course Dan would try to assure us that fears of the Troubles had nothing to do with it – but we knew.

This time, however, he would need to come up with a pretty spectacular excuse not to go and be godfather for Maggie.

"Okay," he said hesitantly, sitting up and looking at me. "If I can get away from work."

"Dan Jones, you have been working your socks off without leave for months now. Of course you can get off work. For one thing, it's over a weekend."

"I'll see," he said and lay back down.

"You'll love it, Dan. The scenery is gorgeous. The bars are top notch. They feed you enough in one sitting to keep you going for a month and the craic is always good."

He smiled. "I do enjoy the craic, begorrah," he said in a fake Northern Irish accent.

"If Aoife hears you talking like that she'll kill you," I laughed, throwing a pillow at his face.

"Go easy, Beth. What kind of impression will I make in chapel with a black eye?"

50

Aoife

"How is the carrot cake? I would kill for some." I typed in the words and pressed Send on my mobile.

It was a fairly innocuous text but it meant a lot to me to send it. It felt weird to send messages to Tom Austin even if they were only about the moistness of Mrs Morelli's carrot cake.

I was sitting in my mother's living-room while Maggie played in her baby gym. Daddy had gone to pick my mother up from the hospital and now seemed as good a time as any to send a few messages to Tom. I couldn't really deny it. I missed him. It was strange really, because I didn't actually know him all that well but there were times over the last week when I needed to talk to him and have him make me laugh. Anna was lovely, but she was starting to live her own life again now after years of loneliness and it wasn't fair of me to make demands on her to stay in and keep me company.

And even if she were there all the time, I knew I would still miss Tom. It was hard to explain, he just listened to me in a different way to Anna. Even though he didn't know me all that well, sometimes I felt he knew me more than most people did.

"Should I post you some over?" came the reply.

"Oooh. Good thinking, Eejit Man. Beth is coming over at the end of the week for Maggie's christening. Could you send some over with her?"

"I'm sure that can be arranged," he texted, with two x's on the end for kisses.

That made me blush. I smiled to Maggie. "That Tom is a nice man, yes, he is," I cooed and she kicked her legs and chomped on her fists in what I liked to think of as a sign of approval.

"Can you make it an extra big bit?" I texted.

"What *exactly* are you referring to? ;)" he replied and I blushed. He was flirting with me. Surely that was a flirtatious text.

"Carrot cake, of course" I texted back, but added a wink.

I lifted the phone and speed-dialled Instant Karma where Beth answered.

"Tom Austin is flirting with me," I said excitedly.

"Are you always going to refer to him as Tom Austin? Surely just Tom would work."

"Sure what's that got to do with the price of eggs? Beth, he's flirting with me!"

"Aoife, my dear," she drawled, "Tom Austin has been flirting with you since the first time he laid eyes on you. How can you only be realising it now?"

"No, he hasn't," I said indignantly.

"Oh yes, he has," she replied and I could hear the smile in her voice.

"You are being ridiculous."

"No, I am not. Aoife, the man is dying about you. He has been moping about like a lost puppy dog since you've been away. He says he is down because he's waiting for the gardening business to take off, but I've seen the way he looks forlornly in the shop window every time he walks past and if he asks me one more time when you will be back I will scream."

I smiled. All this was music to my ears.

"And another thing, Miss McLaughlin, since he has been on the scene, since he has been sending text messages and generally being besotted with you, you have barely mentioned that fuckwit Jake. And I know you still have a daughter by him and everything, but you are happy, Aoife. And do you know how long it has been since you were happy?" Beth's voice started to break and I heard her sniff.

"Are you okay?" I asked, my smile turning to concern,

"I'm fine." She sobbed. "I'm just very, very happy for you and very, very premenstrual."

"Oh shit, Beth, I'm sorry."

"Don't be sorry. I'm okay. Really, I'm very happy for you and things will happen for us when they will."

"Atta girl," I said, wishing I could reach down the phone and rub her arm gently.

"But anyway," she said composing herself, "how exactly has Tom Austin been flirting with you?"

"Well, it all involves a big wadge of cake," I smiled and she laughed.

When my mother arrived home I helped her to her chair, put her slippers on her feet and set about making a cup of tea.

"Do you want one too?" I asked my father but he was busy strapping Maggie into her pram.

"No, I'm fine, love. I'm going to take this little one out for a walk. I want to get some of that good Derry air in her lungs before you take her back to smoggy old London town," he said with a wink.

Already he was getting used to having Maggie around. He wasn't keen on us going back to London but we hoped that things had changed enough that my mother would eventually make the trip over to see us (of course I would have to completely overhaul my flat before I let her cast her eye over it), which meant that Maggie and I would be seeing more of my parents in the future.

I brought a cup of tea in a fine china cup with two Rich Tea biscuits resting on the saucer in to my mother. She was a creature of habit and if I heard her tell me that "tea doesn't taste good unless it's in a china cup" once when I was small, I'd heard it a million times.

"Thanks, love," she said, shifting back in her seat and putting her feet up on the footstool and I smiled at the use of the word "love".

"Are you okay?" I asked. It felt like I was asking her that a lot at the moment. I suppose, if I'm honest, I was waiting for her to tell me that yes, she was okay and she was going to continue to be okay and nothing bad or nasty was ever going to happen ever, ever, ever again.

She nodded. "Just tired, Aoife. I feel as if I've been in the wars."

"Well, it's not been easy," I said, sitting down beside her.

"No, but I've realised I didn't do myself any favours – getting so wound up over things."

"Mum, you know you've always been like that," I smiled. "But I think we would all like it if you would take it nice and easy for a while. We've had enough scares for now."

"You are one to talk, missy. Your father has told me about your little collapse. Low on iron indeed? Did I not teach you right about eating lots of red meat and all your greens. Goodness, lady, what have you been eating over there?"

I smiled quickly as I thought of Mrs Morelli's carrot cake, and Tom Austin, and then took my telling-off on the chin.

"I know. I promise I'm being good now. I've had lots of decent home-cooked food since I've been back."

"Don't tell me Anna has actually been cooking? I didn't think she knew how."

In the past I would have stormed off in the mother of all huffs that my mother had dared criticise my precious Auntie Anna, but now I conceded Anna was not famed for her cookery skills. And I could step back from it all now and see that my mother didn't really mean any harm with her words.

"She's not the worst," I laughed, "and I've done my share. I'm quite good at cooking, you know. All those Home Economic classes at Thornhill really paid off."

My mother grimaced. "God, I hated your cookery days at that bloomin' school. Do you remember you would come home with all manner of inedible rubbish and expect us to eat it for tea? God love your father, he would try."

I laughed, blushing at the memory of stale scones, sludgy fish pie and lumpy soups.

"Okay, well, maybe Home Economics did me no favours but I've come on a long way since then."

"I'll test you on that later," she said, sipping from her cup and taking a bite from her biscuit, cupping her hand under her mouth to stop the crumbs from falling on her.

She sat back and I took the cup from her hand.

"I'm tired, Aoife," she said and I went to fetch a blanket for her. As I tucked it around her she smiled – a watery smile with soft tears rolling down her cheeks.

"I'm glad we can talk now," she said as she closed her eyes to sleep.

I sat on the floor beside her and rested my head on her lap and she stroked my hair. She didn't criticise its frizziness, or pull it back from my face, she just twirled it and stroked it until we both fell asleep.

When we woke my father was staring at us, a proud look on his face as he cuddled Maggie.

"Here," he said, handing my daughter to me, "let me get a picture of my three girls together."

Anna decided to bring John over for tea that night. She called me before and asked me if I would mind. It would have been churlish for me to say that I did – given that I had basically been acting very much like a thirty-one-year-old gooseberry over the last ten days. Not only that, but I had a brought a tiny baby gooseberry with me too to double the damage to Anna's reawakening sex life.

"Of course I don't mind, you eejit," I laughed. "Do you want me to cook something?"

"That would be perfect," she said, "but don't go to any trouble. We are plain eaters and sure it's all about company anyway."

Anna had used the "sure, it's the company that matters" excuse many times as she served up burnt offerings or takeaway, all washed down with loads of decent wine and bundles of warmth and humour. And I guess she was right. I started peeling potatoes and preparing vegetables while looking at the steaks I had bought earlier in Tesco. I had put a bottle of white wine in the fridge to cool.

"I can do this," I said, looking at Maggie who looked back at me with a gaze similar to Matilda's stony stares as if to say "Aye, right!"

"I can," I repeated. "Sure didn't I tell your granny that cooking was wee buns to me at the moment?"

She stared at me, not convinced.

Anna arrived home a short time later, flustered and face blazing red with a mixture of nerves and embarrassment.

"You will be honest with me?" she called down from the

bathroom as she ran a bath. "I mean, not painfully honest. Don't smack him or anything or tell me I'm mad, but tell me please if you think he is worth the effort."

"Of course I will," I replied.

"Because your opinion matters to me," she called. "I mean, what do I know about men and how these modern-day relationships work? And Maeve, well, she has her head in the clouds and her daddy on a pedestal – which is fair enough – so I don't feel I can trust her. But I can trust you? Can't I? You're a good judge of character, Aoife."

I choked back a laugh, thinking of my train-wreck of a love life. If I was such a good judge of character then I would have seen Jake Gibson for the arsehole he was a long time ago. Then again, if I had done, then I wouldn't have Maggie in my life and that wasn't something I wanted to contemplate.

When it came to judging characters I was about as far off the mark as they come. And that is why, despite the flirtatious text messages from Tom Austin, the growing friendship, I was still keeping my cards very close to my chest.

"Anna, I'm sure he is perfectly lovely. I'm looking forward to meeting him actually and warning him that if he even thinks about hurting you I will have his knackers in a vice."

Anna looked down the stairs at me, a towel wrapped around her body. "Would you ever mind letting me have a wee use of his knackers before you smoosh them? It's been a while and I'm not getting any younger. This could be my last chance."

John seemed nice. He was handsome in a newsreader kind of a way, with a warm smile and clean shoes. I liked the fact his shoes were polished – it made me think he was making an effort for my aunt.

He said hello while smiling at Maggie and then returned his glance to me to shake my hand and say it was lovely to make my acquaintance. He had a nice handshake, strong and masculine. A handshake was a good indicator of character, I figured.

"Anna has told me a lot about you," he said.

I nodded. "Well, she hasn't told me a whole lot about you but, now that you are here I can carry out the interrogation for myself."

He looked slightly alarmed before I smiled.

"Don't worry, John. I have a new baby. I don't have the energy for interrogations but I am duty bound to warn you to be nice to Anna."

"I have no intentions of doing anything other than be very nice to your aunt," he said, putting an arm around her waist.

"Good," I replied. "Now let's have some wine."

It was both delightful and difficult to watch the game played out between Anna and John. If I'm honest I was jealous. How did Anna manage to have two men in her life who clearly adored her when I was yet to find even one who would adore me with even a fifth of what she got to experience?

After dinner I made my excuses and went to bed early. Feeding Maggie, I lifted my phone and called Tom Austin.

He answered, his voice gruff with sleepiness.

"Did I wake you? God, I'm sorry Tom. I'll let you go back to sleep."

"No, no, it's fine," he said. "What can I do for you?"

Now there's a loaded question if ever I heard one.

"I just wanted to say hello. If I'm honest I feel a little silly now. Seriously, it's okay. Go back to sleep."

"You're a strange one, Aoife McLaughlin," he said and my heartbeat quickened at how he said my name, his delicious country accent. And it wasn't lost on me that he said Aoife – not Aoifs like that twat-on-legs Jake.

"I'm not strange at all," I blushed.

"It's okay, Your strangeness has a certain appeal, and I've no intention of going back to sleep just yet – not when an attractive Irish lady has called me in the night."

"You're an awful flirt, Tom Austin."

"I thought I was quite good at it actually," he said and I could hear the smile in his voice. "But anyway, what can I do for you? Are you okay? Is Maggie fine?"

"I'm fine. We're fine. I, well, this is going to sound weird but I just fancied talking to you."

"I can't tell you how much that happens to me," he said.

"Really?"

"Well, no. Never really," he laughed, "but I'll never turn down a phone call like this."

"That's good to know."

"So," he said, "do you know when you might be home? I thought, if you didn't mind, I could cook dinner for you some night? I know getting out won't be easy because of Maggie."

"I'd like that," I said. "I would really like that." I could not hide the smile in my voice.

"And Aoife," he said, "in case you wondered, I would want our dinner to be a date – not just friends. I can't make you any promises but I'd like to see what could happen with us."

"I'd like that too," I said. "I'd like that a lot, but I'm not sure when I'll be back. It will be a week or two yet, maybe more. I have to make sure my mum is okay."

"I understand," he said, "but the High Street just isn't the same without you and I swear Mrs Morelli's takings are down a good fifty per cent. She asked me to beg you to come back!"

"You cheeky bugger!" I teased but, feeling my loosening waistbands, I knew he probably had a point.

"You know I'm only teasing," he said, "but it would be nice to see you soon."

"I'll be back soon, I promise," I said.

51

Aoife

Dan and Beth arrived looking more relaxed than I had seen them look in months. I met them at the airport and brought them back to Anna's where we made a cup of tea and chatted – just like the old days before we had settled down and got proper jobs.

The only difference was the not-so-tiny-anymore baby gnawing on my nipples. Still, it was funny to watch Dan try and not look at my breasts while Maggie fed.

After a while, leaving my daughter in the tender care of her great-auntie, I took Beth and Dan to the hotel where they would be staying. (Anna had of course offered to put them up but her box room was even more floral and claustrophobic than the room I was staying in.) Then Dan offered to stay out of our way while Beth and I shared a bottle of wine in the hotel bar and caught up on the gossip.

"So things are well mended with your mum then?" Beth asked, sipping her wine.

"It's getting better. She is getting better and we don't want to kill each other as much. It's not quite Walton's Mountain, but it's a start. She has even taken to calling Maggie her wee lamb."

"That's nice," Beth said smiling. "I'm glad things are starting to come good for you."

I looked at her and wondered if she resented things 'coming good'. I so wanted things to come good for her too. "How are things with you anyway?" I asked.

"Better, thanks. The shop has been going great guns since you left, and Elena and I had a great day browsing through Selfridges for knickknacks. You know how she loves her bits and pieces. Oh, and Aoife, you really have to see our yard. It's amazing. I had a few client meetings out there and it was just glorious."

I found myself blushing. I knew when it came to talking about the garden, it would soon come about that we would talk about Tom Austin. I took a deep gulp of my wine and sat back.

"I look forward to seeing it," I said.

"Is that all you look forward to seeing?" Beth asked, smiling.

"You know full well that it isn't. Oh, Beth, am I mad? It's not right to have feelings for him. And besides we both said we would just be friends. And besides again, I have a child."

"I think he knows that," Beth said.

"Yes, but it means we couldn't date as such, could we? There would always be someone else to consider – a tiny screaming gooseberry of a thing? It would never be just him and me. There wouldn't be lazy Sunday mornings in bed reading the paper and having sex. There would be bottles and leaky boobs and teething and my jelly belly."

Beth looked at me, her eyes misting over, and I clamped my hand to my mouth.

"Jesus, I'm sorry. I'm such an insensitive twat."

"Don't worry about it," she half smiled. "I might want a baby but that doesn't mean I never worry about the loss of freedom we would have. Dan and I do enjoy our time alone together."

"Bless you," I said, topping up her glass. "So you know what I mean then? Even if I was interested in Tom – could I really expect him to be interested in me with all my baggage?"

Sitting forward, and gesturing for me to come near, Beth said: "You may be interested to know that Tom Austin isn't actually opposed to the idea of children."

"What do you mean?" I looked at the bottle of wine at our table, quickly assessed how much of it had been drunk, and wondered if Beth was under the influence.

"Let's just say I happen to know that he wants kids, except he's a bit like me. You know, infertile or whatever, so he can't have them. His marriage broke up over it all so Maggie could actually be a big plus tick in your desirable partner column."

I didn't sleep well that night. It wasn't that I wasn't tired. Physically my very bones ached, but my mind refused to shut off.

"Please," I pleaded with myself, "she'll be awake in an hour for a feed and then you will be fucked. Go to sleep, Aoife, go to sleep."

I even tried my relaxation exercises – letting the muscles from my head to my toes contract and relax, taking myself to my peaceful place – but no, I was still awake. I got up and padded downstairs and made some warm milk but, even though my eyelids were drooping, each time I lay down and closed my eyes the thought would come into my head: Tom Austin doesn't want me: he wants his ready-made family. He wants Maggie. He has been nice to me because I can offer him the one thing Kate couldn't. He doesn't really care. And Jake didn't care either – and my mother certainly didn't care for a long time and all I wanted was someone to care.

Eventually I drifted off, just as Maggie started to whine. I hauled myself from my sleep to feed her, trying to fight the growing resentment of both my daughter and Tom fecking-Eejit-fecking-Man Austin.

By morning I was as ratty as a bag of cats. I was tired, my hair had taken on a weird nest-like quality thanks to copious amounts of tossing and turning, and I was contemplating commissioning Anna to make a couple of new voodoo dolls.

"You okay, pet?" my aunt asked as she boiled the kettle.

"Just tired," I lied, staring out the kitchen window.

"Well, you'll have to rest, with the big day tomorrow you want to be feeling good."

Feeling good? Ha! That was a laugh. I snorted and rolled my eyes, while Anna looked on confused.

"Are you sure you're just tired?" she asked and I nodded.

"Yep, tired of everything. Tired of being a means to an end rather than an end in myself."

Anna sat down, poured the tea and I spilled my guts out to her.

An hour, and half a box of tearsoaked tissues later, I had resolved to phone Tom and tell him I knew what he was playing at. I had needed someone to be honest with me lately and he had been hiding something just so very huge from me that I could not pretend not to know.

Poor Tom. He really hadn't seen hormonal me in full flow yet and he was in for a shock.

"You said you had no agenda," I snapped down the line as he said hello.

"I don't," he said, "and I'm fine, thanks for asking." There was still a jovial tone to his voice. He didn't realise just how pissed off I was.

"Don't lie, Tom. Don't you know that the worst thing you could have done to me was lie?"

"Aoife, are you on drugs? Who has lied to you?"

"You have, Tom. You said you had no agenda. You wanted to be my friend and then you flirted with me. Damn it, you made me have feelings for you when all the time you were just pretending to be something you aren't."

"You have feelings for me?" he asked, his voice thick with confusion.

"Oh don't pretend you don't know, Tom, and don't pretend you don't know what I'm so angry about."

"I'm not pretending anything."

"Well, I'm not going to pretend not to know that you can't have kids and are only interested in me because I have one. I want someone who wants me for me, not for my child."

There was a silence – a long silence.

"If you want to think that of me, Aoife, then by all means go ahead and think that. I didn't want to have feelings for you either, as it happens – and that is in spite of you having a child. I didn't throw myself at you. How can you even say that?"

His voice was angry – his words tumbling together in rage.

I wanted to reply "You have feelings for me?" but the conversation wasn't salvageable now. I had said too much.

"Yes, I can't have children, but I came to terms with that when I left Kate to her new life. I'm not that sad that I went on a mission to bag myself a single mother. I thought you knew me better than that, Aoife. I thought *I* knew *you* better than this." He sighed. "I have to go."

And I apologised to a dead line.

52

Aoife

The sun shone brightly on the day of Maggie's christening and for the first time in recorded history the McLaughlin connection, including Perfect Jacqueline, Anna and her new man, managed to make it through the day without a major row.

Jacqueline had called earlier that week with the christening robe that both Joe and I had worn as children. A simple gown, in raw silk with a delicate lace detail around the hem. I looked at it and tried to imagine that I ever fitted in it. Maggie would look like an angel.

My mother made her first post-op trip into town to buy a candle in the Holy Shop and according to my daddy had spent a good half hour talking to the wee woman behind the counter, showing her pictures of her latest grandchild.

"Of course, she'll do well for herself. My daughter is a fancy interior designer in London, you know. She's just decorated my bedroom and is planning on redesigning the rest of my house. I'm

411

very lucky," mum had said, while daddy nodded beside her. The woman had, Dad said, looked suitably impressed.

"And why wouldn't she be?" he added with a smile.

Anna had picked Beth and Dan up from the hotel that morning and brought them to Mum's house. Beth had made her hellos – handing my mother a bunch of freshly cut flowers. Dan stood to the side – I think he was, if truth be told, utterly terrified of my mother and afraid to speak – and now was not the time to gently take him to one side and let him know she had softened considerably in recent weeks.

"Lovely to welcome you both here for such a special occasion," my father said, dressed in his best (and only) suit. "Youse are both very welcome to Derry, especially you, Dan. Don't worry, we've told the local terrorists to leave their guns behind today. You'll be safe with us, son."

Dan tried to laugh it off, but his face flushed with concern. My father burst out laughing.

"Jeez, you are terribly easy wound up for a big fancy London lawyer."

Dan smiled uneasily until Beth gave him a gentle dig in the ribs and told him to lighten up.

Then Joe walked in and handed him a beer, garnering a look of utter disapproval from my mother who could not believe her precious son was drinking alcohol before going to church. Dan, however, appreciated the gesture and the menfolk made their way into the kitchen to talk about man stuff.

"Right, I'd need to be getting this one ready," I said, lifting Maggie from Beth and making for the stairs.

"Wait a minute, love, I'll come and help," my mother said, following me.

"You need to take it easy, Mum," I chided and she gave me a gentle push upwards.

"I'm fine, madam, now let's get a move on or else we'll be late for church and the priest won't be one bit impressed."

We went into my mother's room and the christening gown lay, pristinely pressed, on the bed. She handed me Maggie's white tights and stared in awe at my daughter's chubby legs as I dressed her.

"She is gorgeous, you know," Mum said.

"I know."

"Look, darling, I don't know much about her daddy and I have a notion I don't want to know but I know you will do the best job you can to raise her to be a great girl."

"I'll do my best," I said, feeling suddenly emotional.

"Now, none of that crying," Mum said. "This is a day for celebration." She got up and walked to her dresser. "I have a little something here," she said and turned and handed me two parcels, both wrapped in gold paper. She nodded to one and said "That's for Maggie, the other one is for you."

I opened Maggie's present first and uncovered a gorgeous ceramic cross with a little girl kneeling and praying. Under it was folded a beautifully delicate lace bib.

"It's not much," Mum said and I shook my head.

"It's perfect, Mum, really perfect."

"Now open yours," she said, wiping a tear from her eye.

I opened the small box and recognised the ring immediately. "Your granny would have wanted you to have this," Mum said, staring at the ruby and diamond ring that I knew as my grandmother's engagement ring.

I slipped it on and then the three of us hugged – well, Mum and I hugged. Maggie just wriggled uncomfortably in her lacy gown wondering where her comfy babygros had gone.

The ceremony went well. Maggie slept for most of it and only cried for a few seconds when she was doused with cold water. Beth and Dan managed to pass themselves as practising Catholics even though it had been a while since either of them had set foot in a church and Odhran had made everyone laugh by singing the *Bob the Builder* theme tune as we walked away from the font. Jacqueline had blushed for a moment but when I smiled at her she relaxed and smiled too. I'm sure under it all she probably was still a god-awful bitch, but at least for today we could pretend to be an eeny bit functional.

Afterwards we went back to Mum's house, where she had gone all out by hiring a catering company to bring in some food. Ordinarily we would have had to make do with soggy egg and onion sandwiches and Pringles (the fancy crisps), but her near-death experience had made my mother almost reckless with money and the caterers had been called in. She had even sprung for a six-pack of beer and a bottle of wine. Of course we managed to sneak in an extra few drinks when she wasn't looking, which Daddy had put out in the fridge in the garage to lessen her suspicion. By the time we were onto our secret stash we knew Mum would be doolally on her medication and we would be able to get away with it.

As Jacqueline was pregnant and not able to partake, she had offered to keep an eye on Maggie to allow me a chance to let my hair down – something I fully intended to do.

The April night was balmy and Beth, Anna and I escaped to the garden to get a breath of air.

"It's been a lovely day, hasn't it?" Anna sighed contentedly.

"Really lovely," I answered looking down at the new ring on my finger.

Beth sighed. "It has been nice. Maggie is so gorgeous. It's been nice to get away from work for a day or two as well."

I blushed. "Look, I'm really sorry for leaving you in the lurch like that. I'll be back soon – Mum is getting better." Although if I was honest, now that Tom and I had fallen out, I wasn't looking forward to my return as much as I had been.

"Oh, I wasn't having a go," said Beth defensively. "Sorry. It's just been really bloody busy and I'm worn out with everything."

"Are you okay?" Anna said, putting her arm around my friend's shoulder.

"I'm grand. Just tired and emotional. Bloody PMT," sighed Beth. "And it has been a lovely day and I don't want to ruin it."

Something started to tick over in my head. This didn't sound right. Last week Beth had told me she had PMT – that her period was imminent and sure wasn't she grand about it because it meant once it was over they could move forward with the whole getting-pregnant-by-whatever-means malarky. We'd had a great laugh making jokes about turkey-basters and the like.

"Beth," I said as gently as I could because I knew she must have been utterly scunnered over the last year with people assuming she was up the duff, "look, I might be way off here, but are you sure you aren't pregnant?"

"Don't be daft," she laughed. "My period is due any time now."

"Wasn't it due last week?"

Anna looked at me, slightly alarmed at my line of questioning. I'm sure she was willing me to shut the feck up and not make things worse for Beth.

"No, it's due now. It's been . . ." Beth started counting in her head and then she paled and sat down on the back step. "Five weeks. Well, that's just the icing on the bleedin' cake, isn't it? Not only can we not get pregnant but now my period decides to play silly buggers on me too."

Anna knelt down beside her. "But Beth, are you sure you aren't pregnant? I mean, that is what it could be, couldn't it?"

Beth shook her head. "Of course not," she said with determination before looking up at me. "Could it?" She looked at us both with wide-open eyes and we each held a hand.

"Only one way to find out, babe," I said.

53

Beth

If this was in the movies I would have peed on a stick and then sat it on the windowsill and gone out of the room for a few moments to talk to my loving husband about what might lie ahead of us. We would have chatted and then realised – silly us – that more than five minutes had elapsed and our test was more than ready. Then we would have walked back into the bathroom and had an argument about who would look at the stick.

"You look at it," I would say, my hand resting on my tummy.

"No, you look at it," he would say and on we would go until one of us would snap and lift the stick before comparing it with the picture on the box and announcing that we were pregnant – or not.

As it happened this is not the movies and things were slightly different. I went home with Anna and Aoife, and while Dan – blissfully unaware – sat downstairs and opened another beer we had crowded upstairs with the paper bag containing a pregnancy test we had bought on the way home.

"This is daft," I protested. "I'm infertile, remember."

"There is nothing wrong with you," Aoife reminded me. "You just haven't got pregnant yet."

"Exactly, so what are the chances that this month I am?"

"Just pee on the fecking stick," Aoife ordered and walked out of the room.

I sat on the toilet seat, with my head in my hands. How on earth had I not realised my period was late? I had lived by my cycle for the guts of two years and this time it had passed me by. Was I losing it entirely? Admittedly life had been busy. Elena Kennedy had announced she wanted her guest rooms done as well and the shop had become busy with people recommended by Tom – who was starting to do a roaring trade in yardens. He seemed more upbeat lately, and I knew he had been talking to Aoife on the phone a lot.

"Have you peed yet?" Aoife stage-whispered outside the door, shaking me from my thoughts.

"Okay, boss," I said and unwrapped the testing kit.

There was no way I would be sitting it on the windowsill to wait for the result. I would be doing what I always did, watching the liquid (okay, my pee) move across the window on the front of the test, wondering if a line was appearing and then throwing the stick in the bin when the single, lonely line control appeared declaring that nope, no baby for me.

I peed, thinking how undignified the whole testing process was, before staring at the wand.

I looked, watching the stick darken waiting for a line and then, as I saw it, I started to cry – mad, hysterical tears.

"Well, fuck me pink!" I blurted as Aoife walked through the door a look of concern on her face.

54

Beth

Eight months later

A cheerful midwife called Peggy walked into the room as my contraction reached its painful crescendo. I had been trying to visualise my vagina opening like a flower, just as my pregnancy book had taught me, but no matter how I tried all I could visualise was me turning completely inside out.

This hurt. This really hurt.

"Breathe, just breathe," Aoife said, mopping my brow,

Dan paled beside me, and reached for my hand.

"It's fine, Betsy, it will all be fine," he said.

I looked at him, ready to shout and scream 'What the fuck would you know?' but then I thought of all the times he had told me it would be fine and he was right.

"You're doing brilliantly," Aoife said, a smile across her face. "This is just where it starts getting good for you, darling. It's all ahead of you now."

Good for me? I could almost feel my perineum tearing and this

419

was the part where it was supposed to get good?

But then I looked at her again and saw her eyes were moist with tears.

Peggy was hovering between my legs.

"Okay, lovely. A nice big push for me, please?" she said.

And I knew, instinctively, as I sucked deep on the gas and air, that Aoife was right – even if, as she said, my poor fandango was fanning as we spoke.

Aoife

Lucas Jones was born on December 18, weighing in at a gorgeous 7lb and 5oz. I saw him come into the world and I saw my two best friends sob happy, ecstatic tears at his arrival.

And Peggy had smiled at me – a secret smile which seemed to say 'You see, Aoife, I knew that first time I saw you that you would learn to love babies more than anything.'

Beth took to motherhood like a duck to water. Of course she had been shocked to find herself pregnant in the first place, but Dr Browne had explained that sometimes the very act of a dye test can make you extra fertile. It was ironic really.

Anna and I had hidden upstairs while Beth told Dan and hugged each other closely as we heard the whoops of delight from them. Dan had rushed right out and bought some cigars – which in fairness we still had because none of us smoked, but it was the gesture that mattered.

Maggie of course loved her little friend. She loved to pull herself up to standing by his crib and try to brain him with her pudgy baby hands.

Beth and I were as happy as we ever had been – and I didn't for one second think it could have got better from there on.

As Christmas Day dawned I watched Maggie crawl to the tree and tear paper off her presents before crawling back to me for a hug. We had already phoned my mother to tunelessly sing "Away in a Manger" down the phone. (I was going to sing "We Wish You a Merry Christmas", but realised just in time my mother would prefer something a little bit more religious.)

Anna was full of Christmas spirit when I phoned her at eight thirty. She was spending the day with John and his family and Maeve would also be joining them. "This is the best Christmas I've had in years," she cooed.

And the day was yet to begin.

As I put the kettle on, I kept singing – now on a delightful chorus of "Do They Know It's Christmas?"

"All this and she sings," Tom said, wrapping his arms around my waist and kissing my neck. I melted into him.

"Happy Christmas, Aoife," he said and sighed contentedly.

It had been wonderful to wake up next to him on Christmas morning.

Jake hadn't been too impressed that his daughter was spending Christmas with another man, but then again, he hadn't been falling over himself to spend any time with her himself. His feckwittedness continued to reach new levels, but Tom, he was different. Yes, things had worked out between us.

As Dan and Beth had cried their tears of joy in Anna's living-room, crushing guilt had swept in on me. How could I have thought Tom was only after my child? How could I have been so bloody callous to him when all he had done was show me friendship? I thought back to how he had smiled at me (me, not Maggie) in Morelli's. I thought back to how he had listened to me rant and rave about Jake – how he had cooked me dinner and walked me home. I thought of how we had laughed, felt at ease, of how he had moved to reassure me after Elena's attempt at pimping me out. Most of all I thought of our flirting and of how my skin tingled when he kissed my cheek.

I had left the happy scene and phoned him from my bedroom.

Before he could say anything I launched into my apology. "I have no right to expect anything from you and I'm more sorry than words can say. I have no excuse to offer, Tom, but I'm sorry for being such a bitch. I was scared, you see, because yes I do have feelings and I so don't want to get hurt. But I was still wrong, so wrong, and if you could forgive me I would really like that because I miss you and I want you in my life."

When I stopped talking, there was silence and it was only when the silence was followed by a beep telling me my time was up that I realised I had been talking to his answerphone.

Shortly after I'd returned from Derry we had met in my garden. I had gone down to admire it. Then I heard movement behind me. Figuring it was either Matilda come to life in a mad modern-day version of the *Chucky* films or that we were about to burgled, I lifted a plant pot and turned to knock the head off my potential attacker.

"Hold fire!" he shouted and I dropped the pot in shock, narrowly missing my foot and making me jump the height of myself.

"Holy Mother of God, how on earth did you get in here?" I shouted, trying to cover my embarrassment.

"Beth gave me a key," he said, "when I was working here so that I could show clients round."

Suddenly I was very worried that we were not alone and my embarrassing plant-pot incident would have been seen by strangers as well as the more-tanned-than-usual-looking Tom Austin.

I looked behind him and was relieved to see that there were no traumatised customers with him – until of course I realised that we were *on our own* and that my heart was beating faster than normal and I didn't know whether he had come to reciprocate my feelings or tell me to stay away forever.

"I'm sorry," he said. "I heard you were back and I just had to call around."

I nodded.

"I missed you," he said and I nodded again. "And I'm sorry I didn't tell you everything from the outset but it's not exactly a desirable quality in a man, is it? The lack of lead in a pencil? And besides we were just friends and that is all I ever intended us to be."

"But things change," I said, reaching my hand out to touch the smooth warm skin of his arm.

"Yes," he said with a smile stepping closer, "things change."

"We'd better get a move on," I said, turning to kiss him. "I promised Beth we would be over early to help with dinner. If you ask me she is out of her head making Christmas dinner for us lot so soon after giving birth."

"You know that Dan and I will be lumbered while you two sit cooing over Lucas and Maggie," he said and I smiled.

"Well, you do tell me my cooking is rubbish."

"More reason to practise then," he said. "No wife of mine can be a shoddy cook."

"Wife? I'm not your wife, Mr Austin."

"No," he said before dropping to one knee, "but who's to say what the future holds?"

THE END

If you enjoyed *Feels Like Maybe* try
Rainy Days & Tuesdays also published by Poolbeg

Here's a sneak preview of Chapter one

I

Rainy Days & Tuesdays

I used to be glamorous once. Honestly I was. I went to the hairdresser's every six weeks and had my roots done. I wore boot-cut jeans, suit jackets and fitted T-shirts which hugged my contours perfectly. I had a dressing-table overflowing with Clarins and L'Oréal and a selection of funky jewellery to jazz up any outfit. I was a babe – but somewhere between being a babe and having a baby I lost my mojo. Now I'm the ultimate slummy mummy.

This thought dances through my mind as I wake up – hair damp with sweat, skin greasy from last night's takeaway. I toy with the idea of hiding under the duvet, ducking my responsibilities and going back to sleep, but then it dawns on me – I'm a grown-up. I can't just do that. It's not like when I was at school and I could feign a cough or grab my stomach and perform my dying-swan routine for my unimpressed mammy who would eventually give in to my pitiful whinges and allow me a day under the blue blanket on the sofa. You can't just refuse to go to work – not when

427

there are bills to pay and stories to write.

You can't go back to sleep when you can hear a wee voice from the nursery next door giving a rather amusing rendition of "Jingle Bells" (despite it being July), letting you know that your toddler is awake and will soon be demanding breakfast.

The dream I had been having was so nice too. It was sunny and bright and I felt gloriously relaxed. I was cycling to a local dress shop to pick a dress to wear to accompany *dish-du-jour* Dermot Murnaghan, TV News Presenter Extraordinaire, to the BAFTAS.

Himself is snoring beside me and I realise this is my reality. A stuffy, too bright room. A snoring husband, who bears not even a passing resemblance to the delectable Dermot, and a child who has started to reach fever pitch with his singing.

Oh yes, and there is work. I have to go to work. I pull myself out of bed and blearily reach for the cow-print slippers which are hiding on the floor. After pulling on my dressing-gown, I give a cursory glance at the mirror. T – minus sixty minutes (in NASA-speak) until I have to be dressed and out of the house. T – minus 60 minutes to make this face, this crumpled, wrinkly, bed-headed vision before me, respectable enough to face my public. It almost makes me laugh.

When I walk into the nursery I am greeted with a "Mammeeee!" Jack is grinning ear to ear from his cot. "My want breakfass!" he cheeps, and I smile again, realising that when my son looks at me he sees nothing but his very own mammy and he loves me.

He is not one bit bothered about my bed-head and the saggy pyjama bottoms I'm wearing. He thinks I am the bee's knees, one yummy mummy, a foxy mamma. He reaches out his chubby arms and I reach in to lift him up, envelop him in my arms and feel his cuddly body against mine. Until, of course, he tries to bite me and the spell is somewhat broken.

This morning, like almost every other, I manage to get myself and Jack out the door in time. At least, I manage to get out the door ten minutes after I wanted to, which is a record for this year. Aidan is still snoring comfortably, having worked long into the night, and I have spent my precious sixty minutes trying to entertain my two-year-old, getting us dressed and getting into the car without totally losing my cool.

I choose to ignore the Weetabix stain I know is on my trousers. It's not that I don't care about my appearance but I know no one gives me a second glance any more anyway, so they are hardly going to notice one wee stain. Grooming is a thing of the past when you have to get a child to the childminder and yourself to work on time.

Where once I would practically dance into the office, throw my (designer) handbag onto my desk and set about working on the features for next month's issue, now I saunter in the back door, sit down, bury my head in organising my desk and offer to cover all the boring, respectable features that don't actually require me to leave the office or speak to anyone face to face.

This morning is no different. I say a few hellos to the team before plonking myself down with my morning coffee and sausage roll to open the post. Somehow in the proper daylight the Weetabix stain on my trousers has morphed from an eeny-weeny mark to one not too dissimilar to that birthmark on Gorbachov's head.

Running my fingers through my hair, I realise, not for the first time, that I have forgotten to brush it again before leaving home. No wonder Susie, the normally very friendly childminder, had looked at me in an alarmed way as I dropped Jack off. Searching through my tatty Dunnes Stores Better Value handbag for a mini-hairbrush, I am needless to say more than a little dismayed to find the bottle of Calpol I keep for emergencies has sprung a leak and, yes, I can still brush my hair, but only if I don't mind it being strawberry-flavoured and slightly pink in colour all day.

I give my hair a quick detangle with my fingers, hoping that everyone is thinking I'm trying the new just-fell-out-of-bed look, and go back to my hiding place behind my monitor. From the other end of the office I can hear Louise laughing uproariously. She was at some launch or other last night and apparently everyone who was anyone was there. It was a scream, she says, and she had a hundred admiring comments for her new dress which she bought in some boutique in Belfast. I try to look interested but all I really want to do is staple her head to her desk so I don't have to look at her smug and gorgeous face any more.

I shouldn't be jealous. I attended a launch myself yesterday. One of the local supermarkets was launching their new improved Mother and Baby Club and I was invited along to find out all about their groovy new parking facilities and padded trolleys. All the best mummies were there. And I stress, they were *mummies* – the posh version of mammies.

The post generates its usual share of gems. At least, being Parenting Editor, I can always expect some interesting samples. There is a book on raising your toddler to be politically correct, some toilet wipes and a dummy which promises to soothe even the most fractious of children.

And for the glamorous mummy-on-the-go, well, there was a sample of Tena Lady because we all know the busy working mum can't smell of wee. I switch on my computer and smile as an image of the lovely Dermot flickers onto the screen. Dermot is my escape – my little fantasy where I can pretend I am still me and not just a mammy or Grace Adams, Parenting Editor of *Northern People* magazine. Amid the cute pictures of Jack grinning at me from the gaudy-coloured frames proclaiming '*I love Mummy!*', beside the piles of parenting magazines, nappies and nipple-creams (again, samples) which clutter my desk, there is Dermot – all be-suited and handsome. He looks at me, his eyebrow raised in that quizzical and sexy manner of his, and I wish, oh really wish, we really were heading out to the BAFTAS for a date. I sigh, sip my coffee and finish the sausage roll. I cannot lose myself in another daydream today. There is work to be done. I have to come face to face with thirty screaming toddlers at Cheeky Monkeys Day Care Centre for a feature on 'Messy Play'. And when all that is done, I have to find the answers to the parenting problems submitted to me by overwrought mummies and daddies all across Ireland. Oh, if only my readers knew that Jack had cheese and ham for breakfast this morning because today his favourite Weetabix was "Icky, Mammy, icky!" or that I'd let him watch *CBeebies* videos until nine-thirty last night just to get some peace and quiet.

I already know this is one of those days when I will need two Nurofen and a power nap in the toilets before lunch-time. If Louise keeps on screeching in her high-pitched giggle, it might even be before tea break.

I open my email and find my daily reminder from *lifecoaches.com* to take each day as a new challenge, relax, breathe and remember: **"I am a strong, confident woman. I can do this!"** Breathing in, holding for five and breathing out, I feel myself relax and get ready for another day.

And then the phone rings.

I would say it is a pretty poor reflection of my ability to be an award-winning journalist that I mentally cringe when the phone rings at my desk. I frequently toy with the idea of not answering it and doing that oh-so-American thing of screening my calls. I imagine that wouldn't go down the best with the powers that be.

"Good morning, Grace Adams speaking!" I trill down the phone.

"Hi, Grace."

Sighing with relief, I realise it is only Aidan – fresh from his slumbers and ready for another day of scratching himself on the PlayStation before heading out for his bar job in the evening.

"Do you know where my phone is?" he asks.

"No," I reply. "Where have you looked for it?"

"I haven't yet. I thought you might know," he says.

My blood pressure rises.

We have this conversation every morning. Sure enough, it might not be the phone we are talking about – it might be the keys, the bills that need paying, the wee doodah you use to bleed the fecked radiator in the front room – but the premise is the same. He asks, I tell him to look, he looks, he finds. Why he can't realise he would be better served to just cut out the middle-woman and look himself is beyond me.

But this morning, in a remarkable turn of events, I don't need to answer. By now he has looked around him and found said item two feet from where he is standing. He informs me of this and I get ready to hang up and go somewhere to faint with shock.

However, just then an unexpected noise comes shooting down the phone line.

"Do you want to go out tomorrow night, Grace?" he asks and I start to wonder if my cholesterol-stuffed heart can really take the impact of two such shocks in one day.

We don't go out. Not any more. Not since we became parents. We tried it once when Jack was one and it was an unmitigated disaster. I spent the whole night worrying about whether or not Jack would settle without me, and himself spent the whole evening telling me why we needed to get out more. Both of us drank ourselves silly, talked shite about the wee man, ignoring the real issues in our relationship, before going home and falling straight to sleep. As I threw my considerable guts up the next day, I vowed never again. Seeing my whiter-than-white pallor, himself agreed that was not a sight he ever wished to see again either so we became Mr and Mrs Bottle-of-Wine-on-a-Saturday-Night. In other words, we became so boring we even bored ourselves.

Soon the bottle of wine would involve him on the PlayStation and me watching a chick flick on my own in the other room, and even that went by the wayside when he got the bar job. So, if I'm honest, I've become a sad old wino on a Saturday night on my own and he has become the life and soul of the staff-party scene at Jackson's Bar.

How we manage to survive as a couple is slightly beyond me so I guess, if I'm trying to operate in the spirit of willingness to save what's left of our marriage, I'll have to say yes to his night out – even though I have nothing to wear.

"Okay then," I mumble, closely followed by a litany of who, what, where questions that any woman needs to know the answer to before she can even think about picking out an outfit. For one brief moment I wonder if we are going somewhere nice, just the two of us.

"It's one of the new bosses at work," Aidan replies. "He wants to talk to me about my job prospects. He thought it might be nice for us to go out for dinner."

I agree, hang up and contemplate suicide. You see, I don't like going out for dinner with strangers. (Strike Two against my ability to be a fabulous journalist.) There is always a great deal of awkwardness when deciding whether or not to have that extra garlic bread or dessert, and I inevitably end up choosing the most unappetising salad on the menu as I don't want to appear a greedy gulpen.

And of course, the menfolk will be talking business – of which I know nothing and care even less for. (Strike Three against my ability to be a renowned journalist – apparently I should be very interested in business and politics etc.)

As I get in the car and leave for Cheeky Monkeys, I'm already frantically trying to figure out what to wear. I have two problems. The first is that when it comes to suitable evening attire, I'm pretty limited to cosy pyjamas and, second of all, even if I do find some treasure lurking in the back of my wardrobe, I'm not sure how to get out of the door without Jack leaving a special food-stain reminder on it.

I think about this, while driving along the Foyle Road towards Cheeky Monkeys. I have approximately twenty-three pairs of tatty tracksuit bottoms and a million T-shirts, but when it comes to glamming it up I realise it will have to be the RBTs again (Reliable Black Trousers), some killer heels (as we will be in a restaurant and therefore not required to walk any further than the toilet and back) and perhaps my nice turquoise satin vest-top would finish it off nicely. (I don't know why I say 'perhaps': it is in fact the only dressy top I have that still fits.)

Congratulating myself on my quick outfit-choosing decisions, I park my car, head inside and immerse my arms in a bowl of jelly.

Whoever said being a journalist wasn't glamorous?

Apparently I am growing too fond of my evening glass of wine. Mammy is concerned. She has been surfing the net, reading about working mums under stress and has even suggested in her ever-so-subtle-as-a-brick way that perhaps I might want to "write a wee feature on parents who hit the sauce".

It was never this way in her day. Oh no, you made do and you survived on a fiver a week and you were there for your children and you didn't want it all. You didn't need to drink and, even if you did, you couldn't afford it anyway. As I listen to The Speech, as my friend Daisy has dubbed it, I pour myself another glass and start to fill the bath.

This is my salvation – my Me Time. A glass of wine, a bubble bath, a good book or, if I'm feeling too tired to read a book, a cheesy weekly magazine to soak away my troubles and forget about the stresses of the day that has passed.

It has only been in the last few months that I've actually been able to get away with a soak. Before then it would be almost guaranteed that no sooner would bum hit bubbles than Jack would wake screaming and I would run, soaking and dripping, to his room where he would then stare at my nakedness with a strange mixture of curiosity, disgust and humour. By the time he was settled the bath would be cold, the wine would be warm and the magazine would be soggy so I'd opt for a quick shower before climbing into my jammies.

I don't drink too much, honestly I don't. Well, not unless Daisy and I have dumped the children for the night and we are on the proverbial piss. But I suppose mammies will always be mammies and mine is as prone to worrying as I am. It is a genetic curse.

Aidan, for those who are interested, is working tonight. He doesn't normally work on a Thursday but, as he isn't working tomorrow night for the big dinner meeting, he has to make up his hours. I decide to make the most of the peace and quiet and climb into the bath and try to lose myself in the latest Marian Keyes while trying to de-fuzz, exfoliate and moisturise all at the same time. I realise that, much as I am not used to pampering myself, I'm actually quite good at multi-tasking and I even manage to tidy that delicate bikini area without clipping a vein.

Climbing out of the bath I start the arduous task of applying self-tanning lotion. Trust me, when you are on the larger side it takes some time to smooth it into your skin. The smell is cloying, but then I tell myself it will all be worth it when I look like a tanned goddess as I step into the restaurant tomorrow night.

Checking the RBTs are clean, and the turquoise top is back from the dry-cleaner's I find myself then faced with an array of shoes of various heights, styles and colours and the real decision-making process has to start.

"Three-inch, four-inch, sparkly or black?" I ask down the phone without even saying hello.

"Occasion? Location? Water-retention levels?" Daisy counters – she knows me so well.

"Dinner with Aidan's bosses," I reply. "Swanky new Italian beside the river, mid-cycle-ankles decidedly unpuffy."

"Outfit?" she counters.

"RBTs," (Daisy knows all my code words as I do hers) "and satin top."

"Three-inch sparkly, with that silver cross I bought for your birthday and your hair swept up at one side with that wee sparkly clip."

"Love you," I answer.

"Love you too," she replies, and hangs up.

The thing with Daisy is that there is no bullshit. She knows me, I know her and there is no need for small-talk – no need to pepper every sentence with pauses and niceties. She is like the modern-day ghostbuster: she comes, she sees, she kicks my arse.

I've only known Daisy two years. We met when I was heavy with child as opposed to being just ordinarily heavy. She was the little ray of Scottish sunshine who phoned the office one day to ask me to feature her nursery in the magazine. We met for coffee, swapped pregnancy stories and became friends.

She assures me she is not merely my friend for the copious amounts of free publicity I can offer her – and, after feeling hormonally paranoid for the first year of Jack's life, I now believe her.

Lifting the sparkly shoes out of the cupboard, I realise Daisy has indeed made the right decision and I could look half-respectable after all.

I climb into bed, close my eyes and drift off to sleep, hoping that Dermot and I get to go to the BAFTAS again tonight.

Poolbeg wishes to

THANK YOU

for buying a Poolbeg book.

If you enjoyed this why not
visit our website:

www.poolbeg.com

and get another book delivered straight
to your home or to a friend's home!

All books despatched within 24 hours.

POOLBEG

WHY NOT JOIN OUR MAILING LIST
@ www.poolbeg.com and get some
fantastic offers on Poolbeg books

ALSO BY PUBLISHED BY POOLBEG

It's got to be Perfect

Claire Allan

All Annie Delaney wants is her happy ever after. A big dress. A big day. A big commitment. She even has a scrapbook filled to bursting with ideas for her dream day, her dream home and her dream man. But the man on her arm is less a dream than a nightmare and as for the sexy man currently in her bed — well, that's a whole other disaster in the making.

With her life heading into a tailspin (what else is new?), Annie realises she has to rethink her blueprint for happiness, while trying (and failing dramatically) not to make things worse.

It was never going to be easy, especially as her friend Fionn is heading straight towards the altar with her own Mr Right. But Annie misjudges Fionn's problems with Mr Right's very own Little Miss, not to mention the ex waiting in the wings for a big comeback.

Turning to her sister Darcy for support, Annie has her eyes opened in an unwelcome way, which forces her to ponder that age-old question: is there ever such a thing as the perfect relationship?

ISBN 978-1-84223-457-0